The Northern Stories of Charles W. Chesnutt

The
NORTHERN STORIES
of Charles W. Chesnutt

Edited by CHARLES DUNCAN

OHIO UNIVERSITY PRESS

ATHENS

Ohio University Press, Athens, Ohio 45701

© 2004 by Ohio University Press

Printed in the United States of America

All rights reserved

Ohio University Press books are printed on acid-free paper ∞™

12 11 10 09 08 07 06 05 04   5 4 3 2 1

Library of Congress Cataloging-in-Publication Data

Chesnutt, Charles Waddell, 1858-1932.
 The northern stories of Charles W. Chesnutt / edited by Charles Duncan.
   p. cm.
 Includes bibliographical references.
 ISBN 0-8214-1542-5 (acid-free paper) — ISBN 0-8214-1543-3 (pbk. : acid-free paper)
 1. Northeastern States—Fiction. 2. African Americans—Fiction. 3. Race relations—
Fiction. I. Duncan, Charles, 1962- II. Title.
 PS1292.C6A6 2004
 813'.4—dc22
                                                        2004002173

To my son, Graham, and my wife, Rebecca

CONTENTS

PREFACE

For the most part, the stories in this collection appear in chronological order, so far as that is possible to determine; as the dates of composition can only be estimated for four of the fictions included here, the chronology is not altogether certain. I have placed "The Passing of Grandison" as the first story because I believe it provides a useful thematic context for the rest of Charles W. Chesnutt's Northern fictions. In another deviation from strict chronological order, I have included an appendix, which contains four brief stories. I have chosen to gather these four together in the appendix because I view them as less substantial (as well as shorter) works than the fourteen fictions that comprise the main body of this collection. They do, however, provide four more examples of Chesnutt's notions of Northern living at the turn of the last century.

As a matter of editorial consistency, I have chosen to modernize Chesnutt's punctuation practices. Several of the stories collected here originally appeared in newspapers and magazines around the turn of the last century, and thus follow a range of punctuation conventions. Rather than remain true to the originals and sacrifice the internal consistency of this collection, I have instead followed contemporary orthographic conventions.

ACKNOWLEDGMENTS

My interest in the work of Charles W. Chesnutt began more than ten years ago, and I have since then benefited enormously from the help of others, only a few of whom I can properly thank here. At Peace College, Jean Arrington, Carol Hiscoe, Nina Pollard, Bes Spangler, Janet Wester, Kim Hocking, Diane Jensen, Paul King, and Charles Yarbrough have helped me in ways they cannot begin to imagine. Without the financial support and general assistance of Peace College, this book would not have been possible. I would specifically like to thank Laura and Warren Bingham, whose ongoing interest in Chesnutt and support of my work have been greatly appreciated. I have also been lucky enough to have first-rate editorial and organizational assistance from Stacy Johnson, Tiffany Watkins, Emily Keplar, and Allison Merkle.

Over the years, I have likewise incurred a great many debts to those whose friendship and wisdom have doubtless shaped my thinking and writing. Whatever I have done wrong here is not the fault of Joseph McElrath, Dean McWilliams, Jesse Crisler, Carl Weitman, Carl Bean, and Jeren Goldstein. I would also like to thank David Sanders, who, from what I can tell, possesses about twice his fair share of patience and loyalty. I am likewise grateful for the thoughtful editorial guidance of Nancy Basmajian.

My son Graham H. Duncan provided much-needed help at every stage of this book's development, and his expert editorial assistance I gratefully acknowledge. As always, my wife, Rebecca Duncan, made this work possible. Her unfailingly insightful responses to Chesnutt's stories helped shape this book in ways that transcend easy description.

INTRODUCTION

Charles Waddell Chesnutt spent most of his life in Ohio—he
was born in Cleveland in 1858 and lived there again from 1883
until his death in 1932—but he continues to be associated primarily with the South. His initial fame derived principally from a
group of folklore-based dialect stories (later collected as *The
Conjure Woman*), which, much like Joel Chandler Harris's *Uncle
Remus* tales, feature an ex-slave raconteur describing the ante-
and postbellum South to a curious Northern white audience.[1] But
Chesnutt had a deep interest in the North as well, and many of
his fictions provide nuanced accounts of how Northerners—
both black and white—lived at the turn of the twentieth century.
Chesnutt produced a large body of what might be called "Northern" or even "Ohio" writings, and those works are profoundly
suggestive not only about African Americans living in the North,
but about the way America itself was shaping, and being shaped
by, its vibrant blend of citizens as it entered the modern era.
Thus, although Chesnutt gained a reputation in part as a reteller
of Southern stories, this collection of short fiction will, I hope,
help to establish his importance as a chronicler of the turn-of-
the-century North as well.

Although his depictions of antebellum North Carolina offer
telling insights into the lives of blacks and whites before and
after the Civil War, his Northern stories, I believe, deserve consideration in a new context, one that accounts for Chesnutt's
deep concern for the ways in which America was evolving into
an urban, multiracial, thoroughly democratized, economically
driven community. In fact, one can find a "new" Chesnutt in his
Northern writings. In these stories he offers startlingly rich and
varied accounts of Americans, particularly black Americans, as
they made their way in a world very different from that of the

antebellum South. By 1900, readers and reviewers had grown increasingly familiar with, and ultimately weary of, stories about the pre–Civil War South, slavery, and its grindingly persistent consequences. One anonymous reviewer of *The Wife of His Youth and Other Tales of the Color Line* (1899), for example, lauds Chesnutt for turning away from those topics: "We have had stories in negro dialect. . . . We want a consideration of the struggle which has already begun in the North" ("Book-Buyer's Guide," 48). In the stories collected in this volume, Chesnutt undertakes precisely that "consideration." For in his Northern fictions, he writes of whites and blacks working—a crucially important concept for him—to make lives for themselves in the newly reconstituted America, one recommitted to the freedoms inherent in our national heritage.

After undergoing a prolonged period of uncertainty,[2] Chesnutt's reputation seems now reasonably secure. During his lifetime (1858–1932), he enjoyed the sometimes uneasy status of being the first African American fiction writer to earn national attention for his works. Writing in 1901, an early reviewer, John Livingston Wright, asserts, for example, that "Charles W. Chesnutt is undoubtedly destined to reach a prominent position in American Literature" (Wright, 78). Indeed, several decades before the Harlem Renaissance of the 1920s, Chesnutt's pioneering work on nonstereotypical African Americans had won him acclaim and respect. As the first well-known African American to articulate the lives of black and mixed-race people in fiction, Chesnutt enjoyed a short-lived but impressive literary prominence from the mid-1880s through the turn of the century.

During those years, Chesnutt published his works in the most prestigious venues open to an aspiring writer. Seven of his stories appeared in the *Atlantic Monthly*, for example, between 1887 ("The Goophered Grapevine") and 1904 ("Baxter's *Procrustes*"), and his novels were brought out by two of the leading American publishing houses: Houghton Mifflin (*The House Behind the Cedars* and *The Marrow of Tradition*) and Doubleday, Page (*The Colonel's Dream*). And, despite the comparatively poor sales of all his books, his writings received generally positive reviews; indeed, no less than the "dean" of American literature—William Dean Howells (another Ohioan)—acclaimed his work:[3]

> Mr. Chesnutt seems to know quite as well what he wants to do in a given case as Maupassant, or Tourguenief, or Mr. James, or Miss Jewett, or Miss Wilkins, in other cases, and has done it with an art of kin-

dred quiet and force. He belongs, in other words, to the good school,
the only school, all aberrations from nature being so much truancy and
anarchy. He sees his people very clearly, very justly, and he shows them
as he sees them, leaving the reader to divine the depth of his feeling for
them. He touches all the stops, and with equal delicacy in stories of real
tragedy and comedy and pathos. (Howells, 53)

An anonymous reviewer for the *Bookman* offered similar praise: "Mr. Chesnutt is a colored man, and that is one reason why his stories are so good. The
other reason is that he knows how to make literature" ("Chronicle," 34).
Thus, while Chesnutt was certainly not a best-selling author, he could point
with pride to a well-earned, impressive reputation among his peers.

But Chesnutt's literary fortunes fell. His works did not sell well enough
for him to make a living as a writer, and by 1902 he had recommitted himself
to his thriving court stenography business in Cleveland, a decision which, of
course, left him little time to write. Although he published one of his novels
and a handful of stories after his return to business, he could never again generate the sort of focused authorial energy that had enabled him to publish five
books between 1899 and 1901. By the 1920s, Chesnutt had apparently been
consigned to the back bench of the American literary establishment, in part
because of the ascendency of the black writers associated with the Harlem
Renaissance, whose works seemed spectacularly more "modern" than his.
Despite, or perhaps because of, the celebrity of so many black writers and
artists during the Renaissance, Chesnutt's literary career would seem to have
run its course: once considered a daring voice on race matters, he had not
published a book since 1905. And the prospects for his legacy looked more
and more bleak as the years passed, his name eliciting the same sort of puzzled looks—even from those professionally engaged in sorting out literary
history—that one comes to expect upon mentioning, say, Timothy Flint, a
figure famous in the early nineteenth century but now little more than a historical footnote.

Late in Chesnutt's life, however, a minor revival began, although it
lasted only briefly. In a 1930 essay, John Chamberlain wrote that "Negro
fiction in America properly commences with Charles Waddell Chesnutt, a
Clevelander who is still living, but whose writing falls mainly into the period
of the 'eighties and 'nineties" (Chamberlain, 134). While such recognition
no doubt gratified the then-seventy-two-year-old Chesnutt,[4] Chamberlain's
historical reconsideration was both wrong and right. He was wrong in that

he underestimated the effects of the slave narrative tradition on African American literature. For, though the writings of such ex-slaves as Frederick Douglass, Harriet Jacobs, and William Wells Brown were autobiographical—and thus not "fiction"—they formed the basis for much subsequent African American (and indeed American) fiction.[5] But Chamberlain was also profoundly right in identifying Chesnutt as a crucial shaper of the African American tradition of fiction writing. Although the lives of black Americans had been the subject of numerous stories and novels by white writers—including Harriet Beecher Stowe,[6] Joel Chandler Harris, Mark Twain, and the now nearly forgotten Thomas Dixon, among many others—Chesnutt became the first widely known African American fiction writer to depict the lives of black Americans.

Despite the attempts of Chamberlain and a handful of others to reconsider Chesnutt as a significant contributor to the African American literary tradition, he once again lapsed into obscurity, this time until the 1960s, an era that reshaped the intellectual and cultural landscape of America. Indeed, the social turbulence of the mid-twentieth century, with its emphasis on civil rights, wrought a profound change in the American literary culture, fostering an interest in previously underexamined writers from the past, especially those whose viewpoints challenged social, racial, and political orthodoxy. During this "rediscovery" period—which commenced in the late 1960s—Chesnutt's reputation began to wax once more, his racialized accounts of turn-of-the-century American life striking a chord with a country reexamining itself and, just as importantly, its past. Chesnutt's life and works suddenly attracted attention again, resulting in a smattering of books and several articles, nearly all of which sought to contextualize this inscrutable figure—one who wrote about ex-slaves living "free" on the same plantations they had worked before the Civil War and about Northerners struggling to understand the enigmatic geography of Southern hearts—for twentieth-century readers. For all the renewed interest in Chesnutt, however, this era of his "fame" generated only a handful of significant book-length publications: Sylvia Lyons Render's edited collection, *The Short Fiction of Charles W. Chesnutt* (1974); J. Noel Heermance's biocritical study, *Charles W. Chesnutt; America's First Great Black Novelist* (1974); Curtis W. Ellison and E. W. Metcalf Jr.'s *Charles W. Chesnutt: A Reference Guide* (1977); Frances Richardson Keller's biography, *An American Crusade: The Life of Charles Waddell Chesnutt* (1978); and William L. Andrews's biocritical study, *The Literary Career of Charles W. Chesnutt* (1980).

Although the social upheaval of the 1960s brought about renewed interest in previously underrepresented writers—especially women and African Americans—the interest in some of those "rediscovered" figures once again began to wane as the second half of the twentieth century unfolded, and Chesnutt seemed destined for the same fate. After Andrews's *Literary Career* appeared in 1980, Chesnutt received only fragmented attention over the next decade: indeed, no books with him as their focus appeared between 1981 and 1991, a relative eternity in the universe of literary culture.

But something happened. Chesnutt's reputation has been reestablished and, I suspect, for good now. Two of his works, for example, appear in the *Norton Anthology of American Literature* (a near-Bible for measuring a writer's status), the same number of selections allotted to such figures as William Dean Howells, Edith Wharton, Jack London, and William Faulkner. In addition, there is now a Charles W. Chesnutt Association, an organization committed to his life and works. And, perhaps most telling, consider the book-length contributions to Chesnutt scholarship only since 1992: William L. Andrews (ed.), *Collected Stories* (1992); Eric Sundquist, a 164-page chapter in *To Wake the Nations: Race in the Making of American Literature* (1993); Richard Brodhead (ed.), *The Journals of Charles W. Chesnutt* (1993); and again Brodhead (ed.), *Conjure Woman and Other Conjure Tales* (1993); Ernestine Pickens, *Charles W. Chesnutt and the Progressive Movement* (1994); Joseph R. McElrath Jr. and Robert G. Leitz III (eds.), *"To Be an Author": Letters of Charles W. Chesnutt, 1889–1905* (1997) and its sequel, *An Exemplary Citizen: Letters of Charles W. Chesnutt, 1906–1932;* Charles Hackenberry (ed.), *Mandy Oxendine* (1997); Charles Duncan, *The Absent Man: The Narrative Craft of Charles W. Chesnutt* (1998); Henry Wonham, *Charles W. Chesnutt: A Study of the Short Fiction* (1998); Dean McWilliams (ed.), *Paul Marchand, F.M.C.* (1999); again McWilliams (ed.), *The Quarry* (1999); McElrath, Jesse Crisler, and Leitz (eds.), *Charles W. Chesnutt: Essays and Speeches* (1999); again McElrath (ed.), *Critical Essays on Charles W. Chesnutt* (1999); SallyAnn Ferguson, *Charles W. Chesnutt: Selected Writings* (2001); again McWilliams, *Charles W. Chesnutt and the Fictions of Race* (2002); Werner Sollors (ed.), *Charles W. Chesnutt: Stories, Novels, & Essays* (2002). By my count, that makes seventeen book-length works by and about an author whose life and works had generated none between the years 1906 and 1973, and none again between 1981 and 1991. As one of Chesnutt's best and most prolific critics points out, "Given such obvious signs of burgeoning interest in Chesnutt's life and writing, what was unthinkable just a few decades ago—that virtually everything he wrote will eventually see print—is rapidly being realized" (McElrath, *CE*, 5). Thus, Chesnutt's status as a prominent American writer seems to have been secured.

Much of that prominence, however, continues to derive from his fiction-alized accounts of Southern life, both before and after the Civil War. In his first collection of short fiction, *The Conjure Woman* (1899), he borrowed from African American folklore to produce seven stories designed to resemble in tone and structure Joel Chandler Harris's *Uncle Remus* tales, although Chesnutt's stories carried a far more subversive message.[7] In his version of "plantation" stories, a white Northerner and his wife who have recently bought a North Carolina vineyard listen cautiously to tales of slavery as narrated by Uncle Julius, a skillful and apparently manipulative storyteller who had lived and worked on the plantation before the Civil War. Told in dialect, the stories rendered by Julius include a colorful blend of Southern history, magic, and the ongoing consequences of slavery. Indeed, Julius's (and Chesnutt's) intention in these tales seems to be both to entertain and to instruct: most of the stories depict the brutalities of the "peculiar institution" in vivid terms not encountered in the works of figures such as Harris, Thomas Nelson Page, or Thomas Dixon, other late-nineteenth-century authors (albeit white ones) who wrote about the antebellum South.

If the seven stories in *The Conjure Woman* established his reputation as a crafty exploiter of Southern life and superstition, the three novels he published in his lifetime similarly reflected his penchant for writing about the South. In fact, *The House Behind the Cedars* (1900), *The Marrow of Tradition* (1901), and *The Colonel's Dream* (1905) are all set primarily in North Carolina, and each describes the various social and cultural changes the South underwent during Reconstruction. *The House Behind the Cedars,* for example, recounts the attempts of two young people of mixed race, John Walden and his sister, Rena, to "pass" as white and thus make their way in the New South. While John succeeds spectacularly well—at least for much of the novel—Rena becomes entangled in a romantic liaison that ultimately reveals her secret and seals her fate: she dies an early death. *The Marrow of Tradition* depicts the New South as well, fictionalizing the Wilmington, North Carolina, race riot of 1898 as the backdrop for a story about the deep divisions within a prestigious family with race-based secrets. And *The Colonel's Dream* similarly features the New South, focusing on a former Confederate officer and successful businessman who returns to his Southern hometown of

Clarendon (based on Fayetteville, North Carolina) and tries to rejuvenate the local economy while simultaneously addressing social, racial, and economic inequalities. The protagonist ultimately abandons the project in disgust after the opposition to his insistence on economic equality culminates in race-motivated violence. All three novels ultimately reveal Chesnutt's impatience—indeed bitterness—with the pace of political change in Southern culture, and he came openly to scorn the South for its intractability.[8]

The three Chesnutt novels published in the last decade of the twentieth century—long after his death—similarly reflect the author's meticulous attention to the importance of geography. *Mandy Oxendine* (first published 1997), like *The House Behind the Cedars*, explores the possibilities for those of mixed race. In it, Chesnutt self-consciously ponders the advantages for African Americans of going "to the North, where there was larger opportunity and more liberal environment" (112). *Paul Marchand, F.M.C.* ["Free Man of Color"] (first published 1999) likewise considers issues of blood and racial identity,[9] but it is a bit of an oddity in Chesnutt's writings in that it takes place almost exclusively in Louisiana. Perhaps the most interesting of these three novels—at least in terms of geography—is *The Quarry* (first published 1999), a novel which, as Dean McWilliams has noted, represents its author's most comprehensive discussion of the North-South dichotomy. The protagonist, Donald Glover, is both Chesnutt's idealized version of a new African American leader and an inveterate *picaro*, living in communities in Ohio, Tennessee, Kentucky, and Harlem. Ultimately, *The Quarry*, written late in Chesnutt's life,[10] seems to be his most optimistic work, and part of that optimism clearly derives from the work's apparent insistence that many of the dichotomies that inform virtually all of its author's writings—North and South, white and black, rich and poor—can somehow be reconciled.

Long before he wrote *The Quarry*, however, Chesnutt also produced a significant—and as yet largely unexplored[11]—body of writings about the North. Many of those works derive from his second collection of short fiction, *The Wife of His Youth and Other Tales of the Color Line*, which includes several stories that explore the lives of mixed-race characters living in the North. Chesnutt also published extensively (nearly one hundred fictions and essays) in periodicals between 1885 and 1930, and many of the stories—several of which appeared in Cleveland newspapers and magazines—depict the Northern lives of both black and white characters of various social classes. Indeed, Chesnutt stands virtually alone as a turn-of-the-century

African American chronicler of Northern culture, anticipating such figures as James Weldon Johnson, Langston Hughes, Richard Wright, Ralph Ellison, James Baldwin, and Toni Morrison. For Chesnutt was fascinated by the ways in which the North went about its business (both literally and figuratively) as the country struggled to enact, in the post-Reconstruction era, the ideals of freedom and economic opportunity intrinsic to America as he conceived of it.

It is important to recognize, I believe, the extent to which Chesnutt's Northern writings differ from his other works, and those differences form the basis of this collection of his short fiction. By collecting and commenting upon these stories, I hope to cast him in a different light, as a subtle interpreter of the dramatic struggles of his Northern characters to make a life for themselves in the turbulent, stimulating milieu of the North of a hundred years ago. Indeed, in the stories collected here, Chesnutt presents an array of characters navigating the landscape of the turn-of-the-century North. It is a place where men and women make life-altering decisions based on the marketplace as well as on love, where choices to marry (or not) can have calamitous or laughable consequences, where truths concealed can save or destroy a life, where social status can be determined by appearance, money, or a few well-placed advertisements in the newspaper. It is a place very much like the one where we all live.

For this collection, I have selected eighteen of Chesnutt's short stories that most clearly reflect his deep interest in depicting the "Northern" experience, as enacted by both black and white characters. Most of the stories included here have explicitly Northern settings, usually "Groveland"— Chesnutt's pseudonym for Cleveland. A few of the works to be found within these pages do not mention specifically Northern settings—one even seems to be set in Europe—but have been included because they were published in Northern periodicals or focus on issues typical of Chesnutt's Northern fiction (especially the concerns of the business world). Taken together, the eighteen short stories offer a representative sample of the ways in which Chesnutt conceived of the North between the 1880s and the early part of the twentieth century. They also present, I believe, a broader notion of the author's range than would a similar collection of his Southern works. These fictions have as subjects, for example, the courtship rituals of both wealthy whites and ex-slaves; the business acumen of book collectors, undertakers, and barbers; and the mysteries of racial identity. As a group, they constitute the universe of the North, as Chesnutt knew it and wrote about it.

In an essay he published late in his life, Chesnutt described the situation of African Americans relative to the ideals of America: "For they still have a long and hard road to travel to reach that democratic equality upon the theory of which our government and our social system are founded" ("The Negro in Cleveland," 27). Such a commentary perfectly captures the tone of six of the stories included in this collection. Those six—"An Eloquent Appeal," "The Wife of His Youth," "A Matter of Principle," "Uncle Wellington's Wives," "The Doll," and "Mr. Taylor's Funeral"—focus specifically on the lives of African Americans working to make a life for themselves and their families in the North. The six stories in this group were published between 1898 and 1915 and present a range of black families as they navigate racial and social terrain typical of Northern cities at the turn of the century. "The Wife of His Youth" and "A Matter of Principle," for example, portray upper-class African Americans living in "Groveland." Both stories trace the complexities of attempting to balance the demands of love, marriage, racial responsibility, social mobility, and the burdens of history. Both "The Doll" and "Mr. Taylor's Funeral," although vastly different from one another in mood and message, examine the challenges that black businessmen confront, a set of challenges central to Chesnutt's understanding of the profound changes underway in America. "Uncle Wellington's Wives," on the other hand, farcically monitors the quest of a married black Southerner who decides to run away to the North and take a Northern wife; the experiment goes comically awry, however, and he eventually returns to his Southern (and presumably forgiving) wife. While the six stories vary in tone, each depicts black Americans coming to terms with their confusing, ultimately invigorating (if not always liberating) Northern worlds.

Conversely, nine of the eighteen stories included in this collection make no mention of race whatsoever, and thus might be characterized as "colorless" or even "white" fiction, a class of stories not often associated with Chesnutt. While none of the nine has a single character explicitly delineated as African American, however, each story resonates with issues—economic opportunity, social and political realities, and notions of individual responsibility—that form the cornerstone of how Chesnutt envisioned America, particularly the North. Thus, the situations he presents in these nine stories speak to his conception of how people enact democracy; each of the nine, that is, focuses on the extent to which its protagonist struggles to define himself or herself in a tumultuous, ever-changing economic, social, and political milieu. So, while "A Bad Night," "How He Met Her," "A Metropolitan Experience," "A Grass Widow," "Cartwright's Mistake," "How a Good Man Went Wrong," "The Shadow of My Past," "The Kiss," and "Baxter's *Procrustes*" all situate their presumably white characters in Northern locations and render no explicit commentary on race matters, they nevertheless address issues faced by both blacks and whites living at the turn of the century, and they do so across a startling range of plots and tones. Although "A Bad Night," for example, seems initially to be about a drunken businessman's comic misadventures, the story ultimately suggests that a man's identity is far less secure than most of us would like to think. "Cartwright's Mistake" depicts how the courtship of an overweight man and a slim woman goes swimmingly until the man undergoes medical treatment that results in his reappearance as "a tall, symmetrical young man, without an ounce of superfluous flesh on him" (41)[12] —at which point the woman mysteriously breaks off the engagement. The story may well be a sly commentary on the nature of prejudice, but at the least it emphasizes, in typically complex Chesnutt fashion, the inexplicability of human judgment. One of Chesnutt's least appreciated stories, in my view, is "The Shadow of My Past," a funny, pointedly satirical look at the ways in which a man might reinvent himself (and his past) in the world of business. And "Baxter's *Procrustes*," considered by many to be Chesnutt's best story, is a tour de force, a multilayered satire of book collectors, literary critics, and his reading audience, set in a Cleveland book club (The Rowfant) one can still visit today. Despite the absence of literally black characters, these stories work on their own terms or, in some cases, as racial allegories.

The other three stories in this collection form a class of their own, addressing such controversial subjects as mixed race, slavery, and miscegenation, and they tackle those divisive subjects from a variety of directions. In "Her Virginia Mammy," the protagonist, a dance instructor named Clara, refuses to marry a Boston Brahmin until she can satisfy herself that she possesses only "good" blood. When her fiancé learns that Clara has, in fact, a black mother, he withholds the information from her—indeed, he seems intent at the end of the story on marrying her. "White Weeds," on the other hand, traces the disintegration of a couple's relationship when, just before his wedding, Professor Carson receives an anonymous note accusing his fiancée of having "Negro blood cours[ing] through [her] veins" (241). Rather than ignore the missive or ask his fiancée about the matter before the wedding, Professor Carson marries her, and then asks her to deny the charge. But Mrs. Carson refuses to do so, and within a year, her husband dies, apparently devastated by his inability to know the truth, and, as the Hawthornesque narrator tells us, "in his doubt he found his punishment." (7). Thus, both stories might certainly be read as endorsements of miscegenation, not a particularly safe suggestion for a turn-of-the-century black writer to make. The position does seem, however, to square with Chesnutt's views on the matter of racial mixing, as he articulated them in other writings. In "The Future American: What the Race Is Likely to Become in the Process of Time," a 1900 essay in the *Boston Evening Transcript*, for example, Chesnutt shares his notions of how America's racial dilemma will ultimately be resolved: "Proceeding then upon the firm basis laid down by science and the historic parallel, it ought to be quite clear that the future American race—the future American ethnic type—will be formed of a mingling, in a yet to be ascertained proportion, of the various racial varieties which make up the present population of the United States" (20). For Chesnutt, then, stories such as "Her Virginia Mammy" and "White Weeds"—as well as "Uncle Wellington's Wives" and a handful of his other fictions—simply enact what he took to be an evolutionary certainty, and in that view he seems to have been prescient.

The first story in this collection might seem, at first thought, out of place here, because it is a story of slavery, and would thus seem to have little in common with what I am calling Chesnutt's Northern fictions. But, as I try to make clear later, "The Passing of Grandison" offers entry into a group of fictions about what the North meant for African Americans.

Although published over a span of decades and often seemingly unrelated in tone or subject, Chesnutt's Northern fictions share less controversial features as well. Indeed, while the stories collected here reveal themes apparent throughout Chesnutt's career—the burdens of history and the vicissitudes of personal identity, to name two—they also lay out a vision surprisingly different than the one that emerges from *The Conjure Woman* or his other Southern writings. Virtually all of his works set in the North emphasize the importance of work to the lives of his characters, both black and white. The action of "Her Virginia Mammy," for example, takes place almost exclusively in the studio in which Clara Hohlfelder gives dancing lessons, and her economic calculations comprise an important subtext throughout the story. Indeed, note the terms in which Clara weighs whether or not to teach a "colored class":

> So when she was asked if she would take a class of twenty or thirty, she had hesitated, and begged for time to consider the application. She knew that several of the more fashionable dancing-schools tabooed all pupils, singly or in classes, who labored under social disabilities—and this included the people of at least one other race who were vastly farther along in the world than the colored people of the community where Miss Hohlfelder lived. . . . Again, a class of forty pupils was not to be despised, for she taught for money, which was equally current and desirable, regardless of its color. (85)

Such a focus emphasizes the centrality of economic considerations to the lives of ordinary Americans at the turn of the century. And, here, no less, is a female entrepreneur, making her way in a story about the nature of personal and social identity. Chesnutt similarly locates financial matters at the heart of such stories as "Mr. Taylor's Funeral," "The Doll," "Uncle Wellington's Wives," and "Baxter's *Procrustes.*"

But Chesnutt's Northern characters are not all stick-in-the-mud workaholics; many of them seek love as well. Several of the stories collected here explore the nature of love, or at least the ways in which relationships work (or, just as often, do not work). Stories such as "The Wife of His Youth" and "Her Virginia Mammy" expose the complexities of modern love in a multiracial world and yet still affirm the possibility that people can behave well while courting. "Cartwright's Mistake," "Uncle Wellington's Wives," "A Grass Widow," and "White Weeds," on the other hand, might make one wonder whether living alone in a cave would not be the wiser course, after all. And, interestingly, virtually all of these Northern "love" stories take place in public forums, as opposed to the privacy, say, of the drawing room. In "The Wife of His Youth," for example, the narrator hosts a ball during which he hopes to propose to a woman (until an earlier love commitment intervenes). And "The Shadow of My Past" chronicles the comic attempts of a man to reinvent his past via speeches and newspaper articles so that his fiancée's father will approve the marriage. In short, Chesnutt's take on love at the turn of the century is surprisingly fresh and appealing, if not always for the faint of heart. For he is no weak-kneed sentimentalist—his characters have scars to prove their love.

Ultimately, though, the stories in this collection do far more than simply offer a sociological treatise on Northern life at the turn of the last century; they also make for engaging and entertaining reading. In an 1898 letter to the editor of the *Atlantic Monthly*, James Lane Allen (1849–1925), a widely respected novelist and short story writer himself, has this to say about Chesnutt's writing:

> Who—in the name of the Lord!—is Charles W. Chesnutt? Half an hour ago, or an hour, I came in from the steaming streets and before beginning my day's work, picked up your ever faithful *Atlantic*. I . . . then turned to the wife of my youth—I beg your pardon—to "The Wife of His Youth." I went through it without drawing breath—except to laugh out two or three times. It is the freshest, finest, most admirably held in and wrought out little story that has gladdened—and moistened—my eyes in many months. (qtd. in H. Chesnutt, 96)

More than a hundred years later, those qualities still, I think, define Chesnutt's work, especially the stories collected here. For the Northern works especially reflect his vision that the world was changing in profound and fascinating ways, and it is our good fortune that he was there, taking notes.

NOTES

1. The so-called "plantation tradition"—works devoted to describing, often in fondly nostalgic terms, the lives of the masters and the slaves who lived on antebellum plantations—featured the works of several white writers, including Harris, Thomas Nelson Page, and Thomas Dixon.

2. For a far more thorough discussion of the trajectory of Chesnutt's reputation, see McElrath's introduction to *Critical Essays on Charles W. Chesnutt*.

3. See "Mr. Charles W. Chesnutt's Stories" for Howells's full appraisal of Chesnutt's stories. Later, Howells would find Chesnutt's novels less enchanting, in part because of what Howells termed an excess of "bitterness."

4. Chamberlain's account of his writing inspired Chesnutt to correspond with his critic. In the 1930 letter, Chesnutt refers to Chamberlain's commentary on his writings "as a very friendly appreciation" (*EC*, 258).

5. In fact, a number of writers—both black and white—have written fictionalized versions of so-called slave narratives, including Stowe, Melville, Chesnutt, Styron, Reed, and Morrison, among others.

6. Indeed, Stowe's *Uncle Tom's Cabin* is one of the best-selling American novels of all time.

7. Two of the seven stories published in *The Conjure Woman*, "The Goophered Grapevine" and "Po' Sandy," originally appeared more than a decade earlier in the *Atlantic Monthly*.

8. In a 1908 letter to Booker T. Washington, for example, Chesnutt writes: "Things must be in a very bad way down there when even your helpful and pacific utterances create such a feeling. I very much fear that the South does not mean, if it can prevent it, to permit education or business or anything else to make of the Negro anything more than an agricultural serf" (*EC*, 52–53).

9. See Dean McWilliams, *Charles W. Chesnutt and the Fictions of Race*, for his detailed and convincing chapter-length discussions of *Mandy Oxendine; Paul Marchand, F.M.C.;* and *The Quarry*, three recently published novels that did not reach print in the author's lifetime.

10. Chesnutt apparently completed the manuscript in 1928 and submitted it to the publishing firm Alfred A. Knopf. See his letters—June 8, 1928, and February 9, 1929—to Harry C. Bloch, an editor at Knopf, in *EC*.

11. Even today, the bulk of criticism on Chesnutt's short stories focuses on the "conjure" tales.

12. Page references in parenthetical citations of Chesnutt's Northern stories are to the present edition.

ABBREVIATIONS

CE *Critical Essays on Charles W. Chesnutt.* Ed. by Joseph R. McElrath Jr. New York: G. K. Hall, 1999.

CS *Collected Stories of Charles W. Chesnutt.* Ed. and intro. by William L. Andrews. New York: Mentor, 1992.

EC *An Exemplary Citizen: Letters of Charles W. Chesnutt, 1906–1932.* Ed. by Joseph R. McElrath Jr., Jesse Crisler, and Robert C. Leitz III. Stanford: Stanford University Press, 2002.

The Passing of Grandison

The Wife of His Youth (1899)

At first glance, "The Passing of Grandison" might seem an odd—perhaps even a mystifying—choice to include in a collection of Chesnutt's "Northern" writings. The primary characters, after all, consist of a Kentucky plantation owner, his lazy and romantic son, and one of his slaves. And in many ways the story seems intended primarily to skewer the racial views and cultural assumptions of Southerners. Nevertheless, I have chosen, for several reasons, not only to include "Grandison," but also to have it appear first in this collection. For, despite its initial setting in Kentucky, the story traces a comically remarkable journey two of the characters take through the North, resulting in descriptions of New York City, Boston, Niagara Falls, and even, briefly, Canada—indeed, one character ultimately chides another for "chasing all over the North" (18). And, as he does elsewhere in his Northern fictions, Chesnutt focuses those descriptions on the social and economic possibilities of the North, especially for black Americans. In addition, the story draws upon and comically modifies the traditional slave narrative, the form of writing on which the African American literary tradition is based.[1] "The Passing of Grandison" works brilliantly, I think, to introduce, both thematically and geographically, the ways in which Chesnutt envisioned the promise and opportunity of the North for African Americans, before and after the Civil War.

Originally published in *The Wife of His Youth and Other Stories of the Color Line* in 1899, "The Passing of Grandison" easily ranks as one of Chesnutt's best short fictions. The action of the story derives from the attempts of Dick Owens, the spoiled and indolent son of a wealthy Kentucky plantation owner (Colonel Owens), to participate in freeing one of his father's slaves as the least troublesome method for impressing the woman—Charity

Lomax—he wants to marry. When Charity, who has just read a newspaper account of an abolitionist "hero" imprisoned for helping a slave escape, mentions that she "'could love a man who would take such chances for the sake of others'" (7), Dick has an idea to speed the couple's courtship: "'Will you love me,'" he asks, "'if *I* run a negro off to Canada?'" (8, italics in original).

Based on her ambiguously encouraging response, Dick devises his plot: to travel to the North, accompanied by one of his father's slaves, who, during the course of the trip, will be "lost" (or "passed" to freedom), an act that will, Dick hopes, win Charity's heart. But his quest proves far more difficult than he imagines, in part because Grandison, the slave he plans to "free," refuses every chance—no matter how elaborately planned by the younger Owens—to escape. Indeed, the slave seems so loyal to his masters that the frustrated Dick ultimately hires thugs to *kidnap* Grandison at Niagara Falls and take him forcibly to his "freedom" in the Canadian wilderness. Even that contingency works only temporarily, as Grandison subsequently "escapes" from his Canadian captors and—in a stunningly comic inversion—travels *South* (with the help of the North Star, no less), back to the Owens plantation in Kentucky, where he is greeted by Colonel Owens as the very epitome of slave fidelity. But only three weeks later, "the colonel's faith in sable humanity was rudely shaken, and its foundations almost broken up" (20) when he learns that Grandison has re-escaped (quite properly, to the North this time), taking with him his wife and several other members of his family. His return to the Kentucky plantation—and indeed his demeanor as a loyal slave—had been an exquisitely plotted hoax, one calculated to create conditions favorable to the far "grand"-er escape he ultimately executes.

In "The Passing of Grandison," Chesnutt makes use of—but significantly modifies—a distinctly African American literary tradition: the slave narrative. The term "slave narrative" generally refers to the autobiographical productions of ex-slaves, documenting the author's experiences as a slave and, usually, his or her escape.[2] Thousands of these accounts of slavery written by American ex-slaves appeared in print between 1760 and the Civil War. Charles T. Davis and Henry Louis Gates Jr. fundamentally define the slave narrative as "[t]he written and dictated testimonies of the enslavement of black human beings" (xii), and until 1865 slave narratives comprised, for a variety of reasons, a substantial part of the African American literary tradition. As James Olney and others have pointed out, traditional slave narratives, which are generally autobiographical in form, have a number of shared characteristics: an account of the slave's life in bondage, a "description of successful attempt(s) to escape, . . . guided by the North Star" (Olney, 153), and a brief commentary of the ex-slave's life in the North.

Although far shorter—and, as the account above suggests, much less predictable—than the typical book-length slave narrative, "The Passing of Grandison" nevertheless conforms in significant ways to the paradigm established by such ex-slave authors as Frederick Douglass, Solomon Northrup, Henry Bibb, William Wells Brown, Harriet Jacobs, and others.[3] Like most slave narratives, the story records, for example, the circumstances defining the lives of slaves on a plantation in the antebellum South, and it subsequently describes the travails of a particular slave, Grandison, as he copes with his enslavement. Indeed, Chesnutt's depiction of Grandison as an apparently stereotypical, fawning slave might initially make modern readers more than a bit uncomfortable.[4] Ultimately, though, Grandison emerges as a far more complicated figure, one who engineers his own eventual escape to the North with his family, a feature not unknown in slave narratives. And, like many of its generic relatives, "The Passing of Grandison" shares central references or rhetorical strategies: it seems intentionally oblique, for instance, about the details of the actual escape, a textual reticence explained by Douglass and Jacobs as an attempt to protect future fugitives. The story likewise includes a reference to Grandison's (seemingly perverse) use of the North Star as navigational aid (but to travel South!), another element characteristic (even archetypal) of literal slave narratives.[5]

In refitting, more than thirty years after the abolition of slavery, the slave narrative form for a comic—though important—story, Chesnutt thus emphasizes the significance of the North for African Americans, whether they lived before or after the Civil War. Put another way, the story establishes the terms of the relationship, as envisioned by Chesnutt, between black Americans and the North.

And, indeed, it is Chesnutt's conception of the North in "The Passing of Grandison" that makes this story resonate as one of the author's "Northern" fictions despite its Southern characters. When Dick and Grandison first arrive in New York, for example, the white plotter decides to rely on the free blacks working at the hotel to convince the slave to seek his liberty there:

> But there were negro waiters in the dining-room, and mulatto bell-boys, and Dick had no doubt that Grandison, with the native gregariousness and garrulousness of his race, would foregather and palaver with them sooner or later, and Dick hoped that they would speedily inoculate him

with the virus of freedom. . . . If . . . he should merely give Grandison
sufficient latitude, he had no doubt he would eventually lose him. (12–13)

As he does in so many of his Northern fictions, Chesnutt—in the midst of
a comic tale—contemplates the ways in which the economic and social
environment of the North had a formative role for African Americans. For,
while the North might not be the sole province of "negro waiters" and
"mulatto bell-boys," here (in a New York hotel) they have the capacity to
"inoculate" a fellow-being with "the virus of freedom." Their jobs and
social interactions, that is, carry enormous responsibilities as well as the
promise of opportunity: personal autonomy as free citizens.

"The Passing of Grandison" also includes an element of Northern life
(before the Civil War) not found anywhere else in Chesnutt's short fictions:
the influence of abolitionists. During the time Dick and Grandison stay
in Boston—the hub of abolitionist activity during the 1830s and 1840s—
the narrator twice describes what appear to be abolitionists, although
the descriptions are interestingly enigmatic. When Dick realizes that his
"ebony encumbrance" (17) won't simply run away on his own, he writes
an anonymous letter to "several well-known abolitionists" (14), urging
them to take steps "in the name of liberty to rescue a fellow-man from
bondage" (14). Apparently, the letters work, and two shadowy figures—
apparently abolitionists who have heeded Dick's anonymous letter—
approach Grandison. The first makes contact with the slave outside his
Boston hotel:

> Grandison had scarcely left the hotel when a long-haired, sharp-
> featured man came out behind him, followed him, soon overtook him,
> and kept along beside him until they turned the next corner. Dick's
> hopes were roused by this spectacle, but sank correspondingly when
> Grandison said nothing about the encounter. (14)

The second encounter is presented in equally mysterious terms:

> Dick sent [Grandison] on further errands from day to day, and upon
> one occasion came squarely up to him—inadvertently of course—
> while Grandison was engaged in conversation with a young white man
> in clerical garb. When Grandison saw Dick approaching, he edged
> away from the preacher and hastened toward his master, with a very
> evident expression of relief upon his countenance. (14)

Although neither of these suspicious figures is identified explicitly as an abolitionist, the text offers suggestions that, indeed, they are such. Later in the story, for example, when Grandison really does escape—with his entire family in tow—the narrator tells us that "strangely enough, the underground railroad seemed to have had its tracks cleared and signals set for this particular train" (20), a reference to meticulous advance planning that goes into Grandison's ultimate "passing." Chesnutt's depiction, even in such shadowy terms, of a pair of Northern abolitionists underscores another element of the North's social landscape that favored African Americans in the early and mid-nineteenth century.

Ultimately, "The Passing of Grandison" offers a series of fascinating paradoxes for contemplating Chesnutt's Northern fictions. First, the story traces the relationships of three Southern characters, each of whom is finally forced to recognize the extent to which the very idea of the North was reshaping the world in which they lived. In addition, while most of the stories in this collection focus on the "new," post–Civil War North, a place of economic and social opportunity for African Americans, this work—alone among Chesnutt's Northern short fictions—instead explores the North as it existed before the Civil War, a place, that is, to which a slave might escape. Thus, it functions as a sort of "prequel," a story that establishes the terms of Chesnutt's fascination with the North and all of its opportunities.

NOTES

1. Charles T. Davis and Henry Louis Gates Jr., in their introduction to *The Slave's Narrative*, argue that "the Afro-American literary tradition, and especially its canonical texts, rests on the framework built, by fits and starts and for essentially polemical intentions, by the first-person narratives of black ex-slaves" (xxxiii).

2. See Davis and Gates, *The Slave's Narrative*, and, more recently, the foreword by Charles Johnson and the introduction to *I Was Born a Slave*, edited by Yuval Taylor, for much fuller descriptions of slave narratives.

3. While "The Passing of Grandison" clearly derives from the slave narrative tradition, it does differ in significant ways. It has, for example, a comic tone, which virtually no traditional slave narrative, for obvious reasons, would use. Indeed, after "Grandison" (1899), the next comic slave narrative is Ishmael Reed's *Flight to Canada* (1976). Also, traditional slave narratives are usually told by first-person narrators, a convention Chesnutt chooses not to use here.

4. Various commentators have expressed discomfort with Chesnutt's intentions, especially in regard to racial and social doctrine. SallyAnn Ferguson, for example, calls

Chesnutt's fictions "racial propaganda." A more sympathetic reader, J. Saunders Redding, also seems on the point of exasperation in interpreting Chesnutt's motives: "Of what is he trying to convince us? In this and other stories one seems always at the point of making a discovery about the author, but the discovery never matures" (*To Make a Poet Black,* 71). See, too, Joel Taxel for his discussion of Chesnutt's varied use of the "Sambo" myth in his fictions.

5. See James Olney and Richard O. Lewis for highly specific details of slave narratives, several of which Chesnutt includes in "The Passing of Grandison." Lewis, for example, focuses on the striking irony of Chesnutt's use of the North Star.

The Passing of Grandison

WHEN IT IS SAID that it was done to please a woman, there ought perhaps to be enough said to explain anything; for what a man will not do to please a woman is yet to be discovered. Nevertheless, it might be well to state a few preliminary facts to make it clear why young Dick Owens tried to run one of his father's negro men off to Canada.

In the early fifties, when the growth of anti-slavery sentiment and the constant drain of fugitive slaves into the North had so alarmed the slave-holders of the border States as to lead to the passage of the Fugitive Slave Law, a young white man from Ohio, moved by compassion for the sufferings of a certain bondman who happened to have a "hard master," essayed to help the slave to freedom. The attempt was discovered and frustrated; the abductor was tried and convicted for slave-stealing, and sentenced to a term of imprisonment in the penitentiary. His death, after the expiration of only a small part of the sentence, from cholera contracted while nursing stricken fellow prisoners, lent to the case a melancholy interest that made it famous in anti-slavery annals.

Dick Owens had attended the trial. He was a youth of about twenty-two, intelligent, handsome, and amiable, but extremely indolent, in a graceful and gentlemanly way; or, as old Judge Fenderson put it more than once, he was lazy as the Devil,—a mere figure of speech, of course, and not one that did justice to the Enemy of Mankind. When asked why he never did anything serious, Dick would good-naturedly reply, with a well-modulated drawl, that he didn't have to. His father was rich; there was but one other child, an unmarried daughter, who because of poor health would probably never marry, and Dick was therefore heir presumptive to a large estate.

Wealth or social position he did not need to seek, for he was born to both. Charity Lomax had shamed him into studying law, but notwithstanding an hour or so a day spent at old Judge Fenderson's office, he did not make remarkable headway in his legal studies.

"What Dick needs," said the judge, who was fond of tropes, as became a scholar, and of horses, as was befitting a Kentuckian, "is the whip of necessity, or the spur of ambition. If he had either, he would soon need the snaffle to hold him back."

But all Dick required, in fact, to prompt him to the most remarkable thing he accomplished before he was twenty-five, was a mere suggestion from Charity Lomax. The story was never really known to but two persons until after the war, when it came out because it was a good story and there was no particular reason for its concealment.

Young Owens had attended the trial of this slave-stealer, or martyr,— either or both,—and, when it was over, had gone to call on Charity Lomax, and, while they sat on the veranda after sundown, had told her all about the trial. He was a good talker, as his career in later years disclosed, and described the proceedings very graphically.

"I confess," he admitted, "that while my principles were against the prisoner, my sympathies were on his side. It appeared that he was of good family, and that he had an old father and mother, respectable people, dependent upon him for support and comfort in their declining years. He had been led into the matter by pity for a negro whose master ought to have been run out of the county long ago for abusing his slaves. If it had been merely a question of old Sam Briggs's negro, nobody would have cared anything about it. But father and the rest of them stood on the principle of the thing, and told the judge so, and the fellow was sentenced to three years in the penitentiary."

Miss Lomax had listened with lively interest.

"I've always hated old Sam Briggs," she said emphatically, "ever since the time he broke a negro's leg with a piece of cordwood. When I hear of a cruel deed it makes the Quaker blood that came from my grandmother assert itself. Personally I wish that all Sam Briggs's negroes would run away. As for the young man, I regard him as a hero. He dared something for humanity. I could love a man who would take such chances for the sake of others."

"Could you love me, Charity, if I did something heroic?"

"You never will, Dick. You're too lazy for any use. You'll never do anything harder than playing cards or fox-hunting."

"Oh, come now, sweetheart! I've been courting you for a year, and it's the hardest work imaginable. Are you never going to love me?" he pleaded.

His hand sought hers, but she drew it back beyond his reach.

"I'll never love you, Dick Owens, until you have done something. When that time comes, I'll think about it."

"But it takes so long to do anything worth mentioning, and I don't want to wait. One must read two years to become a lawyer, and work five more to make a reputation. We shall both be gray by then."

"Oh, I don't know," she rejoined. "It doesn't require a lifetime for a man to prove that he is a man. This one did something, or at least tried to."

"Well, I'm willing to attempt as much as any other man. What do you want me to do, sweetheart? Give me a test."

"Oh, dear me!" said Charity, "I don't care what you *do,* so you do *something.* Really, come to think of it, why should I care whether you do anything or not?"

"I'm sure I don't know why you should, Charity," rejoined Dick humbly, "for I'm aware that I'm not worthy of it."

"Except that I do hate," she added, relenting slightly, "to see a really clever man so utterly lazy and good for nothing."

"Thank you, my dear; a word of praise from you has sharpened my wits already. I have an idea! Will you love me if *I* run a negro off to Canada?"

"What nonsense!" said Charity scornfully. "You must be losing your wits. Steal another man's slave, indeed, while your father owns a hundred!"

"Oh, there'll be no trouble about that," responded Dick lightly; "I'll run off one of the old man's; we've got too many anyway. It may not be quite as difficult as the other man found it, but it will be just as unlawful, and will demonstrate what I am capable of."

"Seeing's believing," replied Charity. "Of course, what you are talking about now is merely absurd. I'm going away for three weeks, to visit my aunt in Tennessee. If you're able to tell me, when I return, that you've done something to prove your quality, I'll—well, you may come and tell me about it."

II

Young Owens got up about nine o'clock next morning and while making up his toilet put some questions to his personal attendant, a rather bright looking young mulatto of about his own age.

"Tom," said Dick.

"Yas, Mars Dick," responded the servant.

"I'm going on a trip North. Would you like to go with me?"

Now, if there was anything that Tom would have liked to make, it was a trip North. It was something he had long contemplated in the abstract, but had never been able to muster up sufficient courage to attempt in the concrete. He was prudent enough, however, to dissemble his feelings.

"I wouldn't min' it, Mars Dick, ez long ez you'd take keer er me an' fetch me home all right."

Tom's eyes belied his words, however, and his young master felt well enough assured that Tom needed only a good opportunity to make him run away. Having a comfortable home, and a dismal prospect in case of failure, Tom was not likely to take any desperate chances; but young Owens was satisfied that in a free State but little persuasion would be required to lead Tom astray. With a very logical and characteristic desire to gain his end with the least necessary expenditure of effort, he decided to take Tom with him, if his father did not object.

Colonel Owens had left the house when Dick went to breakfast, so Dick did not see his father till luncheon.

"Father," he remarked casually to the colonel, over the fried chicken, "I'm feeling a trifle run down. I imagine my health would be improved somewhat by a little travel and change of scene."

"Why don't you take a trip North?" suggested his father. The colonel added to paternal affection a considerable respect for his son as the heir of a large estate. He himself had been "raised" in comparative poverty, and had laid the foundations of his fortune by hard work; and while he despised the ladder by which he had climbed, he could not entirely forget it, and unconsciously manifested, in his intercourse with his son, some of the poor man's deference toward the wealthy and well-born.

"I think I'll adopt your suggestion, sir," replied the son, "and run up to New York; and after I've been there awhile I may go on to Boston for a week or so. I've never been there, you know."

"There are some matters you can talk over with my factor in New York," rejoined the colonel, "and while you are up there among the Yankees, I hope you'll keep your eyes and ears open to find out what the rascally abolitionists are saying and doing. They're becoming altogether too active for our comfort, and entirely too many ungrateful niggers are running away. I hope the conviction of that fellow yesterday may discourage the rest of the breed. I'd just like to catch any one trying to run off one of my darkeys. He'd get short shrift; I don't think any Court would have a chance to try him."

"They are a pestiferous lot," assented Dick, "and dangerous to our institutions. But say, father, if I go North I shall want to take Tom with me."

Now, the colonel, while a very indulgent father, had pronounced views on the subject of negroes, having studied them, as he often said, for a great many years, and, as he asserted oftener still, understanding them perfectly. It is scarcely worth while to say, either, that he valued more highly than if he had inherited them the slaves he had toiled and schemed for.

"I don't think it safe to take Tom up North," he declared, with promptness and decision. "He's a good enough boy, but too smart to trust among those low-down abolitionists. I strongly suspect him of having learned to read, though I can't imagine how. I saw him with a newspaper the other day, and while he pretended to be looking at a woodcut, I'm almost sure he was reading the paper. I think it by no means safe to take him."

Dick did not insist, because he knew it was useless. The colonel would have obliged his son in any other matter, but his negroes were the outward and visible sign of his wealth and station, and therefore sacred to him.

"Whom do you think it safe to take?" asked Dick. "I suppose I'll have to have a body-servant."

"What's the matter with Grandison?" suggested the colonel. "He's handy enough, and I reckon we can trust him. He's too fond of good eating, to risk losing his regular meals; besides, he's sweet on your mother's maid, Betty, and I've promised to let 'em get married before long. I'll have Grandison up, and we'll talk to him. Here, you boy Jack," called the colonel to a yellow youth in the next room who was catching flies and pulling their wings off to pass the time, "go down to the barn and tell Grandison to come here."

"Grandison," said the colonel, when the negro stood before him, hat in hand.

"Yas, marster."

"Haven't I always treated you right?"

"Yas, marster."

"Haven't you always got all you wanted to eat?"

"Yas, marster."

"And as much whiskey and tobacco as was good for you, Grandison?"

"Y-a-s, marster."

"I should just like to know, Grandison, whether you don't think yourself a great deal better off than those poor free negroes down by the plank road, with no kind master to look after them and no mistress to give them medicine when they're sick and—and"——

"Well, I sh'd jes' reckon I is better off, suh, dan dem low-down free niggers, suh! Ef anybody ax 'em who dey b'long ter, dey has ter say nobody, er e'se lie erbout it. Anybody ax me who I b'longs ter, I ain' got no 'casion ter be shame' ter tell 'em, no suh, 'deed I ain', suh!"

The colonel was beaming. This was true gratitude, and his feudal heart thrilled at such appreciative homage. What cold-blooded, heartless monsters they were who would break up this blissful relationship of kindly protection on the one hand, of wise subordination and loyal dependence on the other! The colonel always became indignant at the mere thought of such wickedness.

"Grandison," the colonel continued, "your young master Dick is going North for a few weeks, and I am thinking of letting him take you along. I shall send you on this trip, Grandison, in order that you may take care of your young master. He will need some one to wait on him, and no one can ever do it so well as one of the boys brought up with him on the old plantation. I am going to trust him in your hands, and I'm sure you'll do your duty faithfully, and bring him back home safe and sound—to old Kentucky."

Grandison grinned. "Oh yas, marster, I'll take keer er young Mars Dick."

"I want to warn you, though, Grandison," continued the colonel impressively, "against these cussed abolitionists, who try to entice servants from their comfortable homes and their indulgent masters, from the blue skies, the green fields, and the warm sunlight of their Southern home, and send them away off yonder to Canada, a dreary country, where the woods are full of wildcats and wolves and bears, where the snow lies up to the eaves of the houses for six months of the year, and the cold is so severe that it freezes your breath and curdles your blood; and where, when runaway niggers get sick and can't work, they are turned out to starve and die, unloved and uncared for. I reckon, Grandison, that you have too much sense to permit yourself to be led astray by any such foolish and wicked people."

"'Deed, suh, I would n' low none er dem cussed, low-down abolitioners ter come nigh me, suh. I'd—I'd—would I be 'lowed ter hit 'em, suh?"

"Certainly, Grandison," replied the colonel, chuckling, "hit 'em as hard as you can. I reckon they'd rather like it. Begad, I believe they would! It would serve 'em right to be hit by a nigger!"

"Er ef I didn't hit 'em, suh," continued Grandison reflectively, "I'd tell Mars Dick, en *he'd* fix 'em. He'd smash de face off'n 'em suh, I jes' knows he would."

"Oh yes, Grandison, your young master will protect you. You need fear no harm while he is near."

"Dey won't try ter steal me, will dey, marster?" asked the negro, with sudden alarm.

"I don't know, Grandison," replied the colonel, lighting a fresh cigar. "They're a desperate set of lunatics, and there's no telling what they may resort to. But if you stick close to your young master, and remember always that he is your best friend, and understands your real needs, and has your true interests at hear, and if you will be careful to avoid strangers who try to talk to you, you'll stand a fair chance of getting back to your home and your friends. And if you please your master Dick, he'll buy you a present, and a string of beads for Betty to wear when you and she get married in the fall."

"Thanky, marster, thanky, suh," replied Grandison, oozing gratitude at every pore; "you is a good marster, to be sho', suh; yas, 'deed you is. You kin jus' bet me and Mars Dick gwine git 'long jes' lack I wuz own boy ter Mars Dick. En it won't be my fault ef he don' want me fer his boy all de time, w'en we come back home ag'in."

"All right, Grandison, you may go now. You needn't work any more to-day, and here's a piece of tobacco for you off my own plug."

"Thanky, marster, thanky, marster! You is de bes' marster any nigger ever had in dis worl'." And Grandison bowed and scraped and disappeared round the corner, his jaws closing around a large section of the colonel's best tobacco.

"You may take Grandison," said the colonel to his son. "I allow he's abolitionist-proof."

III

Richard Owens, Esq., and servant, from Kentucky, registered at the fashionable New York hostelry for Southerners in those days, a hotel where an atmosphere congenial to Southern institutions was sedulously maintained. But there were negro waiters in the dining-room, and mulatto bellboys, and Dick had no doubt that Grandison, with the native gregariousness and garrulousness of his race, would foregather and palaver with them sooner or later, and Dick hoped that they would speedily inoculate him with the virus of freedom. For it was not Dick's intention to say anything to his servant about his plan to free him, for obvious reasons. To mention one of them, if Grandison should go away, and by legal process be recaptured, his young master's part in the matter would doubtless become known, which would be embarrassing to Dick, to say the least. If, on the other hand, he should merely give Grandison sufficient latitude, he had no doubt he would eventually lose him. For while not exactly skeptical about Grandison's perfervid loyalty, Dick had been a somewhat keen observer of human nature, in his own indolent way, and based his expectations upon the force of the example and argument that his servant could scarcely fail to encounter. Grandison should have a fair chance to become free by his own initiative; if it should become necessary to adopt other measures to get rid of him, it would be time enough to act when the necessity arose; and Dick Owens was not the youth to take needless trouble.

The young master renewed some acquaintances and made others, and spent a week or two very pleasantly in the best society of the metropolis, easily accessible to a wealthy, well-bred young Southerner, with proper introductions. Young women smiled on him, and young men of convivial habits pressed their hospitalities; but the memory of Charity's sweet, strong face and clear blue eyes made him proof against the blandishments of the one sex and the persuasions of the other. Meanwhile he kept Grandison supplied with pocket-money, and left him mainly to his own devices. Every night when Dick came in he hoped he might have to wait upon himself, and every morning he looked forward with pleasure to the prospect of making his toilet unaided. His hopes, however, were doomed to disappointment, for every night when he came in Grandison was on hand with a bootjack, and a nightcap mixed for his young master as the colonel had taught him to mix it, and every morning Grandison appeared with his master's boots blacked and his clothes brushed, and laid his linen out for the day.

"Grandison," said Dick one morning, after finishing his toilet, "this is the chance of your life to go around among your own people and see how they live. Have you met any of them?"

"Yas, suh, I's seen some of 'em. But I don' keer nuffin fer 'em, suh. Dey're diffe'nt f'm de niggers down ou' way. Dey 'lows dey're free, but dey ain' got sense 'nuff ter know dey ain' half as well off as dey would be down Souf, whar dey'd be 'preciated."

When two weeks had passed without any apparent effect of evil example upon Grandison, Dick resolved to go on to Boston, where he thought the atmosphere might prove more favorable to his ends. After he had been at the Revere House for a day or two without losing Grandison, he decided upon slightly different tactics.

Having ascertained from a city directory the addresses of several well-known abolitionists, he wrote them each a letter something like this:—

DEAR FRIEND AND BROTHER:—

A wicked slaveholder from Kentucky, stopping at the Revere House, has dared to insult the liberty-loving people of Boston by bringing his slave into their midst. Shall this be tolerated? Or shall steps be taken in the name of liberty to rescue a fellow-man from bondage? For obvious reasons I can only sign myself,

A FRIEND OF HUMANITY.

That this letter might have an opportunity to prove effective, Dick made it a point to send Grandison away from the hotel on various errands. On one of these occasions Dick watched him for quite a distance down the street. Grandison had scarcely left the hotel when a long-haired, sharp-featured man came out behind him, followed him, soon overtook him, and kept along beside him until they turned the next corner. Dick's hopes were roused by this spectacle, but sank correspondingly when Grandison returned to the hotel. As Grandison said nothing about the encounter, Dick hoped there might be some self-consciousness behind this unexpected reticence, the results of which might develop later on.

But Grandison was on hand again when his master came back to the hotel at night, and was in attendance again in the morning, with hot water, to assist at his master's toilet. Dick sent him on further errands from day to day, and upon one occasion came squarely up to him—inadvertently of course—while Grandison was engaged in conversation with a young white man in clerical garb. When Grandison saw Dick approaching, he edged away from the preacher and hastened toward his master, with a very evident expression of relief upon his countenance.

"Mars Dick," he said, "dese yer abolitioners is jes' pesterin' de life out er me tryin' ter git me ter run away. I don' pay no 'tention ter 'em, but dey riles me so sometimes dat I'm feared I'll hit some of 'em some er dese days, an' dat mought git me inter trouble. I ain' said nuffin' ter you 'bout it, Mars Dick, fer I did n' wanter 'sturb yo' min'; but I don' like it, suh; no, suh, I don'! Is we gwine back home 'fo' long, Mars Dick?"

"We'll be going back soon enough," replied Dick somewhat shortly, while he inwardly cursed the stupidity of a slave who could be free and would not, and registered a secret vow that if he were unable to get rid of Grandison without assassinating him, and were therefore compelled to take him back to Kentucky, he would see that Grandison got a taste of an article of slavery that would make him regret his wasted opportunities. Meanwhile he determined to tempt his servant yet more strongly.

"Grandison," he said next morning, "I'm going away for a day or two, but I shall leave you here. I shall lock up a hundred dollars in this drawer and give you the key. If you need any of it, use it and enjoy yourself,—spend it all if you like,—for this is probably the last chance you'll have for some time to be in a free State, and you'd better enjoy your liberty while you may."

When he came back a couple of days later and found the faithful Grandison at his post, and the hundred dollars intact, Dick felt seriously annoyed. His vexation was increased by the fact that he could not express his feelings adequately. He did not even scold Grandison; how could he, indeed, find fault with one who so sensibly recognized his true place in the economy of civilization, and kept it with such touching fidelity?

"I can't say a thing to him," groaned Dick. "He deserves a leather medal, made out of his own hide tanned. I reckon I'll write to father and let him know what a model servant he has given me."

He wrote his father a letter which made the colonel swell with pride and pleasure. "I really think," the colonel observed to one of his friends, "that Dick ought to have the nigger interviewed by the Boston papers, so that they may see how contented and happy our darkeys really are."

Dick also wrote a long letter to Charity Lomax, in which he said, among many other things, that if she knew how hard he was working, and under what difficulties, to accomplish something serious for her sake, she would no longer keep him in suspense, but overwhelm him with love and admiration.

Having thus exhausted without result the more obvious methods of getting rid of Grandison, Dick was forced to consider more radical measures. Of course he might run away himself, and abandon Grandison, but this would be merely to leave him in the United States, where he was still a slave, and where, with his notions of loyalty, he would speedily be reclaimed. It was necessary, in order to accomplish the purpose of his trip to the North, to leave Grandison permanently in Canada, where he would be legally free.

"I might extend my trip to Canada," he reflected, "but that would be too palpable. I have it! I'll visit Niagara Falls on the way home, and lose him on the Canada side. When he once realizes that he is actually free, I'll warrant that he'll stay."

So the next day saw them westward bound, and in the course of time, by the somewhat slow conveyances of the period, they found themselves at Niagara. Dick walked and drove about the Falls for several days, taking Grandison along with him on most occasions. One morning they stood on the Canadian side, watching the wild whirl of the waters below them.

"Grandison," said Dick, raising his voice above the roar of the cataract, "do you know where you are now?"

"I's wid you, Mars Dick; dat's all I keers."

"You are now in Canada, Grandison, where your people go when they run away from their masters. If you wished, Grandison, you might walk away from me this very minute, and I could not lay my hand upon you to take you back."

Grandison looked around uneasily.

"Let's go back ober de ribber, Mars Dick. I's feared I'll lose you ovuh heah, an' den I won' hab no marster, an' won't nebber be able to git back home no mo'."

Discouraged, but not yet hopeless, Dick said, a few minutes later,—

"Grandison, I'm going up the road a bit, to the inn over yonder. You stay here until I return. I'll not be gone a great while."

Grandison's eyes opened wide and he looked somewhat fearful.

"Is dey any er dem dadblasted abolitioners roun' heah, Mars Dick?"

"I don't imagine that there are," replied his master, hoping there might be. "But I'm not afraid of *your* running away, Grandison. I only wish I were," he added to himself.

Dick walked leisurely down the road to where the white-washed inn, built of stone, with true British solidarity, loomed up through the trees by the roadside. Arrived there he ordered a glass of ale and a sandwich, and took a seat at a table by a window, from which he could see Grandison in the distance. For a while he hoped that the seed he had sown might have fallen on fertile ground, and that Grandison, relieved from the restraining power of a master's eye, and finding himself in a free country, might get up and walk away; but the hope was vain, for Grandison remained faithfully at his post, awaiting his master's return. He had seated himself on a broad flat stone, and, turning his eyes away from the grand and awe-inspiring spectacle that lay close at hand, was looking anxiously toward the inn where his master sat cursing his ill-timed fidelity.

By and by a girl came into the room to serve his order, and Dick very naturally glanced at her; and as she was young and pretty and remained in attendance, it was some minutes before he looked for Grandison. When he did so his faithful servant had disappeared.

To pay his reckoning and go away without the change was a matter quickly accomplished. Retracing his footsteps toward the Falls, he saw, to his great disgust, as he approached the spot where he had left Grandison, the familiar form of his servant stretched out on the ground, his face to the sun, his mouth open, sleeping the time away, oblivious alike to the grandeur of the scenery, the thunderous roar of the cataract, or the insidious voice of sentiment.

"Grandison," soliloquized his master, as he stood gazing down at his ebony encumbrance. "I do not deserve to be an American citizen; I ought not to have the advantages I possess over you; and I certainly am not worthy of Charity Lomax, if I am not smart enough to get rid of you. I have an idea! You shall yet be free, and I will be the instrument of your deliverance. Sleep on, faithful and affectionate servitor, and dream of the blue grass and the bright skies of old Kentucky, for it is only in your dreams that you will ever see them again!"

Dick retraced his footsteps towards the inn. The young woman chanced to look out of the window and saw the handsome young gentleman she had waited on a few minutes before, standing in the road a short distance away, apparently engaged in earnest conversation with a colored man employed as hostler for the inn. She thought she saw something pass from the white man to the other, but at that moment her duties called her away from the window, and when she looked out again the young gentleman had disappeared, and the hostler, with two other young men of the neighborhood, one white and one colored, were walking rapidly towards the Falls.

IV

Dick made the journey homeward alone, and as rapidly as the conveyances of the day would permit. As he drew near home his conduct in going back without Grandison took on a more serious aspect than it had borne at any previous time, and although he had prepared the colonel by a letter sent several days ahead, there was still the prospect of a bad quarter of an hour with him; not, indeed, that his father would upbraid him, but he was likely to make searching inquiries. And notwithstanding the vein of quiet recklessness that had carried Dick through his preposterous scheme, he was a very poor liar, having rarely had occasion or inclination to tell anything but the truth. Any reluctance to meet his father was more than offset, however, by a stronger force drawing him homeward, for Charity Lomax must long since have returned from her visit to her aunt in Tennessee.

Dick got off easier than he had expected. He told a straight story, and a truthful one, so far as it went.

The colonel raged at first, but rage soon subsided into anger, and anger moderated into annoyance, and annoyance into a sort of garrulous sense of injury. The colonel thought he had been hardly used; he had trusted this negro, and he had broken faith. Yet, after all, he did not blame Grandison so much as he did the abolitionists, who were undoubtedly at the bottom of it.

As for Charity Lomax, Dick told her, privately of course, that he had run his father's man, Grandison, off to Canada, and left him there.

"Oh, Dick," she had said with shuddering alarm, "what have you done? If they knew it they'd send you to the penitentiary, like they did to that Yankee."

"But they don't know it," he had replied seriously; adding, with an injured tone, "you don't seem to appreciate my heroism like you did that of the Yankee; perhaps it's because I wasn't caught and sent to the penitentiary. I thought you wanted me to do it."

"Why, Dick Owens!" she exclaimed. "You know I never dreamed of any such outrageous proceeding.

"But I presume I'll have to marry you," she concluded, after some insistence on Dick's part, "if only to take care of you. You are too reckless for anything; and a man who goes chasing all over the North, being entertained by New York and Boston society and having negroes to throw away, needs some one to look after him."

"It's a most remarkable thing," replied Dick fervently, "that your views correspond exactly with my profoundest convictions. It proves beyond question that we were made for one another."

They were married three weeks later. As each of them had just returned from a journey, they spent their honeymoon at home.

A week after the wedding they were seated, one afternoon, on the piazza of the colonel's house, where Dick had taken his bride, when a negro from the yard ran down the lane and threw open the big gate for the colonel's buggy to enter. The colonel was not alone. Beside him, ragged and travel-stained, bowed with weariness and upon his face a haggard look that told of hardship and privation, sat the lost Grandison.

The colonel alighted at the steps.

"Take the lines, Tom," he said to the man who had opened the gate, "and drive round to the barn. Help Grandison down,—poor devil, he's so stiff he can hardly move!—and get a tub of water and wash him and rub him down, and feed him, and give him a big drink of whiskey, and then let him come round and see his young master and his new mistress."

The colonel's face wore an expression compounded of joy and indignation,—joy at the restoration of a valuable piece of property; indignation for reasons he proceeded to state.

"It's astounding, the depths of depravity the human heart is capable of! I was coming along the road three miles away, when I heard someone call me from the roadside. I pulled up the mare, and who should come out of the woods but Grandison. The poor nigger could hardly crawl along, with the help of a broken limb. I was never more astonished in my life. You could have knocked me down with a feather. He seemed pretty far gone,—he could hardly talk above a whisper,—and I had to give him a mouthful of whiskey to brave him up so he could tell his story. It's just as I thought from the beginning, Dick; Grandison had no notion of running away; he knew when he was well off, and where his friends were. All the persuasions of abolition liars and runaway niggers did not move him. But the desperation of those fanatics knew no bounds; their guilty consciences gave them no rest. They got the notion somehow that Grandison belonged to a nigger-catcher, and had been brought North as a spy to help capture ungrateful runaway servants. They actually kidnapped him—just think of it!—and gagged him and bound him and threw him rudely into a wagon, and carried him into the gloomy depths of a Canadian forest, and locked him in a lonely hut, and fed him on bread and water for three weeks. One of the scoundrels wanted to kill him, and persuaded the others that it ought to be done; but they got to quarreling about how they should do it, and before they had their minds made up Grandison escaped, and, keeping his back steadily to the North Star, made his way, after suffering incredible hardships, back to the old plantation, back to his master, his friends, and his home. Why, it's as good as one of Scott's novels! Mr. Simms or some other one of our Southern authors ought to write it up."

"Don't you think, sir," suggested Dick, who had calmly smoked his cigar throughout the colonel's animated recital, "that that kidnaping yarn sounds a little improbable? Isn't there some more likely explanation?"

"Nonsense, Dick; it's the gospel truth! Those infernal abolitionists are capable of anything—everything! Just think of their locking the poor, faithful nigger up, beating him, kicking him, depriving him of his liberty, keeping him on bread and water for three long, lonesome weeks, and he all the time pining for the old plantation!"

There were almost tears in the colonel's eyes at the picture of Grandison's sufferings that he conjured up. Dick still professed to be slightly skeptical, and met Charity's severely questioning eye with bland unconsciousness.

The colonel killed the fatted calf for Grandison, and for two or three weeks the returned wanderer's life was a slave's dream of pleasure. His fame spread throughout the county, and the colonel gave him a permanent place among the house servants, where he could always have him conveniently at hand to relate his adventures to admiring visitors.

About three weeks after Grandison's return the colonel's faith in sable humanity was rudely shaken, and its foundations almost broken up. He came near losing his belief in the fidelity of the negro to his master,—the servile virtue most highly prized and most sedulously cultivated by the colonel and his kind. One Monday morning Grandison was missing. And not only Grandison, but his wife, Betty the maid; his mother, aunt Eunice; his father, uncle Ike; his brothers, Tom and John, and his little sister Elsie, were likewise absent from the plantation; and a hurried search and inquiry in the neighborhood resulted in no information as to their whereabouts. So much valuable property could not be lost without an effort to recover it, and the wholesale nature of the transaction carried consternation to the hearts of those whose ledgers were chiefly bound in black. Extremely energetic measures were taken by the colonel and his friends. The fugitives were traced, and followed from point to point, on their northward run through Ohio. Several times the hunters were close upon their heels, but the magnitude of the escaping party begot unusual vigilance on the part of those who sympathized with the fugitives, and strangely enough, the underground railroad seemed to have had its tracks cleared and signals set for this particular train. Once, twice, the colonel thought he had them, but they slipped through his fingers.

One last glimpse he caught of his vanishing property, as he stood, accompanied by a United States marshal, on a wharf at a port on the south shore of Lake Erie. On the stern of a small steamboat which was receding rapidly from the wharf, with her nose pointing toward Canada, there stood a group of familiar dark faces, and the look they cast backward was not one of longing for the fleshpots of Egypt. The colonel saw Grandison point him out to one of the crew of the vessel, who waved his hand derisively toward the colonel. The latter shook his fist impotently—and the incident was closed.

A Bad Night

Cleveland News and Herald (1886)

Early in his literary career—during the mid- to late 1880s—
Chesnutt published a number of brief, usually comic stories
clearly intended as light amusements. Classified by William L.
Andrews as "apprenticeship" works, stories such as "Busy Day in
a Lawyer's Office" (*Tid-bits*, 1887), "A Metropolitan Experience"
(*Chicago Ledger*, 1887), "A Midnight Adventure" (*New Haven
Register*, 1887), and "An Eloquent Appeal" (*Puck*, 1888) seem
curious detours for an author who would later devote himself to
often-gloomy depictions of race relations in turn-of-the-century
America. On closer analysis, however, one can recognize the emer-
gent patterns of Chesnutt's storytelling in even the briefest, most
whimsical of his early writings. While "A Bad Night," for example, amusingly documents how a man's indulgence in Kentucky
whiskey leads to comically embarrassing consequences, the story
nevertheless anticipates some of the "darker" concerns—especially the instability of personal and social identity—one associates with Chesnutt's mature fiction.

Serialized in the *Cleveland News and Herald* in July 1886, "A
Bad Night" features an apparently well-bred narrator, Paul
_____, who relates, in an urbane and witty style quite unlike
Chesnutt's usual form, the events subsequent to a drinking binge
with an old college friend. Through a series of comic misassumptions by his wife, the police, and his attorney, the narrator
suffers a series of embarrassing incidents, culminating in his
arrest and a brief, happily concluded trial for burglarizing his
own house. At the basic level, then, the story functions as a pleasant joke, relying as it does upon the narrator's droll account of
his "inebriated condition" and his wife's easily aroused, surprisingly vigorous suspicions.

Despite its comic sensibility and light-hearted style, "A Bad Night" paradoxically previews Chesnutt's more serious, mature writings. For, if the story exploits boozy disorientation for light amusement, it ultimately focuses on the ways in which the narrator, Paul, and his wife revise their impressions of how a person's identity forms and is sustained, a theme crucial to Chesnutt's novels and his race-based short fiction. Because his wife fails to recognize the narrator—a function partly of his drunken condition and partly of the uncertain lighting—the story lays out a collection of details that emphasizes the mutability of Paul's identity and, indeed, his character. After his arrest, for example, he gives a false name to the police; near the end of the story, he studies himself in the mirror to see if his "hair had not turned gray in a single night" (31); after his one night of incarceration, he says to his wife, "'In me you see a nervous wreck, a blasted reputation, blighted prospects, and a ruined life'" (31); and finally, after his release from jail he remakes himself with a new suit and other cosmetic changes, claiming that "the wretched creature who had appeared in the Police Court would never have been recognized as the elegant Paul _____" (32). "A Bad Night," then, although not one of Chesnutt's more accomplished short stories, anticipates his interest in the ways people construct, understand, and revise their conceptions of themselves. This focus recurs repeatedly through Chesnutt's most compelling works, including *The Conjure Woman* (1899), *The Wife of His Youth and Other Stories of the Color Line* (1899), *The House Behind the Cedars* (1900), and *The Marrow of Tradition* (1901), all of which include characters whose public personae differ markedly from the ways they envision themselves and, indeed, the ways they are presented to the reader. While more trenchant in their investigations of the complex web of racial, social, and personal bases upon which the "self" is formed, these later fictions all question, as does "A Bad Night," the very nature of what constitutes identity.

This notion of unstable or evolving identity not only pervades much of Chesnutt's fiction but also in many ways describes his own literary reputation. As a self-identified African American—he ponders in his journal whether he ought to attempt to pass, but rejects the idea—attempting to write himself into a mostly white literary tradition, Chesnutt often found himself pre- and misjudged by white readers,[1] and he makes "misjudgment" a central concern in several of his best works. In such Northern short fictions as "The Passing of Grandison" (1899) and "Baxter's *Procrustes*" (1904), for example, he depicts figures who brilliantly encourage and capitalize on the misassumptions of those who presume too much. Nevertheless, his subsequent inability to earn a substantial living as a writer deepened his mistrust of the very readers on whom his career depended.

"A Bad Night" also contains some Chesnutt trademarks. Despite the fact that the narrator and the major characters speak in standard English—thus seeming to rule out the need for dialect—Chesnutt chooses here to audition the knack for capturing speech modes that characterizes his dialect work in *The Conjure Woman* (1899). In presenting the dialect of an Irish policeman, Chesnutt emphasizes the man's accent: "Oi'll have the nippers ready whin ye've grabbed the spalpeen" (28). Perhaps even more surprisingly, the other officer—an African American—speaks in precisely the sort of dialect that recalls the stereotypical representations of black characters Chesnutt found so repulsive. When, for example, the policemen first arrive on the scene, the "colored policeman" asks, "Whar is de bugglar, ma'am?" (28). Just as striking, though subtly done, is Chesnutt's use of this pair of police officers, or what the narrator calls "two guardians of the peace" (28). Thus, he imagines a Northern city (Cleveland) in which a black figure can wield the same sort of civic and official authority as a white man. Indeed, it is certainly a deliberate, if typically subtle, gesture that here, in fact, an African American—even in a minor role within the story—functions within the social universe of the North as an enforcer of the law.

In that light, "A Bad Night," almost in spite of its lighthearted tone and urbane wordplay, offers compelling insights into some of the formative impulses of Chesnutt's writing sensibilities. In his description of the narrator's wife, for example, he uses the ancient Greek standards of beauty as the basis for comparison, concluding that while she falls short of that measure, she nevertheless exceeds the average in what he calls "these degenerate days" (25). For Chesnutt, any such allusion carried a powerful and unsavory connotation—the mixing of white and black blood in so-called "mulattoes," a subject he relentlessly pursued, to the great peril of his career and indeed his life, in later works. Thus, even in a story one can only place among Chesnutt's least controversial works, the seeds for his later career are provocatively evident.

NOTES

1. See, for example, the breathtaking review of Chesnutt's *The Marrow of Tradition*, in which the reviewer writes, "Chesnutt should print his picture with his book in order to

allow his readers to know whether he is a white man or a negro" (*CE*, 84). Another reviewer rather startlingly writes, "Despite the fact that we have not seen the book, we have seen it reviewed and so know the truth of it" (qtd. in Ellison and Metcalf, 53).

A Bad Night

MY WIFE HAS PERHAPS more good qualities than any woman I am acquainted with. I shall not attempt to enumerate them, but will merely say for the purposes of this story that she has only one fault. In accordance, however, with the universal law of compensation, she possesses that one fault in such measure as to counterbalance a great many of her virtues—she is the most suspicious of women.

Nature has given her a fairly symmetrical figure and a very pleasant face. Her features are not cast exactly in the Greek mold, but are above the average in these degenerate days, and on the whole she is a very good-looking woman. She does not wear the finest fabrics, but always dresses in good taste. Yet whenever she sees anyone looking at her intently, she at once becomes indignant because she imagines that her appearance is being criticized—that her dress does not fit smoothly, or her hat is awry. She has a mortal terror of dogs and canine beauty and fidelity have no existence for her, for in every dog she sees either an actual or a probable case of hydrophobia. The pleasure of rapid motion, which Dr. Johnson so long ago stamped with his approval, she never enjoys, for if the horse gets out of a walk, she thinks he is running away.

Beggars and peddlers never come to our house but once, for in every one of them she sees a tramp or a sneak thief. She has had a wicket put in the kitchen door, through which she can look at anyone knocking and transact any business she may have with strangers. She has even had iron bars put on the lower windows, and nearly bankrupted me once by putting burglar alarms and a telephone into the house—a rented house at that. In vain I have assured her that there is nothing in our humble establishment for the sake of which even an amateur burglar would risk his life or his liberty. She cannot be convinced that my silver watch, the plated teaspoons, and the silver ice pitcher, which was the most valuable of our wedding presents, are not a standing temptation to thieves. We once, during the temporary illness attendant upon the birth of our first child, hired a girl to help with the housework; but my wife kept such a close surveillance over Biddy that the high-spirited scion of Hibernian royalty left in a huff, forgetting to pay back the two-weeks' wages I had advanced her to buy a new bonnet.

On one occasion my venerable uncle, who lives in the country and whom my wife had never met, came in to pay us a visit. He modestly went round to the back door and knocked. My wife opened the wicket, have him a hasty glance, jumped at the conclusion that he was a tramp or a peddler, ordered him out of the yard, and slammed the wicket in his face before the astonished old gentleman had time to introduce himself. We have since had to buy all our Christmas and Thanksgiving turkeys, and did not spend the next summer on my uncle's farm, a visit we had looked forward to with pleasant anticipation.

But these were small matters, and I could afford to laugh at most of them, until the incident occurred which would have rendered my wife's fault unbearable and compelled me to resort to extreme measures (the nature of which it is unnecessary for me to state) if it had not at the same time opened her eyes to her own folly, the first step, I hope, to a permanent cure.

This incident took place one evening in summer. I had said to my wife at noon that I might not be home for supper, as I should probably be detained at the office an hour or two in the evening, and if so, would get a lunch downtown. As it happened I did not have to stay down in the evening, but started home about the usual hour. While I was waiting for a street car I heard a gruff voice pronounce my name, and before I could turn felt a stunning blow on my shoulder—evidently intended for a friendly clap—and as I wheeled around in some trepidation, found myself face to face with Spratt. Spratt was an old college classmate and former chum of mine whom I had not seen for a year as he had been running a cattle ranch in Texas.

"Hello, Spratt, old man," I exclaimed, as soon as I had recovered my breath, "I haven't seen you since the flood!"

Spratt immediately consigned me to the infernal regions in the emphatic language of the Texas cowboy, while the painful grasp of his hand and the unaffected cordiality of his manner showed the pleasure he felt at meeting me. My first impulse was to ask Spratt to supper. But then I remembered that my wife hardly expected me to supper; and while I was mentally balancing the pros and cons, Spratt thrust his hand in my arm and exclaimed:

"I'm stopping at the National, and I'm going up to dinner. Come up and have a bite. I want to talk to you, and I've got to leave the city in the morning."

Under ordinary circumstances I would not, by remaining away from supper, have subjected myself to the unjust and degrading suspicions to which my unexplained absence would have surely given rise; yet, reflecting that my wife did not expect me, I thought I might risk it in this instance. I went with Spratt to the hotel, and we had supper served in a private room where we could talk over old times without restraint. The soup was good, the fish was excellent, the roast was superb. We had a couple of bottles of wine, and Spratt, who had acquired the tastes of the frontiersman with marvelous facility, must have some Kentucky whiskey. I merely took the least bit of this at Spratt's request to try the flavor.

When I parted from Spratt about nine o'clock, I felt extremely comfortable and never was in better spirits in my life. I took a streetcar and soon reached home. In a fit of absent-mindedness I tried to open the door with my pocket knife for a while, but discovering my mistake, applied the latch-key and gained admittance. I hung, or meant to hang, my hat on a hook, but it fell on the floor and rolled over into a corner. I did not think it worthwhile to pick it up, as a slight feeling of languor stealing over me made me disinclined to any unnecessary exertion. I took off my overcoat and hung it over the back of a chair which stood in a corner. It slipped off the chair and fell behind it on the floor, but as it was just as safe there, I did not think it necessary to pick it up. I was feeling very sleepy by this time, and lay down on the lounge in the sitting room.

That is to say, I meant to lie down on the lounge, but through some miscalculation or mistake, or misfortune, I missed the lounge and lay on the floor. My memory is a little indistinct about the matter now, but I remember I thought it would require a good deal of exertion to get up and lie down on the lounge, to say nothing of the possibility of another failure. I concluded that under the circumstances the floor was good enough for me. As the position I lay in was not very comfortable, I turned over toward the lounge and rolled under it; the chintz cover, which fell in a curtain to the floor, shaded my eyes from the light, and I went to sleep almost immediately. My memory is almost an utter blank as to the subsequent events of the evening, and what happened during the next hour I relate as it was told to me afterwards.

My wife, not expecting me home until somewhat late in the evening, had stepped across the street to a progressive euchre party at the house of an intimate friend, where she stayed until about eleven o'clock. On coming home, she did not, for reasons above stated, see my hat or overcoat, and naturally supposed I had not yet come in. My sister-in-law, who was staying with us, had gone to a party with her young man, and thus leaving my wife alone in the house. As time passed and I did not put in an appearance, she became a little restless and nervous, as was but natural for a woman of her disposition. In looking around the room for some object that was misplaced she caught site of my feet protruding from under the lounge. She had no idea that I was in the house, and she needed but a glance at the boots, which had become very dirty in my homeward meandering, to convince her that a burglar had secreted himself under the lounge with the intention of robbing the house when all the inmates were asleep.

Most women, under like circumstances, would have screamed or fainted, or in some way exhibited their emotions. But my wife, as I have said, was no ordinary woman, but possessed a firmness and strength of character which is by no means common, even among the sterner sex, and rarely met with in women. She did not scream or faint, but went quietly out of the room, ran upstairs to the library, closing the doors behind her softly, so as to prevent the noise from being heard below, and telephoned the nearest police station, stating that a burglar was concealed in the house and asking that a policeman be sent to arrest him. Then she got my revolver out of a bureau drawer, went downstairs, and sat down by the worktable, within ten feet of the supposed burglar. I question whether one woman in a thousand would have been capable of as much.

In about five minutes a knocking was heard at the door, and my wife admitted the two guardians of the peace—an Irishman and a Negro.

"Whar is de bugglar, ma'am?" whispered the colored policeman.

"Under the sofa in the next room," she said, pointing to the open door of the sitting room.

"Go in front," suggested the Irishman to the colored man, "and Oi'll have the nippers ready whin ye've grabbed the spalpeen."

They entered the room, and my wife's nerves not being equal to any further tension, she fainted. When she came to, the Irishman was holding a glass of water to her lips, and as she opened her eyes he said:

"Faith, mum, an' we arrested 'im. The spalpeen attempted to resist the officers of the law, and we clubbed him over the head a bit. It'll make him sleep the sounder tonight."

My wife's sister came in a few minutes later, and the two women sat and waited for me far into the night. My sister-in-law first went to bed, and my wife followed shortly after, but not to sleep, as she was worried at my non-appearance and tormented with fears for my safety.

In the cold gray dawn I awoke from a troubled sleep. I was not at first sure that I was awake. My head felt very queer, and, as I discovered by passing my hand over it, was covered with contusions of various degrees of magnitude and tenderness. My clothes were torn and muddy, and taking me altogether, I looked as though I had been tossed by an angry bull or run over by a fire engine. I found myself in a small apartment, with a narrow, grated window and an iron door in the stone wall. It required no second glance to show me that I was in prison. I was, in fact, immured in a cell of the Central Police Station.

I endeavored to recall the events of the previous evening. I remembered, somewhat vaguely, all that took place up to the time when I went to sleep under the lounge. What happened afterwards I could recall only as a dream, in which, like a lost spirit, I had been tormented by devils who clubbed me with telegraph poles and prodded me with red-hot pitchforks.

But why was I here? Had I imbibed too freely of Spratt's Kentucky whiskey, and in a fit of alcoholic mania murdered my wife or one of the children, or the whole family? I pictured to myself the bloody corpses of my children, slain by a father's ruthless hand. Had I gone out in my sleep and unwittingly committed arson or burglary or some other heinous offense? Or had I merely been run in for disorderly conduct? I gave it up, but my reflections were not pleasant while I waited for enlightenment.

About eight o'clock a turnkey put in an appearance with a plate of coarse food and a brown mug of what purported to be coffee, and shoved them through a wicket in the door of my cell.

"I say," I anxiously inquired, "where am I anyway?"

"You're in a very fine place compared with where you will be before long," was the gruff response. "You're in the Central Station now, but the chances are that you will be in jail in about two hours."

This information was not very reassuring. "But what am I in for?" I asked.

"Burglary and resisting the officers. You know what you're in for; the old thing, no doubt. Hurry up and eat your breakfast, if you want any, for the court will open in half an hour, and your case is the first or second on the docket."

I was horror-struck—crushed—almost annihilated! What a position! A life which so far had been at least honest, a reputation without a flaw, to be blasted in a single night by the well-meant, but ill-timed hospitality of Spratt! I am afraid that in the excitement of the moment I referred to Spratt in language which would not bear repetition.

But the all-important question was, how to get out of the scrape, if possible. Of course a lawyer was the first thing needed, and after some solicitation I induced the turnkey, who was naturally inclined to consider me a rather desperate and irresponsible character, to send for an attorney of my acquaintance, on whose skill and secrecy I could rely.

I had hardly time to give my attorney a hasty and somewhat incoherent account of such events of the preceding evening as I could recollect, when the presiding genius of the institution reappeared, and called out in a sing-song tone:

"Number three, burglary and resisting officers," and I was hurried up a flight of stone steps, through a long corridor, and into a dingy court room, where sat a somewhat austere-looking judge, with hair and whiskers slightly streaked with gray, and a mustache clipped straight across the upper lip. As the day was wet and disagreeable, the number of spectators was small, for which I was devoutly thankful.

"What is your name?" asked the court.

"John Smith," whispered my legal adviser, and I unblushingly gave the time-honored response.

"You are charged with two offenses. The first charge against you is burglary. Are you guilty or not guilty?"

"Not guilty," I answered, at the instance of my attorney.

"Mr. Bailiff, call Patrolman Sullivan."

Patrolman Michael Sullivan, being first sworn, testified that on the evening before he had been on duty at the Forest Street Police Station; that at eleven o'clock he had been detailed by Sergeant Donnelly, in response to a telephone call, to go with Patrolman Caesar Johnson to No. 375 Birch Street and arrest a burglar who was concealed on the premises; that they had been admitted to the house by the front door, and had found the prisoner concealed or partly concealed under a lounge in the sitting room; that he was evidently under the influence of liquor at that time; that—

When I heard the number of the house I began to understand the situation, and the subsequent disclosures made it all clear to me. I remembered rolling under the lounge, and knowing my wife's peculiar temperament, I saw that I had been the innocent victim of circumstances. I hurriedly whispered to my lawyer, and as I told him how things were, a broad grin slowly diffused itself over his face. Interrupting the witness exclaimed:

"May it please the court, this whole affair is a most ridiculous mistake, as I can convince your honor in two minutes' private conversation, if your honor will grant me that."

Our police court is not very ceremonious and the coveted two minutes was granted; and in the adjacent witness room the court was soon informed that I had been arrested in my own house, on the complaint of my own wife. The judge was a little incredulous at first, but on the assurance of my attorney the cases against me were dismissed. The court gave me a few words of advice which I received in a spirit of proper humility, and I was once more a free man.

I begged my attorney to call a hack for me, as an appearance on the street in my condition at that time would have occasioned some remarks to say the least, even if some zealous policeman had not re-arrested me on general principles. Even the hackman was suspicious, and demanded his fare in advance. I paid it and was soon driven home.

I alighted from the vehicle and ran up the steps as quickly as possible, to avoid the eyes of inquisitive neighbors. A jerk at the doorbell brought my wife, who uttered a shriek of joy and literally threw herself upon me. In my weakened physical condition I was obliged to brace myself up against the wall in order to sustain the shock.

"Oh, Paul, Paul, my dear husband! Where have you been? Oh, my poor husband! How did you escape?"—and so on, kissing me hysterically the while.

I calmly endured these demonstrations of joy for a few moments, and then putting her from me, I said sternly:

"Madam, behold the consequences of your folly! You have accomplished your work! In me you see a nervous wreck, a blasted reputation, blighted prospects, and a ruined life. Unhand me, madam," and I stalked as majestically as was possible under the circumstances into the house.

I glanced hastily into the first mirror I came to, to see if my hair had not turned gray in a single night; and I cannot tell yet whether it was a relief or a disappointment to find that it had not. I shall always hereafter be a little skeptical about the time-honored literary expedient; for according to all the canons of fiction, my sufferings certainly ought to have had that result.

While I was dressing my wounds and changing my clothes, my wife and I were mutually enlightened as to the events of the night. Of course I heaped reproaches upon her head, and with such a pointed illustration at hand, I was not slow in pointing out to her the absurdity of that suspiciousness which was her one fault. In her mortification at my arrest and the possible social and financial consequences, she did not, as I feared she would, make any allusion to my inebriated condition at the time that I came home; which was, I am reluctantly forced to admit, the primary cause of this unfortunate affair. I need not here stop to say that she has mentioned it several times since then.

But this was not the end. Some sharp-nosed reporter had learned of the arrest of a supposed burglar at No. 375 Birch Street the night before, and had the whole disgusting details dished up in the *Morning Swill Barrel*, together with several circumstances which seemed to connect me with a notorious band of criminals. This brought the scavengers of the evening papers around to learn more about the matter, and in the course of their inquiries they learned that I had not been seen since leaving the hotel the night before. This fact was duly chronicled in the evening papers under the conspicuous title of "A Mysterious Disappearance," and the theory was put forward that I had been put out of the way by the burglar before reaching home, in order to facilitate the commission of the burglary. When I hurried down to the office about three o'clock I found the proprietor and the assistant bookkeeper deeply immersed in the accounts, and I knew from the look of relief that came into the proprietor's face that my reappearance had lifted a load from his mind.

I remained closeted with him for half an hour. I made a clean breast of the matter, for I did not want to have him hear a garbled edition of it from some other source. He was a fair man—not too good to sympathize with the weakness of others—and the matter was overlooked. I took a week's vacation while my wounds were healing and while a tailor was making me a new suit. I am happy to state that the story never got out. My lawyer was discreet, and the wretched creature who had appeared in the Police Court would never have been recognized as the elegant Paul_____. My disappearance was accounted for to inquisitive acquaintances by sudden summons to a neighboring town to attend the dying bed of my aged great-grandfather.

As I remarked at the beginning of this story, which I publish as a warning to young married people, the most important result of the affair—and one which consoles me for all the annoyance and expense in the way of doctor's, lawyer's, and tailor's bills—has been a gradual change for the better in my wife's disposition. At the present rate of improvement, I hope to see her one vice thoroughly eradicated, when I shall be able to present to the world that rarest of creatures:

> *"A perfect woman, nobly planned,*
> *To warn, to comfort, and command."*

Cartwright's Mistake

Cleveland News and Herald (1886)

As an educated, extremely well-read African American—one who had read *The Iliad* in Latin—growing up in the Reconstruction South, Charles Chesnutt certainly came to understand isolation. Describing his early adulthood in North Carolina, for example, Chesnutt writes in his *Journals,* "I occupy here a position similar to that of the Mahomet's Coffin. I am neither fish[,] flesh, nor fowl—neither 'nigger,' poor white, nor 'buckrah.' Too 'stuck-up' for the colored folks, and, of course, not recognized by the whites" (157). Given Chesnutt's background as a black intellectual in a culture only a generation removed from slavery, one can easily comprehend why his short fiction repeatedly derives from the perspectives of outsiders, a position with which the author had broad experience. In fact, it is not at all surprising that an aspiring African American writer struggling to write himself into an almost exclusively white American literary tradition would frequently fashion stories about figures one might classify as outsiders, especially outsiders made so because of their appearances. Many of his works contemplate the attempts of ex-slaves or mulattoes to craft a meaningful place for themselves in the rapidly evolving social and economic milieu of the United States at the close of the nineteenth century. His first published novel, *The House Behind the Cedars* (1900), traces, for example, the experiences of a family whose attempts to "pass" into white society require a clandestine lifestyle reflected in the title of the book; the family does what it can to keep its machinations hidden from prying eyes. In a startling but altogether logical preview of that inclination, one of Chesnutt's first published short stories likewise focuses on a character marginalized because of his appearance. What is surprising, though, is that the story—"Cartwright's Mistake" (1886)—seems to have nothing to do with race. The story nevertheless provides an early clue to Chesnutt's impatience with those who would too quickly judge others only by appearance.

While race is never mentioned in "Cartwright's Mistake," Chesnutt clearly intends to satirize the human impulse to discriminate on the basis of corporeal differences. In this case, the subject of the narrative is the over-weight Cartwright, whose physical appearance seems initially to make him an unlikely protagonist of a romantic quest. First appearing in the *Cleveland News and Herald* in 1886, the story explores the quirkiness of human inter-action by tracing the budding romance of Cartwright and Florence Gay-lord. Although her mother characterizes the suitor as "'ridiculously fat'" (39), Florence becomes enamored and agrees to marry Cartwright. Prob-lems arise, however, when the prospective groom—using the pretense of a long business trip—secretly seeks medical help to lose weight. When Cartwright returns after a prolonged absence as "a tall, symmetrical young man, without an ounce of superfluous flesh upon him" (41), Florence abruptly (and inexplicably) calls off the engagement, much to the bafflement of the narrator, Walton. While the story might be read as an allegory of racial prejudice—Cartwright is defined in large part by his appearance, as are many of Chesnutt's African American characters—it works on a broader level to expose the unaccountable nature of personal bias. Beyond its appeal as an oddly comic commentary on what drives attraction, the work also recounts the extent to which Walton, who serves as a kind of proxy for the reader, develops a respect for Cartwright that transcends the latter's appear-ance. In this way, Walton represents Chesnutt's ideal "reader": one who can put aside prejudice and judge others on their merits rather than their weight (or skin color).

By so doing, "Cartwright's Mistake" emphasizes the enigmatic and indeed perilous nature of interpretation, pointing out that even an intelli-gent, sympathetic reader like Walton can be overmatched by a puzzling text, a theme to which Chesnutt returns in stories such as "White Weeds," "The Passing of Grandison," and "Baxter's *Procrustes*." One rationale for weav-ing such a thesis into his fiction, of course, is his continued interest in per-suading white readers to reevaluate their judgments of African Americans, but the story works as a commentary on the nature of interpretation as well. As in many of his other fictions—both Northern and not—"Cartwright's Mistake" encodes Chesnutt's subtle indictment of a (mostly white) reading audience too willing to rely on visual criteria for their judgments. Chesnutt returned frequently in his fiction to this vein of epistemological inquiry.

The strategy of having sympathetic narrators like Walton relate incidents of prejudice grants rhetorical power to a black author interested in unseating the race prejudice at work in the United States. For, while narrators who also function as protagonists might offer compelling and highly personal accounts of their trials, the use of "witness-narrators"—those who look on more or less disinterestedly while the events unfold—allows Chesnutt to engage readers' sense of reason as well as their emotions. In stories such as "Cartwright's Mistake," the witness-narrator often functions as a proxy for readers, a compassionate yet reasonable commentator on the injustices meted out to individual characters. And, perhaps most significantly for Chesnutt, these narrators—"readers" themselves, after all—come to recognize the inadequacy of their previously unexamined principles of interpretation. Chesnutt thus implicitly calls on his primarily white audience to reconsider the assumptions underlying their own conceptions of the world, and particularly, we might imagine, their understanding of race: for, in Chesnutt's canon, it is skin color that most often generates the sort of reductive judgment that these witness-narrators learn to question. Indeed, "A Fool's Paradise," "Aunt Mimy's Son," "A Grass Widow," and "Baxter's *Procrustes*" all similarly depict witness-narrators who are forced to reevaluate their interpretive skills when they learn that their initial assessments of people or situations have been startlingly inaccurate.

Thus, Chesnutt rehearses in "Cartwright's Mistake" a writing strategy that recurs throughout his more mature works. As in those later works, the author exposes the illogic that attends prejudice based on appearance, although in a significantly disguised form. For Cartwright's liability is not his skin color, but rather his abundance of flesh. It is thus strikingly ironic that Cartwright is at his most attractive to Florence in a form that grants him the least social privilege: as a fat man. When he sheds the extra weight and conforms to the social norms of physical beauty—even Florence's mother seems surprised by her daughter's revulsion for the now-slim Cartwright—he becomes, if *only* for her, less attractive. Whether Chesnutt offers this story as a figural shaking of his head at the mystifying ways in which humans regard one another or as a biting satire on racial prejudice, it seems clear that, even as early as 1886, he was fascinated by the extent to which our lives are determined by visual signals we emit, intentionally or not.

Whatever Chesnutt's intentions with "Cartwright's Mistake," it is vital to recognize the significance of the narrator, Walton, to our understanding of the story. For, while Cartwright ultimately loses the object of his affection—

ironically because of his suddenly svelte form—he does trigger a meta-morphosis in his new friend, Walton, who overcomes his own aversion to the obese Cartwright when he learns that the man is "no mere vulgar bun-dle of adipose tissue. He possessed a strong and vigorous mind, and . . . [h]is frank good-nature was irresistible" (37). Despite the failed romance, then, the story does function as an entertaining tribute to the attractiveness of the unprejudiced mind. While Florence can't get past the "different" (her word for her now-ex-fiancé) Cartwright, Walton—who presumably represents Chesnutt's ideal reader—comes to accept his friend in whatever form the latter takes.

Readers picking up a copy of the *Cleveland News and Herald* in Sep-tember of 1886 might have been initially puzzled by this quirky story about the failed romance of a (literally) re-formed man. "Cartwright's Mistake" must have seemed to those readers an enigmatic tale of found and lost love, and perhaps they shook their heads in wonderment at the apparently inex-plicable revulsion a woman is portrayed as feeling for her newly trim fiancé. But the story makes perfect sense as a precursor to Chesnutt's later writings. It lights, for example, on the notion of the self-made man, a concept found also in such works as "The Wife of His Youth" and, more comically, "The Shadow of My Past." While Chesnutt generally embraced the concept enthu-siastically—as a man of humble beginnings who became a wealthy Cleveland businessman—"Cartwright's Mistake" offers a cautionary tale about the haz-ards of reinventing oneself.

And, though putatively about a white couple beginning the end of their relationship, the story also previews Chesnutt's interest in exploring how various outsiders position themselves in an evolving, turn-of-the-century society. Further, through his experimentation with narrative strategies using witness-narrators to describe their shadowy worlds, Chesnutt also calls into question the very nature of interpretation, whether the subject is a literary text or a social one.

Cartwright's Mistake

I WAS SITTING ON the hotel piazza, following with my glass the movements of a steamer in the offing. As she disappeared around a distant bend of the shore, I turned my head toward the left, from which I heard footsteps approaching. My gaze rested upon the portly figure of a gentleman who stood a short distance from me, his hand resting on top of the balustrade. My eye instinctively settled upon the broad abdominal expanse which the skill of a fashionable tailor had not been able to prevent from being the most striking feature of the gentleman's appearance, for he was very fat.

The gentleman evidently perceived the objective point of my glance, for he gave a faint apologetic sort of a smile, as though he were somewhat ashamed of himself, and advanced toward me.

"Well, Walton," he said, extending his hand, "don't you know me?"

I had not recognized his figure, but the voice was the familiar one of an old college friend.

"Why, it's Cartwright! How are you, old boy? I'm ever so glad to see you," I exclaimed, grasping his outstretched hand and shaking it with genuine pleasure. I had been at this particular hotel of this particular seaside resort (which we will call Cliffdale) for two whole days without meeting a single acquaintance. Cartwright's advent was a decided relief to what threatened to be a solitary exile instead of a pleasant vacation. There were many people at the hotel, but I am not much of a hand at making new acquaintances.

"No wonder you didn't recognize me," said Cartwright, glancing downward at himself as far as his waistband, which formed his horizon in that direction. "I am getting so abominably fleshy that life is almost a burden to me. I thought a course of sea-bathing might reduce my weight somewhat and so I concluded to run down here for a few weeks. I'm ever so glad to meet you, Walton. What have you been doing with yourself since we left old Yale?"

We conversed awhile on topics of mutual interest and then went to walk along the beach. Though Cartwright's weight, as he informed me, was two hundred and fifty pounds, yet he was no mere vulgar bundle of adipose tissue. He possessed a strong and vigorous mind, and carried his flesh in such a way that after the novelty of his appearance wore off it did not provoke mirth or even remark. He was very well proportioned, and while his chin was not disproportionate to the rest of his body, it had not put on the extra folds which disfigure so many fat people. His walk was dignified, at least, if not graceful. His frank good-nature was irresistible.

We parted at bedtime, to meet at breakfast next morning. After a cigar on the piazza, we took a stroll along the beach together. A short distance from the hotel an open carriage dashed by, in which were seated two ladies, one middle-aged and of rather distinguished appearance, the other young and beautiful. I had scarcely time to lift my hat before the carriage had passed us.

"What a beautiful girl!" exclaimed Cartwright, looking after the phaeton; the hood was down, and over it he could see the nodding plume of the young lady's hat. "Who is she?"

"That," I replied, calmly, "is Miss Florence Gaylord, of Clearport. She is rich and accomplished; her charms of person speak for themselves; she is an excellent catch, and so far as I can learn, is still unappropriated."

"She is certainly very beautiful," he rejoined, with a thoughtful air.

The Gaylords, mother and daughter, had arrived at Cliffdale the night before, and this was my first sight of them. They were old acquaintances of mine. We saw them every day during the next few weeks. Cartwright became very attentive to Miss Gaylord, and it soon grew obvious that he was very much in love. I do not know what tricks my own heart might have played me, for Florence was very charming; but there was another young woman, then spending the summer in Europe, who had a first mort-gage on my affections, and the arrangements had been made for a foreclo-sure shortly after her return in October. I was therefore out of the race, and Cartwright had nothing to fear from my rivalry. Of course he would have had no chance whatever had I been in a position to enter the contest.

I could see with half an eye that Miss Gaylord was partial to Cartwright. She walked with him, talked with him, rode with him, danced with him—he could dance well, in spite of his obesity; she sang to him, and discussed books and authors with him, for they were both cultivated people, and fond of lit-erature. I could not see how any self-respecting, modest young woman could offer a man more encouragement than she gave Cartwright.

But he was singularly obtuse. He labored under the impression that no woman could love him with a genuine affection.

"No, Walton," he would say, "no young and pretty woman could love such a mountain of flesh as I am. A widow with a large family, or an old maid who had exhausted all her hopes, might put up with me. A young woman might pity me, and in her generosity seem to encourage me, but she wouldn't mean anything by it. They smile on me for the same reason that they pat the back of a prize ox at a county fair."

"Nonsense," I said, "the woman who catches you will win a prize in the matrimonial lottery and Florence Gaylord knows it. You are worth half a dozen of these feather-weight dudes who are fluttering around her."

"Yes," he rejoined with a rueful smile, "I suppose I would be, by the pound."

One afternoon I strolled down the beach with a paper novel in my hand, and finding a comfortable seat in a rustic pagoda a little way from my hotel, I settled myself for a quiet half hour. I had not read more than one chapter when two ladies approached the pavilion and seated themselves on the other side of the lattice-work, vine-covered screen that divided the pavilion into two parts. I was lying stretched on the seat, the back of which concealed the most of my body, while a mass of vines hid my head from observation. I glanced up from my novel, but did not stir, nor did I recognize the ladies until one of them spoke, with the voice of Florence Gaylord.

"I love Mr. Cartwright very much, and I think he loves me in return, although he is awfully shy. I mean to catch him if I can though it sounds dreadfully vulgar for me to say so." She glanced around her quickly as she made the remark, but fortunately did not perceive me.

Of course the proper thing for me to do would have been to make my presence known. But she had already spoken, and I had already heard, and I spared her blushes by remaining quiet, hoping they would go away before burdening my conscience with any further weight of ill-gotten information. I could not now escape without being seen by them; the most I could do was to feign sleep, to provide against possible discovery.

"He is so ridiculously fat," said Mrs. Gaylord, who was evidently on very familiar terms with her daughter, "that everybody will laugh at you for marrying him. Charlie Puddinghead is just as rich, and much better looking, and is dying for you."

"Why, mamma! How shameful for you to speak of Mr. Cartwright in that way! What you find fault with only makes him more attractive to me. I have always intended to marry a fat man. Charlie Puddinghead is no larger than a well-grown sparrow. Fat men are always good-natured; and one can feel, during the storms of life, that one is anchored to something substantial, that the first rough wind of sorrow or misfortune will not blow away. I despise lean men."

I could scarcely restrain my laughter at this unique confession. I ought perhaps to have been angry, for I myself am lean almost to emaciation, but Miss Gaylord's views were too deliciously droll to wound my sensibilities.

The ladies finally went away, and after waiting until they were some distance away, I went back to the hotel.

I meant to tell Cartwright a part at least of what I had heard. But he had latterly grown somewhat sensitive on the subject of his obesity, and I went up to my room after supper to mediate upon the best way in which to give him the benefit of what I had heard, without disclosing too much, or the exact manner in which I had acquired my information. An hour or two later I went to his room, but he was not there, and I did not see him until morning.

"Walton," he exclaimed, grasping my hand with painful warmth, "congratulate me. Florence has promised to be mine."

"I congratulate you from the bottom of my heart," I said, "I am sure you will be happy."

In my surprise at the suddenness of the announcement, I forgot all about the conversation I had overheard on the bench, which, of course, was now of no consequence. The lovers were quite as much absorbed in each other as lovers usually are, and I was left to a certain extent to my own devices. I had utilized my opportunity by making some sketches which I had planned, but had up to this time been too lazy to execute.

A few days after the announcement of the engagement, Cartwright was called away from Cliffdale on urgent business. He went immediately, promising to return in two weeks.

My vacation lasted somewhat longer than I had originally intended. I was still at the hotel when the two weeks of Cartwright's expected absence had elapsed. The Gaylords had been away a week, visiting some friends, but had returned to the hotel, where they expected to remain until September. When Cartwright had been away two weeks I received from him the following letter:

> "My Dear Walton! I shall be detained here a week or two longer than I expected. I could perhaps finish up my business and get back sooner, but I am preparing a surprise for Florence and my other friends. You will hardly guess the nature of it, but you will open your eyes when you see what it is. Don't say anything about it, for I mean it to be a complete surprise to the others.
>
> > "Yours, etc.,
> > D. CARTWRIGHT"

There was nothing in this mysterious communication that would afford a clue to the nature of the projected surprise. I said nothing to Miss Gaylord about the letter. Cartwright himself kept her informed of his movements.

The last two weeks of my vacation passed pleasantly enough. A day or two before I left Cliffdale, I received the following note from Cartwright:

"Dear Walton: Will be down on the eight o'clock express. Arrange it so that I can meet you alone with Florence and her mother. Leave word with the clerk what room you are in. Don't let them know you expect me.

"Yours, Cartwright"

More mystery, and no clue to unravel it! As fortune would have it, I had received by express that morning a portfolio of etchings and engravings which I had purchased for a certain house I had built for a certain young woman (already mentioned) who was expected to return from Europe in a few weeks. By some mistake they had been sent to me at the seaside. I invited the ladies down to my sitting room at eight o'clock to look at the engravings, and left word at the clerk's desk that Mr. Cartwright would find us there.

The ladies came promptly. They examined the pictures and criticized them with rare good taste, for they had both traveled widely and were familiar with art and the relative merit of artists.

At a quarter past eight I heard a quick step, which sounded somewhat familiar, pass along the hall and stop at my door, at which there was a knock.

"Come in," I exclaimed.

The door was opened, and a gentleman stood in the doorway—a tall, symmetrical young man, without an ounce of superfluous flesh upon him, attired in a faultlessly fitting suit of gray tweed. The ladies and I looked at him for a moment in puzzled curiosity; there was something familiar about him though he was evidently a stranger. There was no sign of recognition on the part of anyone, nor could I imagine who he was until he spoke.

"Well?" he exclaimed, "I thought I would surprise you!"

The wish was father to the thought, for up to that time we had not shown any signs of surprise.

It was Cartwright. He beamed upon us in an ecstasy of pleasure, and laughed gleefully at our evident amazement as we realized who he was.

Meanwhile I watched the effect of his changed appearance upon Florence. She had started at the sound of his voice. When the fact dawned fully upon her that the slender boy before her was but a few weeks before the man whom she loved, she turned as pale as though she had seen a ghost.

"Mamma," she said, in a voice scarcely audible, "take me to my room. The gentlemen will excuse us."

"Why, Florence," answered her mother, "you will be better in a moment. Mr. Cartwright's return was so sudden. You should have prepared us," she said, with a note of reproach, addressing Cartwright.

"Take me to my room, please," urged Florence.

Mrs. Gaylord led her away with murmured excuses. Cartwright offered his arm to assist her.

"No thanks," she said, with a perceptible shudder, "mamma will help me."

When they had gone, Cartwright turned to me, his face white and miserable, his elation all departed.

"What does it all mean?" he groaned. "I thought she would like it." He cast a comprehensive look over his altered person.

"What have you been doing with yourself?" I inquired.

"I've been under treatment for obesity," he replied. "I found a famous physician who has reduced my weight about half in four weeks. But what's the matter with Florence?"

"The surprise was too great for her," I said. "She will be all right in the morning." But I remembered the conversation I had overheard on the beach, and I feared for the result of Cartwright's experiment.

At nine the next morning Cartwright came into my room.

"They have gone," he said; "read this."

He tossed me this note, which I opened and read:

"Dear Mr. Cartwright:—Pardon my seeming rudeness of last evening. But permit me to explain it by saying that my feelings were beyond control. We leave this morning on the early train, and I beg of you to release me from my engagement. It is difficult for me to express my meaning, but you are so different from what you were when we met and when we became engaged, that it is hard to realize that you are the same person. I fear I could never be happy with you now. Feeling as I do, I think it best for us not to meet. I only wish you greater happiness than I could ever have brought you.

FLORENCE GAYLORD"

A Grass Widow

Family Fiction (1887)

Like several of the Northern writings in this collection, "A Grass Widow" was published early in Chesnutt's career. While this story previews some of its author's later tendencies, especially his narrative sophistication, it also differs from his more mature works in significant ways. Although set in the North (Chicago), the story, in fact, resonates with issues one rarely finds in Chesnutt's fictions. First, it focuses self-consciously on the struggles of a young writer to craft a novel, a process to which this author rarely subjects his readers. Second, the story explores some of the less tasteful elements of upper-class life in the late nineteenth century, including a description of a marriage so unpleasant that the husband "had exiled himself to Japan in order to get as far away from [his wife] as possible" (60). And, finally, the plot of "A Grass Widow" hinges on an adulterous affair, a focus nothing short of shocking for an author deemed by Joseph R. McElrath Jr. an "earnest Victorian" (1). Indeed, the story differs so profoundly from other Chesnutt fictions that one wonders how he came to write it.

One of eight Chesnutt stories to appear in a journal titled *Family Fiction* between 1886 and 1888,[1] "A Grass Widow" is an "apprentice" work that foreshadows its author's sophisticated understanding of storytelling strategies.[2] The plot of the story begins with a newspaper account suggestive of the kind of lurid mystery one hardly associates with Chesnutt's other fictions:

> "The body of an unknown woman, well-dressed, but having a dissipated look on her face, was found in an alley, near West Wood street, Thursday. No marks of violence were found on the body, and a post-mortem will be necessary to determine the cause of death. The woman was apparently about twenty-five years of age, slightly above the middle

height, with wavy brown hair, and strikingly beautiful in face and figure.
. . . A peculiar cross-shaped birthmark, high on the left temple and
partly covered by her hair, may give a clue to the friends, if she has any.
The body will remain at Holmes & Hartman's morgue during tomorrow." (46)

While one might expect this sort of first paragraph from a work by Raymond Chandler or Dashiell Hammett, it is enough to startle a reader anticipating a typically discreet Chesnutt story. And, this newspaper account—as
titillating a passage as there is in his writings—drives the plot of "A Grass
Widow."

Curious about the description of the dead woman, the narrator of the
story visits the morgue and learns that "it was the woman I had known. And
now I will tell when and where" (47). Thus, his identification of the body,
formerly Mrs. Wharton, engenders a retrospective narrative of the events
in her life (and his) that he presumes led to her "dissipation." Most of the
rest of the plot is told in flashback, depicting the narrator's experiences with
his brother's family over the course of a summer several years earlier. Also
a guest with the family at that time is Mrs. Wharton, a young wife whose
husband is "away" on business in Japan. During their summer together, the
narrator, Frank, works to compose his first novel, an action romance for
which he plans to use the "divinely tall" Mrs. Wharton as a model for his
heroine. But, as the summer progresses, he begins to have second thoughts
about her, and eventually the married woman shocks his romantic sensibilities when she tries (unsuccessfully) to seduce him. She finds the narrator's
brother, the heretofore happily married George, a more pliable companion,
and eventually the two of them plot to run away together. Only when Frank
discovers the scheme—by intercepting a love note—and confronts the adulterous pair at the train station with news of a potentially calamitous family
crisis is the affair halted, and the unfaithful Mrs. Wharton is sent on her way.
(The unfaithful George, on the other hand, apparently is shocked into his
senses and returns wholeheartedly to his wife and business.)

While the narrative of "A Grass Widow"—with its flashbacks and tem-
poral layering—anticipates Chesnutt's typically sophisticated craft, the focus
on an extramarital affair and its seamy accoutrements seems completely out
of place among the author's other works. Only "The Kiss," also included in
this collection, includes any sort of contemplation of sexual impropriety, and
indeed it is difficult to find an example of physical passion anywhere else in
Chesnutt's oeuvre, which is a fascinating paradox. For, while he apparently

had no compunction about shocking his late-nineteenth-century reading audience with tales of the brutality of slavery or with his gritty insistence on the consequences of racial injustice, he rarely mentioned sex directly in his fictions.[3] Even when dealing with miscegenation—which frequently carried with it a sexual connotation, especially for his contemporaries—Chesnutt makes sure in his fictions ("Her Virginia Mammy" and *The House Behind the Cedars,* to name two) to imply that while racial boundaries had been crossed, the relationships that had produced the "mulatto" children nevertheless have an air of legitimacy (usually in the form of secret marriage).[4] It is therefore quite surprising to come across a passage such as this in his works: "The wicked woman who was with him had wound her toils about his weak nature, and a wife's love, a successful business career, even honor itself, had been thrown to the winds for a pretty face" (59).

Even the manner in which the narrator ultimately handles the discovery that the body of the "dissipated" woman in the morgue is indeed the same Mrs. Wharton who had played such a tawdry role in his life has a distinctly un-Chesnutt-like feel to it. After confirming her identity, he contemplates her life in provocative terms:

> What kind of life she led, through what vicissitudes of fortune or misfortune she passed, how she sank step by step from respectability to shame, I never knew. The look on the marble face in the morgue; the mysterious death in the worst quarter of a great city; the shabby finery of her attire—these things furnished the outline of a story which the imagination may fill in. (60)

Such a description has connotations of misbehavior of a sort one rarely finds documented (or even hinted at) in Chesnutt's fictions. Ultimately, though, the narrator allows the reader's "imagination" to "fill in" the lurid details. Even here, in perhaps his raciest story, Chesnutt can only go so far.

And, finally, the narrator of "A Grass Widow" does share a few characteristics with other figures who appear in Chesnutt's Northern fictions. His manner of resolving his "recognition of the body" (60) is to send "an unsigned letter to the undertaker, enclosing an amount sufficient to pay for her decent burial" (60). Thus, the final act of an atypical story is a burial, one that takes place on at least two levels. First, the narrator manages to bury an unpleasant episode from his past. Equally important, I think, Chesnutt—that "earnest Victorian"—can lay to rest a story he cannot have been especially comfortable imagining, much less writing.

NOTES

1. See Carol B. Gartner for a discussion of Chesnutt's early literary career in Cleveland, especially his writing for S. S. McClure: "S.S. McClure had organized the first newspaper syndicate in the United States and sponsored a contest to attract new and inexpensive material. Chesnutt entered 'Uncle Peter's House,' which did not win, but was published in the *Cleveland News and Herald*. He sold other stories to McClure, published poems in a weekly, *The Cleveland Voice*, and in 1886 began writing for *Family Fiction*" (*CE*, 159).

2. I use William L. Andrews's term—"apprenticeship"—for Chesnutt's early writings, especially those produced in the 1880s.

3. One glaring exception to Chesnutt's skittishness about sex is "The Kiss," a Northern story in which he explores an affair with uncharacteristic forthrightness.

4. For an alternative view, see Eric J. Sundquist, who argues, for example, that *The House Behind the Cedars* ultimately "capitulates to conventions of racialized, gothic sexuality" (399).

⟐⟐⟐

A Grass Widow

I

"CHICAGO, APRIL 14—The body of an unknown woman, well-dressed, but having a dissipated look on her face, was found in an alley, near West Wood street, Thursday. No marks of violence were found on the body, and a post-mortem will be necessary to determine the cause of death. The woman was apparently about twenty-five years of age, slightly above the middle height, with wavy brown hair, and strikingly beautiful in face and figure. There are no marks on the clothing and no papers were found on the person of the deceased by which she might be identified. A peculiar cross-shaped birthmark, high on the left temple and partly covered by her hair, may give a clue to the friends, if she has any. The body will remain at Holmes & Hartman's morgue during tomorrow."

An ordinary newspaper item, which some poor hack of a reporter had picked up on his daily round among the purlieus of a great city. Ordinarily I should have glanced casually over the paragraph, and then have turned my attention to the next column of the paper.

But there was something in it which caught my attention. And, as I reread, the description grew more familiar, and I remembered a woman who had not been twenty-five nor dissipated when I knew her, but who was a little above the middle height (I had described her once as "divinely tall"), with wavy brown hair, and "strikingly beautiful in face and figure." I remembered, too, that once when I had been in her company, a passing breeze had lifted the fringe of hair worn low upon her broad, white forehead, and had revealed a tiny, blood-red cross high upon the temple. I determined to go and look at the body of this unknown woman. It might be the woman I knew; stranger things had happened.

The next morning, after breakfast, I started to the office a little earlier than usual, going a few streets out of the way in order that I might pass the morgue, which was an attachment of a large undertaking establishment. I took my place in the line of waiting visitors. There were morbid curiosity seekers, the same class who frequent murder trials and police courts—intellectual ghouls, feeding their depraved imaginations on the dead and decaying things of society; sharp-eyed young reporters, plying their nimble pencils in little red-covered notebooks; one or two old people, shabbily clad, who went in with anxious looks, and came out with lighter steps and more cheerful countenances—they had not found something they had feared to find.

I passed into the room. There were several bodies there, each lying on a marble slab, with a stream of water trickling over its face. One of these was the body of a woman. The newspaper description was correct; she had been young and fair. My presentiment had also been correct; it was the woman I had known. And now I will tell when and where.

* * * *

I had finished my course at college. I had read for honors and achieved them, but at the imminent risk of my health. I graduated at the head of my class, but I left college pale and nerveless. My physician said that I had been on the verge of brain fever, and advised me to take a long rest, and to spend the summer if possible either in the country or at the seaside. I chose the former and went to visit my brother, who lived in a village twenty miles from the city where I had attended college.

George and I were the only surviving members of a once numerous family. Two of our brothers had been killed in the civil war. Our mother and two sisters had gone the way of all the earth, and only recently had our beloved father joined the silent circle of the dead, snatched away by a remorseless disease, just when the active labors of his life were over, and he was preparing to enjoy the leisure and freedom from care which the training of a large family and the exacting demands of a professional career had hitherto kept beyond his reach. My brother and I were drawn closer together by each of the successive losses, and concentrated on each other the affections that we had shared with the larger family circle. George had married several years before I left college, and his home thenceforth became mine whenever I chose to make it so. He had invested the greater part of his modest patrimony in a stone quarry, on the line of a great railroad, and was doing a flourishing business. He had a wife, handsome, accomplished and lovable; gentle in demeanor, generous in sentiment, and worshipping in her husband an ideal quite different from what he really was. For while affectionate and good-tempered, George had one or two vulnerable points in his character, and was easily tempted in certain directions. Though I was several years his junior my influence had more than once kept him out of serious entanglements. Since he had married, however, he had led an exemplary life, and the most exacting wife could not have demanded greater devotion than he had displayed to Madge.

Their house was situated some distance from the business part of the town, on a suburban continuation of the main street of the town, and behind it, at the rear of the large kitchen garden, ran a shallow brook. A lane ran from the street to the brook, which it crossed by a rustic bridge. I mention these details of the location because they have an important bearing on my story.

The place was old-fashioned in construction and appearance. It was a charming old fashion, however, and George had wisely determined not to disfigure it with modern additions, and except for such interior changes as comfort had demanded the house remained unaltered. A profusion of shrubbery adorned the spacious yard, and a broad piazza, in front of which grew two stately elms, furnished a pleasant lounging place for summer days.

For several weeks I did nothing but read newspapers. The rest of the time I spent rambling about the woods and fields, reveling in the pure country air and the beauty of sky and verdure.

After a few weeks of idleness, however, my health grew better, the color returned to my cheek, and I felt equal to the task of beginning my novel, a work which I had long contemplated and which I imagined I could dash off in a few weeks. I set to work on it, and had completed the first two or three chapters, when the introduction of a new member into our household interfered somewhat with my plans.

"George," said Madge one morning as we sat at a late breakfast. "I am going to invite Laura Wharton to visit us. Poor dear! I know she must find it dreadfully lonely out there among strangers."

"Where is she?" asked George, indifferently.

"In San Francisco. Her husband is in Japan, you know."

"Oh, yes. I remember now. He went over as agent for a firm. When is he coming back?"

"Laura says he will be gone for a year, as the condition of the firm's Japanese business will require his presence at least that much longer."

"Wonder why he didn't take her with him?" asked George.

"Oh, her letter explains that. She was dreadfully anxious to go, but she is rather delicate, and her physician feared that the long voyage and the unaccustomed surroundings might have an unfavorable effect upon her health."

"Well," remarked George, as he rose from the table, "invite her by all means. An interesting young grass widow, in delicate health, will make an excellent companion for our pale student here. Besides, she'll furnish him with literary material; he can put her in his novel." Thus the matter was settled. The invitation was sent and promptly accepted. The letter of acceptance brought a request for George's aid in securing passes over the railroads. The large shipping business of the quarry gave George a claim on the railway companies to courtesies of this description. In due time he handed two handsomely engraved bits of pasteboard to Madge, who forwarded them to her distant friend.

One afternoon, a few weeks later, Madge drove down to the depot to meet the visitor. I was seated in the library, my table drawn close to the long window, and working hard on a personal description of the heroine of my novel; I was still debating the point whether to make her a statuesque blonde or a magnificent brunette, when I heard the crunching of wheels on the graveled drive, and looked up from my manuscript. The window in front of which I sat was open, and on the other side of the piazza a climbing vine had been trained, forming a leafy screen, through which I could gratify my curiosity unperceived. As I looked out a clear, musical voice exclaimed, in tones of unmistakable sincerity:

"Oh, do stop, Madge! What a lovely old place! It looks just like a picture."

I looked at the speaker through my leafy veil, and mentally exclaimed: "What a beautiful woman! I will use her for my heroine!"

Seated by Madge, and leaning slightly forward in the eagerness of her admiration, she did not appear to be nineteen; a half brunette; with wavy brown hair peeping coquettishly from beneath a charming bonnet; her dark eye sparkling with artistic appreciation of the quaint old brick house in its setting of flowers and shrubbery.

"Oh, Madge!" she exclaimed. "How delightful it must be to live in such a charming old place."

Then Madge drove up to the steps, and the guest alighted, and I saw her no more until evening. When she appeared at supper my first impression was strengthened. The traces of travel had been removed, and a becoming evening dress set off to advantage her charms of person. Her conversation was cultivated and witty. I began to think that this delicate grass widow would prove a delightful adjunct to a summer vacation, and that Mrs. Wharton's grace and beauty would add immeasurably to the somewhat colorless abstraction which had hitherto done duty as the heroine of my novel.

II

Mrs. Wharton's presence caused several changes in our domestic habits, but principally in my own. As the only unencumbered person about the house, it naturally came about that the entertainment of the visitor devolved largely upon me. I went out riding with her, and found her by no means averse to a sharp canter along a smooth stretch of road. She rode so well that I immediately inserted an equestrian scene in my novel. I went driving with her, and she handled the reins so well that I wrote up a runaway episode, in which my heroine's skill and presence of mind prevented what might have been a dire catastrophe.

On rainy days we read together in the old library. George was generally absent at the quarry, which lay on the other side of the town. Madge was usually occupied with household affairs. On warm afternoons Mrs. Wharton reclined in a Mexican hammock swing in the piazza, and dawdled over a novel or a book of poems.

Of course it would have been unnatural for a young man, thus thrown in daily and familiar intercourse with a young and pretty woman, not to become more or less interested in her. I will confess that I thought her charming. There was a clinging tenderness in the manner in which she held my arm, for instance, when we visited the quarry and walked too near the edge of a stonepit, that was quite exhilarating. I should doubtless have fallen violently in love with her if she had been a widow or unmarried. There were several reasons why I did not. In the first place, I had been well bred. In the second place, my novel acted as an escape valve for my imagination. Besides, there was a blue-eyed little fairy with whom I had taken many long walks during my last year at college, and her image was too recently and too firmly impressed upon my youthful heart to be driven out even by the charming Mrs. Wharton. I no more dreamed of scaling the barrier which matrimony had built between us than I would have dreamed of scaling Mt. Shasta.

One day I asked her if she had heard from her husband recently.

"Have I a husband?" she asked dreamily, shooting a glance at me from beneath her long eyelashes.

"Twelve thousand miles is a long distance."

Several other remarks, uttered at various times when we were alone together, led me to think that her relations with her husband might not be as pleasant as perfect connubial bliss would require.

"George," I said one evening, when we were smoking on the piazza and Mrs. Wharton and Madge were indoors, "what sort of fellow is Mrs. Wharton's husband?"

"Don't know," he replied laconically. He was a man of few words and many cigars.

"Do you get many letters for her?" The mail for the family always went to the office.

"Haven't got any from Japan so far."

"I imagine she don't care much for her husband," I remarked, stating my reasons for this opinion.

"Likely enough," said George. "It's a beastly shame. A woman like that ought not to be running about the world alone. A woman like that was made to be loved. Wonder you aren't in love with her yourself before now."

I denied the soft impeachment with a blush.

A week or two after this conversation George met with an accident. A heavy fall of rain had softened the earth around the top of one of his quarry-pits, and, stepping carelessly too near the edge, the earth caved, and he was precipitated ten or fifteen feet to the bottom of the pit. His injuries were not serious, but several bruises and a sprained ankle made it necessary for him to keep quiet for a week or two. He therefore remained at home, and I attended to as much of his business at the quarry as could be done in his absence. This kept me away from the house, except for a short time before and after meals.

I noticed that during the week Mrs. Wharton occupied her usual place on the verandah, and I suppose she did her best to entertain George during his convalescence. As for George, he did not seem to take his enforced inactivity as hard as he usually would have done. Ordinarily he would have fretted and fumed, would have smoked innumerable cigars, would have read a few novels and a great many newspapers. He would probably have begun to hobble about before his ankle had gained sufficient strength, with the result of making him somewhat surly and short of speech.

On the contrary, however, his confinement to the house produced none of these results. He was cheerful and even animated. The occasional hitches in his business, resulting from my inexperience, did not disturb his equanimity. I even found him reading Byron one afternoon.

"Cultivating the muses, George?" I inquired.

"Reading about this fellow Beppo," he replied carelessly. "Deuced interesting thing. Didn't know Byron had so much life in him." From which it may be inferred that George's tastes were not strictly literary.

I sat down on the chair which Mrs. Wharton had risen from before I came out on the piazza.

"Don't you think Mrs. Wharton has a beautiful voice?" he said, knocking the ashes from his cigar.

"Decidedly so," I said. "She sang with spirit and understanding to Madge's accompaniment."

"Her figure is perfect," he added, reflectively.

I assented to this.

"And then she has such a charming manner, and dresses in such exquisite taste."

"Have you expressed your opinion to Madge?" I inquired with a tinge of sarcasm.

"I can't say I have," he answered shortly. "Women are peculiar about these things. A man can admire a handsome woman without making a fool of himself about her. Madge is all well enough in her way, but she hasn't got Laura's chic."

"Look out, old boy," I said, laughing, "you know your weakness."

A few days later I came from the quarry a littler earlier than usual. Instead of entering at the front gate, I came down the lane which ran alongside of the yard, leading to the brook below, and came in at the side gate. As I stopped to pluck a flower, I heard Mrs. Wharton's voice speaking in a low tone. The voice came from the piazza, and on the other side of the screen of vines I could see the glimmer of her white dress.

"He was too slow," she was saying. "If he had been more like you,

George, I might have loved him. He has been with me every day for three weeks, and he has not said a word of love, or even kissed so much as my hand. He's a good little fellow, too good for this world. I'm afraid your brother Frank will die early, George."

This conversation promised to become interesting. I kept quiet.

"Frank is young yet, Laura. He'll grow wiser as he grows older. Your love would be wasted on a boy, even so good a boy as Frank."

I crept a little further away from the piazza, and then went around to the front steps. When I went upon the piazza George was deeply absorbed in his volume of Byron, and Mrs. Wharton was knitting with more than usual energy on the fancy sacque she was making for Madge's child, while a slight blush heightened the glow of her cheek.

Of course I said nothing of my discovery. It was clear as day to me now that Mrs. Wharton had been making love to me ever since she had been in our house. It was equally clear that she had used her charms on George with greater effect. I felt oppressed by the weight of my secret, so much so, indeed, that I did not even think of the dramatic effect which I could work it up in my novel. I had no right to speak to Mrs. Wharton; I would not for the world have spoken to Madge, for I instinctively felt that a nature like hers would not overlook such a fault in a husband. I imagined how terrible it must be for a woman to have her dearest ideal shattered. I spoke to George. I did not tell him what I had overheard, but I intimated that I saw the drift of things very clearly. He turned the subject of conversation as soon as he could, and ridiculed the idea that there was anything serious between himself and Mrs. Wharton.

III

A week passed. I saw no further indications of any secret understanding between George and Laura, and I began to think that my advice had borne fruit in recalling George to his senses. It is true that they were much together for several days. Then George's ankle got better, though it seemed to me longer in recovering its strength than the nature of the injury required. At length, however, he got out to his business again, and his tete-a-tetes with the fair Laura were after that less frequent. Of course they met at table and in the family circle, and occasionally, when Mrs. Wharton had some shopping to do, she would accept a seat in George's buggy when he drove through the business part of the town on his way to the quarry.

My novel was progressing finely, and I had got the heroine involved in a position from which it would require something decidedly improbable to extricate her, when, one morning at breakfast, Mrs. Wharton announced that she had received a letter from her husband.

"I am afraid," she said, regrettably, "that I must bring my visit to an end. Ralph writes that he will arrive on *The Mikado*, which is due in San Francisco next week."

"How happy you must be at the prospect of meeting your husband," said Madge. "But I shall be awfully sorry to lose you," she continued.

"It's too bad you can't finish your visit," remarked George, politely, but with almost too apparent unconcern. I observed, however, that he did not look at her as he spoke.

"I'm sure I never spent a more delightful summer," she murmured, leaning over to feed a lump of sugar to Madge's little boy, Johnnie, of which precocious infant Laura seemed very fond. This stuffing with sweets was a breech of domestic discipline only allowed in view of Mrs. Wharton's approaching departure.

"You'll want passes, of course," remarked George as he unfolded his napkin.

"Pray don't trouble yourself," she cried, deprecatingly, "I could not allow you to bother so much on my account."

"Oh, it's no trouble at all," protested George as we rose from the table. "When do you go?"

"I think I had better leave Friday," she replied. "*The Mikado* is due at San Francisco the latter part of next week, and that will give me plenty of time to get there before the steamer arrives."

During the two or three days intervening before Mrs. Wharton's departure I worked away diligently on my novel, and made some progress in extricating the heroine from the disagreeable predicament into which her enemies had forced her. To accomplish this intellectual feat required a great deal of thought on my part, and I therefore did not trouble myself about Mrs. Wharton's affairs.

Thursday evening we all met at supper. Mrs. Wharton was somewhat pale and distrait. Madge was regretfully sympathetic—the regret at losing her visitor—the sympathy in Laura's anticipated pleasure at meeting her husband after such a long absence. George seemed somewhat preoccupied, and gave random answers to several questions which I asked during the meal. The conversation turned on Mrs. Wharton's journey.

"By the way," George remarked, "I have your passes," and he drew out of his pocket an envelope from which he took several papers. One was yellow, and as he opened the envelope I noticed another slip like it in color and size, which he returned to his pocket.

The next morning Mrs. Wharton, assisted by Madge, was busy with preparations for her departure. I did not feel like working on my novel that morning so I went over to the quarry to spend an hour in watching the workers blasting out the solid rock. To my surprise I found very few at work. I spoke to a workman standing near.

"What's the matter?" I asked. "Why are not the men at work?"

"We haven't been doing anything for several days," he replied. "There don't seem to be any contracts on hand, and business has been slack ever since the boss was laid up with his sprained ankle. The men don't like it either."

This was news to me. George had said nothing at home about the condition of his business, or I would surely have heard of it. I walked up to the office. George was seated at his desk, an open letter before him. As I came in he carelessly threw the letter on the desk face downward.

"What's the matter with the business, George?" I asked. "The men say they haven't been doing anything for several weeks."

"Awfully dull for the past three weeks or so," he answered. There was a note in his voice, however, which somehow savored of insincerity.

"I have just got an order, though," he continued, "which will keep us busy for three months. I made a bid to furnish the stone for a new public building at Caldwell, and I think I'll get it. I have just received a letter from the contractor, asking for a conference at his office tomorrow morning. I guess I shall have to run down there tonight."

"You can see Mrs. Wharton a part of the way on her journey," I remarked.

"Yes, that's a fact; so I can. She'll be pleasant company. I wish you would ask Madge to have my valise packed for me."

When I went home to lunch I delivered the message to Madge. She did not evince any surprise, as George's business frequently called him away from home. "It will be pleasant for Laura to have company as far as Caldwell," she said.

When George came home to dinner he explained more fully the object of his journey. He seemed very much elated, but there was a suppressed excitement in his manner, which was very unusual, and which a successful stroke of business seemed hardly sufficient to account for; and I still noticed that tone of insincerity in his voice. I do not think that Madge perceived it. It was like a slight discord in a piece of music is to an unmusical ear. I was conscious of it, but could not define it nor account for it.

The hour for the departure of the travelers approached. The train left at seven, and the depot was at least a mile from the house, on the other side of the town. Just before the time to start it began to rain. This necessitated a change in our plan, which had been to walk to the depot in a family party. It was therefore decided that Madge and I should remain at home, and George would drive Mrs. Wharton to the depot in his covered buggy. The buggy would be brought back by a servant who had gone with the trunks on an express wagon. Mrs. Wharton came down, clad in a gray traveling dress of some clinging material, which fitted her elegant figure perfectly.

"Good-by, dear Madge," she murmured, as the two women embraced. "I cannot find the words to tell you how I have enjoyed my visit."

I bade Mrs. Wharton farewell, and assisted her into the buggy, which rolled off down the graveled drive and out into the street. As we turned to go into the house Madge called her little boy.

"Johnnie! where are you? Come to mamma!"

The child did not come nor answer. He had been in the hall a few minutes before, and Mrs. Wharton had kissed him before she went out on the piazza. Madge went into the house to look for her child. A few minutes later she reappeared.

"Frank," she said anxiously, "I wish you would help me look for Johnnie. I don't know where he can have gone. Please look out in the lane and down toward the brook; he may have strayed in that direction."

I went out of the side gate and down the lane toward the brook. As I neared the rustic bridge I heard a splash and a faint scream. Fear lent wings to my feet, and I reached the bridge in a moment. Looking down the stream I saw a small figure floating a few rods away. The water was shallow, but the child was only three years old. Besides there was an eddy a short distance below, and beyond it a pool of deep water where the boys of the neighborhood were wont to disport themselves. If I could only reach the child before he got to this spot I might save him.

Springing over the low railing I made my way down the stream as rapidly as possible. Every swimmer knows how hard it is to run even in shallow water. But I could not have reached the boy any quicker by running on the bank, for the brook was fenced on each side, and I would have lost more time climbing fences than I would have gained by running on land. My efforts were only partially successful. The child reached the eddy, was whirled around once or twice, and sank, coming up a moment later in the deep water beyond. By this time I had reached the spot and caught his little skirt as he came up. A moment later and I had drawn the dripping and apparently lifeless body to the bank. I knew that prompt measures must be taken, and clasping the limp little frame in my arms I ran as fast as I could homeward.

Madge met me at the gate. She looked at me approaching, and she divined from the manner in which I held the child that something was wrong. With a wild scream she sprang toward me, and seizing the lifeless form of her child, ran toward the house.

"Don't be excited," I exclaimed as calmly as my own excitement would permit. "A few simple steps will restore him to consciousness. He was under the water only a minute."

My familiarity with the books in the library was such that I could put my hand on book or page where instructions were given for resuscitating drowned persons. By the time I found them Madge had recovered somewhat of composure, and her strong good sense asserted itself in the manner in which she carried out the instructions I gave.

"The girl will help you," I said, "and I will go at once for Dr. Greene, and then go to the depot and see if I can catch George before the train leaves."

These events had not occupied a quarter of an hour from the time George and Mrs. Wharton had left for the depot. They had fully half an hour to reach it, and I hoped I could get there on foot in the fifteen minutes remaining. I dashed out of the house and down the street. The doctor's residence was but a half dozen doors from our own. As I drew near I saw his buggy standing at the gate and his rotund figure disappearing in the shrubbery.

"Doctor!" I screamed; "for God's sake, come quick!"

He turned and came back to the gate.

"George's child is drowned," I said, "and they are trying to resuscitate him. His father is going away on the seven o'clock train, and I have but fifteen minutes to reach him."

"Have you a horse?"

"No."

"Take my buggy and I will go to the house on foot. Bring him back if you can. It is not always easy to restore drowned people."

I sprang into the buggy, and seizing the whip, astonished the good doctor's easy-going old gray mare. She seemed to recognize the seriousness of the emergency, however, and responded nobly.

We reached the depot in ten minutes. I sprang out, and ran into the station house. There was no train there. I glanced at the depot clock, and it marked five minutes after train time.

"Plenty of time, sir," said a blue-clad porter, coming up behind me. "Train twenty minutes late."

I ran to the waiting room. There were several people sitting there, but all were strangers.

"Have you seen a lady and a gentleman together?" I inquired of the porter.

"Lady in gray-blue bonnet?" he asked.

"Yes."

"They've gone up the park," he answered. "Those are their things." He pointed to a pile of valises and bundles. I recognized them.

"In what direction did they go?" I asked.

"Didn't notice. Best way to catch 'em now is to wait right here. Train'll be along pretty soon now, and if you go one way they may come another, and you'll miss 'em."

This was true. I could only wait. The depot stood at one side of an ornamental park, used for picnic parties and excursions. The light rain had ceased by this time, and George and Mrs. Wharton, tempted by the delicious coolness of the evening air, and having plenty of time, had strolled off down one of the winding paths. I sat down by the pile of luggage, and instinctively put my hand in my pocket for something to read—I remembered having stuck a newspaper in the inner pocket of the light overcoat which I had snatched up as I left the house. Instead of the newspaper I drew out a folded paper, which I opened with some curiosity, not remembering to have seen it before. It was a letter addressed to my brother George. I involuntarily glanced at the first few lines, when I became interested, and read the letter through. It ran as follows:

> DEAR SIR: Your figures for the quarry are pretty steep. However, it is a valuable property, and we think we can get our money out of it by prudent management. As requested by you, we will have deed prepared according to your instructions, and will be at depot with notary

public to meet the ten o'clock train. We have procured draft on Denver, which will be delivered on execution of deed.

Yours truly,

The letter was signed by a prominent stone merchant in Caldwell, with whom George had frequently had business transactions.

My first sensation was one of astonishment, and it was several moments before the full meaning of the situation dawned upon me. George's alleged business in Caldwell was fictitious. He had been closing up his own business, and had sold out the quarry. He had procured passes for himself as well as for Mrs. Wharton. There could be but one reason for so much deception and secrecy. The wicked woman who was with him had wound her toils about his weak nature, and a wife's love, a successful business career, even honor itself, had been thrown to the winds for a pretty face.

I heard the whistle of the approaching train. The porter ran into the waiting room and gathered up the luggage.

"This way, sir. Lady and gentleman just steppin' on train."

In a moment I was in the car. "George," I cried. "Johnnie has fallen into the brook and drowned. For God's sake, come home."

He turned a ghastly white with emotion, while a look, which I cannot define, came into Mrs. Wharton's eyes. Reading it in the light of my recent discovery, it expressed baffled love and disappointed hopes.

"I will go at once," said George, in a voice which sounded strange and unnatural. "Good-by," he added, turning to Laura. "I—I will—"

"I will go back with you," she said. "I ought not to leave Madge in her affliction."

George had already left the car.

"I do not think it necessary," I said coldly, as she rose from her seat. "Perhaps you had better go on and meet your husband. And as you pass through Caldwell, you might explain to the gentleman at the depot why George is not there to sign the deed for the quarry."

She saw that I knew all. She sank back into her seat, and her eyes blazed with hatred and pent-up rage. The train started and I left the car. I sprang into the buggy and soon overtook George, who had started up the street on foot. The doctor's mare made a record that evening which she has not beaten since.

The doctor and Madge were still working at the child, and it was some minutes after we arrived before the first faint signs of returning animation rewarded their efforts. Finally, however, the child breathed, then opened his eyes, and the danger was over.

George stood looking on with haggard face. When Madge had carried the child off to bed, and the good doctor had gone to his well-earned supper, I drew the letter from my pocket and handed it to George.

"You have on the wrong overcoat," I said, "You left this in your pocket."

He took the letter mechanically, but as he recognized it, his face fell.

"You read it?" he asked. I nodded assent.

He did not attempt to blame me or to excuse himself. "For God's sake, do not tell Madge," he whispered hoarsely. "It's all over now and it would kill her to know."

I never told Madge. The sale of the quarry fell through, and George had to pay a round sum to avoid a lawsuit.

I did not see Mrs. Wharton again. We learned more of her afterwards—that her marital relations were not pleasant, and that her husband had exiled himself to Japan in order to get as far away from her as possible. Madge received a note from her a week or two later to the effect that her husband had been met by dispatches in Honolulu and had turned back to Japan. Madge did not invite her to resume her visit.

I lost sight of her from that time. What kind of life she led, through what vicissitudes of fortune or misfortune she passed, how she sank step by step from respectability to shame, I never knew. The look on the marble face in the morgue; the mysterious death in the worst quarter of a great city; the shabby finery of her attire—those things furnished the outline of a story which the imagination may fill in.

I wrote an unsigned letter to the undertaker, enclosing an amount sufficient to pay for her decent burial. I did not wish to appear personally in the matter, nor did I make my recognition of the body known to the public. She had long been lost to the world in which her early life had been passed. Better let her disappear, like a fallen star, in the darkness of oblivion.

The Wife of His Youth

Atlantic Monthly (1898)

In many ways, "The Wife of His Youth" epitomizes Chesnutt's "Ohio" or Northern stories. Set in the Ohio city of "Groveland" (Cleveland), the story focuses exclusively on the interaction of middle-class African Americans—most of them light-skinned—navigating their own unique social terrain of the late nineteenth century. As a consequence of illuminating the lives of economically successful African American Northerners, the story introduces a figure new to American letters: the black self-made man. Despite its setting in the North and its emphasis on the social relations of a new class of black Americans, however, "The Wife of His Youth" also features elements typical of all of Chesnutt's fictions: the inescapable consequences of the past, the profound influence of race on those with any amount of "black blood," and the extent to which storytelling both shapes and reveals human experiences.

In many ways, "The Wife of His Youth" signaled Chesnutt's ascendance into a significant role as an American writer and a preeminent position as an African American writer. Originally appearing in the *Atlantic Monthly* in 1898, the story attracted enthusiastic attention from a range of sources. W.E.B. Du Bois, for example, said of the story that "Chesnutt wrote powerfully, but with great reserve and suggestiveness, touching a new realm in the borderland between the races and making the world listen with one short story" ("Possibilities," 2). Similarly, James Lane Allen, a fellow writer at the turn of the century, called "The Wife of His Youth" the "freshest, finest, most admirably held in and wrought out little story that has gladdened—and moistened—my eyes in many months" (qtd. in H. Chesnutt, 96). An anonymous reviewer in *Chronicle and Comment* (and the first source to make public Chesnutt's racial make-up) wrote that "Mr. Charles W. Chesnutt, whose touching story, 'The Wife of His Youth,' published in the July *Atlantic* has, perhaps, caused more favourable comment than any other story of the month, is more than a promising new writer in a new field" (*CE*, 29). And even the "Dean of American Literature," William Dean Howells, commented on the power of the story: "Any one accustomed to study methods in fiction," he wrote, "to distinguish between good and bad art, to feel the joy which the delicate skill possible only from a love of truth can give, must have known a high pleasure in the quiet self-restraint of the performance" (Howells, 52).

The plot of "The Wife of His Youth" examines how the past complicates the ways in which African Americans go about trying to build new lives for themselves in the turn-of-the-century North. The protagonist of the story, Mr. Ryder, shares many characteristics with several protagonists of Chesnutt's other Northern writings. Like such figures as Tom Taylor of "The Doll," Cicero Clayton of "A Matter of Principle," and David Taylor of "Mr. Taylor's Funeral," Ryder has prospered economically in the North by means of self-education and hard work:

> He had come to Groveland a young man, and obtaining employment in the office of a railroad company as messenger had in time worked himself up to the position of stationery clerk, having charge of the distribution of the office supplies for the whole company. Although the lack of early training had hindered the orderly development of a naturally fine mind, it had not prevented him from doing a great deal of reading or from having decidedly literary tastes. (66)

As this description makes clear, Ryder exemplifies in many ways Chesnutt's ideal of the black self-made man, a figure with which the author could easily relate. Indeed, the passage cited above describes, in suggestive detail, Chesnutt's own biography.[1]

In addition to his apparently successful business ventures, though, Ryder also attempts to shape the social landscape for his peers by means of his influence in the "Blue Vein Society," an exclusive (and excluding) society of light-skinned, well-educated African Americans. The purpose of the organization—which probably had as its inspiration the Cleveland Social Circle, Chesnutt's own club[2]—"was to establish and maintain correct social standards among a people whose social condition presented almost unlimited room for improvement" (65). By means of "his genius for social leadership" (66), Ryder has become the club's "recognized adviser and head, the custodian of its standards, and the preserver of its traditions" (66).

In establishing Ryder as the "dean" of the Blue Vein Society, Chesnutt has created an inviting target of his satirical impulse. Disturbed to have "been forced to meet in a social way persons whose complexions and callings in life were hardly up to the standard which he considered proper for the society to maintain" (67), Ryder intends to exploit his leadership role in the community precisely "to counteract leveling tendencies"—specifically, the social mixing of light- and dark-skinned African Americans (68). The plot thus allows Chesnutt to explore tensions *within* the black community of the middle-class North, and by so doing "gives us," according to Hamilton Wright Mabie, "new aspects of American life" (51). Despite providing insights into such previously unexplored subjects, Chesnutt nevertheless remains true to his earlier renunciation of bigotry in any form. Indeed, by the end of the story, Mr. Ryder's peculiar form of prejudice—the preference for light skin over dark—has been emphatically, if not comfortably, overturned.

While Chesnutt certainly satirizes those, like Mr. Ryder, who would redraw racial boundaries in their own favor, the story nevertheless remains gently ironic, in part because the author traveled in a social universe very much like the one he describes in this story. In a 1930 letter to John Chamberlain, Chesnutt writes,

> I note your comment on the stories in *The Wife of His Youth*, in which I am somewhat ironical about the racial distinctions among colored people and the "Blue Vein Society," but it is very kindly irony, for I belonged to the "Blue Vein Society," and the characters in "The Wife of His Youth" and "A Matter of Principle" were my personal friends. I shared their sentiments to a degree, though I could see the comic side of them. (*EC*, 258)

Indeed, the story, though initially critical of Ryder's intraracial prejudice, ultimately presents him as a man of high principle. In fact, encased within this mild satire is a remarkably—and for Chesnutt, surprisingly—sentimental love story.

Unlike Chesnutt's conjure tales, stories like "The Wife of His Youth" and "A Matter of Principle" would have been, as Mabie suggests, new to the American reading public. Focusing not on slaves' lives (although Ryder had been a slave in the distant past) or African Americans in menial jobs, Chesnutt instead explores the complex social and cultural lives of middle-class black Northerners. In this way, he anticipates the sociological writings of subsequent generations of African American writers—James Weldon Johnson, Richard Wright, Ralph Ellison, James Baldwin, and Toni Morrison, to name only a few—depicting the lives of a broad array of black characters living in Northern cities. In his 1912 *The Autobiography of an Ex-Coloured Man*—which John Chamberlain calls "the precursor to the Harlem movement" (137)—Johnson chronicles the existence of what he suggests is a third class of African Americans,

> comprised of the independent workmen and tradesmen, and of the well-to-do and educated coloured people; and, strange to say, for a directly opposite reason they are as far removed from the whites as the members of the first class I mentioned. These people live in a little world of their own; in fact, I concluded that if a coloured man wanted to separate himself from his white neighbours, he had but to acquire some money, education, and culture, and to live in accordance. (Johnson, 436).

Chesnutt's depiction of Mr. Ryder, in fact, perfectly typifies Johnson's description of this "third" class of black Americans (a class which, by 1898, had been virtually ignored in American literature). As "The Wife of His Youth" unfolds, we learn that

> [Mr. Ryder] was economical, and had saved money; he owned and occupied a very comfortable house on a respectable street. His residence was handsomely furnished, containing among other things a good library, especially rich in poetry, a piano, and some choice engravings. . . . In the early days of his connection with the Blue Veins he had been regarded as quite a catch. (66)

For turn-of-the-century readers, then, Ryder constituted an entirely new African American subject: businessman, landowner, and social creature. As one can see in "The Wife of His Youth," Chesnutt had already begun, by 1898, to document these African Americans who had "acquire[d] some money, education, and culture," and he does so repeatedly in the Northern fictions collected in this volume. The same sort of focus appears in "A Matter of Principle," "The Doll," and "Mr. Taylor's Funeral," to name only three.

"The Wife of His Youth" brilliantly lays out the conflicts inherent for a black self-made man trying to build a new life for himself in the urban North. Mr. Ryder occupies a fascinating role in Chesnutt's universe of characters, both as the ideal of the self-made man and as the agent of integration. For, as his interactions with the "wife of his youth" indicate, the North is not simply a place to escape responsibilities. The story, though, ultimately suggests that African Americans living there might both recover their past and build their future.

NOTES

1. Chesnutt was also a young man when he first came to Cleveland and, like Ryder, for example, worked for a "railroad company," the Nickel Plate Railroad Company. Nevertheless, the biographies of Chesnutt and Mr. Ryder do not, of course, match exactly.

2. See Helen Chesnutt's description of the Cleveland Social Circle as "a group of young colored people who wanted to promote social intercourse and cultural activities among the better educated people of color" (61).

The Wife of His Youth

I

MR. RYDER WAS GOING to give a ball. There were several reasons why this was an opportune time for such an event.

Mr. Ryder might aptly be called the dean of the Blue Veins. The original Blue Veins were a little society of colored persons organized in a certain Northern city shortly after the war. Its purpose was to establish and maintain correct social standards among a people whose social condition presented almost unlimited room for improvement. By accident, combined perhaps with some natural affinity, the society consisted of individuals who were, generally speaking, more white than black. Some envious outsider made the suggestion that no one was eligible for membership who was not white enough to show blue veins. The suggestion was readily adopted by those who were not of the favored few, and since that time the society, though possessing a longer and more pretentious name, had been known far and wide as the "Blue Vein Society," and its members as the "Blue Veins."

The Blue Veins did not allow that any such requirement existed for admission to their circle, but, on the contrary, declared that character and culture were the only things considered; and that if most of their members were light-colored, it was because such persons, as a rule, had had better opportunities to qualify themselves for membership. Opinions differed, too, as to the usefulness of the society. There were those who had been known to assail it violently as a glaring example of the very prejudice from which the colored race had suffered most; and later, when such critics had succeeded in getting on the inside, they had been heard to maintain with zeal and earnestness that the society was a life-boat, an anchor, a bulwark and a shield,—a pillar of cloud by day and of fire by night, to guide their people through the social wilderness. Another alleged prerequisite for Blue Vein membership was that of free birth; and while there was really no such requirement, it is doubtless true that very few of the members would have been unable to meet it if there had been. If there were one or two of the older members who had come up from the South and from slavery, their history presented enough romantic circumstances to rob their servile origin of its grosser aspects.

While there were no such tests of eligibility, it is true that the Blue Veins had their notions on these subjects, and that not all of them were equally liberal in regard to the things they collectively disdained. Mr. Ryder was one of the most conservative. Though he had not been among the founders of the society, but had come in some years later, his genius for social leadership was such that he had speedily become its recognized adviser and head, the custodian of its standards, and the preserver of its traditions. He had shaped its social policy, was active in providing for its entertainment, and when the interest fell off, as it sometimes did, he fanned the embers until they burst again into a cheerful flame.

There were still other reasons for his popularity. While he was not as white as some of the Blue Veins, his appearance was such as to confer distinction upon them. His features were of a refined type, his hair was almost straight; he was always neatly dressed; his manners were irreproachable, and his morals above suspicion. He had come to Groveland a young man, and obtaining employment in the office of a railroad company as messenger had in time worked himself up to the position of stationery clerk, having charge of the distribution of the office supplies for the whole company. Although the lack of early training had hindered the orderly development of a naturally fine mind, it had not prevented him from doing a great deal of reading or from forming decidedly literary tastes. Poetry was his passion. He could repeat whole pages of the great English poets; and if his pronunciation was sometimes faulty, his eye, his voice, his gestures, would respond to the changing sentiment with a precision that revealed a poetic soul and disarmed criticism. He was economical, and had saved money; he owned and occupied a very comfortable house on a respectable street. His residence was handsomely furnished, containing among other things a good library, especially rich in poetry, a piano, and some choice engravings. He generally shared his house with some young couple, who looked after his wants and were company for him; for Mr. Ryder was a single man. In the early days of his connection with the Blue Veins he had been regarded as quite a catch, and ladies and their mothers had manoeuvred with much ingenuity to capture him. Not, however, until Mrs. Molly Dixon visited Groveland had any woman ever made him wish to change his condition to that of a married man.

Mrs. Dixon had come to Groveland from Washington in the spring, and before summer was over she had won Mr. Ryder's heart. She possessed many attractive qualities. She was much younger than he; in fact, he was old enough to have been her father, though no one knew exactly how old he was. She was whiter than he, and better educated. She had moved in the best colored society of the country, at Washington, and had taught in the schools of that city. Such a superior person had been eagerly welcomed to the Blue Vein Society, and had taken a leading part in its activities. Mr. Ryder had at first been attracted by her charms of person, for she was very good looking and not over twenty-five; then by her refined manners and by the vivacity of her wit. Her husband had been a government clerk, and at his death had left a considerable life insurance. She was visiting friends in Groveland, and, finding the town and the people to her liking, had prolonged her stay indefinitely. She had not seemed displeased at Mr. Ryder's attentions, but on the contrary had given him every proper encouragement; indeed, a younger and less cautious man would long since have spoken. But he had made up his mind, and had only to determine the time when he would ask her to be his wife. He decided to give a ball in her honor, and at some time during the evening of the ball to offer her his heart and hand. He had no special fears about the outcome, but, with a little touch of romance, he wanted the surroundings to be in harmony with his own feelings when he should have received the answer he expected.

Mr. Ryder resolved that this ball should mark an epoch in the social history of Groveland. He knew, of course,—no one could know better,—the entertainments that had taken place in past years, and what must be done to surpass them. His ball must be worthy of the lady in whose honor it was to be given, and must, by the quality of its guests, set an example for the future.

He had observed of late a growing liberality, almost a laxity, in social matters, even among members of his own set, and had several times been forced to meet in a social way persons whose complexions and callings in life were hardly up to the standard which he considered proper for the society to maintain. He had a theory of his own.

"I have no race prejudice," he would say, "but we people of mixed blood are ground between the upper and the nether millstone. Our fate lies between absorption by the white race and extinction in the black. The one doesn't want us yet, but may take us in time. The other would welcome us, but it would be for us a backward step. 'With malice towards none, with charity for all,' we must do the best we can for ourselves and those who are to follow us. Self-preservation is the first law of nature."

His ball would serve by its exclusiveness to counteract leveling tendencies, and his marriage to Mrs. Dixon would help to further the upward process of absorption he had been wishing and waiting for.

II

The ball was to take place on Friday night. The house had been put in order, the carpets covered with canvas, the halls and stairs decorated with palms and potted plants; and in the afternoon Mr. Ryder sat on his front porch, which the shade of a vine running up over a wire netting made a cool and pleasant lounging-place. He expected to respond to the toast "The Ladies," at the supper, and from a volume of Tennyson—his favorite poet—was fortifying himself with apt quotations. The volume was open at "A Dream of Fair Women." His eyes fell on these lines, and he read them aloud to judge better of their effect:—

> *"At length I saw a lady within call,*
> *Stiller than chisell'd marble, standing there;*
> *A daughter of the gods, divinely tall,*
> *And most divinely fair."*

He marked the verse, and turning the page read the stanza beginning,—

> *"O sweet pale Margaret,*
> *O rare pale Margaret."*

He weighed the passage a moment, and decided that it would not do. Mrs. Dixon was the palest lady he expected at the ball, and she was of a rather ruddy complexion, and of lively disposition and buxom build. So he ran over the leaves until his eye rested on the description of Queen Guinevere:—

"She seem'd a part of joyous Spring:
A gown of grass-green silk she wore,
Buckled with golden clasps before;
A light-green tuft of plumes she bore
Closed in a golden ring.

• • • • •

"She look'd so lovely, as she sway'd
The rein with dainty finger-tips,
A man had given all other bliss,
And all his worldly worth for this,
To waste his whole heart in one kiss
Upon her perfect lips."

As Mr. Ryder murmured these words audibly, with an appreciative thrill, he heard the latch of his gate click, and a light footfall sounding on the steps. He turned his head, and saw a woman standing before the door.

She was a little woman, not five feet tall, and proportioned to her height. Although she stood erect, and looked around her with very bright and restless eyes, she seemed quite old; for her face was crossed and recrossed with a hundred wrinkles, and around the edges of her bonnet could be seen protruding here and there a tuft of short gray wool. She wore a blue calico gown of ancient cut, a little red shawl fastened around her shoulders with an old-fashioned brass brooch, and a large bonnet profusely ornamented with faded red and yellow artificial flowers. And she was very black,—so black that her toothless gums, revealed when she opened her mouth to speak, were not red, but blue. She looked like a bit of the old plantation life, summoned up from the past by the wave of a magician's wand, as the poet's fancy had called into being the gracious shapes of which Mr. Ryder had just been reading.

He rose from his chair and came over to where she stood.

"Good-afternoon, madam," he said.

"Good-evenin', suh," she answered, ducking suddenly with a quaint curtsy. Her voice was shrill and piping, but softened somewhat by age. "Is dis yere whar Mistuh Ryduh lib, suh?" she asked, looking around her doubtfully, and glancing into the open windows, through which some of the preparations for the evening were visible.

"Yes," he replied, with an air of kindly patronage, unconsciously flattered by her manner, "I am Mr. Ryder. Did you want to see me?"

"Yas, suh, ef I ain't 'sturbin' of you too much."

"Not at all. Have a seat over here behind the vine, where it is cool. What can I do for you?"

"'Scuse me, suh," she continued, when she had sat down on the edge of a chair, "'scuse me, suh, I's lookin' for my husban'. I heerd you wuz a big man an' had libbed heah a long time, an' I 'lowed you wouldn't min' ef I'd come roun' an' ax you ef you'd eber heerd of a merlatter man by de name er Sam Taylor 'quirin' roun' in de chu'ches er emongs' de people fer his wife 'Liza Jane?"

Mr. Ryder seemed to think for a moment.

"There used to be many such cases right after the war," he said, "but it has been so long that I have forgotten them. There are very few now. But tell me your story, and it may refresh my memory."

She sat back farther in her chair so as to be more comfortable, and folded her withered hands in her lap.

"My name's 'Liza," she began, "'Liza Jane. W'en I wuz young I us'ter b'long ter Marse Bob Smif, down in old Missoura. I wuz bawn down dere. W'en I wuz a gal I wuz married ter a man named Jim. But Jim died, an' after dat I married a merlatter man named Sam Taylor. Sam wuz free-bawn, but his mammy and daddy died, an' de w'ite folks 'prenticed him ter my marster fer ter work fer 'im 'tel he wuz growed up. Sam worked in de fiel', an' I wuz de cook. One day Ma'y Ann, ole miss's maid, come rushin' out ter de kitchen, an' says she, "Liza Jane, ole marse gwine sell yo' Sam down de ribber.'

"'Go way f'm yere,' says I; 'my husban's free!'

"'Don' make no diff'ence. I heerd old marse tell ole miss he wuz gwine take yo' Sam 'way wid 'im ter-morrow, fer he needed money, an' he knowed whar he could git a t'ousan' dollars fer Sam an' no questions axed.'

"W'en Sam come home f'm de fiel', dat night, I tole him 'bout ole marse gwine steal 'im, an' Sam run erway. His time wuz mos' up, an' he swo' dat w'en he wuz twenty-one he would come back an' he'p me run erway, er else save up de money ter buy my freedom. An' I know he'd 'a' done it, fer he

thought a heap er me, Sam did. But w'en he come back he did n' fin' me, fer
I wuz n' dere. Ole marse had heerd dat I warned Sam, so he had me whip'
an' sol' down de ribber.

"Den de wah broke out, an' w'en it was ober de cullud folks wuz scattered. I went back ter de ole home; but Sam wuz n' dere, an' I could n' l'arn
nuffin' 'bout 'im. But I knowed he'd be'n dere to look fer me an' had n'
foun' me, an' had gone erway ter hunt fer me.

"I's be'n lookin' fer 'im eber sence," she added simply, as though twenty-
five years were but a couple of weeks, "an' I knows he's be'n lookin' fer me.
Fer he sot a heap er sto' by me, Sam did, an' I know he's be'n huntin' fer me
all dese years,—'less'n he's be'n sick er sump'n, so he could n' work, er out'n
his head, so he could n' 'member his promise. I went back down de ribber, fer
I 'lowed he'd gone down dere lookin' fer me. I's be'n ter Noo Orleens, an'
Atlanty, an' Charleston, an' Richmon'; an' w'en I'd be'n all ober de Souf I
come ter de Norf. Fer I knows I'll fin' 'im some er dese days," she added
softly, "er he'll fin' me, an' den we'll bofe be as happy in freedom as we wuz
in de ole days befo' de wah." A smile stole over her withered countenance as
she paused a moment, and her bright eyes softened into a far-away look.

This was the substance of the old woman's story. She had wandered a little here and there. Mr. Ryder was looking at her curiously when she finished.

"How have you lived all these years?" he asked.

"Cookin,' suh. I's a good cook. Does you know anybody w'at needs a
good cook, suh? I's stoppin' wid a cullud fam'ly roun' de corner yonder 'tel
I kin fin' a place."

"Do you really expect to find your husband? He may be dead long ago."

She shook her head emphatically. "Oh no, he ain' dead. De signs an'
de tokens tells me. I dremp three nights runnin' on'y dis las' week dat I
foun' him."

"He may have married another woman. Your slave marriage would not
have prevented him, for you never lived with him after the war, and without that your marriage does n't count."

"Would n' make no diff'ence wid Sam. He would n' marry no yuther
'ooman 'tel he foun' out 'bout me. I knows it," she added. "Sump'n's be'n
tellin' me all dese years dat I's gwine fin' Sam 'fo' I dies."

"Perhaps he's outgrown you, and climbed up in the world, where he
wouldn't care to have you find him."

"No, indeed, suh," she replied, "Sam ain' dat kin' er man. He wuz good
ter me, Sam wuz, but he wuz n' much good ter nobody e'se, fer he wuz one

er de triflin'es' han's on de plantation. I 'spec's ter haf ter suppo't 'im w'en I fin' 'im, fer he nebber would work 'less'n he had ter. But den he wuz free, an' he did n' git no pay fer his work, an' I don't blame 'im much. Mebbe he's done better sence he run erway, but I ain' 'spectin' much."

"You may have passed him on the street a hundred times during the twenty-five years, and not have known him; time works great changes."

She smiled incredulously. "I'd know 'im 'mongs' a hund'ed men. Fer dey wuz n' yuther merlatter man like my man Sam, an' I could n' be mistook. I's toted his picture roun' wid me twenty-five years."

"May I see it?" asked Mr. Ryder. "It might help me to remember whether I have seen the original."

As she drew a small parcel from her bosom, he saw that it was fastened to a string that went around her neck. Removing several wrappers, she brought to light an old-fashioned daguerreotype in a black case. He looked long and intently at the portrait. It was faded with time, but the features were still distinct, and it was easy to see what manner of man it had represented.

He closed the case, and with a slow movement handed it back to her.

"I don't know of any man in town who goes by that name," he said, "nor have I heard of any one making such inquiries. But if you will leave me your address, I will give the matter some attention, and if I find out anything I will let you know."

She gave him the number of a house in the neighborhood, and went away, after thanking him warmly.

He wrote down the address on the fly-leaf of the volume of Tennyson, and, when she had gone, rose to his feet and stood looking after her curiously. As she walked down the street with mincing step, he saw several persons whom she passed turn and look back at her with a smile of kindly amusement. When she had turned the corner, he went upstairs to his bedroom, and stood for a long time before the mirror of his dressing-case, gazing thoughtfully at the reflection of his own face.

III

At eight o'clock the ballroom was a blaze of light and the guests had begun to assemble; for there was a literary programme and some routine business of the society to be gone through with before the dancing. A black servant in evening dress waited at the door and directed the guests to the dressing-rooms.

The occasion was long memorable among the colored people of the city; not alone for the dress and display, but for the high average of intelligence and culture that distinguished the gathering as a whole. There were a number of school-teachers, several young doctors, three or four lawyers, some professional singers, an editor, a lieutenant in the United States army spending his furlough in the city, and others in various polite callings; these were colored, though most of them would not have attracted even a casual glance because of any marked difference from white people. Most of the ladies were in evening costume, and dress coats and dancing-pumps were the rule among the men. A band of string music, stationed in an alcove behind a row of palms, played popular airs while the guests were gathering.

The dancing began at half past nine. At eleven o'clock supper was served. Mr. Ryder had left the ballroom some little time before the intermission, but reappeared at the supper-table. The spread was worthy of the occasion, and the guests did full justice to it. When the coffee had been served, the toast-master, Mr. Solomon Sadler, rapped for order. He made a brief introductory speech, complimenting host and guests, and then presented in their order the toasts of the evening. They were responded to with a very fair display of after-dinner wit.

"The last toast," said the toast-master, when he reached the end of the list, "is one which must appeal to us all. There is no one of us of the sterner sex who is not at some time dependent upon woman,—in infancy for protection, in manhood for companionship, in old age for care and comforting. Our good host has been trying to live alone, but the fair faces I see around me to-night prove that he too is largely dependent upon the gentler sex for most that makes life worth living,—the society and love of friends,—and rumor is at fault if he does not soon yield entire subjection to one of them. Mr. Ryder will now respond to the toast,—The Ladies."

There was a pensive look in Mr. Ryder's eyes as he took the floor and adjusted his eyeglasses. He began by speaking of woman as the gift of Heaven to man, and after some general observations on the relations of the sexes he said: "But perhaps the quality which most distinguishes woman is her fidelity and devotion to those she loves. History is full of examples, but has recorded none more striking than one which only to-day came under my notice."

He then related, simply but effectively, the story told by his visitor of the afternoon. He told it in the same soft dialect, which came readily to his lips, while the company listened attentively and sympathetically. For the story had awakened a responsive thrill in many hearts. There were some present who had seen, and others who had heard their fathers and grandfathers tell, the wrongs and sufferings of this past generation, and all of them still felt, in their darker moments, the shadow hanging over them. Mr. Ryder went on:—

"Such devotion and such confidence are rare even among women. There are many who would have searched a year, some who would have waited five years, a few who might have hoped ten years; but for twenty-five years this woman has retained her affection for and her faith in a man she has not seen or heard of in all that time.

"She came to me to-day in the hope that I might be able to help her find this long-lost husband. And when she was gone I gave my fancy rein, and imagined a case I will put to you.

"Suppose that this husband, soon after his escape, had learned that his wife had been sold away, and that such inquiries as he could make brought no information of her whereabouts. Suppose that he was young, and she much older than he; that he was light, and she was black; that their marriage was a slave marriage, and legally binding only if they chose to make it so after the war. Suppose, too, that he made his way to the North, as some of us have done, and there, where he had larger opportunities, had improved them, and had in the course of all these years grown to be as different from the ignorant boy who ran away from fear of slavery as the day is from the night. Suppose, even, that he had qualified himself, by industry, by thrift, and by study, to win the friendship and be considered worthy the society of such people as these I see around me to-night, gracing my board and filling my heart with gladness; for I am old enough to remember the day when such a gathering would not have been possible in this land. Suppose, too, that, as the years went by, this man's memory of the past grew more and more indistinct, until at last it was rarely, except in his dreams, that any image of this bygone period rose before his mind. And then suppose that accident should bring to his knowledge the fact that the wife of his youth, the wife he had left behind him,—not one who had walked by his side and kept pace with him in his upward struggle, but one upon whom advancing years and a laborious life had set their mark,—was alive and seeking him, but that he was absolutely safe from recognition or discovery, unless he chose to reveal himself. My friends, what would the man do? I will suppose that he was one who loved honor, and tried to deal justly with all men. I will even carry the case further, and suppose that perhaps he had set his heart upon another, whom he had hoped to call his own. What would he do, or rather what ought he to do, in such a crisis of a lifetime?

"It seemed to me that he might hesitate, and I imagined that I was an old friend, a near friend, and that he had come to me for advice; and I argued the case with him. I tried to discuss it impartially. After we had looked upon the matter from every point of view, I said to him, in words that we all know:

> *'This above all: to thine own self be true,*
> *And it must follow, as the night the day,*
> *Thou canst not then be false to any man.'*

Then, finally, I put the question to him, 'Shall you acknowledge her?'

"And now, ladies and gentlemen, friends and companions, I ask you, what should he have done?"

There was something in Mr. Ryder's voice that stirred the hearts of those who sat around him. It suggested more than mere sympathy with an imaginary situation; it seemed rather in the nature of a personal appeal. It was observed, too, that his look rested more especially upon Mrs. Dixon, with a mingled expression of renunciation and inquiry.

She had listened, with parted lips and streaming eyes. She was the first to speak: "He should have acknowledged her."

"Yes," they all echoed, "he should have acknowledged her."

"My friends and companions," responded Mr. Ryder, "I thank you, one and all. It is the answer I expected, for I knew your hearts."

He turned and walked toward the closed door of an adjoining room, while every eye followed him in wondering curiosity. He came back in a moment, leading by the hand his visitor of the afternoon, who stood startled and trembling at the sudden plunge into this scene of brilliant gayety. She was neatly dressed in gray, and wore the white cap of an elderly woman.

"Ladies and gentlemen," he said, "this is the woman, and I am the man, whose story I have told you. Permit me to introduce to you the wife of my youth."

Her Virginia Mammy

The Wife of His Youth (1899)

One of Chesnutt's best and most provocative stories, "Her Virginia Mammy" considers the nature of identity—racial, social, and entrepreneurial—for a Northern woman at the turn of the century. Apparently set in "Groveland" (although the protagonist had grown up in Cincinnati),[1] the story explores several controversial topics, including miscegenation, "passing," and the suppression of one's racialized past. Despite the presence of such potentially inflammatory issues, however, Chesnutt also infuses the work with subjects with which all of his readers, black or white, could identify. "Her Virginia Mammy" thoughtfully investigates the ways in which a late-nineteenth-century figure, one who happens to be a woman, reconciles her uncertain past with her plans for the future. And, while it might easily be classified—based on its apparently happy ending—as a sentimental love story, it nevertheless offers unblinking commentary on crucial issues one finds throughout Chesnutt's writings. In many ways similar to "The Wife of His Youth," "A Matter of Principle," and "White Weeds," the story analyzes how even the hint of mixed blood can have momentous consequences in the lives of turn-of-the-century men and women. Like those stories, "Her Virginia Mammy" ultimately represents, I think, Chesnutt's attempt to reimagine the American family as a broader, more inclusive institution, one able to acknowledge, even embrace, the increasingly multiracial composition of America. Whether he could finally convince himself that such a notion of family could prevail against the racial and social pressures of American history is an open question. After reading "Her Virginia Mammy," though, one can more thoroughly appreciate the complexity of Chesnutt's vision regarding the lives of his Northerners.

First published in *The Wife of His Youth and Other Stories of the Color Line* (1899), the story features Clara Hohlfelder, the adopted daughter of German immigrants who postpones her marriage until she can authenticate the merit of her blood family. "'You know I love you, John,'" Clara tells the man who has recently proposed to her, "'and why I do not say what you wish. You must give me a little more time to make up my mind before I consent to burden you with a nameless wife, one who does not know who her mother was'" (81). Clara's refusal to marry a man of "pure" blood—his ancestors include "'the governor and the judge and the Harvard professor and the *Mayflower* pilgrim'" (82)—derives from her fear that she comes from inferior stock. But while the light-skinned Clara worries that her blood family may not measure up to that of her prospective fiancé, it turns out she has vastly underestimated her problem. For we learn, though she never does, that she has black ancestry and is, in fact, the daughter of an ex-slave.

Within the framework of the story, Clara meets Mrs. Harper (really her mother), who has the power to answer her genealogical questions. But when Mrs. Harper learns that Clara's marital hopes depend upon the purity of her blood, she does not refute her daughter's mistaken guess that the older woman is her "Virginia mammy." In another writer's hands, such a plot might easily devolve into mawkish sentimentality, but Chesnutt manipulates the story in such a way as to minimize the importance of the pair's coincidental discovery of one another after so many years of separation. Instead, he focuses on the way Clara and Mrs. Harper deliver their own stories to each other, forming what Susan Fraiman calls "a long, caressing conversation in which the two women piece together their common past" (446).[2] This conversation ultimately misleads Clara, who, by story's end, has a spectacularly inaccurate—but now quite definite—view of her ancestral identity. And because the only impediment to her plans to marry John had been the uncertainty of her bloodlines, the story therefore concludes with the clear implication that the two of them will marry. Mrs. Harper's genealogical lie thus authorizes the wavering Clara to marry and thereby to build a family, while insuring that she'll figure in her daughter's life not as "mother" but as long-lost "mammy." The story, in fact, comes precariously close to endorsing miscegenation,[3] a perilous opinion for a turn-of-the-century African American writer to make so public.

As an example of his Northern fiction, "Her Virginia Mammy" articulates several of Chesnutt's most compelling themes. First, it speaks to his career-long fascination with investigating the concept of "family," and here he lays out, in startling terms for an 1899 story written by an African American author, the blueprint for a new kind of American family, one that includes both black and white members. For, while Clara's obsession with the past forces Mrs. Harper (and, later, John) to mislead her, Chesnutt seems ultimately to dismiss the importance of "blood" as a shaper of identity. Standing in marked contrast to Morrison's *Song of Solomon*, Walker's *The Color Purple*, and Griggs's *Imperium in Imperio*, among many other works by black writers that insist on the importance of tracing one's roots, "Her Virginia Mammy" stresses instead the advantages to be derived from *de-emphasizing* genealogical history. One can almost hear, in fact, Chesnutt's voice in John's speech about the unimportance of ancestry (although it had been spoken before he realizes Clara's lineage):

> "We are all worms of the dust, and if we go back far enough, each of us has had millions of ancestors; peasants and serfs, most of them; thieves, murderers, and vagabonds, many of them, no doubt; and therefore the best of us have but little to boast of. Yet we are all made after God's own image, and formed by his hand, for his ends; and therefore not to be lightly despised, even the humblest of us, least of all by ourselves. For the past we can claim no credit, for those who made it died with it. Our destiny lies in the future." (84)

Significantly, although John had outlined this position while still under the impression that Clara's ancestry was "merely" common, he does not renounce this idealistic philosophy once he recognizes the truth; he still seems eager to marry Clara by the end of the story. Featuring an ex-slave, a Boston Brahmin, and a mixed-race dance instructor, the family composed in this story is an inclusive, indeed a democratic, reimagining of the American family, one that transcends (albeit with a bit of a "white" lie) the boundaries of race.

In emphasizing how Clara and Mrs. Harper exchange and reshape one another's stories about their "family"—and especially the latter's reluctant affirmation of her daughter's incorrect assumptions about her ancestry—Chesnutt examines how the construction of family can move beyond simple notions of "blood" or "duty." Through the telling of her carefully crafted story, which she modifies for Clara's benefit, Mrs. Harper here *composes* a family for her daughter, even at the cost of concealing their true relationship. Rather than rely on literal "blood" connections—as an ex-slave, she had seen her own marriage condemned by her husband's family—Mrs. Harper (and later John) instead expands the very notion of family, translating a genealogical construct into something else altogether. In thus fashioning such an inclusive model of the American family, Chesnutt confirms Eric

Sundquist's assertion about him: "No writer before Faulkner so completely made the family his means of delineating the racial crisis of American history as did Chesnutt" (394).[4] One can see that emphasis throughout such "Northern" stories as "Her Virginia Mammy," "The Wife of His Youth," "Uncle Wellington's Wives," "White Weeds," and "A Matter of Principle."

The second surprising Northern emphasis in "Her Virginia Mammy" has to do with the ways in which Chesnutt defines Clara. Although her dilemma seems pointedly domestic—whether or not to marry—the story unfolds almost exclusively at *her* place of business: the protagonist of the work is thus characterized as a businesswoman. Chesnutt reminds us several times of the significance of her business to Clara. When weighing the pros and cons of taking on a class of "colored" students, for example, she ultimately concludes that "a class of forty students was not to be despised, for she taught for money, which was equally current and desirable, regardless of its color" (85). Thus, like her male counterparts in "The Doll," "Mr. Taylor's Funeral," and "The Wife of His Youth"—other black entrepreneurial figures in Chesnutt's Northern writings—Clara shrewdly calculates her decisions in financial, as well as emotional, terms. Similarly, in stressing her identity as a working woman, the narrator tells us that "[h]er day had been a hard one. There had been a matinee at two o'clock, a children's class at four, and at eight o'clock the class now on the floor had assembled" (80–81). So, while Clara's story finally has to do with her past and her future, Chesnutt nevertheless emphasizes that, for the present, she is a businesswoman. Few other American stories published before 1900 share such an emphasis.

Under the guise of a sentimental love story—John and Clara seem, after all, destined to marry by the end of the story—"Her Virginia Mammy" nevertheless delivers one of Chesnutt's most daring messages: none of us can really know what our past holds. In addition to its seeming endorsement of miscegenation,[5] the story also calls into question the very notion of a fixed identity. Clara's very happiness comes, after all, at the cost of her self-professed goal of "kn[owing] the truth" about her ancestry. By focusing on the deceived but now-content Clara, Chesnutt thus mocks the notion of a secure identity. As in virtually all of his Northern writings, he emphasizes the complexity of modern identity, whether racial, social, or familial.

NOTES

1. Certainly the story is set in the North, and we can safely, I think, assume it takes place in "Groveland" (Cleveland), if for no other reason than the presence of Solomon

Sadler, a member of Clara's dance class. He likewise appears as a character in "A Matter of Principle" and "The Wife of His Youth," which are set explicitly in Groveland.

2. For an extended discussion of the ways in which "Her Virginia Mammy" explores identity—in racial and gender terms—see Susan Fraiman's essay.

3. Although miscegenation was a controversial subject at the time, Chesnutt nevertheless seemed to view it as an inevitable agent of evolution. In such essays as "The Future American: A Complete Race-Amalgamation Likely to Occur," "The White and the Black," and "What Is a White Man?" he repeatedly argues that racial mixing would, over time, eventually eliminate the notion of "race."

4. For a thorough discussion of Chesnutt's place in American literary history, see Sundquist's *To Wake the Nations: Race in the Making of American Literature.*

5. William L. Andrews argues that the seeming betrothal of John and Clara at the end of "Her Virginia Mammy"—which, remember, was originally published in 1899—took "the question of miscegenation out of the realm of abstract moral prohibition and made it a matter of personal ethical decision" (*CS*, xv).

Her Virginia Mammy

THE PIANIST HAD STRUCK up a lively two-step, and soon the floor was covered with couples, each turning on its own axis, and all revolving around a common center, in obedience perhaps to the same law of motion that governs the planetary systems. The dancing-hall was a long room, with a waxed floor that glistened with the reflection of the lights from the chandeliers. The walls were hung in paper of blue and white, above a varnished hard wood wainscoting; the monotony of surface being broken by numerous windows draped with curtains of dotted muslin, and by occasional engravings and colored pictures representing the dances of various nations, judiciously selected. The rows of chairs along the two sides of the room were left unoccupied by the time the music was well under way, for the pianist, a tall colored woman with long fingers and a muscular wrist, played with a verve and a swing that set the feet of the listeners involuntarily in motion.

The dance was sure to occupy the class for a quarter of an hour at least, and the little dancing-mistress took the opportunity to slip away to her own sitting-room, which was on the same floor of the block, for a few minutes of rest. Her day had been a hard one. There had been a matinée at two o'clock, a children's class at four, and at eight o'clock the class now on the floor had assembled.

When she reached the sitting-room she gave a start of pleasure. A young man rose at her entrance, and advanced with both hands extended— a tall, broad-shouldered, fair-haired young man, with a frank and kindly countenance, now lit up with the animation of pleasure. He seemed about twenty-six or twenty-seven years old. His face was of the type one instinctively associates with intellect and character, and it gave the impression, besides, of that intangible something which we call race. He was neatly and carefully dressed, though his clothing was not without indications that he found it necessary or expedient to practice economy.

"Good-evening, Clara," he said, taking her hands in his; "I've been waiting for you five minutes. I supposed you would be in, but if you had been a moment later I was going to the hall to look you up. You seem tired tonight," he added, drawing her nearer to him and scanning her features at short range. "This work is too hard; you are not fitted for it. When are you going to give it up?"

"The season is almost over," she answered, "and then I shall stop for the summer."

He drew her closer still and kissed her lovingly. "Tell me, Clara," he said, looking down into her face,—he was at least a foot taller than she,— "when I am to have my answer."

"Will you take the answer you can get tonight?" she asked with a wan smile.

"I will take but one answer, Clara. But do not make me wait too long for that. Why, just think of it! I have known you for six months."

"That is an extremely long time," said Clara, as they sat down side by side.

"It has been an age," he rejoined. "For a fortnight of it, too, which seems longer than all the rest, I have been waiting for my answer. I am turning gray under the suspense. Seriously, Clara dear, what shall it be? or rather, when shall it be? for to the other question there is but one answer possible."

He looked into her eyes, which slowly filled with tears. She repulsed him gently as he bent over to kiss them away.

"You know I love you, John, and why I do not say what you wish. You must give me a little more time to make up my mind before I can consent to burden you with a nameless wife, one who does not know who her mother was—"

"She was a good woman, and beautiful, if you are at all like her."

"Or her father—"

"He was a gentleman and a scholar, if you inherited from him your mind or your manner."

"It is good of you to say that, and I try to believe it. But it is a serious matter; it is a dreadful thing to have no name."

"You are known by a worthy one, which was freely given you, and is legally yours."

"I know—and I am grateful for it. After all, though, it is not my real name; and since I have learned that it was not, it seems like a garment—something external, accessory, and not a part of myself. It does not mean what one's own name would signify."

"Take mine, Clara, and make it yours; I lay it at your feet. Some honored men have borne it."

"Ah yes, and that is what makes my position the harder. Your great-grandfather was governor of Connecticut."

"I have heard my mother say so."

"And one of your ancestors came over in the Mayflower."

"In some capacity—I have never been quite clear whether as ship's cook or before the mast."

"Now you are insincere, John; but you cannot deceive me. You never spoke in that way about your ancestors until you learned that I had none. I know you are proud of them, and that the memory of the governor and the judge and the Harvard professor and the Mayflower pilgrim makes you strive to excel, in order to prove yourself worthy of them."

"It did until I met you, Clara. Now the one inspiration of my life is the hope to make you mine."

"And your profession?"

"It will furnish me the means to take you out of this; you are not fit for toil."

"And your book—your treatise that is to make you famous?"

"I have worked twice as hard on it and accomplished twice as much since I have hoped that you might share my success."

"Oh! if I but knew the truth!" she sighed, "or could find it out! I realize that I am absurd, that I ought to be happy. I love my parents—my foster-parents—dearly. I owe them everything. Mother—poor, dear mother!—could not have loved me better or cared for me more faithfully had I been her own child. Yet—I am ashamed to say it—I always felt that I was not like them, that there was a subtle difference between us. They were contented in prosperity, resigned in misfortune; I was ever restless, and filled with vague ambitions. They were good, but dull. They loved me, but they never said so. I feel that there is warmer, richer blood coursing in my veins that the placid stream that crept through theirs."

"There will never be any such people to me as they were," said her lover, "for they took you and brought you up for me."

"Sometimes," she went on dreamily, "I feel sure that I am of good family, and the blood of my ancestors seems to call to me in clear and certain tones. Then again when my mood changes, I am all at sea—I feel that even if I had but simply to turn my hand to learn who I am and whence I came, I should shrink from taking the step, for fear that what I might learn would leave me forever unhappy."

"Dearest," he said, taking her in his arms, while from the hall and down the corridor came the softened strains of music, "put aside these unwholesome fancies. Your past is shrouded in mystery. Take my name, as you have taken my love, and I'll make your future so happy that you won't have time to think of the past. What are a lot of musty, mouldy old grandfathers, compared with life and love and happiness? It's hardly good form to mention one's ancestors nowadays, and what's the use of them at all if one can't boast of them?"

"It's all very well of you to talk that way," she rejoined. "But suppose you should marry me, and when you become famous and rich, and patients flock to your office, and fashionable people to your home, and every one wants to know who you are and whence you came, you'll be obliged to bring out the governor, and the judge, and the rest of them. If you should refrain, in order to forestall embarrassing inquiries about *my* ancestry, I should have deprived you of something you are entitled to, something which has a real social value. And when people found out all about you, as they eventually would from some source, they would want to know—we Americans are a curious people—who your wife was, and you could only say—"

"The best and sweetest woman on earth, whom I love unspeakably."

"You know that is not what I mean. You could only say—a Miss Nobody, from Nowhere."

"A Miss Hohlfelder, from Cincinnati, the only child of worthy German parents, who fled from their own country in '49 to escape political persecution—an ancestry that one surely need not be ashamed of."

"No; but the consciousness that it was not true would be always with me, poisoning my mind, and darkening my life and yours."

"Your views of life are entirely too tragic, Clara," the young man argued soothingly. "We are all worms of the dust, and if we go back far enough, each of us has had millions of ancestors; peasants and serfs, most of them; thieves, murderers, and vagabonds, many of them, no doubt; and therefore the best of us have but little to boast of. Yet we are all made after God's own image, and formed by his hand, for his ends; and therefore not to be lightly despised, even the humblest of us, least of all by ourselves. For the past we can claim no credit, for those who made it died with it. Our destiny lies in the future."

"Yes," she sighed, "I know all that. But I am not like you. A woman is not like a man; she cannot lose herself in theories and generalizations. And there are tests that even all your philosophy could not endure. Suppose you should marry me, and then some time, by the merest accident, you should learn that my origin was the worst it could be—that I not only had no name, but was not entitled to one."

"I cannot believe it," he said, "and from what we do know of your history it is hardly possible. If I learned it, I should forget it, unless, perchance, it should enhance your value in my eyes, by stamping you as a rare work of nature, an exception to the law of heredity, a triumph of pure beauty and goodness over the grosser limitations of matter. I cannot imagine, now that I know you, anything that could make me love you less. I would marry you just the same—even if you were one of your dancing-class to-night."

"I must go back to them," said Clara, as the music ceased.

"My answer," he urged, "give me my answer!"

"Not to-night, John," she pleaded. "Grant me a little longer time to make up my mind—for your sake."

"Not for my sake, Clara, no."

"Well—for mine." She let him take her in his arms and kiss her again.

"I have a patient yet to see to-night," he said as he went out. "If I am not detained too long, I may come back this way—if I see the lights in the hall still burning. Do not wonder if I ask you again for my answer, for I shall be unhappy until I get it."

II

A stranger entering the hall with Miss Hohlfelder would have seen, at first glance, only a company of well-dressed people, with nothing to specially distinguish them from ordinary humanity in temperate climates. After the eye had rested for a moment and begun to separate the mass into its component parts, one or two dark faces would have arrested its attention; and with the suggestion thus offered, a closer inspection would have revealed that they were nearly all a little less than white. With most of them this fact would not have been noticed, while they were alone or in company with one another, though if a fair white person had gone among them it would perhaps have been more apparent. From the few who were undistinguishable from pure white, the colors ran down the scale by minute gradations to the two or three brown faces at the other extremity.

It was Miss Hohlfelder's first colored class. She had been somewhat startled when first asked to take it. No person of color had ever applied to her for lessons; and while a woman of that race had played the piano for her for several months, she had never thought of colored people as possible pupils. So when she was asked if she would take a class of twenty or thirty, she had hesitated, and begged for time to consider the application. She knew that several of the more fashionable dancing-schools tabooed all pupils, singly or in classes, who labored under social disabilities—and this included the people of at least one other race who were vastly farther along in the world than the colored people of the community where Miss Hohlfelder lived. Personally she had no such prejudice, except perhaps a little shrinking at the thought of personal contact with the dark faces of whom Americans always think when "colored people" are spoken of. Again, a class of forty pupils was not to be despised, for she taught for money, which was equally current and desirable, regardless of its color. She had consulted her foster-parents, and after them her lover. Her foster-parents, who were German-born, and had never become thoroughly Americanized, saw no objection. As for her lover, he was indifferent.

"Do as you please," he said. "It may drive away some other pupils. If it should break up the business entirely, perhaps you might be willing to give me a chance so much the sooner."

She mentioned the matter to one or two other friends, who expressed conflicting opinions. She decided at length to take the class, and take the consequences.

"I don't think it would be either right or kind to refuse them for any such reason, and I don't believe I shall lose anything by it."

She was somewhat surprised, and pleasantly so, when her class came together for their first lesson, at not finding them darker and more uncouth. Her pupils were mostly people whom she would have passed on the street without a second glance, and among them were several whom she had known by sight for years, but had never dreamed of as being colored people. Their manners were good, they dressed quietly and as a rule with good taste, avoiding rather than choosing bright colors and striking combinations—whether from natural preference, or because of a slightly morbid shrinking from criticism, of course she could not say. Among them, the dancing-mistress soon learned, there were lawyers, doctors, teachers, telegraph operators, clerks, milliners and dressmakers, students of the local college and scientific school, and, somewhat to her awe at the first meeting, even a member of the legislature. They were mostly young, although a few light-hearted older people joined the class, as much for company as for the dancing.

"Of course, Miss Hohlfelder," exclaimed Mr. Solomon Sadler, to whom the teacher had paid a compliment on the quality of the class, "the more advanced of us are not numerous enough to make the fine distinctions that are possible among white people; and of course as we rise in life we can't get entirely away from our brothers and our sisters and our cousins, who don't always keep abreast of us. We do, however, draw certain lines of character and manners and occupation. You see the sort of people we are. Of course we have no prejudice against color, and we regard all labor as honorable, provided a man does the best he can. But we must have standards that will give our people something to aspire to."

The class was not a difficult one, as many of the members were already fairly good dancers. Indeed the class had been formed as much for pleasure as for instruction. Music and hall rent and a knowledge of the latest dances could be obtained cheaper in this way than in any other. The pupils had made rapid progress, displaying in fact a natural aptitude for rhythmic motion, and a keen susceptibility to musical sounds. As their race had never been criticized for these characteristics, they gave them full play, and soon developed, most of them, into graceful and indefatigable dancers. They were now almost at the end of their course, and this was the evening of the last lesson but one.

Miss Hohlfelder had remarked to her lover more than once that it was a pleasure to teach them. "They enter into the spirit of it so thoroughly, and they seem to enjoy themselves so much."

"One would think," he suggested, "that the whitest of them would find their position painful and more or less pathetic; to be so white and yet to be classed as black—so near and yet so far."

"They don't accept our classification blindly. They do not acknowledge any inferiority; they think they are a great deal better than any but the best white people," replied Miss Hohlfelder. "And since they have been coming here, do you know," she went on, "I hardly think of them as any different from other people. I feel perfectly at home among them."

"It is a great thing to have faith in one's self," he replied. "It is a fine thing, too, to be able to enjoy the passing moment. One of your greatest charms in my eyes, Clara, is that in your lighter moods you have this faculty. You sing because you love to sing. You find pleasure in dancing, even by way of work. You feel the *joie de vivre*—the joy of living. You are not always so, but when you are so I think you most delightful."

Miss Hohlfelder, upon entering the hall, spoke to the pianist and then exchanged a few words with various members of the class. The pianist began to play a dreamy Strauss waltz. When the dance was well under way Miss Hohlfelder left the hall again and stepped into the ladies' dressing-room. There was a woman seated quietly on a couch in a corner, her hands folded on her lap.

"Good-evening, Miss Hohlfelder. You do not seem as bright as usual to-night."

Miss Hohlfelder felt a sudden yearning for sympathy. Perhaps it was the gentle tones of the greeting; perhaps the kindly expression of the soft though faded eyes that were scanning Miss Hohlfelder's features. The woman was of the indefinite age between forty and fifty. There were lines on her face which, if due to years, might have carried her even past the half-century mark, but if caused by trouble or ill health might leave her somewhat below it. She was quietly dressed in black, and wore her slightly wavy hair low over her ears, where it lay naturally in the ripples which some others of her sex so sedulously seek by art. A little woman, of clear olive complexion and regular features, her face was almost a perfect oval, except as time had marred its outline. She had been in the habit of coming to the class with some young women of the family she lived with, part boarder, part seamstress and friend of the family. Sometimes, while waiting for her young charges, the music would jar her nerves, and she would seek the comparative quiet of the dressing-room.

"Oh, I'm all right, Mrs. Harper," replied the dancing-mistress, with a brave attempt at cheerfulness, "—just a little tired, after a hard day's work."

She sat down on the couch by the elder woman's side. Mrs. Harper took her hand and stroked it gently, and Clara felt soothed and quieted by her touch.

"There are tears in your eyes and trouble in your face. I know it, for I have shed the one and know the other. Tell me, child, what ails you? I am older than you, and perhaps I have learned some things in the hard school of life that may be of comfort or service to you."

Such a request, coming from a comparative stranger, might very properly have been resented or lightly parried. But Clara was not what would be called self-contained. Her griefs seemed lighter when they were shared with others, even in spirit. There was in her nature a childish strain that craved sympathy and comforting. She had never known—or if so it was only in a dim and dreamlike past—the tender, brooding care that was her conception of a mother's love. Mrs. Hohlfelder had been fond of her in a placid way, and had given her every comfort and luxury her means permitted. Clara's ideal of maternal love had been of another and more romantic type; she thought of a fond, impulsive mother, to whose bosom she could fly when in trouble or distress, and to whom she could communicate her sorrows and trials; who would dry her tears and soothe her with caresses. Now, when even her kind foster-mother was gone, she felt still more the need of sympathy and companionship with her own sex; and when this little Mrs. Harper spoke to her so gently, she felt her heart respond instinctively.

"Yes, Mrs. Harper," replied Clara with a sigh, "I am in trouble, but it is trouble that not you nor any one else can heal."

"You do not know, child. A simple remedy can sometimes cure a very grave complaint. Tell me your trouble, if it is something you are at liberty to tell."

"I have a story," said Clara, "and it is a strange one,—a story I have told to but one other person, one very dear to me."

"He must be very dear to you indeed, from the tone in which you speak of him. Your very accents breathe love."

"Yes, I love him, and if you saw him—perhaps you have seen him, for he has looked in here once or twice during the dancing-lessons—you would know why I love him. He is handsome, he is learned, he is ambitious, he is brave, he is good; he is poor, but he will not always be so; and he loves me, oh, so much!"

The other woman smiled. "It is not so strange to love, nor yet to be loved. And all lovers are handsome and brave and fond."

"That is not all of my story. He wants to marry me." Clara paused, as if to let this statement impress itself upon the other.

"True lovers always do," said the elder woman.

"But sometimes, you know, there are circumstances which prevent them."

"Ah yes," murmured the other reflectively, and looking at the girl with deeper interest, "circumstances which prevent them. I have known of such a case."

"The circumstance which prevents us from marrying is my story."

"Tell me your story, child, and perhaps, if I cannot help you otherwise, I can tell you one that will make yours seem less sad."

"You know me," said the young woman, "as Miss Hohlfelder; but that is not actually my name. In fact I do not know my real name, for I am not the daughter of Mr. and Mrs. Hohlfelder, but only an adopted child. While Mrs. Hohlfelder lived, I never knew that I was not her child. I knew I was very different from her and father,—I mean Mr. Hohlfelder. I knew they were fair and I was dark; they were stout and I was slender; they were slow and I was quick. But of course I never dreamed of the true reason of this difference. When mother—Mrs. Hohlfelder—died, I found among her things one day a little packet, carefully wrapped up, containing a child's slip and some trinkets. The paper wrapper of the packet bore an inscription that awakened my curiosity. I asked father Hohlfelder whose the things had been, and then for the first time I learned my real story.

"I was not their own daughter, he stated, but an adopted child. Twenty-three years ago, when he had lived in St. Louis, a steamboat explosion had occurred up the river, and on a piece of wreckage floating down stream, a girl baby had been found. There was nothing on the child to give a hint of its home or parentage; and no one came to claim it, though the fact that a child had been found was advertised all along the river. It was believed that the infant's parents must have perished in the wreck, and certainly no one of those who were saved could identify the child. There had been a passenger list on board the steamer, but the list, with the officer who kept it, had been lost in the accident. The child was turned over to an orphan asylum, from which within a year it was adopted by the two kind-hearted and childless German people who brought it up as their own. I was that child."

The woman seated by Clara's side had listened with strained attention. "Did you learn the name of the steamboat?" she asked quietly, but quickly, when Clara paused.

"The Pride of St. Louis," answered Clara. She did not look at Mrs. Harper, but was gazing dreamily toward the front, and therefore did not see the expression that sprang into the other's face,—a look in which hope struggled with fear, and yearning love with both,—nor the strong effort with which Mrs. Harper controlled herself and moved not one muscle while the other went on.

"I was never sought," Clara continued, "and the good people who brought me up gave me every care. Father and mother—I can never train my tongue to call them anything else—were very good to me. When they adopted me they were poor; he was a pharmacist with a small shop. Later on he moved to Cincinnati, where he made and sold a popular 'patent' medicine and amassed a fortune. Then I went to a fashionable school, was taught French, and deportment, and dancing. Father Hohlfelder made some bad investments, and lost most of his money. The patent medicine fell off in popularity. A year or two ago we came to this city to live. Father bought this block and opened the little drug store below. We moved into the rooms upstairs. The business was poor, and I felt that I ought to do something to earn money and help support the family. I could dance; we had this hall, and it was not rented all the time, so I opened a dancing-school."

"Tell me, child," said the other woman, with restrained eagerness, "what were the things found upon you when you were taken from the river?"

"Yes," answered the girl, "I will. But I have not told you all my story, for this is but the prelude. About a year ago a young doctor rented an office in our block. We met each other, at first only now and then, and afterwards oftener; and six months ago he told me that he loved me."

She paused, and sat with half opened lips and dreamy eyes, looking back into the past six months.

"And the things found upon you—"

"Yes, I will show them to you when you have heard all my story. He wanted to marry me, and has asked me every week since. I have told him that I love him, but I have not said I would marry him. I don't think it would be right for me to do so, unless I could clear up this mystery. I believe he is going to be great and rich and famous, and there might come a time when he would be ashamed of me. I don't say that I shall never marry him; for I have hoped—I have a presentiment that in some strange way I shall find out who I am, and who my parents were. It may be mere imagination on my part, but somehow I believe it is more than that."

"Are you sure there was no mark on the things that were found upon you?" said the elder woman.

"Ah yes," sighed Clara, "I am sure, for I have looked at them a hundred times. They tell me nothing, and yet they suggest to me many things. Come," she said, taking the other by the hand, "and I will show them to you."

She led the way along the hall to her sitting-room, and to her bed-chamber beyond. It was a small room hung with paper showing a pattern of morning-glories on a light ground, with dotted muslin curtains, a white iron bedstead, a few prints on the wall, a rocking-chair—a very dainty room. She went to the maple dressing-case, and opened one of the drawers.

As they stood for a moment, the mirror reflecting and framing their image, more than one point of resemblance between them was emphasized. There was something of the same oval face, and in Clara's hair a faint suggestion of the wave in the older woman's; and though Clara was fairer of complexion, and her eyes were gray and the other's black, there was visible, under the influence of the momentary excitement, one of those indefinable likenesses which are at times encountered,—sometimes marking blood relationship, sometimes the impress of a common training; in one case perhaps a mere earmark of temperament, and in another the index of a type. Except for the difference in color, one might imagine that if the younger woman were twenty years older the resemblance would be still more apparent.

Clara reached her hand into the drawer and drew out a folded packet, which she unwrapped, Mrs. Harper following her movements meanwhile with a suppressed intensity of interest which Clara, had she not been absorbed in her own thoughts, could not have failed to observe.

When the last fold of paper was removed there lay revealed a child's muslin slip. Clara lifted it and shook it gently until it was unfolded before their eyes. The lower half was delicately worked in a lacelike pattern, revealing an immense amount of patient labor.

The elder woman seized the slip with hands which could not disguise their trembling. Scanning the garment carefully, she seemed to be noting the pattern of the needlework, and then pointing to a certain spot, exclaimed:—

"I thought so! I was sure of it! Do you not see the letters—M.S.?"

"Oh, how wonderful!" Clara seized the slip in turn and scanned the monogram. "How strange that you should see that at once and that I should not have discovered it, who have looked at it a hundred times! And here," she added, opening a small package which had been inclosed in the other, "is my coral necklace. Perhaps your keen eyes can find something in that."

It was a simple trinket, at which the older woman gave but a glance— a glance that added to her emotion.

"Listen, child," she said, laying her trembling hand on the other's arm. "It is all very strange and wonderful, for that slip and necklace, and, now that I have seem them, your face and your voice and your ways, all tell me who you are. Your eyes are your father's eyes, your voice is your father's voice. The slip was worked by your mother's hand."

"Oh!" cried Clara, and for a moment the whole world swam before her eyes.

"I was on the Pride of St. Louis, and I knew your father—and your mother."

Clara, pale with excitement, burst into tears, and would have fallen had not the other woman caught her in her arms. Mrs. Harper placed her on the couch, and, seated by her side, supported her head on her shoulder. Her hands seemed to caress the young woman with every touch.

"Tell me, oh, tell me all!" Clara demanded, when the first wave of emotion had subsided. "Who were my father and my mother, and who am I?"

The elder woman restrained her emotion with an effort, and answered as composedly as she could,—

"There were several hundred passengers on the Pride of St. Louis when she left Cincinnati on that fateful day, on her regular trip to New Orleans. Your father and mother were on the boat—and I was on the boat. We were going down the river, to take ship at New Orleans for France, a country which your father loved."

"Who was my father?" asked Clara. The woman's words fell upon her ear like water on a thirst soil.

"Your father was a Virginia gentleman, and belonged to one of the first families, the Staffords, of Melton County."

Clara drew herself up unconsciously, and into her face there came a frank expression of pride which became it wonderfully, setting off a beauty that needed only this to make it all but perfect of its type.

"I knew it must be so," she murmured. "I have often felt it. Blood will always tell. And my mother?"

"Your mother—also belonged to one of the first families of Virginia, and in her veins flowed some of the best blood of the Old Dominion."

"What was her maiden name?"

"Mary Fairfax. As I was saying, your father was a Virginia gentleman. He was as handsome a man as ever lived, and proud, oh, so proud!— and good, and kind. He was a graduate of the University and had studied abroad."

"My mother—was she beautiful?"

"She was much admired, and your father loved her from the moment he first saw her. Your father came back from Europe, upon his inheritance. But he had been away from Virginia so long, and had read so many books, that he had outgrown his home. He did not believe that slavery was right, and one of the first things he did was to free his slaves. His views were not popular, and he sold out his lands a year before the war, with the intention of moving to Europe."

"In the mean time he had met and loved and married my mother?"

"In the mean time he had met and loved your mother."

"My mother was a Virginia belle, was she not?"

"The Fairfaxes," answered Mrs. Harper, "were the first of the first families, the bluest of the blue-bloods. The Miss Fairfaxes were all beautiful and all social favorites."

"What did my father do then, when he had sold out in Virginia?"

"He went with your mother and you—you were just a year old—to Cincinnati, to settle up some business connected with his estate. When he had completed his business, he embarked on the Pride of St. Louis with you and your mother and a colored nurse."

"And how did you know about them?" asked Clara.

"I was one of the party. I was—"

"You were the colored nurse?—my 'mammy,' they would have called you in my old Virginia home?"

"Yes, child, I was—your mammy. Upon my bosom you have rested; my breasts once gave you nourishment; my hands once ministered to you; my arms sheltered you, and my heart loved you and mourned you like a mother loves and mourns a firstborn."

"Oh, how strange, how delightful!" exclaimed Clara. "Now I understand why you clasped me so tightly, and were so agitated when I told you my story. It is too good for me to believe. I am of good blood, of an old and aristocratic family. My presentiment has come true. I can marry my lover, and I shall owe all my happiness to you. How can I ever repay you?"

"You can kiss me, child, kiss your mammy."

Their lips met, and they were clasped in each other's arms. One put into the embrace all of her new-found joy, the other all the suppressed feeling of the last half hour, which in turn embodied the unsatisfied yearning of many years.

The music had ceased and the pupils had left the hall. Mrs. Harper's charges had supposed her gone, and had left for home without her. But the two women, sitting in Clara's chamber, hand in hand, were oblivious to external things and noticed neither the hour nor the cessation of the music.

"Why, dear mammy," said the young woman musingly, "did you not find me, and restore me to my people?"

"Alas, child! I was not white, and when I was picked up from the water, after floating miles down the river, the man who found me kept me his prisoner for a time, and, there being no inquiry for me, pretended not to believe that I was free, and took me down to New Orleans and sold me as a slave. A few years later the war set me free. I went to St. Louis but could find no trace of you. I had hardly dared to hope that a child had been saved, when so many grown men and women had lost their lives. I made such inquiries as I could, but all in vain."

"Did you go to the orphan asylum?"

"The orphan asylum had been burned and with it all the records. The war had scattered the people so that I could find no one who knew about a lost child saved from a river wreck. There were many orphans in those days, and one more or less was not likely to dwell in the public mind."

"Did you tell my people in Virginia?"

"They, too, were scattered by the war. Your uncles lost their lives on the battlefield. The family mansion was burned to the ground. Your father's remaining relatives were reduced to poverty, and moved away from Virginia."

"What of my mother's people?"

"They are all dead. God punished them. They did not love your father, and did not wish him to marry your mother. They helped to drive him to his death."

"I am alone in the world, then, without kith or kin," murmured Clara, "and yet, strange to say, I am happy. If I had known my people and lost them, I should be sad. They are gone, but they have left me their name and their blood. I would weep for my poor father and mother if I were not so glad."

Just then some one struck a chord upon the piano in the hall, and the sudden breaking of the stillness recalled Clara's attention to the lateness of the hour.

"I had forgotten about the class," she exclaimed. "I must go and attend to them."

They walked along the corridor and entered the hall. Dr. Winthrop was seated at the piano, drumming idly on the keys.

"I did not know where you had gone," he said. "I knew you would be around, of course, since the lights were not out, and so I came in here to wait for you."

"Listen, John, I have a wonderful story to tell you."

Then she told him Mrs. Harper's story. He listened attentively and sympathetically, at certain points taking his eyes from Clara's face and glancing keenly at Mrs. Harper, who was listening intently. As he looked from one to the other he noticed the resemblance between them, and something in his expression caused Mrs. Harper's eyes to fall, and then glance up appealingly.

"And now," said Clara, "I am happy. I know my name. I am a Virginia Stafford. I belong to one, yes, to two of what were the first families of Virginia. John, my family is as good as yours. If I remember my history correctly, the Cavaliers looked down upon the Roundheads."

"I admit my inferiority," he replied. "If you are happy I am glad."

"Clara Stafford," mused the girl. "It is a pretty name."

"You will never have to use it," her lover declared, "for now you will take mine."

"Then I shall have nothing left of all that I have found—"

"Except your husband," asserted Dr. Winthrop, putting his arm around her, with an air of assured possession.

Mrs. Harper was looking at them with moistened eyes in which joy and sorrow, love and gratitude, were strangely blended. Clara put out her hand to her impulsively.

"And my mammy," she cried, "my dear Virginia mammy."

A Matter of Principle

The Wife of His Youth (1899)

One of Chesnutt's funniest stories, the ironically titled "A Matter of Principle" examines, satirically and comically, the social life of a wealthy African American family living in "Groveland" (Cleveland). In fact, the characters depicted in this story are, like Mr. Ryder of "The Wife of His Youth," members of "The Blue Vein Society," an elite social organization for light-skinned African Americans.[1] Originally appearing in *The Wife of His Youth and Other Stories of the Color Line*, "A Matter of Principle" offers a comic but nevertheless incisive commentary on intrarace prejudice. The story also recapitulates many of the themes central to Chesnutt's writings throughout his career, including his fascination with the ways in which families are formed and re-formed, as well as issues such as the color line and the nature of hypocrisy. "A Matter of Principle" differs from many of those stories, however, in investigating the rapidly changing lives of blacks living in Northern cities. Despite the broadly comic tone of the story— which functions to soften the satirical thrusts at those who would practice discrimination—Chesnutt describes the social and cultural universe of figures wholly unfamiliar to turn-of-the-century readers, both black and white. Rather than depict slaves (or ex-slaves) or working-class blacks, this story considers the loves and lives (and failed intrigues) of upper-class African Americans trying to make a life for themselves and their families in the North during Reconstruction.

The fundamental plot of "A Matter of Principle" focuses on Cicero Clayton's attempt to enhance his family's social position by having his daughter Alice marry a light-skinned, successful man. (Mr. Clayton, like Mr. Ryder, "declined to associate to any considerable extent with black people.") The story traces Mr. Clayton's machinations to ascertain the skin color of an African American congressman (and potential suitor of his daughter) who will soon visit Groveland. He repeatedly adjusts his strategies of engagement with Congressman Brown in response to conflicting reports he receives of the latter's hue. Indeed, Brown's name functions as a sort of joke on the story's central dilemma—is the congressman light brown or dark? The question may seem trivial but, for Clayton, it is the primary factor determining whether or not Brown may court his daughter. Indeed, the narrator several times emphasizes Clayton's "principles" on the matter: "'If this man is black,'" he tells his family about the congressman, "'we don't want to encourage him'" (107). At first, Clayton accepts the report of a friend who insists that Brown is light-skinned, prompting Alice's father to conclude that "'we must treat him white'" (108) by having a ball for him that will "'show the darkeys of Groveland how to entertain a Congressman'" (108). Because he believes, early in the story, that Brown is light-skinned, Clayton arranges for the congressman to stay with him and his family in Groveland.

A series of misassumptions—which another of Alice's suitors, Jack, subtly manipulates as a means of advancing his own interests—leads to the comic unraveling of Clayton's plan. When the complexion-obsessed father mistakenly identifies a very dark man at the train station as Brown, the horrified man of "principle" considers his mistake and its potential consequences:

> He had invited to his house, had come down to meet, had made elaborate preparations to entertain on the following evening, a light-colored man,—a white man by his theory, an acceptable guest, a possible husband for his daughter, an avowed suitor for her hand. If the Congressman had turned out to be brown, even dark brown, with fairly good hair, though he might not have desired him as a son-in-law, yet he could have welcomed him as a guest. But even this softening of the blow was denied him, for the man in the waiting-room was palpably, aggressively black, with pronounced African features and woolly hair, without apparently a single drop of *redeeming white blood*. Could he, in the face of his well-known principles, his lifelong rule of conduct, take this Negro into his home and introduce him to his friends? Could he subject his wife and daughter to the rude shock of such a disappointment? (110–11, emphasis added)

As he does in other satirical works—especially "The Wife of His Youth," "Baxter's *Procrustes*," and "The Shadow of My Past"—Chesnutt here comically exaggerates his language as a means of exposing the hypocrisy of his protagonist. The rest of the story focuses on the consequences of Clayton's comic guesses about Brown (and his hue), and the plot ultimately works as both a comedy of manners and a satire of racial prejudice, even if that bigotry is intraracial.

"A Matter of Principle" typifies Chesnutt's Northern fiction in that it reconsiders the role of African Americans living in the North during (or just after) Reconstruction; the narrator tells us that the events he relates take place in Groveland in the spring of 187–).[2] And, like Chesnutt's other stories with Northern settings—including "Mr. Taylor's Funeral" and "The Doll," to name only two—this story emphasizes that, despite his racial narrow-mindedness, Clayton has ascended socially and economically because of his business acumen and hard work. He is, in short, yet another example of the African American "self-made man" in Chesnutt's Northern works:

> [Clayton] had begun life with a small patrimony, and had his money in a restaurant, which by careful and judicious attention had grown from a cheap eating-house into the most popular and successful confectionary and catering establishment in Groveland. His business occupied a double store on Oakwood Avenue. He owned houses and lots, and stocks and bonds, had good credit at the banks, and lived in a style befitting his income and business standard. (102)[3]

Despite the satirical blade Chesnutt wields in this story for Clayton, it is nevertheless a mistake, I think, to underestimate the extent to which the author reveres the notion of the "self-made man" (or woman, as evident in other Chesnutt fictions). Clayton may harbor inane bigotry, but he represents a new class of African Americans—people of business—who were changing the social and economic landscape of the North at the turn of the century.

In "A Matter of Principle," Chesnutt also explores in penetrating detail the social milieu in which members of this new business class of African Americans live. The Claytons, for example,

> had a social refuge in a little society of people like themselves; they attended, too, a church, of which nearly all the members were white, and they were connected with a number of the religious and benevolent associations open to all good citizens, where they came into contact with the better class of white people, and were treated, in their capacity of members, with a courtesy and consideration scarcely different from that accorded to other citizens. (101–2)

While the plot of "A Matter of Principle" stresses the comic miscalculations Mr. Clayton makes as he attempts to navigate the currents of this exclusive society, it nevertheless opens up a new subject for turn-of-the-century readers: the social lives of middle- and upper-class African Americans.

But though Chesnutt maintains a comic tone throughout this story, he offers a few surprising emphases in his depiction of the African American social universe of "Groveland." While most of the story features only gentle satire of the "Blue Veins,"[4] it contains some harsh, racially charged language that one would not expect in an otherwise humorous story. When Mrs. Clayton discovers (mistakenly) that Brown is quite black—and is therefore not an appropriate suitor for young Alice—she reacts in surprising terms: "'That nigger,' said Mrs. Clayton indignantly, 'can never set foot in this house'" (113). The appearance of that particularly offensive epithet in Chesnutt's writings always signals deeply held resentments about race, and its use here hints at the serious—indeed angry—social commentary informing this apparently farcical tale.

Nearly as surprising, "A Matter of Principle" takes up the question of miscegenation, an unlikely topic to appear in a comedy of manners. But then again, Chesnutt has a tendency to infuse even the most comic situations with controversial issues. While describing the marital prospects for young women of Alice's circle, the narrator tells us that

> among Miss Clayton's friends and associates matrimony took on an added seriousness because of the very narrow limits within which it could take place. Miss Clayton and her friends, by reason of their assumed superiority to black people, . . . would not marry black men, and except in rare instances white men would not marry them. They were therefore restricted for a choice to the young men of their own complexion. But these, unfortunately for the girls, had a wider choice. In any State where the laws permit freedom of the marriage contract, a man, by virtue of his sex, can find a wife of whatever complexion he prefers. . . . To the number thus lost by "going on the other side," as the phrase went, add the worthless contingent whom no self-respecting woman would marry, and the choice was still further restricted. (102–3)

Thus, even in a story of clear comic intent, Chesnutt embeds notions that could—and probably did—make his turn-of-the-century readers uneasy. By including potentially offensive language and issues, he can show the extent to which African Americans have advanced socially and yet emphasize the racially charged barriers to full integration that still remain.

Despite the inclusion of such pointed social commentary, "A Matter of Principle" still manages to provide a thoughtful—and often humorous—

look at the lives of successful African Americans in the North. Like "Uncle Wellington's Wives" and the "The Wife of His Youth," the story exemplifies Chesnutt's highly stylized, ironic prose. But like those stories, too, "A Matter of Principle" ultimately explores, albeit in comic terms, how families shape, and are shaped by, the North at the turn of the century.

NOTES

1. Andrews suggests that this fictional organization was based on the Cleveland Social Circle. See, too, Helen Chesnutt and Francis Richardson Keller, both of whom expound on the composition of the Cleveland Social Circle and its relationship to the fictional "Blue Vein Society."

2. Of the Northern stories collected here, four are explicitly set in "Groveland," which is Chesnutt's semi-disguised name for Cleveland. In addition to "A Matter of Principle," "The Wife of His Youth," "Mr. Taylor's Funeral," and (half of) "Uncle Wellington's Wives" take place in this Northern city. And, we can infer that "Her Virginia Mammy" is likewise situated in Groveland, because Solomon Sadler, a member of the "Blue Vein Society," appears in that story as well as in "The Wife of His Youth" and "A Matter of Principle."

3. This description of Clayton's successful career mirrors, in many ways, Chesnutt's own careful nurturing of his court stenography business, which grew substantially over the years and made him one of the wealthiest African Americans in Cleveland during the first part of the twentieth century. See Helen Chesnutt, Frances Richardson Keller, and William L. Andrews (*Literary Career*) for accounts of his financial success in business.

4. In a 1930 letter to John Chamberlain, Chesnutt has this to say about his depictions of those in the "Blue Vein Society," the social organization he satirizes in both "The Wife of His Youth" and "A Matter of Principle": "I note your comment on the stories in *The Wife of His Youth*, in which I am somewhat ironical about the racial distinctions among colored people and the 'Blue Vein Society,' but it is a very kindly irony, for I belonged to the 'Blue Vein Society,' and the characters in 'The Wife of His Youth' and 'A Matter of Principle' were my personal friends. I shared their sentiments to a degree, though I could see the comic side to them" (*EC*, 258).

A Matter of Principle

I

"WHAT OUR COUNTRY NEEDS most in its treatment of the race problem," observed Mr. Cicero Clayton at one of the monthly meetings of the Blue

Vein Society, of which he was a prominent member, "is a clearer conception of the brotherhood of man."

The same sentiment in much the same words had often fallen from Mr. Clayton's lips,—so often, in fact, that the younger members of the society sometimes spoke of him—among themselves of course—as "Brotherhood Clayton." The sobriquet derived its point from the application he made of the principle involved in this oft-repeated proposition.

The fundamental article of Mr. Clayton's social creed was that he himself was not a negro.

"I know," he would say, "that the white people lump us all together as negroes, and condemn us all to the same social ostracism. But I don't accept this classification, for my part, and I imagine that, as the chief party in interest, I have a right to my opinion. People who belong by half or more of their blood to the most virile and progressive race of modern times have as much right to call themselves white as others have to call them negroes."

Mr. Clayton spoke warmly, for he was well informed, and had thought much upon the subject; too much, indeed, for he had not been able to escape entirely the tendency of too much concentration upon one subject to make even the clearest minds morbid.

"Of course we can't enforce our claims, or protect ourselves from being robbed of our birthright; but we can at least have principles, and try to live up to them the best we can. If we are not accepted as white, we can at any rate make it clear that we object to being called black. Our protest cannot fail in time to impress itself upon the better class of white people; for the Anglo-Saxon race loves justice, and will eventually do it, where it does not conflict with their own interests."

Whether or not the fact that Mr. Clayton meant no sarcasm, and was conscious of no inconsistency in this eulogy, tended to establish the racial identity he claimed may safely be left to the discerning reader.

In living up to his creed Mr. Clayton declined to associate to any considerable extent with black people. This was sometimes a little inconvenient, and occasionally involved a sacrifice of some pleasure for himself and his family, because they would not attend entertainments where many black people were likely to be present. But they had a social refuge in a little society of people like themselves; they attended, too, a church, of which nearly all the members were white, and they were connected with a number of the religious and benevolent associations open to all good citizens, where they came into contact with the better class of white people, and were treated, in their capacity of members, with a courtesy and consideration scarcely different from that accorded to other citizens.

Mr. Clayton's racial theory was not only logical enough, but was in his own case backed up by substantial arguments. He had begun life with a small patrimony, and had invested his money in a restaurant, which by careful and judicious attention had grown from a cheap eating-house into the most popular and successful confectionery and catering establishment in Groveland. His business occupied a double store on Oakwood Avenue. He owned houses and lots, and stocks and bonds, had good credit at the banks, and lived in a style befitting his income and business standing. In person he was of olive complexion, with slightly curly hair. His features approached the Cuban or Latin-American type rather than the familiar broad characteristics of the mulatto, this suggestion of something foreign being heightened by a Vandyke beard and a carefully waxed and pointed mustache. When he walked to church on Sunday mornings with his daughter Alice, they were a couple of such striking appearance as surely to attract attention.

Miss Alice Clayton was queen of her social set. She was young, she was handsome. She was nearly white; she frankly confessed her sorrow that she was not entirely so. She was accomplished and amiable, dressed in good taste, and had for her father by all odds the richest colored man—the term is used with apologies to Mr. Clayton, explaining that it does not necessarily mean a negro—in Groveland. So pronounced was her superiority that really she had but one social rival worthy of the name,—Miss Lura Watkins, whose father kept a prosperous livery stable and lived in almost as good style as the Claytons. Miss Watkins, while good-looking enough, was not so young nor quite so white as Miss Clayton. She was popular, however, among their mutual acquaintances, and there was a good-natured race between the two as to which should make the first and best marriage.

Marriages among Miss Clayton's set were serious affairs. Of course marriage is always a serious matter, whether it be a success or a failure, and there are those who believe that any marriage is better than no marriage. But among Miss Clayton's friends and associates matrimony took on an added seriousness because of the very narrow limits within which it could take place. Miss Clayton and her friends, by reason of their assumed superiority to black people, or perhaps as much by reason of a somewhat morbid shrinking from the curiosity manifested toward married people of strongly contrasting colors, would not marry black men, and except in rare instances white men would not marry them. They were therefore restricted for a choice to the young men of their own complexion. But these, unfortunately for the girls, had a wider choice. In any State where the laws permit freedom of the marriage contract, a man, by virtue of his sex, can find a wife of whatever complexion he prefers; of course he must not always ask too much in other respects, for most women like to better their social position when they marry. To the number thus lost by "going on the other side," as the phrase went, add the worthless contingent whom no self-respecting woman would marry, and the choice was still further restricted; so that it had become fashionable, when the supply of eligible men ran short, for those of Miss Clayton's set who could afford it to go traveling, ostensibly for pleasure, but with the serious hope that they might meet their fate away from home.

Miss Clayton had perhaps a larger option than any of her associates. Among such men as there were she could have taken her choice. Her beauty, her position, her accomplishments, her father's wealth, all made her eminently desirable. But, on the other hand, the same things rendered her more difficult to reach, and harder to please. To get access to her heart, too, it was necessary to run the gauntlet of her parents, which, until she had reached the age of twenty-three, no one had succeeded in doing safely. Many had called, but none had been chosen.

There was, however, one spot left unguarded, and through it Cupid, a veteran sharpshooter, sent a dart. Mr. Clayton had taken into his service and into his household a poor relation, a sort of cousin several times removed. This boy—his name was Jack—had gone into Mr. Clayton's service at a very youthful age,—twelve or thirteen. He had helped about the housework, washed the dishes, swept the floors, taken care of the lawn and the stable for three or four years, while he attended school. His cousin had then taken him into the store, where he had swept the floor, washed the windows, and done a class of work that kept fully impressed upon him the fact that he was a poor dependent. Nevertheless he was a cheerful lad, who took what he could get and was properly grateful, but always meant to get more. By sheer force of industry and affability and shrewdness, he forced his employer to promote him in time to a position of recognized authority in the establishment. Any one outside of the family would have perceived in him a very suitable husband for Miss Clayton; he was of about the same age, or a year or two older, was as fair of complexion as she, when she was not powdered, and was passably good-looking, with a bearing of which the natural manliness had been no more warped than his training and racial status had rendered inevitable; for he had early learned the law of growth, that to bend is better than to break. He was sometimes sent to accompany Miss Clayton to places in the evening, when she had no other escort, and it is quite likely that she discovered his good points before her parents did. That they should in time perceive them was inevitable. But even then, so accustomed were they to looking down upon the object of their former bounty, that they only spoke of the matter jocularly.

"Well, Alice," her father would say in his bluff way, "you'll not be absolutely obliged to die an old maid. If we can't find anything better for you, there's always Jack. As long as he doesn't take to some other girl, you can fall back on him as a last chance. He'd be glad to take you to get into the business."

Miss Alice had considered the joke a very poor one when first made, but by occasional repetition she became somewhat familiar with it. In time it got around to Jack himself, to whom it seemed no joke at all. He had long considered it a consummation devoutly to be wished, and when he became aware that the possibility of such a match had occurred to the other parties in interest, he made up his mind that the idea should in due course of time become an accomplished fact. He had even suggested as much to Alice, in a casual way, to feel his ground; and while she had treated the matter lightly, he was not without hope that she had been impressed by the suggestion. Before he had had time, however, to follow up this lead, Miss Clayton, in the spring of 187–, went away on a visit to Washington.

The occasion of her visit was a presidential inauguration. The new President owed his nomination mainly to the votes of the Southern delegates in the convention, and was believed to be correspondingly well disposed to the race from which the Southern delegates were for the most part recruited. Friends of rival and unsuccessful candidates for the nomination had more than hinted that the Southern delegates were very substantially rewarded for their support at the time when it was given; whether this was true or not the parties concerned know best. At any rate the colored politicians did not see it in that light, for they were gathered from near and far to press their claims for recognition and patronage. On the evening following the White House inaugural ball, the colored people of Washington gave an "inaugural" ball at a large public hall. It was under the management of their leading citizens, among them several high officials holding over from the last administration, and a number of professional and business men. This ball was the most noteworthy social event that colored circles up to that time had ever known. There were many visitors from various parts of the country. Miss

Clayton attended the ball, the honors of which she carried away easily. She danced with several partners, and was introduced to innumerable people whom she had never seen before, and whom she hardly expected ever to meet again. She went away from the ball, at four o'clock in the morning, in a glow of triumph, and with a confused impression of senators and representatives and lawyers and doctors of all shades, who had sought an introduction, led her through the dance, and overwhelmed her with compliments. She returned home the next day but one, after the most delightful week of her life.

II

One afternoon, about three weeks after her return from Washington, Alice received a letter through the mail. The envelope bore the words "House of Representatives" printed in one corner, and in the opposite corner, in a bold running hand, a Congressman's frank, "Hamilton M. Brown, M. C." The letter read as follows:—

HOUSE OF REPRESENTATIVES,

WASHINGTON, D.C., March 30, 187–.

MISS ALICE CLAYTON, GROVELAND.

Dear Friend (if I may be permitted to call you so after so brief an acquaintance),—I remember with sincerest pleasure our recent meeting at the inaugural ball, and the sensation created by your beauty, your amiable manners, and your graceful dancing. Time has so strengthened the impression I then received, that I should have felt inconsolable had I thought it impossible ever to again behold the charms which had brightened the occasion of our meeting and eclipsed by their brilliancy the leading belles of the capital. I had hoped, however, to have the pleasure of meeting you again, and circumstances have fortunately placed it in my power to do so at an early date. You have doubtless learned that the contest over the election in the Sixth Congressional District of South Carolina has been decided in my favor, and that I now have the honor of representing my native State at the national capital. I have just been appointed a member of a special committee to visit and inspect the Sault River and the Straits of Mackinac, with reference to the needs of lake navigation. I have made arrangements to start a week ahead of the other members of the committee, whom I am to meet in Detroit on the 20th. I shall leave here on the 2d, and will arrive in Groveland on the 3d, by the 7.30 evening express. I shall remain in Groveland several days, in the course of which I shall be pleased to call, and renew the acquaintance so auspiciously begun in Washington, which it is my fondest hope may ripen into a warmer friendship.

If you do not regard my visit as presumptuous, and do not write me in the mean while forbidding it, I shall do myself the pleasure of waiting on you the morning after my arrival in Groveland.

With renewed expressions of my sincere admiration and profound esteem, I remain,

Sincerely yours,

HAMILTON M. BROWN, M.C.

To Alice, and especially to her mother, this bold and flowery letter had very nearly the force of a formal declaration. They read it over again and again, and spent most of the afternoon discussing it. There were few young men in Groveland eligible as husbands for so superior a person as Alice Clayton, and an addition to the number would be very acceptable. But the mere fact of his being a Congressman was not sufficient to qualify him; there were other considerations.

"I've never heard of this Honorable Hamilton M. Brown," said Mr. Clayton. The letter had been laid before him at the supper-table. "It's strange, Alice, that you haven't said anything about him before. You must have met lots of swell folks not to recollect a Congressman."

"But he wasn't a Congressman then," answered Alice; "he was only a claimant. I remember Senator Bruce, and Mr. Douglass; but there were so many doctors and lawyers and politicians that I couldn't keep track of them all. Still I have a faint impression of a Mr. Brown who danced with me."

She went in to the parlor and brought out the dancing programme she had used at the Washington ball. She had decorated it with a bow of blue ribbon and preserved it as a souvenir of her visit.

"Yes," she said, after examining it, "I must have danced with him. Here are the initials—'H. M. B.'"

"What color is he?" asked Mr. Clayton, as he plied his knife and fork.

"I have a notion that he was rather dark—darker than any one I have ever danced with before."

"Why did you dance with him?" asked her father. "You weren't obliged to go back on your principles because you were away from home."

"Well, father, 'when you're in Rome'—you know the rest. Mrs. Clearweather introduced me to several dark men, to him among others. They were her friends, and common decency required me to be courteous."

"If this man is black, we don't want to encourage him. If he's the right sort, we'll invite him to the house."

"And make him feel at home," added Mrs. Clayton, on hospitable thoughts intent.

"We must ask Sadler about him to-morrow," said Mr. Clayton, when he had drunk his coffee and lighted his cigar. "If he's the right man he shall have cause to remember his visit to Groveland. We'll show him that Washington is not the only town on earth."

The uncertainty of the family with regard to Mr. Brown was soon removed. Mr. Solomon Sadler, who was supposed to know everything worth knowing concerning the colored race, and everybody of importance connected with it, dropped in after supper to make an evening call. Sadler was familiar with the history of every man of Negro ancestry who had distinguished himself in any walk of life. He could give the pedigree of Alexander Pushkin, the titles of scores of Dumas's novels (even Sadler had not time to learn them all), and could recite the whole of Wendell Phillips's lecture on Toussaint l'Ouverture. He claimed a personal acquaintance with Mr. Frederick Douglass, and had been often in Washington, where he was well known and well received in good colored society.

"Let me see," he said reflectively, when asked for information about the Honorable Hamilton M. Brown. "Yes, I think I know him. He studied at Oberlin just after the war. He was about leaving there when I entered. There were two H. M. Browns there—a Hamilton M. Brown and a Henry M. Brown. One was stout and dark and the other was slim and quite light; you could scarcely tell him from a dark white man. They used to call them 'light Brown' and 'dark Brown.' I didn't know either of them except by sight, for they were there only a few weeks after I went in. As I remember them, Hamilton was the fair one—a very good-looking, gentlemanly fellow, and, as I heard, a good student and fine speaker."

"Do you remember what kind of hair he had?" asked Mr. Clayton.

"Very good indeed; straight, as I remember it. He looked something like a Spaniard or a Portuguese."

"Now that you describe him," said Alice, "I remember quite well dancing with such a gentleman; and I'm wrong about my 'H. M. B.' the dark man must have been some one else; there are two others on my card that I can't remember distinctly, and he was probably one of those."

"I guess he's all right, Alice," said her father when Sadler had gone away. "He evidently means business, and we must treat him white. Of course he must stay with us; there are no hotels in Groveland while he is here. Let's see—he'll be here in three days. That isn't very long, but I guess we can get ready. I'll write a letter this afternoon—or you write it, and invite him to the house, and say I'll meet him at the depot. And you may have *carte blanche* for making the preparations."

"We must have some people to meet him."

"Certainly; a reception is the proper thing. Sit down immediately and write the letter and I'll mail it first thing in the morning, so he'll get it before he has time to make other arrangements. And you and your mother put your heads together and make out a list of guests, and I'll have the invitation printed to-morrow. We will show the darkeys of Groveland how to entertain a Congressman."

It will be noted that in moments of abstraction or excitement Mr. Clayton sometimes lapsed into forms of speech not entirely consistent with his principles. But some allowance must be made for his atmosphere; he could no more escape from it than the leopard can change his spots, or the— In deference to Mr. Clatyon's feelings the quotation will be left incomplete.

Alice wrote the letter on the spot and it was duly mailed, and sped on its winged way to Washington.

The preparations for the reception were made as thoroughly and elaborately as possible on so short a notice. The invitations were issued; the house was cleaned from attic to cellar; an orchestra was engaged for the evening; elaborate floral decorations were planned and the flowers ordered. Even the refreshments, which ordinarily, in the household of a caterer, would be mere matter of familiar detail, became a subject of serious consultation and study.

The approaching event was a matter of very much interest to the fortunate ones who were honored with invitations, and this for several reasons. They were anxious to meet this sole representative of their race in the —th Congress, and as he was not one of the old-line colored leaders, but a new star risen on the political horizon, there was a special curiosity to see who he was and what he looked like. Moreover, the Claytons did not often entertain a large company, but when they did, it was on a scale commensurate with their means and position, and to be present on such an occasion was a thing to remember and to talk about. And, most important consideration of all, some remarks dropped by members of the Clayton family had given rise to the rumor that the Congressman was seeking a wife. This invested his visit with a romantic interest, and gave the reception a practical value; for there were other marriageable girls besides Miss Clayton, and if one was left another might be taken.

III

On the evening of April 3d, at fifteen minutes of six o'clock, Mr. Clayton, accompanied by Jack, entered the livery carriage waiting at his gate and ordered the coachman to drive to the Union Depot. He had taken Jack along, partly for company, and partly that Jack might relieve the Congressman of any trouble about his baggage, and make himself useful in case of emergency. Jack was willing enough to go, for he had foreseen in the visitor a rival for Alice's hand,—indeed he had heard more or less of the subject for several days—and was glad to make a reconnaissance before the enemy arrived upon the field of battle. He had made—at least he had thought so—considerable progress with Alice during the three weeks since her return from Washington, and once or twice Alice had been perilously near the tender stage. This visit had disturbed the situation and threatened to ruin his chances; but he did not mean to give up without a struggle.

Arrived at the main entrance, Mr. Clayton directed the carriage to wait, and entered the station with Jack. The Union Depot at Groveland was an immense oblong structure, covering a dozen parallel tracks and furnishing terminal passenger facilities for half a dozen railroads. The tracks ran east and west, and the depot was entered from the south, at about the middle of the building. On either side of the entrance, the waiting-rooms, refreshment rooms, baggage and express departments, and other administrative offices, extended in a row for the entire length of the building; and beyond them and parallel with them stretched a long open space, separated from the tracks by an iron fence or *grille*. There were two entrance gates in the fence, at which tickets must be shown before access could be had to trains, and two other gates, by which arriving passengers came out.

Mr. Clayton looked at the blackboard on the wall underneath the station clock, and observed that the 7.30 train from Washington was five minutes late. Accompanied by Jack he walked up and down the platform until the train, with the usual accompaniment of panting steam and clanging bell and rumbling trucks, pulled into the station, and drew up on the third or fourth track from the iron railing. Mr. Clayton stationed himself at the gate nearest the rear end of the train, reasoning that the Congressman would ride in a parlor car, and would naturally come out by the gate nearest the point at which he left the train.

"You'd better go and stand by the other gate, Jack," he said to his companion, "and stop him if he goes out that way."

The train was well filled and a stream of passengers poured through. Mr. Clayton scanned the crowd carefully as they approached the gate, and scrutinized each passenger as he came through, without seeing any one that met the description of Congressman Brown, as given by Sadler, or any one that could in his opinion be the gentleman for whom he was looking. When the last one had passed through he was left to the conclusion that his expected guest had gone out by the other gate. Mr. Clayton hastened thither.

"Didn't he come out this way, Jack?" he asked.

"No, sir," replied the young man, "I haven't seen him."

"That's strange," mused Mr. Clayton, somewhat anxiously. "He would hardly fail to come without giving us notice. Surely we must have missed him. We'd better look around a little. You go that way and I'll go this."

Mr. Clayton turned and walked several rods along the platform to the men's waiting-room, and standing near the door glanced around to see if he could find the object of his search. The only colored person in the room was a stout and very black man, wearing a broadcloth suit and a silk hat, and seated a short distance from the door. On the seat by his side stood a couple of valises. On one of them, the one nearest him, on which his arm rested, was written, in white letters, plainly legible,—

"H.M. Brown, M.C.
"Washington, D. C."

Mr. Clayton's feelings at this discovery can better be imagined than described. He hastily left the waiting-room, before the black gentleman, who was looking the other way, was even aware of his presence, and, walking rapidly up and down the platform, communed with himself upon what course of action the situation demanded. He had invited to his house, had come down to meet, had made elaborate preparations to entertain on the following evening, a light-colored man,—a white man by this theory, an acceptable guest, a possible husband for his daughter, an avowed suitor for her hand. If the Congressman had turned out to be brown, even dark brown, with fairly good hair, though he might not have desired him as a son-in-law, yet he could have welcomed him as a guest. But even this softening of the blow was denied him, for the man in the waiting-room was palpably, aggressively black, with pronounced African features and woolly hair, without apparently a single drop of redeeming white blood. Could he, in the face of his well-known principles, his lifelong rule of conduct, take this Negro into his home and introduce him to his friends? Could he subject his wife and daughter to the rude shock of such a disappointment? It would be bad enough for them to learn of the ghastly mistake, but to have him in the house would be twisting the arrow in the wound.

Mr. Clayton had the instincts of a gentleman, and realized the delicacy of the situation. But to get out of his difficulty without wounding the feelings of the Congressman required not only diplomacy but dispatch. Whatever he did must be done promptly; for if he waited many minutes the Congressman would probably take a carriage and be driven to Mr. Clayton's residence.

A ray of hope came for a moment to illumine the gloom of the situation. Perhaps the black man was merely sitting there, and not the owner of the valise! For there were two valises, one on each side of the supposed Congressman. For obvious reasons he did not care to make the inquiry himself, so he looked around for his companion, who came up a moment later.

"Jack," he exclaimed excitedly, "I'm afraid we're in the worst kind of a hole, unless there's some mistake! Run down to the men's waiting-room and you'll see a man and a valise, and you'll understand what I mean. Ask the darkey if he is the Honorable Mr. Brown, Congressman from South Carolina. If he says yes, come back right away and let me know, without giving him time to ask any questions, and put your wits to work to help me out of the scrape."

"I wonder what's the matter?" said Jack to himself, but did as he was told. In a moment he came running back.

"Yes, sir," he announced; "he says he's the man."

"Jack," said Mr. Clayton desperately, "if you want to show your appreciation of what I've done for you, you must suggest some way out of this. I'd never dare to take that negro to my house, and yet I'm obliged to treat him like a gentleman."

Jack's eyes had worn a somewhat reflective look since he had gone to make the inquiry. Suddenly his face brightened with intelligence, and then, as a newsboy ran into the station calling his wares, hardened into determination.

"Clarion, special extry 'dition! All about de epidemic er dipt'eria!"

clamored the newsboy with shrill childish treble, as he made his way toward the waiting-room. Jack darted after him, and saw the man to whom he had spoken buy a paper. He ran back to his employer, and dragged him over toward the ticket-seller's window.

"I have it, sir!" he exclaimed, seizing a telegraph blank and writing rapidly, and reading aloud as he wrote. "How's this for a way out?"—

"DEAR SIR,—I write you this note here in the depot to inform you of an unfortunate event which has interfered with my plans and those of my family for your entertainment while in Groveland. Yesterday my daughter Alice complained of a sore throat, which by this afternoon had developed into a case of malignant diphtheria. In consequence our house has been quarantined; and while I have felt myself obliged to come down to the depot, I do not feel that I ought to expose you to the possibility of infection, and I therefore send you this by another hand. The bearer will conduct you to a carriage which I have ordered placed at your service, and unless you should prefer some other hotel, you will be driven to the Forest Hill House, where I beg you will consider yourself my guest during your stay in the city, and make the fullest use of every convenience it may offer. From present indication I fear no one of our family will be able to see you, which we shall regret beyond expression, as we have made elaborate arrangements for your entertainment. I still hope, however, that you may enjoy your visit, as there are many places of interest in the city, and many friends will doubtless be glad to make your acquaintance.

"With assurances of my profound regret, I am

"Sincerely yours,
"CICERO CLAYTON"

"Splendid!" cried Mr. Clayton. "You've helped me out of a horrible scrape. Now, go and take him to the hotel and see him comfortably located, and tell them to charge the bill to me."

"I suspect, sir," suggested Jack, "that I'd better not go up to the house, and you'll have to stay in yourself for a day or two, to keep up appearances. I'll sleep on the lounge at the store, and we can talk business over the telephone."

"All right, Jack, we'll arrange the details later. But for Heaven's sake get him started, or he'll be calling a hack to drive up to the house. I'll go home on a street car."

"So far so good," sighed Mr. Clayton to himself as he escaped from the station. "Jack is a deuced clever fellow, and I'll have to do something more for him. But the tug-of-war is yet to come. I've got to bribe a doctor, shut up the house for a day or two, and have all the ill-humor of two disappointed women to endure until this negro leaves town. Well, I'm sure my wife and Alice will back me up at any cost. No sacrifice is too great to escape having to entertain him; of course I have no prejudice against his color,— he can't help that,—but it is the *principle* of the thing. If we received him it would be a concession fatal to all my views and theories. And I am really doing him a kindness, for I'm sure that all the world could not make Alice and her mother treat him with anything but cold politeness. It'll be a great mortification to Alice, but I don't see how else I could have got out of it."

He boarded the first car that left the depot, and soon reached home. The house was lighted up, and through the lace curtains of the parlor windows he could see his wife and daughter, elegantly dressed, waiting to receive their distinguished visitor. He rang the bell impatiently, and a servant opened the door.

"The gentleman didn't come?" asked the maid.

"No," he said as he hung up his hat. This brought the ladies to the door.

"He didn't come?" they exclaimed. "What's the matter?"

"I'll tell you," he said. "Mary," this to the servant, a white girl, who stood in open-eyed curiosity, "we shan't need you any more to-night."

Then he went into the parlor, and, closing the door, told his story. When he reached the point where he had discovered the color of the honorable Mr. Brown, Miss Clayton caught her breath, and was on the verge of collapse.

"That nigger," said Mrs. Clayton indignantly, "can never set foot in this house. But what did you do with him?"

Mr. Clayton quickly unfolded his plan, and described the disposition he had made of the Congressman.

"It's an awful shame," said Mrs. Clayton. "Just think of the trouble and expense we have gone to! And poor Alice'll never get over it, for everybody knows he came to see her and that he's smitten with her. But you've done just right; we never would have been able to hold up our heads again if we had introduced a black man, even a Congressman, to the people that are invited here tomorrow night, as a sweetheart of Alice. Why, she wouldn't marry him if he was President of the United States and plated with gold an inch thick. The very idea!"

"Well," said Mr. Clayton, "then we've got to act quick. Alice must wrap up her throat—by the way, Alice, how *is* your throat?"

"It's sore," sobbed Alice, who had been in tears almost from her father's return, "and I don't care if I do have diphtheria and die, no, I don't!" and wept on.

"Wrap up your throat and go to bed, and I'll go over to Doctor Pillsbury's and get a diphtheria card to nail up on the house. In the morning, first thing, we'll have to write notes recalling the invitations for to-morrow evening, and have them delivered by messenger boys. We were fools for not finding out all about this man from some one who knew, before we invited him here. Sadler don't know more than half he thinks he does, anyway. And we'll have to do this thing thoroughly, or our motives will be misconstrued, and people will say we are prejudiced and all that, when it is only a matter of principle with us."

The programme outlined above was carried out to the letter. The invitations were recalled, to the great disappointment of the invited guests. The family physician called several times during the day. Alice remained in bed, and the maid left without notice, in such a hurry that she forgot to take her best clothes.

Mr. Clayton himself remained at home. He had a telephone in the house, and was therefore in easy communication with his office, so that the business did not suffer materially by reason of his absence from the store. About ten o'clock in the morning a note came up from the hotel, expressing Mr. Brown's regrets and sympathy. Toward noon Mr. Clayton picked up the morning paper, and was glancing over it casually when his eye fell upon a column headed "A Colored Congressman." He read the article with astonishment that rapidly turned to chagrin and dismay. It was an interview describing the Congressman as a tall and shapely man, about thirty-five years old, with an olive complexion not noticeably darker than many a white man's, straight hair, and eyes as black as sloes.

"The bearing of this son of South Carolina reveals the polished manners of the Southern gentleman, and neither from his appearance nor his conversation would one suspect that the white blood which flows in his veins in such preponderating measure had ever been crossed by that of a darker race," wrote the reporter, who had received instructions at the office that for urgent business considerations the lake shipping interest wanted Representative Brown treated with marked consideration.

There was more of the article, but the introductory portion left Mr. Clayton in such a state of bewilderment that the paper fell from his hand. What was the meaning of it? Had he been mistaken? Obviously so, or else the reporter was wrong, which was manifestly improbable. When he had recovered himself somewhat, he picked up the newspaper and began reading where he had left off.

"Representative Brown traveled to Groveland in company with Bishop Jones of the African Methodist Jerusalem Church, who is *en route* to attend the general conference of his denomination at Detroit next week. The bishop, who came in while the writer was interviewing Mr. Brown, is a splendid type of the pure negro. He is said to be a man of great power among his people, which may easily be believed after one has looked upon his expressive countenance and heard him discuss the questions which affect the welfare of his church and his race."

Mr. Clayton stared at the paper. "'The bishop,'" he repeated, "'is a splendid type of the pure negro.' I must have mistaken the bishop for the Congressman! But how in the world did Jack get the thing balled up? I'll call up the store and demand an explanation of him."

"Jack," he asked, "what kind of a looking man was the fellow you gave the note to at the depot?"

"He was a very wicked-looking fellow, sir," come back the answer. "He had a bad eye, looked like a gambler, sir. I am not surprised that you didn't want to entertain him, even if he was a Congressman."

"What color was he—that's what I want to know—and what kind of hair did he have?"

"Why, he was about my complexion, sir, and had straight black hair."

The rules of the telephone company did not permit swearing over the line. Mr. Clayton broke the rules.

"Was there any one else with him?" he asked when he had relieved his mind.

"Yes, sir, Bishop Jones of the African Methodist Jerusalem Church was sitting there with him; they had traveled from Washington together. I drove the bishop to his stopping-place after I had left Mr. Brown at the hotel. I didn't suppose you'd mind."

Mr. Clayton fell into a chair, and indulged in thoughts unutterable.

He folded up the paper and slipped it under the family Bible, where it was least likely to be soon discovered.

"I'll hide the paper, anyway," he groaned. "I'll never hear the last of this till my dying day, so I may as well have a few hours' respite. It's too late to go back, and we've got to play the farce out. Alice is really sick with disappointment, and to let her know this now would only make her worse. Maybe he'll leave town in a day or two, and then she'll be in condition to stand it. Such luck is enough to disgust a man with trying to do right and live up to his principles."

Time hung a little heavy on Mr. Clayton's hands during the day. His wife was busy with the housework. He answered several telephone calls about Alice's health, and called up the store occasionally to ask how the business was getting on. After lunch he lay down on a sofa and took a nap, from which he was aroused by the sound of the door-bell. He went to the door. The evening paper was lying on the porch, and the newsboy, who had not observed the diphtheria sign until after he had rung, was hurrying away as fast as his legs would carry him.

Mr. Clayton opened the paper and looked it through to see if there was any reference to the visiting Congressman. He found what he sought and more. An article on the local page contained a resume of the information given in the morning paper, with the following additional paragraph:—

"A reporter, who called at the Forest Hill this morning to interview Representative Brown, was informed that the Congressman had been invited to spend the remainder of his time in Groveland as the guest of Mr. William Watkins, the proprietor of the popular livery establishment on Main Street. Mr. Brown will remain in the city several days, and a reception will be tendered him at Mr. Watkins's on Wednesday evening."

"That ends it," sighed Mr. Clayton. "The dove of peace will never again rest on my roof-tree."

Buy why dwell longer on the sufferings of Mr. Clayton, or attempt to describe the feelings or chronicle the remarks of his wife and daughter when they learned the facts in the case?

As to Representative Brown, he was made welcome in the hospitable home of Mr. William Watkins. There was a large and brilliant assemblage at the party on Wednesday evening, at which were displayed the costumes prepared for the Clayton reception. Mr. Brown took fancy to Miss Lura Watkins, to whom, before the week was over, he became engaged to be married. Meantime poor Alice, the innocent victim of circumstances and principles, lay sick abed with a suppositious case of malignant diphtheria, and a real case of acute disappointment and chagrin.

"Oh, Jack!" exclaimed Alice, a few weeks later, on the way home from evening church in company with the young man, "what a dreadful thing it all was! And to think of that hateful Lura Watkins marrying the Congressman!"

The street was shaded by trees at the point where they were passing, and there was no one in sight. Jack put his arm around her waist, and, leaning over, kissed her.

"Never mind, dear," he said soothingly, "you still have your 'last chance' left, and I'll prove myself a better man than the Congressman."

Occasionally, at social meetings, when the vexed question of the future of the colored race comes up, as it often does, for discussion, Mr. Clayton may still be heard to remark sententiously:—

"What the white people of the United States need most, in dealing with this problem, is a higher conception of the brotherhood of man. For of one blood God made all the nations of the earth."

Uncle Wellington's Wives

The Wife of His Youth (1899)

Considered one of Chesnutt's best works by William Dean Howells[1]—a fellow Ohioan and the most influential literary figure of his time—"Uncle Wellington's Wives" vividly illustrates its author's deft but often overlooked comic touch. Despite its broad, almost slapstick humor, the story nevertheless conforms to Chesnutt's career-long interest in examining the forces, especially love and race, that shaped American families at the turn of the century. Like both "A Matter of Principle" and "The Wife of His Youth," "Uncle Wellington's Wives" focuses on a light-skinned African American attempting to capitalize on the social and economic promise of the North. But while "The Wife of His Youth" explores the reunification of a couple married in slavery and separated by the Civil War, "Uncle Wellington's Wives" depicts its title character's comic struggle to *exchange* his longtime black wife for a white one. The central figure of this tale attempts to enhance his social position, and perhaps to lighten his workload, by leaving his hard-working wife, Milly, in the South for the chance to marry a Northern white woman. If other Chesnutt fictions—including *The House Behind the Cedars*, "Her Virginia Mammy," and "Cicely's Dream"—focus on the agonizing consequences of miscegenation, then "Uncle Wellington's Wives" surprisingly makes the same issue the subject of farce.

Originally published in *The Wife of His Youth and Other Stories of the Color Line*, "Uncle Wellington's Wives" has the distinction of being one of the few Chesnutt stories in which the protagonist lives in both the North and the South. Residing initially in a "little frame house in the suburbs of Patesville" (Chesnutt's fictional redesignation of Fayetteville, North Carolina), the protagonist decides to emigrate to "Groveland" (Cleveland), where, he thinks, he'll live out a fantasy life in the North, as described by a visitor from that land of milk and honey:

> The speaker pictured in eloquent language the state of ideal equality and happiness enjoyed by colored people at the North: how they sent their children to school with the white children; how they sat by white people in the churches and theatres, ate with them in the public restaurants, and buried their dead in the same cemeteries. The professor waxed eloquent with the development of his theme, and, as a finishing touch to an alluring picture, assured the excited audience that the intermarriage of the races was common, and that he himself had espoused a white woman. (123)

Based on this compelling vision of the North as the answer to so many inadequacies inherent in Southern living, Wellington Braboy sets off to make a new life for himself—without his black Southern wife—in the Northern city of Groveland.

Thus, "Uncle Wellington's Wives" represents one of Chesnutt's few comic treatments of the importance of the North as a concept for African Americans, especially, but not exclusively, ex-slaves. Chesnutt recognized and often seemed obsessed in his works by the extent to which geography could profoundly dictate a person's fortunes. He repeatedly contrives his plots, in fact, to emphasize how identity and geography had become intertwined for black Americans. While the South frequently represented "home," the North had its own special pull—the possibilities, even the promises, of equality. Though Chesnutt typically treats the matter with grave attention in such works as "The Doll," "The Wife of His Youth," and *The Colonel's Dream,* he deploys a strikingly playful tone in "Uncle Wellington's Wives." Like other Chesnutt characters, Wellington Braboy imagines the North to be rich in opportunity, but this story ultimately satirizes those who would rely too heavily on geographical curatives. In fact, Wellington's conception of the North grows so absurdly exaggerated that he finally envisions it as a utopian social order that encourages miscegenation and rewards laziness:

> The more uncle Wellington's mind dwelt upon the professor's speech, the more attractive seemed the picture of Northern life presented. . . . Giving full rein to his fancy, he saw in the North a land flowing with

> milk and honey,—a land peopled by noble men and beautiful women, among whom colored men and women moved with the ease and grace of acknowledged right. Then he placed himself in the foreground of the picture. What a fine figure he would have made in the world if he had been born at the free North! He imagined himself dressed like the professor, and passing the contribution-box in a white church; and most pleasant of his dreams, and the hardest to realize as possible, was that of the gracious white lady he might have called wife. (123–24)

Hence, the notion that moving to the North will confer a new identity on him proves too difficult a lure to resist, and the protagonist makes his escape from his Southern home and his Southern wife.[2]

And, indeed, Braboy's experiences in the first half of the story seem to confirm Chesnutt's personal preference for the North over the South, although that seeming confirmation is short-lived at best. At first, Uncle Wellington's Northern home lives up to its billing as the promised land. He acquires a well-paying job as a coachman, he learns something of the economics of the North, and, most congenially, he even fulfills his quest to marry a "white lady" (although she turns out to be a tad less "gracious" than he had imagined). Ultimately, his second marriage deteriorates so badly that he

> found himself wondering if his second marriage had been a wise one. Other circumstances combined to change his once rose-colored conception of life at the North. He had believed that all men were equal in this favored locality, but he discovered more degrees of inequality than he had ever perceived at the South. A colored man might be as good as a white man in theory, but neither of them was of any special consequence without money, or talent, or position. . . . On occasions when Mrs. Braboy [the second] would require of him some unusual physical exertion, or when too frequent applications to the bottle had loosened her tongue, uncle Wellington's mind would revert, with a remorseful twinge of conscience, to the *dolce far niente* of his Southern home. (142–43)

Soon enough, bereft of job, money, and finally the white wife (who leaves him and takes everything with her), Braboy is left to contemplate his fate, alone in a suddenly not-so-utopian North: "Instead of the beautiful Northern life he had dreamed of, he found himself stranded, penniless, in a strange land" (147). Ultimately, Braboy returns to his black wife and the South because the trappings of a new identity—an *ungracious* white wife (rather than the "gracious white lady" he had envisioned)—and the economics of responsibility—Braboy is such a poor worker that he models several different employments, from coachman to painter to fisherman—subvert his notion of the "free North."

Perhaps because of its farcical premise and its reliance on what Joseph R. McElrath Jr. calls the "shudder-inducing stereotyping of 'Uncle' Wellington" (*CE*, 17), "Uncle Wellington's Wives" provokes wide-ranging interpretations. An early reviewer argued that the story "has not a redeeming quality! The author should blush to have written it, and the publishers to have published it" (Stephenson, 55). Howells, on the other hand, lists it among his favorites, and a recent critic, Myles Raymond Hurd, finds the story a telling commentary on such social issues as miscegenation and the resettlement of African Americans to the North.[3] Despite the disparity in views of the story, it nevertheless explores, albeit in significantly different ways, issues typical of Chesnutt's Northern writings. Like "A Matter of Principle," for example, "Uncle Wellington's Wives" employs a characteristic Chesnutt thematic framework—the search for family identity—and then plays it for laughs. Clayton and Braboy corrupt the very undertaking of such a quest because they do it for the wrong reasons: to improve social standing, to avoid work, to lighten the black race.

And, although Chesnutt does argue in his essays that "the future American race . . . will be formed by a mingling . . . of the various racial varieties which make up the present population of the United States" ("Future American," 20),[4] this story suggests that there might be bumps along the road. Ultimately, whether one considers "Uncle Wellington's Wives" a telling (if humorous) sociological commentary or a joke in questionable taste, we can agree, I think, that the story explores, in farcically exaggerated terms, a set of new social dynamics in the North. It is about love and family and making a living wage in the North. Of all the stories in this collection, only this one seems to provide a cautionary tale about Northern life.

NOTES

1. See Howells's 1900 essay "Mr. Charles W. Chesnutt's Stories," in which he praises Chesnutt for "touch[ing] all the stops, and with equal delicacy in stories of real tragedy and comedy and pathos" (Howells, 53).

2. In a fascinating reversal, Chesnutt has Uncle Wellington's flight from the South sound remarkably similar to the flights of slaves in so-called slave narratives—so much so that it reads like a parodic retelling of the slave's flight to the North: Braboy clandestinely

travels at night; he takes a literal train (as opposed to the Underground Railway); and he takes refuge in a "safe" house.

3. See Hurd's essay for one of the few extensive commentaries on "Uncle Wellington's Wives."

4. Chesnutt writes much the same thing in a 1906 letter to Booker T. Washington: "I do not believe it possible for two races to subsist side by side without intermingling; experience has demonstrated this fact and there will be more experience along that line" (*EC*, 14).

Uncle Wellington's Wives

I

UNCLE WELLINGTON BRABOY WAS so deeply absorbed in thought as he walked slowly homeward from the weekly meeting of the Union League, that he let his pipe go out, a fact of which he remained oblivious until he had reached the little frame house in the suburbs of Patesville, where he lived with aunt Milly, his wife. On this particular occasion the club had been addressed by a visiting brother from the North, Professor Patterson, a tall, well-formed mulatto, who wore a perfectly fitting suit of broadcloth, a shiny silk hat, and linen of dazzling whiteness,—in short, a gentleman of such distinguished appearance that the doors and windows of the offices and stores on Front Street were filled with curious observers as he passed through that thoroughfare in the early part of the day. This polished stranger was a traveling organizer of Masonic lodges, but he also claimed to be a high officer in the Union League, and had been invited to lecture before the local chapter of that organization at Patesville.

The lecture had been largely attended, and uncle Wellington Braboy had occupied a seat just in front of the platform. The subject of the lecture was "The Mental, Moral, Physical, Political, Social, and Financial Improvement of the Negro Race in America," a theme much dwelt upon, with slight variations, by colored orators. For to this struggling people, then as now, the problem of their uncertain present and their doubtful future was the chief concern of life. The period was the hopeful one. The Federal Government retained some vestige of authority in the South, and the newly emancipated race cherished the delusion that under the Constitution, that enduring rock on which our liberties are founded, and under the equal laws it purported to guarantee, they would enter upon the era of freedom and opportunity which their Northern friends had inaugurated with such solemn sanctions. The speaker pictured in eloquent language that state of ideal equality and happiness enjoyed by colored people at the North: how they sent their children to school with the white children; how they sat by white people in the churches and theatres, ate with them in the public restaurants, and buried their dead in the same cemeteries. The professor waxed eloquent with the development of his theme, and, as a finishing touch to an alluring picture, assured the excited audience that the intermarriage of the races was common, and that he himself had espoused a white woman.

Uncle Wellington Braboy was a deeply interested listener. He had heard something of these facts before, but his information had always come in such vague and questionable shape that he had paid little attention to it. He knew that the Yankees had freed the slaves, and that runaway negroes had always gone to the North to seek liberty; any such equality, however, as the visiting brother had depicted, was more than uncle Wellington had ever conceived as actually existing anywhere in the world. At first he felt inclined to doubt the truth of the speaker's statements; but the cut of his clothes, the eloquence of his language, and the flowing length of his whiskers, were so far superior to anything uncle Wellington had ever met among the colored people of his native State, that he felt irresistibly impelled to the conviction that nothing less than the advantages claimed for the North by the visiting brother could have produced such an exquisite flower of civilization. Any lingering doubts uncle Wellington may have felt were entirely dispelled by the courtly bow and cordial grasp of the hand with which the visiting brother acknowledged the congratulations showered upon him by the audience at the close of his address.

The more uncle Wellington's mind dwelt upon the professor's speech, the more attractive seemed the picture of Northern life presented. Uncle Wellington possessed in large measure the imaginative faculty so freely bestowed by nature upon the race from which the darker half of his blood was drawn. He had indulged in occasional day-dreams of an ideal state of social equality, but his wildest flights of fancy had never located it nearer than heaven, and he had felt some misgivings about its practical working even there. Its desirability he had never doubted, and the speech of the evening before had given a local habitation and a name to the forms his imagination had bodied forth. Giving full rein to his fancy, he saw in the North a land flowing with milk and honey,—a land peopled by noble men and beautiful women, among whom colored men and women moved with the ease and grace of acknowledged right. Then he placed himself in the foreground of the picture. What a fine figure he would have made in the world if he had been born at the free North! He imagined himself dressed like the professor, and passing the contribution-box in a white church; and most pleasant of his dreams, and the hardest to realize as possible, was that of the gracious white lady he might have called wife. Uncle Wellington was a mulatto, and his features were those of his white father, though tinged with the hue of his mother's race; and as he lifted the kerosene lamp at evening, and took a long look at his image in the little mirror over the mantelpiece, he said to himself that he was a very good-looking man, and could have adorned a much higher sphere in life than that in which the accident of birth had placed him. He fell asleep and dreamed that he lived in a two-story brick house, with a spacious flower garden in front, the whole inclosed by a high iron fence; that he kept a carriage and servants, and never did a stroke of work. This was the highest style of living in Patesville, and he could conceive of nothing finer.

Uncle Wellington slept later than usual the next morning, and the sunlight was pouring in at the open window of the bedroom, when his dreams were interrupted by the voice of his wife, in tones meant to be harsh, but which no ordinary degree of passion could rob of their native unctuousness.

"Git up f'm dere, you lazy, good-fuh-nuffin' nigger! Is you gwine ter sleep all de mawnin'? I's ti'ed er dis yer runnin' 'roun' all night an' den sleepin' all day. You won't git dat tater patch hoed ovuh ter-day 'less'n you git up f'm dere an' git at it."

Uncle Wellington rolled over, yawned cavernously, stretched himself, and with a muttered protest got out of bed and put on his clothes. Aunt Milly had prepared a smoking breakfast of hominy and fried bacon, the odor of which was very grateful to his nostrils.

"Is breakfus' done already?" he inquired, tentatively, as he came into the kitchen and glanced at the table.

"No, it ain't ready, an' 't ain't gwine ter be ready 'tel you tote dat wood an' water in," replied aunt Milly severely, as she poured two teacups of boiling water on two tablespoonfuls of ground coffee.

Uncle Wellington went down to the spring and got a pail of water, after which he brought in some oak logs for the fireplace and some lightwood for kindling. Then he drew a chair towards the table and started to sit down.

"Wonduh what's de matter wid you dis mawnin' anyhow," remarked aunt Milly. "You must 'a' be'n up ter some devilment las' night, fer yo' recommemb'ance is so po' dat you fus' fergit ter git up, an' den fergit ter wash yo' face an' hands fo' you set down ter the table. I don' 'low nobody ter eat at my table dat a-way."

"I don' see no use 'n washin' 'em so much," replied Wellington wearily. "Dey gits dirty ag'in right off, an' den you got ter wash 'em ovuh ag'in; it's jes' pilin' up wuk what don' fetch in nuffin'. De dirt don' show nohow, 'n' I don' see no advantage in bein' black, ef you got to keep on washin' yo' face 'n' han's jes' lack w'ite folks." He nevertheless performed his ablutions in a perfunctory way, and resumed his seat at the breakfast-table.

"Ole 'oman," he asked, after the edge of his appetite had been taken off, "how would you lack ter live at the Norf?"

"I dunno nuffin' 'bout de Norf," replied aunt Milly. "It's hard 'nuff ter git erlong heah, whar we knows all erbout it."

"De brother what 'dressed de meetin' las' night say dat de wages at de Norf is twicet ez big ez dey is heah."

"You could make a sight mo' wages heah ef you'd 'ten' ter yo' wuk better," replied aunt Milly.

Uncle Wellington ignored this personality, and continued, "An' he say de cullud folks got all de privileges er de w'ite folks,—dat dey chillen goes ter school tergedder, dat dey sets on same seats in chu'ch, an' sarves on jury, 'n' rides on de kyars an' steamboats wid de w'ite folks, an' eats at de fus' table."

"Dat 'u'd suit you," chuckled aunt Milly, "an' you'd stay dere fer de secon' table, too. How dis man know 'bout all dis yer foolis'ness?" she asked incredulously.

"He come f'm de Norf," said uncle Wellington, "an' he 'speunced it all hisse'f."

"Well, he can't make me b'lieve it," she rejoined, with a shake of her head.

"An' you would n' lack ter go up dere an' 'joy all dese privileges?" asked uncle Wellington, with some degree of earnestness.

The old woman laughed until her sides shook. "Who gwine ter take me up dere?" she inquired.

"You got de money yo'se'f."

"I ain' got no money fer ter was'e," she replied shortly, becoming serious at once; and with that the subject was dropped.

Uncle Wellington pulled a hoe from under the house, and took his way wearily to the potato patch. He did not feel like working, but aunt Milly was the undisputed head of the establishment, and he did not dare to openly neglect his work. In fact, he regarded work at any time as a disagreeable necessity to be avoided as much as possible.

His wife was cast in a different mould. Externally she would have impressed the casual observer as a neat, well-preserved, and good-looking black woman, of middle age, every curve of whose ample figure—and her figure was all curves—was suggestive of repose. So far from being indolent, or even deliberate in her movements, she was the most active and energetic woman in the town. She went through the physical exercises of a prayer-meeting with astonishing vigor. It was exhilarating to see her wash a shirt, and a study to watch her do it up. A quick jerk shook out the dampened garment; one pass of her ample palm spread it over the ironing-board, and a few well-directed strokes with the iron accomplished what would have occupied the ordinary laundress for half an hour.

To this uncommon, and in uncle Wellington's opinion unnecessary and unnatural activity, his own habits were a steady protest. If aunt Milly had been willing to support him in idleness, he would have acquiesced without a murmur in her habits of industry. This she would not do, and, moreover, insisted on his working at least half the time. If she had invested the proceeds of her labor in rich food and fine clothing, he might have endured it better; but to her passion for work was added a most detestable thrift. She absolutely refused to pay for Wellington's clothes, and required him to furnish a certain proportion of the family supplies. Her savings were carefully put by, and with them she had bought and paid for the modest cottage which she and her husband occupied. Under her careful hand it was always neat and clean; in summer the little yard was gay with bright-colored flowers, and woe to the heedless pickaninny who should stray into her yard and pluck a rose or a verbena! In a stout oaken chest under her bed she kept a capacious stocking, into which flowed a steady stream of fractional currency. She carried the key to this chest in her pocket, a proceeding regarded by uncle Wellington with no little disfavor. He was of the opinion—an opinion he would not have dared to assert in her presence—that his wife's earnings were his own property; and he looked upon this stocking as a drunkard's wife might regard the saloon which absorbed her husband's wages.

Uncle Wellington hurried over the potato patch on the morning of the conversation above recorded, and as soon as he saw aunt Milly go away with a basket of clothes on her head, returned to the house, put on his coat, and went uptown.

He directed his steps to a small frame building fronting on the main street of the village, at a point where the street was intersected by one of the several creeks meandering through the town, cooling the air, providing numerous swimming-holes for the amphibious small boy, and furnishing water-power for grist-mills and saw-mills. The rear of the building rested on long brick pillars, built up from the bottom of the steep bank of the creek, while the front was level with the street. This was the office of Mr. Matthew Wright, the sole representative of the colored race at the bar of Chinquapin County. Mr. Wright came of an "old issue" free colored family, in which, though the negro blood was present in an attenuated strain, a line of free ancestry could be traced beyond the Revolutionary War. He had enjoyed exceptional opportunities, and enjoyed distinction of being the first, and for a long time the only colored lawyer in North Carolina. His services were frequently called into requisition by impecunious people of his own race; when they had money they went to white lawyers, who, they shrewdly conjectured, would have more influence with judge or jury than a colored lawyer, however able.

Uncle Wellington found Mr. Wright in his office. Having inquired after the health of the lawyer's family and all his relations in detail, uncle Wellington asked for a professional opinion.

"Mistah Wright, ef a man's wife got money, whose money is dat befo' de law—his'n or her'n?"

The lawyer put on his professional air, and replied:—

"Under the common law, which in default of special legislative enactment is the law of North Carolina, the personal property of the wife belongs to her husband."

"But dat don' jes' tech de p'int, suh. I wuz axin' 'bout money."

"You see, uncle Wellington, your education had not rendered you familiar with legal phraseology. The term 'personal property' or 'estate' embraces, according to Blackstone, all property other than land, and therefore includes money. Any money a man's wife has is his, constructively, and will be recognized as his actually, as soon as he can secure possession of it."

"Dat is ter say, suh—my eddication don' quite 'low me ter understan' dat—dat is ter say"—

"That is to say, it's yours when you get it. It isn't yours so that the law will help you get it; but on the other hand, when you once lay your hands on it, it is yours so that the law won't take it away from you."

Uncle Wellington nodded to express his full comprehension of the law as expounded by Mr. Wright, but scratched his head in a way that expressed some disappointment. The law seemed to wobble. Instead of enabling him to stand up fearlessly and demand his own, it threw him back upon his own efforts; and the prospect of his being able to overpower or outwit aunt Milly by any ordinary means was very poor.

He did not leave the office, but hung around awhile as though there were something further he wished to speak about. Finally, after some discursive remarks about the crops and politics, he asked, in an offhand, disinterested manner, as though the thought had just occurred to him:—

"Mistah Wright, w'ile 's we 're talkin' 'bout law matters, what do it cos' ter git a defoce?"

"That depends upon circumstances. It is n't altogether a matter of expense. Have you and aunt Milly been having trouble?"

"Oh no, suh; I was jes' a-wond 'rin'."

"You see," continued the lawyer, who was fond of talking, and had nothing else to do for the moment, "a divorce is not an easy thing to get in this State under any circumstances. It used to be the law that divorce could be granted only by special act of the legislature; and it is but recently that the subject has been relegated to the jurisdiction of the courts."

Uncle Wellington understood a part of this, but the answer had not been exactly to the point in his mind.

"S'pos'n', den, jes' fer de argyment, me an' my ole 'oman sh'd fall out en wanter separate, how could I git a defoce?"

"That would depend on what you quarreled about. It's pretty hard work to answer general questions in a particular way. If you merely wished to separate, it wouldn't be necessary to get a divorce; but if you should want to marry again, you would have to be divorced, or else you would be guilty of bigamy, and could be sent to the penitentiary. But, by the way, uncle Wellington, when were you married?"

"I got married 'fo' de wah, when I was livin' down on Rockfish Creek."

"When you were in slavery?"

"Yas, suh."

"Did you have your marriage registered after the surrender?"

"No, suh; never knowed nuffin' 'bout dat."

After the war, in North Carolina and other States, the freed people who had sustained to each other the relation of husband and wife as it existed among slaves, were required by law to register their consent to continue in the marriage relation. By this simple expedient their former marriages of convenience received the sanction of law, and their children the seal of legitimacy. In many cases, however, where the parties lived in districts remote from the larger towns, the ceremony was neglected, or never heard of by the freedmen.

"Well," said the lawyer, "if that is the case, and you and aunt Milly should disagree, it wouldn't be necessary for you to get a divorce, even if you should want to marry again. You were never legally married."

"So Milly ain't my lawful wife, den?"

"She may be your wife in one sense of the word, but not in such a sense as to render you liable to punishment for bigamy if you should marry another woman. But I hope you will never want to do anything of the kind, for you have a very good wife now."

Uncle Wellington went away thoughtfully, but with a feeling of unaccustomed lightness and freedom. He had not felt so free since the memorable day when he had first heard of the Emancipation Proclamation. On leaving the lawyer's office, he called at the workshop of one of his friends, Peter Williams, a shoemaker by trade, who had a brother living in Ohio.

"Is you hearn f'm Sam lately?" uncle Wellington inquired, after the conversation had drifted through the usual generalities.

"His mammy got er letter f'm 'im las' week; he's livin' in de town er Groveland now."

"How's he gittin' on?"

"He says he gittin' on monst'us well. He 'low ez how he make five dollars a day w'ite-washin', an' have all he kin do."

The shoemaker related various details of his brother's prosperity, and uncle Wellington returned home in a very thoughtful mood, revolving in his mind a plan of future action. This plan had been vaguely assuming form ever since the professor's lecture, and the events of the morning had brought out the detail on bold relief.

Two days after the conversation with the shoemaker, aunt Milly went, in the afternoon, to visit a sister of hers who lived several miles out in the country. During her absence, which lasted until nightfall, uncle Wellington went uptown and purchased a cheap oilcloth valise from a shrewd son of Israel, who had penetrated to this locality with a stock of notions and cheap clothing. Uncle Wellington had his purchase done up in brown paper, and took the parcel under his arm. Arrived at home he unwrapped the valise, and thrust into its capacious jaws his best suit of clothes, some underwear, and a few other small articles for personal use and adornment. Then he carried the valise out into the yard, and, first looking cautiously around to see if there was any one in sight, concealed it in a clump of bushes in a corner of the yard.

It may be inferred from this proceeding that uncle Wellington was preparing for a step of some consequence. In fact, he had fully made up his mind to go to the North; but he still lacked the most important requisite for traveling with comfort, namely, the money to pay his expenses. The idea of tramping the distance which separated him from the promised land of liberty and equality had never occurred to him. When a slave, he had several times been importuned by fellow servants to join them in the attempt to escape from bondage, but he had never wanted his freedom badly enough to walk a thousand miles for it; if he could have gone to Canada by stage-coach, or by rail, or on horseback, with stops for regular meals, he would probably have undertaken the trip. The funds he now needed for his journey were in aunt Milly's chest. He had thought a great deal about his right to this money. It was his wife's savings, and he had never dared to dispute, openly, her right to exercise exclusive control over what she earned; but the lawyer had assured him of his right to the money, of which he was already constructively in possession, and he had therefore determined to possess himself actually of the coveted stocking. It was impracticable for him to get the key of the chest. Aunt Milly kept it in her pocket by day and under her pillow at night. She was a light sleeper, and, if not awakened by the abstraction of the key, would certainly have been disturbed by the unlocking of the chest. But one alternative remained, and that was to break open the chest in her absence.

There was a revival in progress at the colored Methodist church. Aunt Milly was as energetic in her religion as in other respects, and had not missed a single one of the meetings. She returned at nightfall from her visit to the country and prepared a frugal supper. Uncle Wellington did not eat as heartily as usual. Aunt Milly perceived his want of appetite, and spoke of it. He explained it by saying that he did not feel very well.

"Is you gwine ter chu'ch ter-night?" inquired his wife.

"I reckon I'll stay home an' go ter bed," he replied. "I ain't be'n feelin' well dis evenin', an' I 'spec' I better git a good night's res'."

"Well, you kin stay ef you mineter. Good preachin' 'u'd make you feel better, but ef you ain't gwine, don't fergit ter tote in some wood an' lighterd 'fo' you go ter bed. De moon is shinin' bright, an' you can't have no 'scuse 'bout not bein' able ter see."

Uncle Wellington followed her out to the gate, and watched her receding form until it disappeared in the distance. Then he reentered the house with a quick step, and taking a hatchet from a corner of the room, drew the chest from under the bed. As he applied the hatchet to the fastenings, a thought struck him, and by the flickering light of the pine-knot blazing on the hearth, a look of hesitation might have been seen to take the place of the determined expression his face had worn up to that time. He had argued himself into the belief that his present action was lawful and justifiable. Though this conviction had not prevented him from trembling in every limb, as though he were committing a mere vulgar theft, it had still nerved him to the deed. Now even his moral courage began to weaken. The lawyer had told him that his wife's property was his own; in taking it he was therefore only exercising his lawful right. But at the point of breaking open the chest, it occurred to him that he was taking this money in order to get away from aunt Milly, and that he justified his desertion of her by the lawyer's opinion that she was not his lawful wife. If she was not his wife, then he had no right to take the money; if she was his wife, he had no right to marry another woman. His scheme was about to go to shipwreck on this rock, when another idea occurred to him.

"De lawyer say dat in one sense er de word de ole 'oman is my wife, an' in anudder sense er de word she ain't my wife. Ef I goes ter de Norf an' marry a w'ite 'oman, I ain't commit no brigamy, 'caze in dat sense er de word she ain't my wife; but ef I takes dis money, I ain't stealin' it, 'caze in dat sense er de word she is my wife. Dat 'splains all de trouble away."

Having reached this ingenious conclusion, uncle Wellington applied the hatchet vigorously, soon loosened the fastenings of the chest, and with trembling hands extracted from its depths a capacious blue cotton stocking. He emptied the stocking on the table. His first impulse was to take the whole, but again there arose in his mind a doubt—a very obtrusive, unreasonable doubt, but a doubt, nevertheless—of the absolute rectitude of his conduct; and after a moment's hesitation he hurriedly counted the money—it was in bills of small denominations—and found it to be about two hundred and fifty dollars. He then divided it into two piles on one hundred and twenty-five dollars each. He put one pile into his pocket, returned the remainder to the stocking, and replaced it where he had found it. He then closed the chest and shoved it under the bed. After having arranged the fire so that it could safely be left burning, he took a last look around the room, and went out into the moonlight, locking the door behind him, and hanging the key on a nail in the wall, where his wife would be likely to look for it. He then secured his valise from behind the bushes, and left the yard. As he passed by the wood-pile, he said to himself:—

"Well, I declar' ef I ain't done fergot ter tote in dat lighterd; I reckon de ole 'oman 'll ha' ter fetch it in herse'f dis time."

He hastened through the quiet streets, avoiding the few people who were abroad at that hour, and soon reached the railroad station, from which a North-bound train left at nine o'clock. He went around to the dark side of the train, and climbed into a second-class car, where he shrank into the darkest corner and turned his face away from the dim light of the single dirty lamp. There were no passengers in the car except one or two sleepy negroes, who had got on at some other station, and a white man who had gone into the car to smoke, accompanied by a gigantic bloodhound.

Finally the train crept out of the station. From the window uncle Wellington looked out upon the familiar cabins and turpentine stills, the new barrel factory, the brickyard where he had once worked for some time; and as the train rattled through the outskirts of the town, he saw gleaming in the moonlight the white headstones of the colored cemetery where his only daughter had been buried several years before.

Presently the conductor came around. Uncle Wellington had not bought a ticket, and the conductor collected a cash fare. He was not acquainted with uncle Wellington, but had just had a drink at the saloon near the depot, and felt at peace with all mankind.

"Where are you going, uncle?" he inquired carelessly.

Uncle Wellington's face assumed the ashen hue which does duty for pallor in ducky countenances, and his knees began to tremble. Controlling his voice as well as he could, he replied that he was going up to Jonesboro, the terminus of the railroad, to work for a gentleman at that place. He felt immensely relieved when the conductor pocketed the fare, picked up his lantern, and moved away. It was very unphilosophical and very absurd that a man who was only doing right should feel like a thief, shrink from the sight of other people, and lie instinctively. Fine distinctions were not in uncle Wellington's line, but he was struck by the unreasonableness of his feelings, and still more by the discomfort they caused him. By and by, however, the motion of the train made him drowsy; his thoughts all ran together in confusion; and he fell asleep with his head on his valise; and one hand in his pocket, clasped tightly around the roll of money.

II

The train from Pittsburg drew into the Union Depot at Groveland, Ohio, one morning in the spring of 187–, with bell ringing and engine puffing; and from a smoking-car emerged the form of uncle Wellington Braboy, a little dusty and travel-stained, and with a sleepy look about his eyes. He mingled in the crowd, and, valise in hand, moved toward the main exit from the depot. There were several tracks to be crossed, and more than once a watchman snatched him out of the way of a baggage-truck, or a train backing into the depot. He at length reached the door, beyond which, and as near as the regulations would permit, stood a number of hackmen, vociferously soliciting patronage. One of them, a colored man, soon secured several passengers. As he closed the door after the last one he turned to uncle Wellington, who stood near him on the sidewalk, looking about irresolutely.

"Is you goin' uptown?" asked the hack-man, as he prepared to mount the box.

"Yas, suh."

"I'll take you up fo' a quahtah, ef you want ter git up here an' ride on de box wid me."

Uncle Wellington accepted the offer and mounted the box. The hackman whipped up his horses, the carriage climbed the steep hill leading up to the town, and the passengers inside were soon deposited at their hotels.

"Whereabouts do you want to go?" asked the hackman of uncle Wellington, when the carriage was emptied of its last passengers.

"I want ter go ter Brer Sam Williams's," said Wellington.

"What's his street an' number?"

Uncle Wellington did not know the street and number, and the hackman had to explain to him the mystery of numbered houses, to which he was a total stranger.

"Where is he from?" asked the hackman, "and what is his business?"

"He is f'm Norf Ca'lina," replied uncle Wellington, "an' makes his livin' w'ite-washin'."

"I reckon I knows de man," said the hackman. "I 'spec' he's changed his name. De man I knows is name' Johnson. He b'longs ter my chu'ch. I'm gwine out dat way ter git a passenger fer de ten o'clock train, an' I'll take you by dere."

They followed one of the least handsome streets of the city for more than a mile, turned into a cross street, and drew up before a small frame house, from the front of which a sign, painted in white upon a black background, announced to the reading public, in letters inclined to each other at various angles, that whitewashing and kalsomining were "dun" there. A knock at the door brought out a slatternly looking colored woman. She had evidently been disturbed at her toilet, for she held a comb in one hand, and the hair on one side of her head stood out loosely, while on the other side it was braided close to her head. She called her husband, who proved to be the Patesville shoemaker's brother. The hackman introduced the traveler, whose name he had learned on the way out, collected his quarter, and drove away.

Mr. Johnson, the shoemaker's brother, welcomed uncle Wellington to Groveland, and listened with eager delight to the news of the old town, from which he himself had run away many years before, and followed the North Star to Groveland. He had changed his name from "Williams" to "Johnson," on account of the Fugitive Slave Law, which, at the time of his escape from bondage, had rendered it advisable for runaway slaves to court obscurity. After the war he had retained the adopted name. Mrs. Johnson prepared breakfast for her guest, who ate it with an appetite sharpened by his journey. After breakfast he went to bed, and slept until late in the afternoon.

After supper Mr. Johnson took uncle Wellington to visit some of the neighbors who had come from North Carolina before the war. They all expressed much pleasure at meeting "Mr. Braboy," a title which at first sounded a little odd to uncle Wellington. At home he had been "Wellin'-ton," "Brer Wellin'ton," or "uncle Wellin'ton"; it was a novel experience to be called "Mister," and he set it down, with secret satisfaction, as one of the first fruits of Northern liberty.

"Would you lack ter look 'roun' de town a little?" asked Mr. Johnson at breakfast next morning. "I ain' got no job dis mawnin', an' I kin show you some er de sights."

Uncle Wellington acquiesced in this arrangement, and they walked up to the corner to the street-car line. In a few moments a car passed. Mr. Johnson jumped on the moving car, and uncle Wellington followed his example, at the risk of life or limb, as it was his first experience of street cars.

There was only one vacant seat in the car and that was between two white women in the forward end. Mr. Johnson motioned to the seat, but Wellington shrank from walking between those two rows of white people, to say nothing of sitting between the two women, so he remained standing in the rear part of the car. A moment later, as the car rounded a short curve, he was pitched sidewise into the lap of a stout woman magnificently attired in a ruffled blue calico gown. The lady colored up, and uncle Wellington, as he struggled to his feet amid the laughter of the passengers, was absolutely helpless with embarrassment, until the conductor came up behind him and pushed him toward the vacant place.

"Sit down, will you," he said; and before uncle Wellington could collect himself, he was seated between the two white women. Everybody in the car seemed to be looking at him. But he came to the conclusion, after he had pulled himself together and reflected a few moments, that he would find this method of locomotion pleasanter when he got used to it, and then he could score one more glorious privilege gained by his change of residence.

They got off at the public square, in the heart of the city, where there were flowers and statues, and fountains playing. Mr. Johnson pointed out the court-house, the post-office, the jail, and other public buildings fronting on the square. They visited the market near by, and from an elevated point, looked down upon the extensive lumber yards and factories that were the chief sources of the city's prosperity. Beyond these they could see the fleet of ships that lined the coal and iron ore docks of the harbor. Mr. Johnson, who was quite a fluent talker, enlarged upon the wealth and prosperity of the city; and Wellington, who had never before been in a town of more than three thousand inhabitants, manifested sufficient interest and wonder to satisfy the most exacting *cicerone*. They called at the office of a colored lawyer and member of the legislature, formerly from North Carolina, who, scenting a new constituent and a possible client, greeted the stranger warmly, and in flowing speech pointed out the superior advantages of life at the North, citing himself as an illustration of the possibilities of life in a country really free. As they wended their way homeward to dinner uncle Wellington, with quickened pulse and rising hopes, felt that this was indeed the promised land, and that it must be flowing with milk and honey.

Uncle Wellington remained at the residence of Mr. Johnson for several weeks before making any effort to find employment. He spent this period in looking about the city. The most commonplace things possessed for him the charm of novelty, and he had come prepared to admire. Shortly after his arrival, he had offered to pay for his board, intimating at the same time that he had plenty of money. Mr. Johnson declined to accept anything from him for board, and expressed himself as being only too proud to have Mr. Braboy remain in the house on the footing of an honored guest, until he had settled himself. He lightened in some degree, however, the burden of obligation under which a prolonged stay on these terms would have placed his guest, by soliciting from the latter occasional small loans, until uncle Wellington's roll of money began to lose its plumpness, and with an empty pocket staring him in the face, he felt the necessity of finding something to do.

During his residence in the city he had met several times his first acquaintance, Mr. Peterson, the hackman, who from time to time inquired how he was getting along. On one of these occasions Wellington mentioned his willingness to accept employment. As good luck would have it, Mr. Peterson knew of a vacant situation. He had formerly been a coachman for a wealthy gentleman residing on Oakwood Avenue, but had resigned the situation to go into business for himself. His place had been filled by an Irishman, who had just been discharged for drunkenness, and the gentleman that very day had sent word to Mr. Peterson, asking him if he could recommend a competent and trustworthy coachman.

"Does you know anything erbout hosses?" asked Mr. Peterson.

"Yas, indeed, I does," said Wellington. "I wuz raise' 'mongs' hosses."

"I tol' my ole boss I'd look out fer a man, an' ef you reckon you kin fill de 'quirements er de situation, I'll take yo' roun' dere termorrer mornin.' You wants ter put on yo' bes' clothes an' slick up, fer dey're partic'lar people. Ef you git de place I'll expec' you ter pay me fer de time I lose in 'tendin' ter yo' business, fer time is money in dis country, an' folks don't do much fer nuthin'."

Next morning Wellington blacked his shoes carefully, put on a clean collar, and with the aid of Mrs. Johnson tied his cravat in a jaunty bow which gave him quite a sprightly air and a much younger look than his years warranted. Mr. Peterson called for him at eight o'clock. After traversing several cross streets they turned into Oakwood Avenue and walked along the finest part of it for about half a mile. The handsome houses of this famous avenue, the stately trees, the wide-spreading lawns, dotted with flower beds, fountains, and statuary, made up a picture so far surpassing anything in Wellington's experience as to fill him with an almost oppressive sense of its beauty.

"Hit looks lack hebben," he said softly.

"It's a pootty fine street," rejoined his companion, with a judicial air, "but I don't like dem big lawns. It's too much trouble ter keep de grass down. One er dem lawns is big enough to pasture a couple er cows."

They went down a street running at right angles to the avenue, and turned into the rear of the corner lot. A large building of pressed brick, trimmed with stone, loomed up before them.

"Do de gemman lib in dis house?" asked Wellington, gazing with awe at the front of the building.

"No, dat's de barn," said Mr. Peterson with good-natured contempt; and leading the way past a clump of shrubbery to the dwelling-house, he went up the back steps and rang the door-bell.

The ring was answered by a buxom Irish-woman, of a natural freshness of complexion deepened to a fiery red by the heat of a kitchen range.

Wellington thought he had seen her before, but his mind had received so many new impressions lately that it was a minute or two before he recognized in her the lady whose lap he had involuntarily occupied for a moment on his first day in Groveland.

"Faith," she exclaimed as she admitted them, "an' it's mighty glad I am to see ye ag'in, Misther Payterson! An' how hev ye be'n, Misther Payterson, sence I see ye lahst?"

"Middlin' well, Mis' Flannigan, middlin' well, 'ceptin' a tech er de rheumatiz. S'pose you be'n doin' well as usual?"

"Oh yis, as well as a dacent woman could do wid a drunken baste about the place like the lahst coachman. O Misther Payterson, it would make yer heart bleed to see the way the spalpeen cut up a-Saturday! But Misther Todd discharged 'im the same avenin', widout a charachter, bad 'cess to 'im, an' we've had no coachman sence at all, at all. An' it's sorry I am"—

The lady's flow of eloquence was interrupted at this point by the appearance of Mr. Todd himself, who had been informed of the men's arrival. He asked some questions in regard to Wellington's qualifications and former experience, and in view of his recent arrival in the city was willing to accept Mr. Peterson's recommendation instead of a reference. He said a few words about the nature of the work, and stated his willingness to pay Wellington the wages formerly allowed Mr. Peterson, thirty dollars a month and board and lodging.

This handsome offer was eagerly accepted, and it was agreed that Wellington's term of service should begin immediately. Mr. Peterson, being familiar with the work, and financially interested, conducted the new coachman through the stables and showed him what he would have to do. The silver-mounted harness, the variety of carriages, the names of which he learned for the first time, the arrangements for feeding and watering the horses,—these appointments of a rich man's stable impressed Wellington very much, and he wondered that so much luxury should be wasted on mere horses. The room assigned to him, in the second story of the barn, was a finer apartment than he had ever slept in; and the salary attached to the situation was greater than the combined monthly earnings of himself and aunt Milly in their Southern home. Surely, he thought, his lines had fallen in pleasant places.

Under the stimulus of new surroundings Wellington applied himself diligently to work, and, with the occasional advice of Mr. Peterson, soon mastered the details of his employment. He found the female servants, with whom he took his meals, very amiable ladies. The cook, Mrs. Katie Flannigan, was a widow. Her husband, a sailor, had been lost at sea. She was a woman of many words, and when she was not lamenting the late Flannigan's loss,—according to her story he had been a model of all the virtues,—she would turn the batteries of her tongue against the former coachman. This gentleman, as Wellington gathered from frequent remarks dropped by Mrs. Flannigan, had paid her attentions clearly susceptible of a serious construction. These attentions had not borne their legitimate fruit, and she was still a widow unconsoled,—hence Mrs. Flannigan's tears. The housemaid was a plump, good-natured German girl, with a pronounced German accent. The presence on washdays of a Bohemian laundress, of recent importation, added another to the variety of ways in which the English tongue was mutilated in Mr. Todd's kitchen. Association with the white women drew out all the native gallantry of the mulatto, and Wellington developed quite a helpful turn. His politeness, his willingness to lend a hand in kitchen or laundry, and the fact that he was the only male servant on the place, combined to make him a prime favorite in the servants' quarters.

It was the general opinion among Wellington's acquaintances that he was a single man. He had come to the city alone, had never been heard to speak of a wife, and to personal questions bearing upon the subject of matrimony had always returned evasive answers. Though he had never questioned the correctness of the lawyer's opinion in regard to his slave marriage, his conscience had never been entirely at ease since his departure from the South, and any positive denial of his married condition would have stuck in his throat. The inference naturally drawn from his reticence in regard to the past, coupled with his expressed intention of settling permanently in Groveland, was that he belonged in the ranks of the unmarried, and was therefore legitimate game for any widow or old maid who could bring him down. As such game is bagged easiest at short range, he received numerous invitations to tea-parties, where he feasted on unlimited chicken and pound cake. He used to compare these viands with the plain fare often served by aunt Milly, and the result of the comparison was another item to the credit of the North upon his mental ledger. Several of the colored ladies who smiled upon him were blessed with good looks, and uncle Wellington, naturally of a susceptible temperament, as people of lively imagination are apt to be, would probably have fallen a victim to the charms of some woman of his own race, had it not been for a strong counter-attraction in the person of Mrs. Flannigan. The attentions of the lately discharged coachman had lighted anew the smouldering fires of her widowed heart, and awakened longings which still remained unsatisfied. She was thirty-five years old, and felt the need of some one else to love. She was not a woman of lofty ideals; with her a man was a man—

"For a' that an' a' that;"

and, aside from the accident of color, uncle Wellington was as personable a man as any of her acquaintance. Some people might have objected to his complexion; but then, Mrs. Flannigan argued, he was at least half white; and, this being the case, there was no good reason why he should be regarded as black.

Uncle Wellington was not slow to perceive Mrs. Flannigan's charms of person, and appreciated to the full the skill that prepared the choice tidbits reserved for his plate at dinner. The prospect of securing a white wife had been one of the principal inducements offered by a life at the North; but the awe of white people in which he had been reared was still too strong to permit his taking any active steps toward the object of his secret desire, had not the lady herself come to his assistance with a little of the native coquetry of her race.

"Ah, Misther Braboy," she said one evening when they sat at the supper table alone,—it was the second girl's afternoon off, and she had not come home to supper,—"it must be an awful lonesome life ye've been afther l'adin', as a single man, wid no one to cook fer ye, or look afther ye."

"It are a kind er lonesome life, Mis' Flannigan, an' dat's a fac'. But sence I had de privilege er eatin' yo' cookin' an' 'joyin' yo' society, I ain' felt a bit lonesome."

"Yer flatthrin' me, Misther Braboy. An' even if ye mane it"—

"I means eve'y word of it, Mis' Flanningan."

"An' even if ye mane it, Misther Braboy, the time is liable to come when things 'll be different; for service is uncertain, Misther Braboy. An' then you'll wish you had some nice, clean woman, 'at knowed how to cook an' wash an' iron, ter look afther ye, an' make yer life comfortable."

Uncle Wellington sighed, and looked at her languishingly.

"It 'u'd all be well ernuff, Mis' Flannigan, ef I had n' met you; but I don' know whar I's ter fin' a colored lady w'at 'll begin ter suit me after habbin' libbed in de same house wid you."

"Colored lady, indade! Why, Misther Braboy, ye don't nade ter demane yerself by marryin' a colored lady—not but they're as good as anybody else, so long as they behave themselves. There's many a white woman 'u'd be glad ter git as fine a lookin' man as ye are."

"Now *you're* flattrin' *me*, Mis' Flannigan," said Wellington. But he felt a sudden and substantial increase in courage when she had spoken, and it was with astonishing ease that he found himself saying:—

"Dey ain' but one lady, Mis' Flannigan, dat could injuce me ter want ter change de lonesomeness er my singleness fer de 'sponsibilities er matermony, an' I'm feared she'd say no ef I'd ax her."

"Ye'd better ax her, Misther Braboy, an' not be wastin' time a-wond'rin.' Do I know the lady?"

"You knows 'er better 'n anybody else, Mis' Flannigan. *You* is de only lady I'd be satisfied ter marry after knowin' you. Ef you casts me off I'll spen' de rest er my days in lonesomeness an' mis'ry."

Mrs. Flannigan affected much surprise and embarrassment at this bold declaration.

"Oh, Misther Braboy," she said, covering him with a coy glance, "an' it's rale 'shamed I am to hev b'en talkin' ter ye ez I hev. It looks as though I 'd b'en doin' the coortin'. I did n't drame that I 'd b'en able ter draw yer affections to mesilf."

"I 's loved you ever sence I fell in yo' lap on de street car de fus' day I wuz in Groveland," he said, as he moved his chair up closer to hers.

One evening in the following week they went out after supper to the residence of Rev. Caesar Williams, pastor of the colored Baptist church, and, after the usual preliminaries, were pronounced man and wife.

III

According to all his preconceived notions, this marriage ought to have been the acme of uncle Wellington's felicity. But he soon found that it was not without its drawbacks. On the following morning Mr. Todd was informed of the marriage. He had no special objection to it, or interest in it, except that he was opposed on principle to having husband and wife in his employment at the same time. As a consequence, Mrs. Braboy, whose place could be more easily filled than that of her husband, received notice that her services would not be required after the end of the month. Her husband was retained in his place as coachman.

Upon the loss of her situation, Mrs. Braboy decided to exercise the married woman's prerogative of letting her husband support her. She rented the upper floor of a small house in an Irish neighborhood. The newly wedded pair furnished their rooms on the installment plan and began housekeeping.

There was one little circumstance, however, that interfered slightly with their employment of that perfect freedom from care which ought to characterize a honeymoon. The people who owned the house and occupied the lower floor had rented the upper part to Mrs. Braboy in person, it never occurring to them that her husband could be other than a white man. When it became known that he was colored, the landlord, Mr. Dennis O'Flaherty, felt that he had been imposed upon, and, at the end of the first month, served notice upon his tenants to leave the premises. When Mrs. Braboy, with characteristic impetuosity, inquired the meaning of this proceeding, she was informed by Mr. O'Flaherty that he did not care to live in the same house "wid naygurs." Mrs. Braboy resented the epithet with more warmth than dignity, and for a brief space of time the air was green with choice specimens of brogue, the altercation barely ceasing before it had reached the point of blows.

It was quite clear that the Braboys could not longer live comfortably in Mr. O'Flaherty's house, and they soon vacated the premises, first letting the rent get a couple of weeks in arrears as a punishment to the too fastidious landlord. They moved to a small house on Hackman Street, a favorite locality with colored people.

For a while, affairs ran smoothly in the new home. The colored people seemed, at first, well enough disposed toward Mrs. Braboy, and she made quite a large acquaintance among them. It was difficult, however, for Mrs. Braboy to divest herself of the consciousness that she was white, and therefore superior to her neighbors. Occasional words and acts by which she manifested this feeling were noticed and resented by her keen-eyed and sensitive colored neighbors. The result was a slight coolness between them. That her few white neighbors did not visit her, she naturally and no doubt correctly imputed to disapproval of her matrimonial relations.

Under these circumstances, Mrs. Braboy was left a good deal to her own company. Owing to lack of opportunity in early life, she was not a woman of many resources, either mental or moral. It is therefore not strange that, in order to relieve her loneliness, she should occasionally have recourse to a glass of beer, and, as the habit grew upon her, to still stronger stimulants. Uncle Wellington himself was no teetotaler, and did not interpose any objection so long as she kept her potations within reasonable limits, and was apparently none the worse for them; indeed, he sometimes joined her in a glass. On one of these occasions he drank a little too much, and, while driving the ladies of Mr. Todd's family to the opera, ran against a lamp-post and overturned the carriage, to the serious discomposure of the ladies' nerves, and at the cost of his situation.

A coachman discharged under such circumstances is not in the best position for procuring employment at his calling, and uncle Wellington, under the pressure of need, was obliged to see some other means of livelihood. At the suggestion of his friend Mr. Johnson, he bought a whitewash brush, a peck of lime, a couple of pails, and a handcart, and began work as a whitewasher. His first efforts were very crude, and for a while he lost a customer in every person he worked for. He nevertheless managed to pick up a living during the spring and summer months, and to support his wife and himself in comparative comfort.

The approach of winter put an end to the whitewashing season, and left uncle Wellington dependent for support upon occasional jobs of unskilled labor. The income derived from these was very uncertain, and Mrs. Braboy was at length driven, by stress of circumstances, to the washtub, that last refuge of honest, able-bodied poverty, in all countries where the use of clothing is conventional.

The last state of uncle Wellington was now worse than the first. Under the soft firmness of aunt Milly's rule, he had not been required to do a great deal of work, prompt and cheerful obedience being chiefly what was expected of him. But matters were very different here. He had not only to bring in the coal and water, but to rub the clothes and turn the wringer, and to humiliate himself before the public by emptying the tubs and hanging out the wash in full view of the neighbors; and he had to deliver the clothes when laundered.

At times Wellington found himself wondering if his second marriage had been a wise one. Other circumstances combined to change in some degree his once rose-colored conception of life at the North. He had believed that all men were equal in this favored locality, but he discovered more degrees of inequality than he had ever perceived at the South. A colored man might be as good as a white man in theory, but neither of them was of any special consequence without money, or talent, or position. Uncle Wellington found a great many privileges open to him at the North, but he had not been educated to the point where he could appreciate them or take advantage of them; and the enjoyment of many of them was expensive, and, for that reason alone, as far beyond his reach as they had ever been. When he once began to admit even the possibility of a mistake on his part, these considerations presented themselves to his mind with increasing force. On occasions when Mrs. Braboy would require of him some unusual physical exertion, or when too frequent applications to the bottle had loosened her tongue, uncle Wellington's mind would revert, with a remorseful twinge of conscience, to the *dolce far niente* of his Southern home; a film would come over his eyes and brain, and, instead of the red-faced Irishwoman opposite him, he could see the black but comely disk of aunt Milly's countenance bending over the washtub; the elegant brogue of Mrs. Braboy would deliquesce into the soft dialect of North Carolina; and he would only be aroused from this blissful reverie by a wet shirt or a handful of suds thrown into his face, with which gentle reminder his wife would recall his attention to the duties of the moment.

There came a time, one day in spring, when there was not longer any question about it: uncle Wellington was desperately homesick.

Liberty, equality, privileges,—all were but as dust in the balance when weighed against his longing for old scenes and faces. It was the natural reaction in the mind of a middle-aged man who had tried to force the current of a sluggish existence into a new and radically different channel. An active, industrious man, making the change in early life, while there was time to spare for the waste of adaptation, might have found in the new place more favorable conditions than in the old. In Wellington age and temperament combined to prevent the success of the experiment; the spirit of enterprise and ambition into which he had been temporarily galvanized could no longer prevail against the inertia of old habits of life and thought.

One day when he had been sent to deliver clothes he performed his errand quickly, and boarding a passing street car, paid one of his very few five-cent pieces to ride down to the office of the Hon. Mr. Brown, the colored lawyer whom he had visited when he first came to the city, and who was well known to him by sight and reputation.

"Mr. Brown," he said, "I ain' gitt'n' 'long very well wid my ole 'oman."

"What's the trouble?" asked the lawyer, with business-like curtness, for he did not scent much of a fee.

"Well, de main trouble is she doan treat me right. An' den she gits drunk, an' wuss'n dat, she lays vi'lent han's on me. I kyars de marks er dat 'oman on my face now."

He showed the lawyer a long scratch on the neck.

"Why don't you defend yourself?"

"You don' know Mis' Braboy, suh; you don' know dat 'oman," he replied, with a shake of the head. "Some er dese yer w'ite women is monst'us strong in de wris'."

"Well, Mr. Braboy, it's what you might have expected when you turned your back on your own people and married a white woman. You weren't content with being a slave to the white folks once, but you must try it again. Some people never know when they've got enough. I don't see that there's any help for you; unless," he added suggestively, "you had a good deal of money."

"'Pears ter me I heard somebody say sence I be'n up heah, dat it wuz 'gin de law fer w'ite folks an' colored folks ter marry."

"That was once the law, though it has always been a dead letter in Groveland. In fact, it was the law when you got married, and until I introduced a bill in the legislature last fall to repeal it. But even that law didn't hit cases like yours. It was unlawful to make such a marriage, but it was a good marriage when once made."

"I don' jes' git dat th'oo my head," said Wellington, scratching that member as though to make a hole for the idea to enter.

"It's quite plain, Mr. Braboy. It's unlawful to kill a man, but when he's killed he's just as dead as though the law permitted it. I'm afraid you haven't much of a case, but if you'll go to work and get twenty-five dollars together, I'll see what I can do for you. We may be able to pull a case through on the ground of extreme cruelty. I might even start the case if you brought in ten dollars."

Wellington went away sorrowfully. The laws of Ohio were very little more satisfactory than those of North Carolina. And as for the ten dollars,—the lawyer might as well have told him to bring in the moon, or a deed for the Public Square. He felt very, very low as he hurried back home to supper, which he would have to go without if he were not on hand at the usual supper-time.

But just when his spirits were lowest, and his outlook for the future most helpless, a measure of relief was at hand. He noticed, when he reached home, that Mrs. Braboy was a little preoccupied, and did not abuse him as vigorously as he expected after so long an absence. He also perceived the smell of strange tobacco in the house, of a better grade than he could afford to use. He thought perhaps some one had come in to see about the washing; but he was too glad of a respite from Mrs. Braboy's rhetoric to imperil it by indiscreet questions.

Next morning she gave him fifty cents.

"Braboy," she said, "ye've be'n helpin' me nicely wid the washin', an' I'm going ter give ye a holiday. Ye can take yer hook an' line an' go fishin' on the breakwater. I'll fix ye a lunch, an' ye needn't come back till night. An' there's half a dollar; ye can buy yerself a pipe er terbacky. But be careful an' don't waste it," she added, for fear she was overdoing the thing.

Uncle Wellington was overjoyed at this change of front on the part of Mrs. Braboy; if she would make it permanent he did not see why they might not live together very comfortably.

The day passed pleasantly down on the breakwater. The weather was agreeable, and the fish bit freely. Towards evening Wellington started home with a bunch of fish that no angler need have been ashamed of. He looked forward to a good warm supper; for even if something should have happened during the day to alter his wife's mood for the worse, any ordinary variation would be more than balanced by the substantial addition of food to their larder. His mouth watered at the thought of the finny beauties sputtering in the frying-pan.

He noted, as he approached the house, that there was no smoke coming from the chimney. This only disturbed him in connection with the matter of supper. When he entered the gate he observed further that the window-shades had been taken down.

"'Spec' de ole 'oman's been house-cleanin'," he said to himself. "I wonder she did n' make me stay an' he'p 'er."

He went round to the rear of the house and tried the kitchen door. It was locked. This was somewhat of a surprise, and disturbed still further his expectations in regard to supper. When he had found the key and opened the door, the gravity of his next discovery drove away for the time being all thoughts of eating.

The kitchen was empty. Stove, table, chairs, wash-tubs, pots and pans, had vanished as if into thin air.

"Fo' de Lawd's sake!" he murmured in open-mouthed astonishment.

He passed into the other room,—they had only two,—which had served as bedroom and sitting-room. It was as bare as the first, except that in the middle of the floor were piled uncle Wellington's clothes. It was not a large pile, and on top of it lay a folded piece of yellow wrapping-paper.

Wellington stood for a moment as if petrified. Then he rubbed his eyes and looked around him.

"W'at do dis mean?" he said. "Is I er-dreamin', er does I see w'at I 'pears ter see?" He glanced down at the bunch of fish which he still held.

"Heah's de fish; heah's de house; heah I is; but whar's de ole 'oman, an' whar's de fu'niture? *I* can't figure out w'at dis yer all means."

He picked up the piece of paper and unfolded it. It was written on one side. Here was the obvious solution of the mystery,—that is, it would have been obvious if he could have read it; but he could not, and so his fancy continued to play upon the subject. Perhaps the house had been robbed, or the furniture taken back by the seller, for it had not been entirely paid for.

Finally he went across the street and called to a boy in a neighbor's yard.

"Does you read writin', Johnnie?"

"Yes, sir, I'm in the seventh grade."

"Read dis yer paper fuh me."

The youngster took the note, and with much labor read the following:—

"MR. BRABOY:

"In lavin' ye so suddint I have ter say that my first husban' has turned up unexpected, having been saved onbeknownst ter me from a wathry grave an' all the money wasted I spint fer masses fer ter rist his sole an' I wish I had it back I feel it my dooty ter go an' live wid 'im again. I take the furnacher because I bought it yer close is yors I leave them and wishin' yer the best of luck I remane oncet yer wife but now agin

"MRS. KATIE FLANNIGAN.

"N. B. I'm lavin town terday so it won't be no use lookin' fer me."

On inquiry uncle Wellington learned from the boy that shortly after his departure in the morning a white man had appeared on the scene, followed a little later by a moving-van, into which the furniture had been loaded and carried away. Mrs. Braboy, clad in her best clothes, had locked the door, and gone away with the strange white man.

The news was soon noised about the street. Wellington swapped his fish for supper and a bed at a neighbor's, and during the evening learned from several sources that the strange white man had been at his house the afternoon of the day before. His neighbors intimated that they thought Mrs. Braboy's departure a good riddance of bad rubbish, and Wellington did not dispute the proposition.

Thus ended the second chapter of Wellington's matrimonial experiences. His wife's departure had been the one thing needful to convince him, beyond a doubt, that he had been a great fool. Remorse and homesickness forced him to the further conclusion that he had been knave as well as fool, and had treated aunt Milly shamefully. He was not altogether a bad old man, though very weak and erring, and his better nature now gained the ascendancy. Of course his disappointment had a great deal to do with his remorse; most people do not perceive the hideousness of sin until they begin to reap its consequences. Instead of the beautiful Northern life he had dreamed of, he found himself stranded, penniless, in a strange land, among people whose sympathy he had forfeited, with no one to lean upon, and no refuge from the storms of life. His outlook was very dark, and there sprang up within him a wild longing to get back to North Carolina,—back to the little whitewashed cabin, shaded with china and mulberry trees; back to the woodpile and the garden; back to the old cronies with whom he had swapped lies and tobacco for so many years. He longed to kiss the rod of aunt Milly's domination. He had purchased his liberty at too great a price.

The next day he disappeared from Groveland. He had announced his departure only to Mr. Johnson, who sent his love to his relations in Patesville.

It would be painful to record in detail the return journey of uncle Wellington—Mr. Braboy no longer—to his native town; how many weary miles he walked; how many times he risked his life on railroad trucks and between freight cars; how he depended for sustenance on the grudging hand of backdoor charity. Nor would it be profitable or delicate to mention any slight deviations from the path of rectitude, as judged by conventional standards, to which he may occasionally have been driven by a too insistent hunger; or to refer in the remotest degree to a compulsory sojourn of thirty days in a city where he had no references, and could show no visible means of support. True charity will let these purely personal matters remain locked in the bosom of him who suffered them.

IV

Just fifteen months after the date when uncle Wellington had left North Carolina, a weather-beaten figure entered the town of Patesville after nightfall, following the railroad track from the north. Few would have recognized in the hungry-looking old brown tramp, clad in dusty rags and limping along with bare feet, the trim-looking middle-aged mulatto who so few months before had taken the train from Patesville for the distant North; so, if he had but known it, there was no necessity for him to avoid the main streets and sneak around by unfrequented paths to reach the old place on the other side of the town. He encountered nobody that he knew, and soon the familiar shape of the little cabin rose before him. It stood distinctly outlined against the sky, and the light streaming from the half-opened shutters showed it to be occupied. As he drew nearer, every familiar detail of the place appealed to his memory and to his affections, and his heart went out to the old home and the old wife. As he came nearer still, the odor of fried chicken floated out upon the air and set his mouth to watering, and awakened unspeakable longings in his half-starved stomach.

At this moment, however, a fearful thought struck him; suppose the old woman had taken legal advice and married again during his absence? Turn about would have been only fair play. He opened the gate softly, and with his heart in his mouth approached the window on tiptoe and looked in.

A cheerful fire was blazing on the hearth, in front of which sat the familiar form of aunt Milly—and another, at the sight of whom uncle Wellington's heart sank within him. He knew the other person very well; he had sat there more than once before uncle Wellington went away. It was the minister of the church to which his wife belonged. The preacher's former visits, however, had signified nothing more than pastoral courtesy, or appreciation of good eating. His presence now was of serious portent; for Wellington recalled, with acute alarm, that the elder's wife had died only a few weeks before his own departure for the North. What was the occasion of his presence this evening? Was it merely a pastoral call? or was he courting? or had aunt Milly taken legal advice and married the elder?

Wellington remembered a crack in the wall, at the back of the house, through which he could see and hear, and quietly stationed himself there.

"Dat chicken smells mighty good, Sis' Milly," the elder was saying; "I can't fer de life er me see why dat low-down husban' er yo'n could ever run away f'm a cook like you. It's one er de beatenis' things I ever heared. How he could lib wid you an' not 'preciate you *I* can't understan', no indeed I can't."

Aunt Milly sighed. "De trouble wid Wellin'ton wuz," she replied, "dat he did n' know when he wuz well off. He wuz alluz wishin' fer change, er studyin' 'bout somthin' new."

"Ez fer me," responded the elder earnestly, "I likes things what has be'n prove' an' tried an' has stood de tes', an' I can't 'magine how anybody could spec' ter fin' a better housekeeper er cook dan you is, Sis' Milly. I'm a gittin' mighty lonesome sence my wife died. De Good Book say it is not good fer man ter lib alone, en it 'pears ter me dat you an' me mought git erlong tergether monst'us well."

Wellington's heart stood still, while he listened with strained attention. Aunt Milly sighed.

"I ain't denyin', elder, but what I've be'n kinder lonesome myse'f fer quite a w'ile, an' I doan doubt dat w'at de Good Book say 'plies ter women as well as ter men."

"You kin be sho' it do," averred the elder, with professional authoritativeness; "yas'm, you kin be cert'n sho'."

"But, of co'se," aunt Milly went on, "havin' los' my ole man de way I did, it has tuk some time fer ter git my feelin's straighten' out like dey oughter be."

"I kin 'magine yo' feelin's Sis' Milly," chimed in the elder sympathetically, "w'en you come home dat night an' foun' yo' chist broke open, an' yo' money gone dat you had wukked an' slaved fuh f'm mawnin' 'tel night, year in an' year out, an' w'en you foun' dat no-'count nigger gone wid his clo's an' you lef' all alone in de worl' ter scuffle 'long by yo'self."

"Yas, elder," responded aunt Milly, "I wa'n't used right. An' den w'en I heared 'bout his goin' ter de lawyer ter fin' out 'bout a defoce, an' w'en I heared w'at de lawyer said 'bout my not bein' his wife 'less he wanted me, it made me so mad, I made up my min' dat ef he ever put his foot on my do'-sill ag'in, I'd shet de do' in his face an' tell 'im ter go back whar he come f'm."

To Wellington, on the outside, the cabin had never seemed so comfortable, aunt Milly never so desirable, chicken never so appetizing, as at this moment when they seemed slipping away from his grasp forever.

"Yo' feelin's does you credit, Sis' Milly," said the elder, taking her hand, which for a moment she did not withdraw. "An' de way fer you ter close yo' do' tightes' ag'inst 'im is ter take me in his place. He ain' got no claim on you no mo'. He tuk his ch'ice 'cordin' ter w'at de lawyer tol' 'im, an' 'termine' dat he wa'n't yo' husban'. Ef he wa'n't yo' husban', he had no right ter take yo' money, an' ef he comes back here ag'in you kin hab 'im tuck up an' sent ter de penitenchy fer stealin' it."

Uncle Wellington's knees, already weak from fasting, trembled violently beneath him. The worst that he had feared was now likely to happen. His only hope of safety lay in flight, and yet the scene within so fascinated him that he could not move a step.

"It 'u'd serve him right," exclaimed aunt Milly indignantly, "ef he wuz sent ter de penitenchy fer life! Dey ain't nuthin' too mean ter be done ter 'im. What did I ever do dat he should use me like he did?"

The recital of her wrongs had wrought upon aunt Milly's feelings so that her voice broke, and she wiped her eyes with her apron.

The elder looked serenely confident, and moved his chair nearer hers in order the better to play the role of comforter. Wellington, on the outside, felt so mean that the darkness of the night was scarcely sufficient to hide him; it would be no more than right if the earth were to open and swallow him up.

"An' yet aftuh all, elder," said Milly with a sob, "though I knows you is a better man, an' would treat me right, I wuz so use' ter dat ole nigger, an' libbed wid 'im so long, dat ef he'd open dat do' dis minute an' walk in, I'm feared I'd be foolish ernuff to forgive 'im an' take 'im back ag'in."

With a bound, uncle Wellington was away from the crack in the wall. As he ran round the house he passed the wood-pile and snatched up an armful of pieces. A moment later he threw open the door.

"Ole 'oman," he exclaimed, "here's dat wood you tol' me ter fetch in! Why, elder," he said to the preacher, who had started from his seat with surprise, "w'at's yo' hurry? Won't you stay an' hab some supper wid us?"

The Kiss

Unpublished in Chesnutt's lifetime

Like "A Grass Widow," "The Kiss" might initially confound readers expecting Chesnutt's typically discreet sensibility (at least about all matters other than race). Perhaps the most melodramatic work in this collection, the story recounts the travails of a couple whose relationship has undergone extreme testing. Set presumably in "Groveland" (Cleveland), the story unfolds primarily in a "handsome residence on Euclid Avenue" (154). Unlike virtually all of the Northern writings, however, "The Kiss" focuses on an adulterous affair, the same fundamental premise that informs "A Grass Widow." But while that story—which reached print in 1887—recounts the events that finally lead a "wicked" woman to her lurid death, "The Kiss" describes similar acts of infidelity to introduce the story of a woman who seeks, and ultimately finds, her own redemption.

Unpublished in Chesnutt's life,[1] but written sometime after 1901,[2] "The Kiss" explores a few years in the seemingly proper lives of an upper-class "Groveland" couple, the Cartwrights. Eustace Cartwright marries the vivacious and much younger Hilda, and initially their marriage is a happy one. But when Eustace's nephew, Carroll Deane, arrives to live with the family for several months before attending college, the resulting sexually charged passion seems conspicuously out of place in a Chesnutt story. Indeed, though he had similarly focused on an act of infidelity in "A Grass Widow," Chesnutt seems to have warmed to the task by the time—at least fourteen years later—he wrote "The Kiss." The narrator in the former story can bring himself only to describe the affair as an event in which "a wife's love, a successful business career, even honor itself, had been thrown to the winds for a pretty face" (59), in contrast to the far more explicit description in "The Kiss":

> Carroll was a convenient escort for Hilda when Cartwright did not care to go to a ball or party, a function which Carroll seemed more willing to perform than most young men to wait upon their female relatives. The beauty of the two young people—their vivacity, their youthful zest for pleasure, their freedom of intercourse, brought about the old result. There was a fierce insurrection of primal passions, a few months of guilty pleasure, and then Carroll had gone away to college. (154–55)

Such a description seems positively un-Chesnutt-like. Indeed, even the language of the passage, focusing on "primal passions" and "guilty pleasure," makes one wonder what had gotten into this usually straitlaced, even prudish writer.

After the affair between Hilda and Carroll runs its (surprisingly) passionate course, the young man dies in a train accident—so Victorian is his ex-lover that she concludes "[h]e had, in a sense, deserved his fate" (158)—but leaves behind incriminating letters. Upon learning of his wife's affair, Eustace Cartwright constructs a new marital model for himself and Hilda, one built on maintaining appearances:

> "As I have said, you can no longer be my wife. But neither would I have you leave me. There are the children—I must consider them, if you did not; they must never, by any act of mine, have occasion to hold their mother in disrespect." . . .
>
> "You shall be free . . . to come and go. I shall not interfere with your movements—except that I shall exercise a certain supervision over your company, for both our sakes. Upon formal occasions, when it is conventionally required, I will attend you—perhaps I have neglected my duty in that regard, and am myself to blame, in part, for what has happened." (159–60).

Despite his stern, old-fashioned handling of the messiness, however, Eustace cannot easily maintain the pretense, and he falls seriously ill. The rest of the plot focuses on Hilda's response to his illness, culminating in a death-bed scene in which the wife must decide whether or not to kiss her diptheria-infected husband. Its melodramatic plot notwithstanding, "The Kiss" nevertheless merits attention because of how different it is from the other Northern writings in this collection, despite its setting in "Groveland."

The story, when read in tandem with "A Grass Widow," also reveals a striking dichotomy in Chesnutt's sensibility. He had, after all, lived through (and around) a broad range of cultural phenomena—slavery, the Civil War,

Reconstruction, World War I, the Harlem Renaissance, to name only a few—as well as having witnessed seismic shifts in science and technology. For, as Dean McWilliams notes, "Born and shaped in the nineteenth century, Chesnutt spent the majority of his creative life in the twentieth" (ix). While "A Grass Widow" indicates the extent to which the nineteenth century did "shape" Chesnutt, "The Kiss" has telling signs of twentieth-century thought and vocabulary. Consider, for example, two words in "The Kiss" which may not appear in any of Chesnutt's other short stories: automobile and membrane. Both terms suggest the extent to which the author was himself "passing" into the twentieth century, and this story reflects, I think, his coming to terms with his own old-fashionedness. In the twentieth century, technology and science—represented precisely if unromantically by automobiles and membranes in "The Kiss"—have profoundly more relevance than the horse and buggy of the scene Chesnutt describes at the crisis moment of "A Grass Widow." Thus, the two stories consider the issue of marital faithlessness from two very different perspectives. In "A Grass Widow," the issue is explored (and ultimately buried, along with the offending wife) by a narrator one might describe as a world-weary Victorian moralist. "The Kiss," on the other hand, reflects the views of a more forgiving (and surprisingly romantic) twentieth-century narrator, one who believes in second chances.

Ultimately, both "A Grass Widow" and "The Kiss" explore subjects Chesnutt did not seem particularly comfortable discussing in polite company. Both works also suggest the extent to which the North was undergoing deep and unsettling changes, and he was there to record them. But he did more than merely record. For, in addition to recounting the cultural and social transformations going on around him, he came to terms with those changes, and indeed tried to account for them. As painful in many ways as it must have been for an "earnest Victorian,"[3] Chesnutt knew when it was time to write of automobiles and membranes.

NOTES

1. Like two other fictions collected here—"The Shadow of My Past" and "White Weeds"—"The Kiss" first reached print, thirty-two years after Chesnutt's death in 1932, in Sylvia Lyons Render's *The Short Fiction of Charles W. Chesnutt* (1974).

2. In her bibliography to *Short Fiction*, Sylvia Lyons Render asserts that "The Kiss" was written sometime after September 1901.

3. Joseph R. McElrath Jr., introduction to *Critical Essays on Charles W. Chesnutt*, 1.

The Kiss

MRS. CARTWRIGHT LEFT THE streetcar at the nearest corner, and walked the half of a city block that led to her own gateway, and up the flower-bordered flagged walk across the green lawn to the verandah where her two children, Talbot and Cecile, were playing, under the supervision of a white-capped nurse. They were beautiful children, fashionably dressed. It was a beautiful home, upon a beautiful street, and Mrs. Cartwright was a beautiful woman.

Beautiful, and young. She had been less than twenty when Eustace Cartwright had first met her. Her family had been poor, and in financial difficulties. Cartwright had rescued them from ruin, and, fascinated by Hilda's beauty and her wit, had taken her from an eight-room house in a shabby suburb, had bestowed his old and honored name upon her, and, after a summer in Switzerland, had brought her home to the handsome residence on Euclid Avenue which his grandfather had built forty years before. It was not in the latest style, but was possessed of a spaciousness, a dignity and a comfort which suited Cartwright's quiet, scholarly tastes.

They had been very happy for several years. Hilda's two children had occupied her mind and her time. She appreciated to the full her good fortune; never more than when, while driving in her carriage or her automobile, she passed her former friends on foot, or, when, while shopping, she saw them standing behind the counter. She wore the airs and graces of a fine lady in a manner to satisfy even her husband's friends, who had been not entirely certain that Cartwright had not stooped to marry her.

The serpent had entered Eden when Cartwright's nephew, Carroll Deane, the son of his only sister, became a member of the household, after the death of his mother, already a widow. Cartwright was fond of the handsome, blue-eyed youth, whose liveliness was in marked contrast to his own taciturn sedateness. He showered the boy with benefits, and found a keen pleasure in seeing him enjoy the things for which the older man had never greatly cared. Carroll was a convenient escort for Hilda when Cartwright did not care to go to a ball or party, a function which Carroll seemed more willing to perform than most young men to wait upon their female relatives. The beauty of the two young people—their vivacity, their youthful zest for pleasure, their freedom of intercourse, brought about the old result. There was a fierce insurrection of primal passions, a few months of guilty pleasure, and then Carroll had gone away to college.

Carroll and Hilda corresponded during his absence. He came home for the Christmas holidays. He went away again, and the correspondence continued. He returned for the Easter vacation, and had left that morning, a day late, for the East. She had accompanied him to the station, on a streetcar, and they had parted with a handclasp and a few whispered words—their real parting had taken place, an hour before, at the house. She was conscious, when the train pulled out, of a loss, and yet of a relief. The mantle of deceit did not rest lightly upon her shoulder—she had not sinned without suffering.

She was glad, as she went up the walk that day, that Carroll was gone. She had quite decided to break off their affair. It was too wicked, too treacherous, too dangerous. Eustace had been easy to deceive, but once enlightened, was not the man to endure lightly such an offense at the hands of the objects of his own bounty. Carroll had agreed with her. He was going to Europe in June, to be gone all summer. They would write, now and then, friendly letters—that was all.

As an earnest of her reformation, which was to begin as soon as he had gone, she had given him his letters and demanded hers.

"I destroyed them," he said, "last night."

She was obliged to take his word, though she had not always found him truthful—light love is apt to take liberties with truth. A lingering doubt had assailed her at the railroad station.

"You are sure, dear," she said, "that you burnt my letters?"

"Quite sure," he returned. "I hated to, but we had agreed that it was best."

It was sweet to have him hate to; but it was best, and she felt relieved, and tried to be glad—that he had burnt her letters, and that he was gone, and that she would not see him again for many months, by which time it would be easy for them to meet as friends and relatives, and with no other thought.

This feeling had grown in strength during her return homeward on the streetcar. The sight of her beautiful home, the outward and visible sign of physical comfort and assured position; the merry greeting of her rosy-cheeked children—the pledges of her wifehood—strengthened her renewed sense of virtue and conjugal fidelity.

She had laid off the last of her wraps, together with the last lingering consciousness of her sins, and had entered upon her role of ideal wife, when the telephone bell rang. She was near the instrument and took down the receiver.

"Hello, is this East 897-B?"

"Yes, is that you, Eustace?"

"Yes, Hilda. I have had bad news, Carroll's train met with an accident, about twenty miles out. Many were killed or injured."

Her heart stopped beating.

"And Carroll?" she breathed.

"Is among the killed."

She dropped the receiver and sat for a moment like one dazed. Then the instinct of self-preservation returned, and she picked up the receiver and placed it to her ear.

"Hello, hello, hello!" came her husband's voice. "Are you there, Hilda?"

"Yes—yes!"

"I thought they'd cut us off. I wanted to say that a relief train is leaving the Union Station in ten minutes, and I am going out on it. If he is dead, I will bring his body home. It is terrible—poor boy, just on the threshold of life—facing its struggles and its joys—my sister's only child, whom I loved as my own son."

Hilda had been thinking with lightning-like rapidity (an electric wave, it is said, would flash around the earth an incredible number of times a second, could it last so long). Carroll was dead, and he had not destroyed her letters—she knew instinctively that he had not destroyed them—and they were either on his person or in his luggage. Eustace would go to the scene of the wreck, and he would find them, and she would be disgraced and ruined. A wild thought seized her.

"Can I go with you?" she demanded anxiously.

She would go with him, and perhaps she could get the letters, so that Eustace would never see them.

"I don't think it necessary, dear. The scene would only harrow your feelings."

"I might be of some use," she insisted.

"You can be of more use in preparing for our reception. And you haven't time. I've barely five minutes to make the station, and it would take you twenty, if you had an automobile at the door."

She hung up the receiver, despair in her heart. Never before had her sin appeared so hideous. She felt a foreboding, not dim and distant, but vivid and imminent, that her punishment was at hand—that she would lose everything that made her life worth living. She would lose husband, children, home—her position, her good name—all the things for which women strive, and which not even few of whom attain in such full measure as they had come to her. She could not even retain the solace of guilty love—for her lover was dead—dead in his youth and his beauty and his sins, with the proofs of his treachery upon his person. She would have nothing left, except her beauty, and the flower of that was gone; nor was it a commodity that could go twice to such a market. She wished that she were dead.

But she took no steps to carry out the wish. Perhaps, after all, Carroll had destroyed the letters. They might have been lost in the wreck. Perhaps Eustace would not search Carroll's luggage. She would hope against hope—even against the cold fear which clutched her heart and told her there was no escape.

Cartwright returned home in the afternoon, bringing the body of his nephew. Hilda awaited her fate in agonized suspense. But there was nothing unusual in Cartwright's manner, unless it were an added gravity, for which the occasion was sufficient to account. Hilda had very little opportunity for conversation with him during the day—he was fully occupied with preparations for the funeral and with communications from and to friends of Carroll.

Carroll's trunk and valise had been brought to the house, and Hilda, during her husband's absence, examined their contents thoroughly. She found many souvenirs of their love—a lock of hair, a ring, half a dozen photographs, a ribbon, a glove, a stolen slipper—each with its tender associations. Had she been less anxious, she would have wept her eyes out, but even the tragedy of death faded in importance beside the tragedy of the life which would face her should Eustace find her letters.

She felt a measure of relief when she did not find them. Would she have felt more relieved at finding them? She did not know—there was always the possibility that Eustace might have found them first and read them. On the whole, she thought she would rather have found them; she would have destroyed them, and the chances were that her husband had not examined Carroll's luggage.

She even overcame her emotions enough to make sure that the letters were not upon Carroll's body. He must have destroyed them, as he had said. She had misjudged the poor boy. He had told the truth, and had made a sacrifice, for her sake. She would cherish a tender memory of him, for their love's sake.

The funeral took place next day. Eustace's manner reassured Hilda. Nothing was omitted which the dignity and position of the family required. Eustace wore a band of crepe upon his hand, and, with Hilda and the children in deep mourning, followed the body to the family vault in Lake View Cemetery.

Hilda felt greatly relieved when all was over. Her husband had shown no sign of suspicion. It was inconceivable that he could have done what he had that day, with knowledge of the dead youth's treachery. Hilda swore a silent and solemn oath that never again would she run such a risk—never again would she be tempted to deceive this loyal and courteous gentleman who had done so much for her. She would prove, by her devotion, how much she loved and respected him, and she would atone, so far as in her lay, for the wrong she had already done him. The atonement, of course, must be secret, as the sin had been. Confession would be worse than useless; it could do no one any good—it would not only destroy her husband's happiness but deprive her of opportunity for reparation.

She felt, as she sat opposite Eustace at dinner that night, a chastened gladness that Carroll was gone. He had, in a sense, deserved his fate, and she was free, from her sin and from its consequences—free to tread the straight and pleasant path of honest happiness by the side of a gentleman who loved her—free through no merit of her own, it was true, but by the decree of a kind fate which had spared her while taking her fellow sinner.

When the dessert was served, she rang for the nurse, who took the children away.

"Will you come into my study?" said Eustace, quietly, when they were gone. "I have something to say to you."

The color left her face, the light forsook her eyes. Her panoply of self-absolution and future immaculateness slipped, like a dropped garment, from her sinful soul and left it bare, as she rose mechanically and followed the accusing figure of her husband from the room.

His study lay across the hall. As she entered, he placed a chair for her, with formal courtesy. He then unlocked a drawer of his desk and took from it a bundle of letters, tied with narrow blue ribbon. She recognized the ribbon and remembered vividly when and from where it had been taken.

"These, I think" said Cartwright, in calm and even tones, "are yours—it is the law, I believe, that letters belong, first to the recipient, then to the writer. My interest, I think, was sufficient to justify my having read them—or some of them—enough of them. I now return them—to their lawful owner."

He put out his hand. She took the letters mechanically and laid them on her lap. An hour earlier, had she laid hands on them, she would have concealed them in her bosom. Now they had been read. Then they had been pregnant with immense possibilities—now they were dead—a spent rocket—dead as the body of her lover in the vault—dead as her hope for future happiness. They might lie on her lap, or on the floor, or in Eustace's desk, so far as he and she were concerned.

She heard him speaking, as though from a distance, and it was with an effort, at first, that she grasped the purport of his speech.

"Of course you realize, Hilda, what the result of this discovery must be. You can no longer be wife of mine, or I husband of yours. I have lost, at one blow, wife and nephew—both of whom I loved—what more I have lost I leave for you to imagine; you have a keen mind and a judgment riper than your years.

"I shall not attempt to fix or to distribute the blame for this deplorable affair which has worked my misfortune. Carroll is dead—as the result of his own folly, in all likelihood, for had he left yesterday, as he ought to have done, he would not have been a passenger upon the wrecked train. But you were the older of the two. You were a mother—you had your children to consider. And you were a wife, and held my honor in your hands."

He had not lifted his voice in the least, but upon her quivering conscience every word fell like the lash of a whip. She shrank together, and almost cowered before him, while her eyes sought the floor, but could get no further than the damning bundle of letters upon her lap.

"I shall not reproach you," he went on, "now or ever. When this interview is ended, I shall never mention the matter again—it will not be a pleasant subject. As I have said, you can no longer be my wife. But neither would I have you leave me. There are the children—I must consider them, if you did not; they must never, by any act of mine, have occasion to hold their mother in disrespect. Carroll was my sister's child; to blacken his memory would be to reflect upon her and upon all of us; nor do I care to become a subject of pity or ridicule."

She wondered vaguely, and dully, what he was going to—what he *could* do that would carry out his purpose and yet leave undone the things he did not wish to do.

"You will continue," he said, "that is, if my wishes prevail—to occupy your place in the household. To the world—to the servants even, there will be no change. If there should be at first some slight and inevitable constraint, and you think the servants might take notice, you can discharge them all and take on new ones who will know no past with which to compare our future. You will doubtless be glad to share with me the effort to keep the children in the dark—for their sakes?"

He seemed to wait for an answer, and she murmured something inarticulate which he apparently took for acquiescence.

"This, of course, will limit our intercourse. The house is large, and we need not interfere at all with one another. A very slight difference of arrangement will effect all the change that is necessary."

Her fingers were mechanically picking at the folds of her gown. The bundle of letters had slipped to the floor. Something within her shrank from what the life to which he condemned her might become. Nor had her husband ever seemed so noble, so worthy of love and respect as now when he sat in judgment upon her, and she had lost him.

Perhaps he noticed her change of expression.

"You shall be free," he said, "to come and go. I shall not interfere with your movements—except that I shall exercise a certain supervision over your company, for both our sakes. Upon formal occasions, when it is conventionally required, I will attend you—perhaps I have neglected my duty in that regard, and am myself to blame, in part, for what has happened.

"If you find life unendurable under these terms," he added, rising as though to dismiss her, "doubtless we can find a remedy. You could travel, or reside abroad, for your health. Or if you should wish, sometime, to seek a divorce—such things can be quietly arranged, with no scandal.

"And now, if there is nothing you wish to say, or ask, shall we terminate this painful interview?"

She rose, and with desperate effort, stepped firmly forward—had she faltered, he would, she knew, have offered her his arm—and she was unworthy to take it. He stooped, however, picked up the packet of letters, and, as he opened the door of the library with one hand, extended the bundle with the other.

"Permit me," he said, "you were leaving your letters."

How many lifetimes Hilda Cartwright lived in the next five years, she never stopped to figure out, but the time was long. From the very beginning she accepted, as a finality, the situation and her husband's terms. To the outside world, they were husband and wife, living in conventional harmony—if conjugal harmony be any longer conventional. If friends of their own social circle suspected anything between them, they were courteous enough not to mention it—to their faces; and when curiosity had nothing new to feed upon, it soon died away.

Their divided life was rendered easier by a gradual change in their habits. Cartwright had never cared a great deal for society, and Hilda began to go out less and less, until she became, in time, almost as much a recluse as her husband.

As the best atonement she could make for her offense, she sought to become what she imagined Eustace would have liked her to be, had she never disappointed him. She was a perfect housekeeper, an ideal mother. Such social duties as she still undertook were performed with effectiveness, grace and dignity, and Mrs. Cartwright became known as one of the most respected and admired of the younger matrons of her set. She was active in the work of her church, and a liberal contributor, both of time and money, to a number of good charities. Her benefactions fell like dew upon many a thirsty soul, because they felt in what she did the subtle sympathy with weakness or misfortune which comes only from those who have trod the same path.

Time dealt gently with her. She grew in the noble virtues which take their root in self-sacrifice. They left their impress upon her face, which became more beautiful with the passing years. At thirty she was in a young matronly prime which put her youthful and more immature beauty to the blush.

During all the years of her atonement, Cartwright had never, by a single word, recalled the subject of their estrangement. Nor were they much together, except in the presence of others. He was always courteous—too courteous, one shrewd lady said, for a man who loved his wife—and sometimes almost kind. But while Hilda loved him well enough to have thrown herself at his feet and placed his heel upon her neck, she was ever conscious of the impalpable barrier which separated them—a barrier as impenetrable as the shirt of chain mail which gentlemen of the romantic past wore under their silken doublets when dining with their friends. She did not attempt to pass this barrier—it would turn a smile, or a fond word, she felt instinctively, as surely as the steel jacket would stop a dagger-thrust. If he would ever change she did not know. If so, she would be there, beside him; if not, she must bear her punishment as best she could.

She knew he was not happy—and the knowledge was part, the greater part—of her punishment. Nor had he quite her resources to ward off unhappiness. Companionship was in large measure denied him. She had her children, nor did she realize, in her absorption, the extent to which she monopolized their society. He threw himself eagerly into affairs, and devoted himself, in his hours of relaxation, to the studies of which he was so fond.

But Hilda saw he was not happy, and, at last, that he was not well. His cheeks grew thinner, his hair was more than touched with gray, he lost some of the spring of life. Hilda watched him silently, with a yearning love, and with a growing fear. If he should die, it would be of unhappiness, and she would have murdered him as surely as though she had dropped poison in his cup.

In the spring of the fifth year of their estrangement, Cartwright fell ill. The doctor diagnosed the case as one of fever, possibly malignant, and ordered isolation and a trained nurse.

"I shall nurse him myself," said Hilda firmly.

"Impossible, madam. You will be liable to infection. And there are the children to consider."

"They can be sent away, if necessary," she declared. "For myself I do not care—and I am strong. I shall nurse him."

She could not be dissuaded, but took her place by Cartwright's bedside. At the height of the fever he became delirious, and said some things which tore her heart—not altogether with pain. She had a trained nurse assist her, but at these times she sent the nurse out of the room.

He seemed to be mending, when, one morning, he took a turn for the worse. The doctor made a careful examination.

"Astonishing," he said, as he finished. "I never knew of such a combination. He has developed diphtheria, of a malignant type."

She knew what this implied. "Is there no hope?" she whispered hoarsely.

"None," he replied, "without a miracle—and the age of miracles is past. At his age, he could scarcely hope to recover even in good health; in his present weakened condition there is no power of resistance whatever— it is only a matter of a day or two. Meanwhile it is dangerous for you to be near him—you have denied yourself sleep and rest—you are in none too good condition yourself to resist disease."

"I shall stay beside him," she declared, "to the last moment. I wish to be near him when he—if he—recovers consciousness. If it were only for a moment, and I were away, I should never forgive myself."

He protested, but in vain. Finding she would stay, he gave her minute directions how to avoid infection.

"Above all things, guard your mouth. Don't let your lips touch anything—not even your hands—that could possibly convey the contagion. I think you are running an unnecessary risk, but willful woman—"

"Must have her way," said Hilda, closing the conversation.

The doctor went away, but returned in an hour, remained two, and went away again.

"I'll be back in another hour. He'll last till morning, perhaps."

While the doctor was gone, Cartwright opened his eyes and looked up at his wife. The nurse was asleep in the next room.

"Hilda," he said, "is it you, dear?"

"Yes, Eustace," she returned, dropping on her knees beside the bed and taking his thin hand in hers.

"I am going to die, Hilda. I haven't cared a great deal about living, for several years."

"Spare me, Eustace, and spare yourself. If you die, I shall not care to live."

His face lit up with a rare smile.

"Do you love me?" he whispered, with his failing breath.

"I would give my life for you—and give it twice for one word of love."

"One word, my darling—one word? I have loved you always—I have never ceased to love you, and I am dying of my love. I wish now that I could live, but I suppose it is too late. But kiss me, Hilda, before I die!"

Then bravely, and without a moment's hesitation, she took her life into her hands and bent her face to his. He threw his arms, hot with fever, about her neck, and their lips met in a long, lingering caress.

They ought to have died, of course, and given their story a dramatic ending. But the doctor came back, an hour later, with a new culture which dissipated the gathering membrane.

They spent their new honeymoon in the Engadine—it was long before the war—and were as happy as chastened remorse, upon one side, and complete forgiveness, upon the other, and fervent love, upon both, would permit.

The Shadow of My Past

Unpublished in Chesnutt's lifetime

"The Shadow of My Past" constitutes a singular paradox in the writing career of Charles Chesnutt. Although unpublished in his life and despite its apparent lack of racialized subject matter—unlike most of his fiction, the story seems to feature only white characters—"The Shadow of My Past" nevertheless exemplifies its author's non-dialect short fiction. Like so many of his other fictions, this story examines the challenges faced by a character as he tries to translate his past into a viable identity in turn-of-the-century America. But while most of Chesnutt's examinations of that topic explicitly focus on the lives of black or mulatto protagonists, "The Shadow of My Past" considers the vicissitudes of identity construction—both social and personal—through the perspective of a love-struck, white narrator-protagonist, Hal/ Hank Skinner. As Skinner (who's known in his youth as "Hank" but presently calls himself, among other things, "Hal") attempts both to understand and to reshape his past for several demanding audiences, Chesnutt comically exaggerates the machinations of identity formation, but with serious intent. Despite both its comic tone and the absence of literally black characters, "The Shadow of My Past" resonates as both a racial allegory and a satirical interpretation of the American concept of the self-made man. Although the story has received very little critical attention,[1] it nevertheless represents one of Chesnutt's most fascinating commentaries on the American experience.

The basic plot of "The Shadow of My Past" combines two of Chesnutt's most fundamental themes: the search for identity and the role of the past. When the protagonist and narrator, Hal, proposes to the daughter of his employer, Mr. Parker, the prospective father-in-law devises a plan to investigate the past of his daughter's suitor. As Hal's fiancée explains, Mr. Parker "'has a theory that a man's character is a unit, and must be a harmonious unit; that if it is defective or weak at one point, or at any time in his life, it is marred all the way through'" (170). Although Parker will not commence his inquiries for several months, the idea prompts the narrator to spend his vacation in the town of his youth, Greenville, as a means of previewing what Mr. Parker will learn about him and his presumably "spotless" past: "It occurred to me," he writes, "that it might be well to anticipate Ethel's father's investigation and visit the old town and learn for myself whether I was remembered, and in what manner" (171). To those ends, Hal disguises himself—he becomes "John H. Smith, Chicago" (173), tellingly a Northerner—so that, without revealing his identity, he can ascertain his own reputation. By having his protagonist assume a false identity to explore his own past, Chesnutt establishes a figurative duality that pervades many of his fictions, a strategy that reflects Du Bois's notion of the "twoness" of African Americans.[2]

The results of Skinner's search have both comic and meaningful implications for Chesnutt (and his readers). While much of the humor of "Shadow" derives from the disjunction between Hal's account of his youth and townspeople's version of the same events, that disjunction also illuminates one of Chesnutt's favorite dilemmas: the extent to which individual identities depend upon public opinion. In fact, the townspeople's characterization of Hal's early life completely reverses his own conception of himself during that period. Chesnutt exploits the situational humor engendered by the narrator's smug confidence that his return will be greeted with affection and fond memories. Instead, each "witness" he speaks with describes a more wicked version of "Hank" (his nickname as a boy) than the last. While Hal speculates, for example, how "heartily" Mr. Gormully—his ex-employer and father to two children young Hank had wrestled with—"would laugh at the memory of my little 'scrap' with the children" (171), the man instead announces his willingness "to appear as a witness in the trial" of the "depraved" Hank Skinner (174).

Repeatedly faced with depictions of himself contrary to his own—"People whom I had never known gravely bore witness to my precocious depravity" (178), the narrator tells us—Hal decides to make nearly literal the concept of the "self-made man," a concept in which Chesnutt enthusiastically invested.[3] In a literalization of that concept, Hal does successfully rewrite his own life before Mr. Parker hears it: in essence, he remakes himself, or, at the least, he remakes his reputation. The manner by which Hal/Hank accomplishes this feat reveals both Chesnutt's deft comic touch and his more serious concern with the nature (and economics) of public identity. Using very modern notions of public relations, Hal initiates "a campaign for publicity" that redefines reputation:

> Hitherto I had been the most retiring of men. I didn't start a newspaper, but I cultivated the acquaintance of newspaper men. When I attended a ball or reception, I saw that my name was in the list of guests. . . . Seizing every opportunity to speak, I began to develop forensic ability. During the fall I read a paper to the Chamber [of Commerce] on "The Relation of National Banks to National Prosperity," upon which I received many compliments. As my various successes were from time to time mentioned in the newspapers, I sent marked copies to Thomas Gormully, Esq., Editor of the *Greenville Torchlight*. A struggling weekly published my address in full—I confess I paid for the composition—accompanied by a short biography, prepared with an especial view to its reaching the eyes of the Greenville public, and so worded as to make clear my identity with the Hank Skinner who had formerly worked for the mayor. (179)

Thus, the narrator "composes," or indeed recomposes, his own biography. Other Chesnutt fictions—including "Uncle Wellington's Wives," "The Wife of His Youth," "A Matter of Principle," and "Cicely's Dream"—render the attempts of characters to remake themselves to improve their social positions, but "The Shadow of My Past" differs from most of the author's fictions in that it features a narrator who *successfully* rewrites his public reputation. Hal/Hank has a great deal in common with Chesnutt, who, according to Richard H. Brodhead, thought "of writing largely as a way *out*, a way to achieve a selfhood not bounded by his local scene" (20). Hank Skinner, on the other hand, conceives of writing precisely as a way back *in* to his social community, and as a way into the heart of his prospective father-in-law.

The extent to which the initially befuddled protagonist-narrator pensively explores the construction of his identity—by both himself and others—resonates throughout this otherwise humorous tale. When he discovers, for example, that the stories of his erstwhile "friends" share many key elements, Hal begins to question the very fabric of his self-conception:

Had I really been such a scoundrel as my old friends pictured me? Of course I had not poisoned my brother, or shot my father, or burned my mother; but brushing aside these absurdities, had I been so much worse than other boys as to forfeit the toleration extended toward the faults of youth? Had I possessed no single redeeming trait? It was strange that they should all have misjudged me so greatly; and yet it would have been more remarkable that a sane person could have so greatly misjudged himself. A fool may not perceive his own folly, but a liar must know when he lies, and a thief when he steals. (178)

Although the tone of this story remains comic even through this meditative analysis, the consequences of his sullied reputation threaten both his domestic life and his dream "of a public career. Could I hope for either with such a cloud hanging over me?" (179). Through Hal's quandary Chesnutt explores potential consequences of public opinion, even when inaccurately formed, on one's life. As a light-skinned African American businessman who negotiated a variety of social circles—both black and white—in Cleveland,[4] Chesnutt had a great deal of experience with precisely this dilemma.

But the story works as more than a mirror of the author's social trajectory. As he does in such Northern fictions as "The Wife of His Youth," "Uncle Wellington's Wives," and "Mr. Taylor's Funeral," Chesnutt grapples with the complexities of identity construction. And, as those fictions and "The Shadow of My Past" attest, he seems to have concluded that identity is not a fixed matter, but instead a fluid, constantly shifting process, a conception that stands, of course, in utter opposition to Mr. Parker's rigid theory that one's character forms "a harmonious unit" (170).

Despite its humor—which at times takes on a slapstick appeal—and its lack of literally black characters, "The Shadow of My Past" thus depicts Chesnutt's own anxieties about social identity in terms of black and white. After speaking with a few preliminary "witnesses" who detail his alleged youthful misdemeanors, for example, Hal tells us, "My record was growing blacker and blacker" (177). The absence of literally black characters here seems to suggest that Chesnutt has recast his interest in race-identity issues in metaphoric terms, or it could be instead that he had broadened his interest to the identities of Northern whites as well. Certainly, the search for identity, as well as the emphasis on composing one's own identity, functions as a shaping motif of Chesnutt's work, especially his Northern fictions. Stories such as "The Wife of His Youth," "Uncle Wellington's Wives," and "Her Virginia

Mammy" all explore the tension between characters who want to define themselves and the various social and racial pressures they face. But as the experiences of the characters in those works repeatedly demonstrate, Chesnutt usually focuses on the costs of redefining one's identity. This story is quite different. One might argue, in fact, that "The Shadow of My Past" forms, for Chesnutt, the ideal allegorical representation of the self-made man, one in which the protagonist determines his own place in the social landscape.[5] Hal's "publicity campaign" ultimately works, that is, and he is "able to face [his] *fiancée* and [his] future without fear" (181). Despite its uniqueness in Chesnutt's fiction as an examination of a self-made man who succeeds in unqualified fashion, "The Shadow of My Past" does rely on a tactic familiar to readers of Chesnutt and other African American writers. The quest to find or construct one's identity often includes the use of disguises or masks in black writings, a strategy apparent in the works of such diverse authors as Harriet Jacobs and Ralph Ellison, as well as throughout Chesnutt's canon.

In focusing on the extent to which one might reinvent oneself, Chesnutt celebrates the notion of the self-made man while simultaneously sounding a cautionary note about the means by which a society comes to understand the individuals who compose it (and, indeed, are composed by it). That he can do so behind the cloak of a putatively comic narrative attests to his mature powers of craft. "The Shadow of My Past" rests on a typical Chesnutt paradox: unlike most of his fiction in profound ways, it is nevertheless a true accounting of his work.

NOTES

1. "The Shadow of My Past," like "The Kiss" and "White Weeds," was unpublished in Chesnutt's lifetime. All three works appeared for the first time in Sylvia Lyons Render's essential collection, *The Short Fiction of Charles W. Chesnutt* (1974).

2. In *The Souls of Black Folk*, Du Bois speaks of the doubleness of African Americans, who must regard themselves both as Americans and as blacks.

3. See, for example, Chesnutt's speech on "Self-Made Men" in *Essays and Speeches*. And, Chesnutt's Northern stories repeatedly emphasize the extent to which his characters create an identity for themselves. In such diverse works as "The Wife of His Youth," "The Doll," and "Mr. Taylor's Funeral," he rehearses the theme.

4. Although not by nature a "mixer," Chesnutt belonged to an astounding variety of social and political groups, including the Cleveland Social Circle (apparently the model for the "Blue Vein Society" of such Northern works as "The Wife of His Youth" and "A Matter of Principle"), the Rowfant Club (a Cleveland club for bibliophiles), and the Committee of Twelve for the Advancement of the Interests of the Negro Race.

5. Especially in his racialized versions of Chesnutt's "self-made man" stories, the protagonist usually makes far more compromises. Consider, for example, Tom Taylor of "The Doll," who, for the sake of his family and his business, must suppress the urge to avenge his father's death.

❖❖❖

The Shadow of My Past

WHEN I HAD KNOWN Ethel about a year, I declared my love, and found, to my intense joy, that it was returned.

"I will speak to your father at once," I said.

Her face took on a thoughtful expression.

"I shouldn't be precipitate," she said. "It will be real nice to be engaged, but papa has very decided notions about marriage, and you'd better let me handle him."

I deferred to her wishes. Indeed I was glad to be relieved of a formidable task. I had been employed for a year or two as teller in the bank of which her father was a stockholder and director. He was a rather reserved and stern-looking old gentleman, and our occasional communications at the bank had been of the briefest. I had met Ethel at an evening party, and had been calling at the house for some time, but had seldom met Mr. Parker. He, it seemed, had a library upstairs where he spent most of his time. When I had run across him in the hall now and then he had nodded curtly, and had thrown me a glance which seemed to ask what the devil I was doing there. I was a self-made man, however, and used to overcoming difficulties. As long as he did not translate his looks into words and forbid me the house, I continued to go. I was therefore secretly relieved that Ethel should undertake the labor of bringing him around.

When I saw her next evening, I inquired how matters were progressing.

"Be patient, Hal," she said. "Papa is a man of moods, and must be approached carefully. As soon as I think it safe, I will bring the subject up."

It was a week before she reported.

"I have spoken to papa," she said, "and while he doesn't say no—he doesn't say yes."

"What does he say?" I asked in pained suspense.

"He says I'm too young."

"Preposterous! You are twenty-two."

"He doesn't believe that girls should marry before they are twenty-five.

Now, Hal, don't look as though you were sentenced to death. I'm not going to wait until I am twenty-five."

"My darling!" I ejaculated, intensely relieved.

"But I'll tell you," she continued, "what I *am* going to do. Papa, mamma and I are going to Europe in May. We shall be back in October. After we return, papa is going down to the town you came from, and if he finds that your career from the beginning has been a consistently worthy one, he will take up the question of our marriage say a year hence. He has a theory that a man's character is a unit, and must be a harmonious unit; that if it is defective or weak at one point, or at any time in his life, it is marred all the way through."

There was nothing to do but submit. I made some tentative suggestion about her being old enough to know her own mind and about the loneliness of a summer without her; but she did not choose to see the drift of my remarks.

"I expect to have a lovely time, Hal, and you'll be too busy with your work to do more than answer my letters. I told papa where you were born and spent your boyhood. I'm not afraid of anything he may find out about you."

"You will have no cause to be," I replied with conviction.

I was a self-made man, not entirely finished, but not ashamed of the job, so far as it had gone. As I looked back over my career, after my last conversation with Ethel, I could recall no place at which an accusing finger could be pointed. I had begun my business career as a district messenger, had become an office boy. I had worked hard, and had risen in proportion, doubtless, to my merits. Certainly nothing but merit had helped me on, for I had no influential relatives or friends.

But if my life in the city had been an open book, my life before was a closed chapter; at least I had not opened it for thirteen years. My recollections of it were none too distinct, and some of them none too pleasant. Suppose Ethel's father should be absurd enough to go down to Greenville to look up my early life, what would people say of me—the people who had known me only as a child and had lost sight of me so long?

My childhood had not been fortunate. My father, a man of more than average intelligence, and of considerable energy, had lacked the judgment to combine these effectively, and had therefore remained always a poor man. My mother, I have been told, was a woman of fine parts, and fitted by nature for something better than the life of drudgery to which her condition as a poor man's wife condemned her. I had three brothers and two sisters, of whom all but one brother died while children.

When I was about twelve our family met with a series of misfortunes which seemed to mock at the doctrine of chances and the laws of life. My father, while out hunting, accidentally shot and killed himself. The sod on his grave had not taken root before my brother was poisoned by eating ice cream at a Sunday-school picnic. While we were at his funeral our house took fire and burned to the ground. My mother, bereft of her husband and her home, was obliged to take in sewing for a living. My own support was provided for by binding me out to Josiah Gormully, a prosperous butcher who kept a shop in our neighborhood. Gormully had a son, Tom, about two years my senior, and a daughter of about my own age who, to impress upon me their own superiority, conspired to make my life as miserable as possible. I endured this while my mother lived, but when she at last succumbed to her troubles and a hemorrhage, I found my lot too hard to bear. One day when Tom Gormully was more than usually exasperating, I gave him a sound thrashing, notwithstanding that his sister Mary undertook to help him out. Gormully had gone away for several days to buy cattle. After my passion had cooled, I looked forward with some apprehension to his return. The nearer it approached, the more apprehensive I became, and, the night before his expected arrival, I packed my slender wardrobe in an old oilcloth valise, and between two days shook the dust of Greenville from my feet.

Fifteen years had passed, and time had long since softened any animosity I had felt against the Gormullys. When vacation time arrived, it occurred to me that it might be well to anticipate Ethel's father's investigation and visit the old town and learn for myself whether I was remembered, and in what manner. It would be an easy way to dispose of a week of the two to which I was entitled. I bought a ticket to Greenville.

Reclining luxuriously in the parlor car, I felt a pleasant glow of anticipation. I thought of my old master the butcher, and imagined the cordial handclasp with which he would greet me. How heartily he would laugh at the memory of my little "scrap" with the children! I pictured Mary a plump and rosy matron, recalling with pleased surprise, in the handsome and well-dressed gentleman who stood before her, the lean and shabby apprentice upon whom she had looked down so many years before. Old Jim Prout, the village shoemaker, in whose shop, next door to Gormully's, I had spent so many spare hours, would be delighted to see the boy who had listened so patiently to his stories, and whose hard lot he had pitied. There rose before my mind the image of Mrs. Betsy Barker, who kept the little millinery shop of the village and gave me cake and apples and other good things, and sympathized so deeply with my mother on her misfortunes. I should be glad to shake hands with my Sunday-school teacher, Deacon Hardacre, of the Free Will Baptist Church, to which my parents had belonged, and to let him know that his work had not been entirely barren of results. But the person I looked forward with most pleasure to meeting was Miss Celina Hawkins, a distant relative of my mother's and the only individual in Greenville with whom I could claim the tie of blood. Often had I run errands, chopped wood, drawn water, and worked in the garden for Cousin Celina. Once when the roof of her house caught fire I had climbed up and put it out, at the imminent risk of my own physical integrity. I was sure that Miss Hawkins, if living, would be overjoyed to see me; nor had I come to the end of these pleasing reflections when the train drew up at Greenville station.

There were many changes in the town. I left the train at the same little wooden depot that had been there when I went away, but walking up the street I noticed many new buildings, and missed some that I remembered. The modest inn that had sheltered travelers in my boyhood had given place to a pretentious brick building designated by a large sign in gilt letters as the Commercial Hotel.

The service, however, was scarcely in keeping with the exterior. There was no one at the desk when I went in, and the boy who took my valise explained that the clerk had been subpoenaed into court with the register, to give evidence in a lawsuit; that he would return shortly, when I could register. Meantime I could have supper, which was ready.

I had been at the table but a few minutes when I was engaged in conversation by the man opposite me. From his familiarity with the waiters I inferred that he was no stranger to the hotel. We exchanged some remarks about the weather, and then I asked him if he lived in the town.

"Yes, sir," he answered, "my name is Gormully—Thomas J. Gormully, editor of the *Weekly Torchlight*. You're in tobacco, I presume—or are you in liquor?"

I don't know why he should have thought me in tobacco or liquor, unless it might be that they were the principal commodities dealt in by the local trades-people. But the mention of his name diverted my mind from any annoyance I might otherwise have felt at the suggestion that I looked like a whiskey drummer.

I had an inspiration. Tom Gormully had not suspected my identity, nor had he asked my name. Before revealing it, I might, by a question, learn the real estimation in which I was held by the Gormully family.

"No," I replied, "I am not in any commercial line. To be candid," I said, "I am here to look up the record of a man who was brought up in this town, I believe. He was known in those days as Henry, sometimes called Hank Skinner."

My companion leaned forward eagerly, resting both hands on the table, with this knife and fork pointing upward.

"Hank Skinner!" he exclaimed. "Why I know all about Hank Skinner! What is it this time—murder?"

I was so taken aback at this outburst that I could only murmur confusedly that my mission was a confidential one; I simply desired to ascertain the facts.

"I'm the man to give them to you," he said with enthusiasm. "Nothing that he has done or is suspected of will surprise the people of Greenville. To speak the literal truth, Hank Skinner, even as a boy, was a desperate character. Several years my elder, one day he assaulted me and in spite of my feeble resistance, nearly killed me. My sister, who was present, implored him to desist. In an access of brutal rage he turned upon her with such ferocity that she was laid up for a month from the shock. Father was away from home at the time and Skinner escaped before his return. Father offered a reward for his capture, but he was never apprehended. I supposed he had died a violent death or was in the penitentiary long ago. Well, well, I'll take you down to the house after supper. The old man will tell you more about him."

This was a trifle discouraging. To disclose my identity now would likely prove even more embarrassing. I felt curious to know what, if anything more, the old man *could* say to my detriment. If it should prove to be any worse, I might hesitate to make myself known at all. When I had finished supper, I registered as "John H. Smith, Chicago," and then walked with my new acquaintance a couple of blocks to a fine, large new house, which he pointed out as his father's residence.

"Father," he said, introducing me to the portly and well-clad individual who came forward to meet us, "this is Mr. Smith, a gentleman from Chicago, who is looking up the record—the black record—of Hank Skinner, our Hank, you know. Mr. Smith, my father, the Honorable Josiah Gormully, Mayor of Greenville."

"I welcome you to our city, Mr. Smith," said the mayor. "I am indeed glad to know you, and to render you any assistance within my power. Hank Skinner was a most depraved, indeed a most dangerous character."

The mayor then repeated in substance what his son had said, with somewhat fuller detail, and expressed regret that he could not have one more meeting with Hank Skinner—just one.

"I am quite willing," he added, "to appear as a witness in the trial or to give my deposition."

I thanked him, and said I would communicate with him later. As we were getting up to go out, a large, showily dressed woman of twenty-eight or thirty came into the room.

"Good evening, Mary," said Tom Gormully. "Mr. Smith, my sister, Miss Gormully. Mr. Smith is looking up the early record of Hank Skinner, *our* Hank."

Miss Gormully, who had given me a winning smile at first, now frowned and shuddered.

"That is a painful subject with me," she answered. "I can even now see his murderous look bent upon me, and feel the blows he aimed at me with his brutal fists. My poor nerves never recovered fully from the effects of his fury. His very name makes me shudder. Has he murdered somebody, now that he is strong enough?"

I was sufficiently hardened, by this time, to retain my self-possession. I replied that my mission being a confidential one, I was not at liberty to disclose it.

"Oh, I see," said the mayor, nodding sagaciously, "he might take alarm and escape. Well, I hope you may convict him and send him over the road."

The mayor mentioned the names of several of my former acquaintances and suggested that I call on them. I bade him and his interesting offspring good-night, found my way back to the hotel, smoked a cigar, and then went to bed. My past record, as developed so far, was scarcely one to be proud of. But the Gormullys could hardly be expected to hold me in a grateful remembrance, and therefore their statements did not greatly interfere with my night's rest.

After breakfast next morning, I started out to find Mrs. Betsy Barker. The house that had formerly been her millinery shop was now used as a coal office, and in the window where the creations of Mrs. Barker's genius had once been displayed, there now stood a row of pine boxes containing samples of coal. I inquired of the clerk behind the desk the whereabouts of the former tenant.

"I don't know," he said, "I've only been in town a few weeks. But there's an old shoemaker around the corner who seems to know everybody; you'd better ask him."

I found the shoemaker, whom I recognized immediately, in spite of some changes wrought by time, as my old friend, Jim Prout. He made room for me by brushing the waxed ends from the three-legged stool, and asked me to sit down, glancing meanwhile at my feet. But the glossy sheen of my patent leathers must have raised a doubt as to the object of my visit, and he looked at me inquiringly as I sank cautiously down upon the stool. I will own to a slight feeling of disappointment at perceiving that he did not recognize me. A friendship so sincere as his had been should have a keener memory. But of course age might have dulled his faculties. The mention of my name would doubtless open his eyes.

"I am from Chicago," I said with a smile, "and am trying to find out something about the past life of one Henry Skinner—Hank Skinner, they used to call him—who was brought up in Greenville. I am led to believe that you knew him, some fifteen years ago."

The old man turned a blank and lack-luster upon me, took off his glasses, wiped them, put them on again, and planted his elbows on his knees.

"Skinner—Hank Skinner? I disremember any sich name. Who did he work for?"

"I understand he was bound to the mayor, Mr. Gormully."

"Le'me see," he said reflectively. "There wuz a boy by the name of Jeems—Jeems Jinkins, that worked for Gormully when he run the tannery. Mebbe that wuz the boy ye mean?"

"No, this boy's name was Hank—Hank Skinner. He worked for Gormully when he kept a butcher shop down on Jackson Street."

"Oh, I reckon I ricollec' the boy now—a tall, stoop-shouldered boy with red hair, and cross-eyes."

"No," I said, "that isn't the boy. This boy was short and thin, and had black eyes and hair."

"Le'me see. Seems ter me ther wuz sich a boy druv' Gormully's butcher cart 'long 'bout twenty years after the war. Do yer know anything 'bout his folks?"

"His father accidentally shot himself."

"Oh, yes, I remember the boy distinc'ly now. He was a son of ole Joe Skinner, a worthless kind o' cuss, that spent most of his time huntin' an' fishin' an' hangin' roun' barrooms. I did hear it said that Hank shot his daddy and then put out a report about his havin' shot hisself. There was some difficulty 'bout provin' it, an' so there wuz nothin' done. But it wuz more'n likely so, for it wa'n't long before he sot fire to his mammy's house, and run away to 'scape the consequences. He wuz a desp'rit character, and it wuz a good riddance o' bad rubbish when he made hisself skeerce. And so you're lookin' up his record, air ye? What's he be'n doin' now?"

"I am not at liberty to state at present," I replied, "but I thank you for the information. Do you know where I can find a Mrs. Betsy Barker, an old lady who is said to have once kept a millinery store around the corner here?"

"Ole Mis' Betsy Barker? Wal, I sh'd say I could! Mis' Barker lives out by the fair grounds, the fust house on the left-han' side after ye pass Eccles' mill-pond. Just keep on down Gillespie Street, and ye can't miss it. I don't know whether ye can get anything sensible from ole Mis' Barker. She's gettin' on to'ds her second chil'hood, but now an then she has a glimmerin' o' reason an' ricollection. Have ye got any terbacker with ye?"

I gave the old man a cigar, and left his shop decidedly chagrined, comforting myself, however, with the reflection that the old man was in his dotage. Mrs. Barker was ten years younger; her memory could scarcely be worse. I crossed the bridge over the mill-pond, and reached the little cottage to which I had been directed. A knock at the door brought out Mrs. Barker herself, a little thinner, a little more bent, the veins in her hands a little more prominent, but with the same keen eyes peeping out of her wrinkled face. It was clear by this time that I had changed much more in appearance than my former friends, for Mrs. Barker showed no sign of recognition.

I lifted my hat, and stated that I had been directed to her as one who might remember a boy by the name of Henry Skinner, commonly called Hank, who had run away from Gormully the butcher some fifteen years before.

"Laws yes! I remember Hank Skinner perficly well. Won't you sit down? Hank's mother was a friend of mine when I was a gal. But pore Mandy was unfortunate. Her husband wa'n't worth shucks. He got shot in a quarrel down at Bill Syke's barroom, an' left Mandy a wider with two boys, one named Bill, and this Hank. Bill was a good boy, but Hank was the black sheep o' the flock. He p'isoned his brother, and ran away before they could take him up. I believe he did work for Gormully the butcher a little while, but was discharged for stealin'. Is he be'n forgin' a note or robbin' a bank?"

"I am not at liberty to state the exact nature of his offense at present," I replied mechanically, "but I am much obliged to you for your information."

This was appalling. My record was growing blacker and blacker. And yet in spite of my chagrin, there was a certain grim humor about the situation. I felt a reckless curiosity to fathom the greatest depth of depravity I had reached in the memory of my former acquaintances. I had concealed my identity at first upon the impulse of the moment, expecting at each subsequent meeting to declare myself. It now seemed uncertain whether a favorable opportunity would present itself. I still cherished, however, a lingering hope that my old Sunday-school teacher, Deacon Hardacre, would remember some good thing of me, and that my distant relative, Miss Celina Hawkins, had preserved some kindly thought of the orphan boy who had fled from a harsh and cruel service. It was well I did not build upon this hope.

Deacon Hardacre had prospered with the growth of the town. I found him at his office, where he transacted a real estate and insurance business. He glanced at me keenly, and inquired in what way he could serve me. I stated the object of my visit.

"Hennery Skinner?" he said, dropping into what I recognized, even after the lapse of years, as his Sunday-school tone. "Oh, yes, I remember Hennery. Your inquiry confirms my fear that he had succumbed to temptation. No wonder, when his temperament and inherited tendencies were so much against him! How often have I trembled for his future! For I realized that only a large outpouring of divine grace could save him from destruction. But, alas! I could never see any comforting signs in Hennery. He was neglectful of his lessons, and gave me more trouble than any boy in Sabbath school; and I have heard that he was a sore trial to his poor mother. My fears were confirmed when he committed a brutal assault on the children of his employer, our present mayor, and fled from the restraining influences of home and friends. May I inquire the nature—"

I murmured some vague reply and escaped, sick at heart. Could I have been so grossly self-deceived? My last hope of rehabilitation lay in my old friend Cousin Celina. I found her seated on the front porch of the same old house where she had lived when I was a child. The same old elm cast its shade over her. There was a difference, though; twenty years had left their mark on Miss Celina, while the elm did not seem a day older.

I had hardly expected her to know me, and when I had convinced her that I was not a tramp, or an agent of any kind, I made the usual inquiry, whether she remembered anything about Hank Skinner's boyhood.

"Hank Skinner? Yes, I recollec' Hank. I heard there was a detective in town lookin' him up. I reckon you must be the detective? Well, I can tell you this much—none o' the Skinners was ever worth the powder and shot it would take to kill 'em. My third cousin, Amanda Simpson, married this Hank Skinner's father, and it was a sad day for her. He never amounted to anything, and his boys was jus' like him. This Hank used to hang roun' my house for somethin' to eat, and I had to keep things locked up while he was about. As it was, I missed one o' my spoons that's never been accounted for, and I'm positive he took it. This Hank had a fearful temper. He had to run away for somethin'—let me see, what was it? His brother—no, his brother p'isoned a man. Oh, I remember now—my memory ain't as good as it used to be, but I remember quite distinc'ly now! Hank knocked his mother down, and then set fire to the house before she came to. There wa'n't no evidence, but everybody knowed Hank must 'a' done it. And so he's suspected o' killin' somebody else, is he? Well, I always said he'd come to a bad end!"

My last hope had failed. Miss Celina maundered on in a disconnected way, while I sat for a few minutes like one oppressed with a hideous nightmare. How I got out of the house I hardly know, but a little later I found myself sitting on the bridge over the mill-pond, where I had so often gone swimming and fishing in my boyhood. Fixing my eyes upon the quiet water, I reviewed my past in detail.

Had I really been such a scoundrel as my old friends pictured me? Of course I had not poisoned my brother, or shot my father, or burned my mother; but brushing aside these absurdities, had I been so much worse than other boys as to forfeit the toleration extended toward the faults of youth? Had I possessed no single redeeming trait? It was strange that they should all have misjudged me so greatly; and yet it would have been more remarkable that a sane person could have so greatly misjudged himself. A fool may not perceive his own folly, but a liar must know when he lies, and a thief when he steals.

I spent the remainder of the day in finding out all I could about myself. I heard nothing worse than I had heard already, but I collected elaborate details of my misdoings. I learned the motives which had prompted them. Not only was I made out the author of the misfortunes which had overwhelmed my family, but other mysterious crimes occurring about that time were imputed to me. People whom I had never known gravely bore witness to my precocious depravity. Such was my reputation as it would be gathered by my prospective father-in-law, who believed in the unity of character; who maintained that one serious moral lapse argued a permanently defective character.

I left Greenville by the night train, without having disclosed to anyone my identity. I found a quiet place, with good fishing, where I finished my vacation, and thought out a plan for the redemption of my reputation. It was before the war, and the path to fame was not so easy as in peacetime. But it was still four months or more before Ethel and her father would return from Europe, and in four months an energetic man, with his future happiness at stake, can accomplish wonders. Not only was my love in jeopardy from the shadow that rested on my past. I was ambitious for large success; I had dreamed of a public career. Could I hope for either with such a cloud hanging over me?

My plan involved a campaign for publicity. Hitherto I had been the most retiring of men. I didn't start a newspaper, but I cultivated the acquaintance of newspaper men. When I attended a ball or reception, I saw that my name was in the list of guests. I joined the Chamber of Commerce, and deliberately worked for a place on an important committee. Seizing every opportunity to speak, I began to develop forensic ability. During the fall I read a paper to the Chamber on "The Relation of National Banks to National Prosperity," upon which I received many compliments. As my various successes were from time to time mentioned in the newspapers, I sent marked copies to Thomas Gormully, Esq., Editor of the *Greenville Torchlight*. A struggling weekly published my address in full—I confess I paid for the composition— accompanied by a short biography, prepared with an especial view to its reaching the eyes of the Greenville public, and so worded as to make clear my identity with the Hank Skinner who had formerly worked for the mayor. Shortly after I had forwarded copies of this paper to Editor Gormully, I received through the mail a marked copy of the *Greenville Torchlight* containing the following editorial:

A Distinguished Fellow Townsman

The older citizens of Greenville especially, and some of the younger ones as well, will be pleased to note the success which has attended the career of one of our former citizens, the Honorable Henry Skinner. We are proud to number ourselves among the friends of Mr. Skinner's boyhood, and to remember that at one period of his life the same roof sheltered both our heads. The career of Mr. Skinner, the principal events of whose life are set forth elsewhere in this number, in an excerpt from a metropolitan journal, is one that reflects credit upon our city, and should be an incentive to every ambitious young man among us, as well as a matter of local pride. The editor is one of a committee of prominent citizens who have united in requesting Mr. Skinner to deliver an address to the people of Greenville at an early date.

The next week I received the invitation. I accepted, went to Greenville, and delivered an address. I was met at the depot by a committee and escorted in a carriage to the hotel. The hall in which I spoke was filled to overflowing.

The rostrum was decorated with a magnificent bouquet of roses to which was attached the card of Miss Mary Gormully. The Mayor, attired in a suit of black broadcloth, with a glittering diamond in his shirt-front, introduced me in the following language, as reported in the next week's edition of the *Torchlight:*

> Ladies and gentlemen: I have the honor of presenting to you this evening a young man whom some of you have known in other days, a gentleman who typifies in his career the genius of American civilization; who epitomizes in his life the growth and progress of our country. I remember him when but a child, the comfort of his widowed mother, upon whom misfortune had laid its hard hand. It was my privilege at one period of his young life to receive him under my own roof, and I feel proud today of the small share I contributed to his prosperity. But our town was not large enough to hold him. His mind then soared beyond our confines, and sought in the outer world wider opportunities for development. He found them, and made the best use of them. His career has been one of uninterrupted success, and while yet a young man, he is the recipient of honors which most of us consider ourselves fortunate to attain toward the close of life. I have the honor of introducing to you our friend and fellow townsman, the Honorable Henry Skinner, who will now address you.

I spoke and spoke well. My remarks were received with favor, and with each recurring sign of appreciation I waxed more eloquent, until I finally sat down amid a perfect storm of applause. For half an hour after the meeting closed I was surrounded by prominent citizens who came forward to shake my hand and claim old acquaintance. They congratulated me on my address and on my success in life. Old Jim Prout, in his Sunday clothes, was among the first to come forward and shake my hand, his face beaming with pleasure. I may say right here that no one seemed to connect me in the slightest degree with the John H. Smith who had visited Greenville a few months before. I could account for this partly by psychological reasons, partly by some difference in dress, and by my having shaved off my mustache.

"Well, well," said old Jim, "but I am glad to see ye, Hank. I always knowed you'd git along in the world. It was only the other night I was saying to my old woman, 'Liza,' says I, 'I'm goin' ter hear Hank Skinner speak if I have to crawl there on my han's an' knees.'"

I was going out of the hall with Tom Gormully, when we passed an old woman seated near the door.

"You ain't going by without speaking to yo'r old friends, be ye?" said a piping voice which I recognized as that of Mrs. Betsy Barker.

"I'm too old to scrouge up there on the platform," she added, putting out her hand, "but I was determined to speak to ye if I had to be the last one goin' out. Yo'r mother was my best friend, and I remember what a good boy you was and what a help and comfort to her! Old Deacon Hardacre was out to my house the other day tryin' to buy my lot, and we got to talkin' about how smart you used to be, and how you always knowed yo'r Sunday-school lessons, and how he had often wondered what had become of you. I allowed that I always knowed you'd git along; and he said yes, that a boy of yo'r talents and yo'r character couldn't be kep' down, and that you was one of the Lord's chosen vessels. I hear the deacon's sick, else he'd surely be here tonight."

At the hotel I received a note from Miss Celina Hawkins, expressing regret that her rheumatism prevented her from coming to hear me speak, but hoping I would not leave town without visiting my old friend and cousin.

Thus the shadow of my past was lifted and I was able to face my *fiancée* and my future without fear. I never judged my old friends harshly. Human nature is much the same at all times and in all places, and my experience illustrates the consequences of giving a dog a bad name. But the reverse of the proverb is also true, although it takes a little longer time to make, and a little harder work to keep, a good name.

Baxter's *Procrustes*

Atlantic Monthly (1904)

After reading several stories, poems, or novels by any author, a reader might well develop a comfortable sense of what to expect from that writer and his or her works. Certainly, readers of the eighteen Chesnutt stories collected in this volume could easily produce a list of the author's usual themes, issues, and strategies: emphasis on race matters, concern with the ways in which families form and re-form, interest in notions of personal and social identity, and, of course, fascination with the new racial, economic, and social dynamics at play in the North at the turn of the century. And yet, a reader coming to "Baxter's *Procrustes*" would face several surprises. Instead of the accustomed situations, the story appears to feature only white characters; it makes absolutely no mention of anything remotely like a "family" motif; and it apparently has little or nothing to do with racial or social identity. Indeed, "Baxter's *Procrustes*" constitutes a characteristic Chesnutt paradox: seemingly unlike virtually all of his other fictions, it nevertheless may well be his best work.[1]

In brief, the story meticulously traces the execution and consequences of a finely wrought practical joke played on the preoccupied members of a book collectors' club very much like the one to which Chesnutt belonged. Chesnutt drew on his own experiences with Cleveland's Rowfant Club (which is still going strong today) to construct the broadly humorous—and often hilarious—narrative of "Baxter's *Procrustes*." Set entirely within the confines of the Bodleian Club (his fictionalized name for the Rowfant Club), the story thus presents a particularized (and highly exclusive) segment of Cleveland's social order at the turn of the century.

The plot focuses on the attempts of an author to strike back at the literary establishment and, especially, the terms by which books are assessed. When the members of the Bodleian Club learn that one of its members, Baxter, has completed an epic poem, the *Procrustes,* they prevail upon him to allow the club to publish the work as a limited-edition, "rare" book, not out of any particular passion for Baxter's verse but because such a publication, they know, will instantly be of financial value, the only true measure, for them, of literature. Baxter sees in this request the perfect opportunity to skewer the pretensions of his avaricious fellows and especially their predilection for seeking not truth or beauty or wisdom in their books, but instead a tangible economic return on an "investment." The narrator lays out the standards by which he and his fellows calculate a book's value:

> Early in its history [the Bodleian] began the occasional publication of books which should meet the club standard,—books in which emphasis should be laid upon the qualities that make a book valuable in the eyes of collectors. Of these, age could not, of course, be imparted, but in the matter of fine and curious bindings, of hand-made linen papers, of uncut or deckle edges, of wide margins and limited editions, the club could control its own publications. *The matter of contents was, it must be confessed, a less important consideration.* (188, emphasis added)

The members of the club, that is, prefer the accoutrements to the "contents" of the book, a preference that rankled Baxter (and indeed Chesnutt). As a means of retaliating against the club's disregard for literary merit (or "contents"), Baxter contrives to control the printing process—no one in the Bodleian ever actually sees his poem prior to publication—so that the final version of his "book" enacts the club's stated preferences, although perhaps more literally than the members of the Bodleian Club might have wished. Ultimately, the joke, which I won't spoil here, works for both Baxter and Chesnutt as a commentary on the commercialism of literature and the sometimes absurd standards by which serious writers are judged.

In several fascinating ways, "Baxter's *Procrustes*" draws on Chesnutt's own experiences with the Rowfant Club, an association of bibliophiles whose goal was twofold: "Primarily, the critical study of books in their various capacities to please the mind of man; and secondarily, the publication from time to time of privately printed editions of books for its members" (qtd. in Keller, 228). In 1902, some of Chesnutt's friends put him forward for membership in the Rowfant Club, although it chose not to grant him admission at that time. Nevertheless, the process by which the club initially considered him must have appealed to Chesnutt's ironic sensibility at the same time as it offended his principles:

> Two members must propose the name of a candidate in their own hand-writing. The Council of Fellows balloted secretly after a candidate's name had been inscribed for two weeks, using white and black balls. In the first encounter between Chesnutt and members of this *sanctum sanctorum* of literature, Chesnutt received at least two black balls, though he had friends willing to propose his name. Afterwards someone told him that "one or two members thought the time hadn't come" for opening the doors to men of Negro descent, whatever their qualifications. (Keller, 229)

Thus, Chesnutt was initially "blackballed" by the Rowfant Club. It's therefore not much of a stretch to imagine his exacting a sort of literary revenge for this 1902 snub by composing "Baxter's *Procrustes*," which reached print only two years later.

Despite his satirical send-up of the club in 1904, though, Chesnutt's subsequent admission to the Rowfant Club in 1910 after its initial rejection of him eight years earlier would seem to indicate that he harbored no sustained antipathy for bibliophiles, or indeed for the Rowfant. In a 1910 letter to Frederick H. Goff, however, he makes clear his feelings regarding his previous experience with the club:

> A month or two ago, Ginn asked me one day if I would care to join the Rowfant Club, observing that he thought there would be no difficulty about it this time. I replied that if they could stand it, I could, but that I would like to have him feel pretty certain about the matter before he puts my name up, as I would not care to go twice through the same experience. It went through all right, and I anticipate considerable pleasure from the company of the gentlemen with whom I am at last found worthy to associate. (*EC*, 86)

And, in fact, Chesnutt, according to his daughter's biography of him, did derive "considerable pleasure" from his association with the club:

> Chesnutt enjoyed these Saturday nights at the Rowfant Club. There he met, in delightful fellowship, some of the finest and most scholarly men of Cleveland. . . .

When his turn came to contribute to the Saturday night programs he was delighted, and spent a great deal of time in research and in writing. His first paper entitled "Who and Why was Samuel Johnson" was read in November, 1911. (H. Chesnutt, 289)

Chesnutt remained a member through the end of his life in 1932. He also contributed to several more "Saturday night programs," discussing such figures as François Villon, Alexander Dumas, and George Meredith. In short, the Rowfant Club apparently suited him and he suited it.

Ultimately, his relationship to the members of the club and their ideals—as laid out in the witty terms of this story—remains, like Chesnutt himself, enigmatic. For, despite his sardonic jibes at those who value a book's trappings more highly than its contents, he had a few surprising tendencies in that direction of his own. He shared, after all, the passion he satirically attributes to them: Chesnutt too proved a considerable bibliophile, both before and after the publication of "Baxter's *Procrustes*." Houghton, Mifflin published, for example, his first collection of short stories in both a trade edition and a special limited large-paper edition, and his daughter confirms the extent to which her father prized the latter:

> The people of Cleveland were so interested [in the publication of *The Conjure Woman*] that some of the members of the Rowfant Club suggested to Houghton, Mifflin and Company that they issue a special limited Large-Paper Edition of the book. Subscription forms were sent out, and the subscriptions justified the issue of a Large-Paper Edition of one hundred and fifty numbered copies at the same time as the trade edition was issued. This Large-Paper Edition was printed on hand-made linen paper, and bound in linen-colored buckram. . . . Later on when Chesnutt became a member of the Rowfant Club, he had his author's copy of the Large-Paper Edition rebound in blue morocco with hand-tooled designs at the Rowfant bindery; this volume remains a family treasure. (106)

The language of this passage—the book has "hand-made linen paper" and "hand-tooled designs," for example—is strikingly similar to the terms that the narrator of "Baxter's *Procrustes*" uses in outlining the standards by which the club measures the value of books.

Clearly, the members of the Rowfant Club did not hold a grudge against Chesnutt and the "gentle fun" (H. Chesnutt, 208) he made of them, for the club reissued the story as—of all things—a rare book in 1966. According to John B. Nicholson Jr., the editor of the 1966 *Baxter's Procrustes* as a book, Chesnutt delivers "a soft-spoken ribbing of all whose hearts belong more to the physical world of rare tomes than to their spiritual and intellectual contents" (39).[2] Nicholson concludes his essay by claiming that

> the man whose imagination brought this satirical story to life stands behind its printed pages, not as a man of any business or profession, not as a man of some particular race, not even as a man of any faith, but simply as a free creative mind sensing the foolishness of man prejudging man, and reacting with a kindly humorous wisdom to the nonsense in all men. (39)

Nicholson is right, I think, about the "kindly humorous wisdom" of this story, and his introductory essay to the book acknowledges, with grace and good humor, Chesnutt's gentle mocking of bibliophiles, himself included.[3]

But despite the fact that the story seems incongruous in his career, Chesnutt does depict the North (not to mention Cleveland) in "Baxter's *Procrustes*." That he—as a black man living in Cleveland at the turn of the century—felt confident enough to describe the inner workings of an exclusive (and only recently integrated) club speaks to the extent to which the racial and social milieu of the North was evolving. In a 1916 letter to E. J. Lilly, Chesnutt waxes philosophical about Cleveland and the Rowfant:

> I am a member of the Chamber of Commerce, . . . and also of the very exclusive Rowfant Club which belongs among the Clubs, membership in which is noted in *Who's Who in America*. . . . It is needless to say that it is not wealth or blood or birth that makes me acceptable in such company. . . . Indeed in this liberal and progressive Northern city we get most of the things which make life worth living. . . . In the North, race prejudice is rather a personal than a community matter, and a man is not regarded as striking at the foundations of society if he sees fit to extend a social courtesy to a person of color. (*EC*, 127)

While "Baxter's *Procrustes*" might not seem to depict Cleveland as "this liberal and progressive Northern city"—focusing as it does on an elaborately literary practical joke—the story nevertheless refracts Chesnutt's experience with the Rowfant Club into telling social commentary. For, despite the work's ironies, it also traces—albeit in comically fictionalized terms—the ways in which the North was coming to terms with its new identity at the beginning of a new century.

NOTES

1. See, for example, Andrews, who praises Chesnutt's use of multilayered satire in the story to poke fun at book collectors, turn-of-the-century critics, and, perhaps, his own readers. Render similarly praises the story, calling it evidence of his "mastery of the short-story form" (42).

2 See Nicholson's essay for more on his delighted reaction to the satire Chesnutt directs at bibliophiles and his fellow "Rowfanters": "No group of men gathered together under so happy an ordering of bookish pleasure could fail to enjoy exposure of the many-faceted idiosyncracies of their bibliolatrous fellows. Bookmen have for centuries enjoyed literary exposures of their collective weaknesses. . . . Its exposé of Rowfanters is sly but urbane, incisively pricking their precious conceits" (39).

3. Throughout his writing career, Chesnutt very often seems to mock himself, infusing his stories with characters whose biographies match his own and then deflating them. In "Uncle Wellington's Wives," for example, he satirizes the business practices of a lawyer who, in several ways, seems a proxy for himself. And, in several other works—such as "The March of Progress," "A Matter of Principle," and "The Wife of His Youth," among others—he comically punctures the pretensions of characters who seem very much like him.

Baxter's *Procrustes*

BAXTER'S PROCRUSTES IS ONE of the publications of the Bodleian Club. The Bodleian Club is composed of gentlemen of culture, who are interested in books and book collecting. It was named, very obviously, after the famous library of the same name, and not only became in our city a sort of shrine for local worshipers of fine bindings and rare editions, but was visited occasionally by pilgrims from afar. The Bodleian has entertained Mark Twain, Joseph Jefferson, and other literary and histrionic celebrities. It possesses quite a collection of personal mementos of distinguished authors, among them a paperweight which once belonged to Goethe, a lead pencil used by Emerson, an autograph letter of Matthew Arnold, and a chip from a tree felled by Mr. Gladstone. Its library contains a number of rare books, including a fine collection on chess, of which game several of the members are enthusiastic devotees.

The activities of the club are not, however, confined entirely of books. We have a very handsome clubhouse, and much taste and discrimination have been exercised in its adornment. There are many good paintings, including portraits of the various presidents of the club, which adorn the entrance hall. After books, perhaps the most distinctive feature of the club is our collection of pipes. In a large rack in the smoking-room—really a superfluity, since smoking is permitted all over the house—is as complete an assortment of pipes as perhaps exists in the civilized world. Indeed, it is an unwritten rule of the club that no one is eligible for membership who cannot produce a new variety of pipe, which is filed with his application for membership, and, if he passes, deposited with the club collection, he, however, retaining the title himself. Once a year, upon the anniversary of the death of Sir Walter Raleigh, who, it will be remembered, first introduced tobacco into England, the full membership of the club, as a rule, turns out. A large supply of the very best smoking mixture is laid in. At nine o'clock sharp each member takes his pipe from the rack, fills it with tobacco, and then the whole club, with the president at the head, all smoking furiously, march in solemn procession from room to room, upstairs and downstairs, making the tour of the clubhouse and returning to the smoking-room. The president then delivers an address, and each member is called upon to say something, either by way of a quotation or an original sentiment, in praise of the virtues of nicotine. This ceremony—facetiously known as "hitting the pipe"—being thus concluded, the membership pipes are carefully cleaned out and replaced in the club rack.

As I have said, however, the *raison d'être* of the club, and the feature upon which its fame chiefly rests, is its collection of rare books, and of these by far the most interesting are its own publications. Even its catalogues are works of art, published in numbered editions, and sought by libraries and book-collectors. Early in its history it began the occasional publication of books which should meet the club standard,—books in which emphasis should be laid upon the qualities that make a book valuable in the eyes of collectors. Of these, age could not, of course, be imparted, but in the matter of fine and curious bindings, of hand-made linen papers, of uncut or deckle edges, of wide margins and limited editions, the club could control its own publications. The matter of contents was, it must be confessed, a less important consideration. At first it was felt by the publishing committee that nothing but the finest products of the human mind should be selected for enrichment in the beautiful volumes which the club should issue. The length of the work was an important consideration,—long things were not compatible with wide margins and graceful slenderness. For instance, we brought out Coleridge's Ancient Mariner, an essay by Emerson, and another by

Thoreau. Our Rubáiyat of Omar Khayyám was Heron-Allen's translation of the original MS. in the Bodleian Library at Oxford, which, though less poetical than FitzGerald's, was not so common. Several years ago we began to publish the works of our own members. Bascom's Essay on Pipes was a very creditable performance. It was published in a limited edition of one hundred copies, and since it had not previously appeared elsewhere and was copyrighted by the club, it was sufficiently rare to be valuable for that reason. The second publication of local origin was Baxter's Procrustes.

I have omitted to say that once or twice a year, at a meeting of which notice has been given, an auction is held at the Bodleian. The members of the club send in their duplicate copies, or books they for any reason wish to dispose of, which are auctioned off to the highest bidder. At these sales, which are well attended, the club's publications have of recent years formed the leading feature. Three years ago, number three of Bascom's Essay on Pipes sold for fifteen dollars;—the original cost of publication was one dollar and seventy-five cents. Later in the evening an uncut copy of the same brought thirty dollars. At the next auction the price of the cut copy was run up to twenty-five dollars, while the uncut copy was knocked down at seventy-five dollars. The club had always appreciated the value of uncut copies, but this financial endorsement enhanced their desirability immensely. This rise in the Essay on Pipes was not without a sympathetic effect upon all the club publications. The Emerson essay rose from three dollars to seventeen, and the Thoreau, being by an author less widely read, and by his own confession commercially unsuccessful, brought a somewhat higher figure. The prices, thus inflated, were not permitted to come down appreciably. Since every member of the club possessed one or more of these valuable editions, they were all manifestly interested in keeping up the price. The publication, however, which brought the highest prices, and, but for the sober second thought, might have wrecked the whole system, was Baxter's Procrustes.

Baxter was, perhaps, the most scholarly member of the club. A graduate of Harvard, he had traveled extensively, had read widely, and while not so enthusiastic a collector as some of us, possessed as fine a private library as any man of his age in the city. He was about thirty-five when he joined the club, and apparently some bitter experience—some disappointment in love or ambition—had left its mark upon his character. With light, curly hair, fair complexion, and gray eyes, one would have expected Baxter to be genial of temper, with a tendency toward wordiness of speech. But though he had occasional flashes of humor, his ordinary demeanor was characterized by a mild cynicism, which, with his gloomy pessimistic philosophy, so foreign to the temperament that should accompany his physical type, could only be accounted for upon the hypothesis of some secret sorrow such as I have suggested. What it might be no one knew. He had means and social position, and was an uncommonly handsome man. The fact that he remained unmarried at thirty-five furnished some support for the theory of a disappointment in love, though this the several intimates of Baxter who belonged to the club were not able to verify.

It had occurred to me, in a vague way, that perhaps Baxter might be an unsuccessful author. That he was a poet we knew very well, and typewritten copies of his verses had occasionally circulated among us. But Baxter had always expressed such a profound contempt for modern literature, had always spoken in terms of such unmeasured pity for the slaves of the pen, who were dependent upon the whim of an undiscriminating public for recognition and a livelihood, that no one of us had ever suspected him of aspirations toward publication, until, as I have said, it occurred to me one day that Baxter's attitude with regard to publication might be viewed in the light of effect as well as of cause,—that his scorn of publicity might as easily arise from failure to achieve it, as his never having published might be due to his preconceived disdain of the vulgar popularity which one must share with the pugilist or balloonist of the hour.

The notion of publishing Baxter's Procrustes did not emanate from Baxter,—I must do him the justice to say this. But he had spoken to several of the fellows about the theme of his poem, until the notion that Baxter was at work upon something fine had become pretty well disseminated throughout our membership. He would occasionally read brief passages to a small coterie of friends in the sitting-room or library,—never more than ten lines at once, or to more than five people at a time,—and these excerpts gave at least a few of us a pretty fair idea of the motive and scope of the poem. As I, for one, gathered, it was quite along the line of Baxter's philosophy. Society was the Procrustes which, like the Greek bandit of old, caught every man born into the world, and endeavored to fit him to some preconceived standard, generally to the one for which he was least adapted. The world was full of men and women who were merely square pegs in round holes, and *vice versa*. Most marriages were unhappy because the contracting parties were not properly mated. Religion was mostly superstition, science for the most part sciolism, popular education merely a means of forcing the stupid and repressing the bright, so that all the youth of the rising generation might conform to the same dull, dead level of democratic mediocrity. Life would soon become so monotonously uniform and so uniformly monotonous as to be scarce worth the living.

It was Smith, I think, who first proposed that the club publish Baxter's Procrustes. The poet himself did not seem enthusiastic when the subject was broached; he demurred for some little time, protesting that the poem was not worthy of publication. But when it was proposed that the edition be limited to fifty copies he agreed to consider the proposition. When I suggested, having in mind my secret theory of Baxter's failure in authorship, that the edition would at least be in the hands of friends, that it would be difficult for a hostile critic to secure a copy, and that if it should not achieve success from a literary point of view, the extent of the failure would be limited to the size of the edition, Baxter was visibly impressed. When the literary committee at length decided to request formally of Baxter the privilege of publishing his Procrustes, he consented, with evident reluctance, upon condition that he should supervise the printing, binding, and delivery of the books, merely submitting to the committee, in advance, the manuscript, and taking their views in regard to the bookmaking.

The manuscript was duly presented to the literary committee. Baxter having expressed the desire that the poem be not read aloud at a meeting of the club, as was the custom, since he wished it to be given to the world clad in suitable garb, the committee went even farther. Having entire confidence in Baxter's taste and scholarship, they, with great delicacy, refrained from even reading the manuscript, contenting themselves with Baxter's statement of the general theme and the topics grouped under it. The details of the bookmaking, however, were gone into thoroughly. The paper was to be of hand-made linen, from the Kelmscott Mills; the type black-letter, with rubricated initials. The cover, which was Baxter's own selection, was to be of dark green morocco, with a cap-and-bells border in red inlays, and doublures of maroon morocco with a blind-tooled design. Baxter was authorized to contract with the printer and superintend the publication. The whole edition of fifty numbered copies was to be disposed of at auction, in advance, to the highest bidder, only one copy to each, the proceeds to be devoted to paying for the printing and binding, the remainder, if any, to go into the club treasury, and Baxter himself to receive one copy by way of remuneration. Baxter was inclined to protest at this, on the ground that his copy would probably be worth more than the royalties on the edition, at the usual ten per cent, would amount to, but was finally prevailed upon to accept an author's copy.

While the Procrustes was under consideration, some one read, at one of our meetings, a note from some magazine, which stated that a sealed copy of a new translation of Campanella's Sonnets, published by the Grolier Club, had been sold for three hundred dollars. This impressed the members greatly. It was a novel idea. A new work might thus be enshrined in a sort of holy of holies, which, if the collector so desired, could be forever sacred from the profanation of any vulgar or unappreciative eye. The possessor of such a treasure could enjoy it by the eye of imagination, having at the same time the exaltation of grasping what was for others the unattainable. The literary committee were so impressed with this idea that they presented it to Baxter in regard to the Procrustes. Baxter making no objection, the subscribers who might wish their copies delivered sealed were directed to notify the author. I sent in my name. A fine book, after all, was an investment, and if there was any way of enhancing its rarity, and therefore its value, I was quite willing to enjoy such an advantage.

When the Procrustes was ready for distribution, each subscriber received his copy by mail, in a neat pasteboard box. Each number was wrapped in a thin and transparent but very strong paper, through which the cover design and tooling were clearly visible. The number of the copy was indorsed upon the wrapper, the folds of which were securely fastened at each end with sealing-wax, upon which was impressed, as a guarantee of its inviolateness, the monogram of the club.

At the next meeting of the Bodleian a great deal was said about the Procrustes, and it was unanimously agreed that no finer specimen of bookmaking had ever been published by the club. By a curious coincidence, no one had brought his copy with him, and the two club copies had not yet been received from the binder, who, Baxter had reported, was retaining them for some extra fine work. Upon resolution, offered by a member who had not subscribed for the volume, a committee of three was appointed to review the Procrustes at the next literary meeting of the club. Of this committee it was my doubtful fortune to constitute one.

In pursuance of my duty in the premises, it of course became necessary for me to read the Procrustes. In all probability I should have cut my own copy for this purpose, had not one of the club auctions intervened between my appointment and the date set for the discussion of the Procrustes. At this meeting a copy of the book, still sealed, was offered for sale, and bought by a non-subscriber for the unprecedented price of one hundred and fifty dollars. After this a proper regard for my own interests would not permit me to spoil my copy by opening it, and I was therefore compelled to procure my information concerning the poem from some other source. As I had no desire to appear mercenary, I said nothing about my own copy, and made no attempt to borrow. I did, however, casually remark to Baxter that I should like to look at his copy of the proof sheets, since I wished to make some extended quotations for my review, and would rather not trust my copy to a typist for that purpose. Baxter assured me, with every evidence of regret, that he had considered them of so little importance that he had thrown them into the fire. This indifference of Baxter to literary values struck me as just a little overdone. The proof sheets of Hamlet, corrected in Shakespeare's own hand, would be well-nigh priceless.

At the next meeting of the club, I observed that Thompson and Davis, who were with me on the reviewing committee, very soon brought up the question of the Procrustes in conversation in the smoking-room, and seemed anxious to get from the members their views concerning Baxter's production, I supposed upon the theory that the appreciation of any book review would depend more or less upon the degree to which it reflected the opinion of those to whom the review should be presented. I presumed, of course, that Thompson and Davis had each read the book,—they were among the subscribers,— and I was desirous of getting their point of view.

"What do you think," I inquired, "of the passage on Social Systems?" I have forgotten to say that the poem was in blank verse, and divided into parts, each with an appropriate title.

"Well," replied Davis, it seemed to me a little cautiously, "it is not exactly Spencerian, although it squints at the Spencerian view, with a slight deflection toward Hegelianism. I should consider it an harmonious fusion of the best views of all the modern philosophers, with a strong Baxterian flavor."

"Yes," said Thompson, "the charm of the chapter lies in this very quality. The style is an emanation from Baxter's own intellect,—he has written himself into the poem. By knowing Baxter we are able to appreciate the book, and after having read the book we feel that we are so much the more intimately acquainted with Baxter,—the real Baxter."

Baxter had come in during this colloquy, and was standing by the fireplace smoking a pipe. I was not exactly sure whether the faint smile which marked his face was a token of pleasure or cynicism; it was Baxterian, however, and I had already learned that Baxter's opinions upon any subject were not to be gathered always from his facial expression. For instance, when the club porter's crippled child died, Baxter remarked, it seemed to me unfeelingly, that the poor little devil was doubtless better off, and that the porter himself had certainly been relieved of a burden; and only a week later the porter told me in confidence that Baxter had paid for an expensive operation, undertaken in the hope of prolonging the child's life. I therefore drew no conclusion from Baxter's somewhat enigmatical smile. He left the room at this point in the conversation, somewhat to my relief.

"By the way, Jones," said Davis, addressing me, "are you impressed by Baxter's views on Degeneration?"

Having often heard Baxter express himself upon the general downward tendency of modern civilization, I felt safe in discussing his views in a broad and general manner.

"I think," I replied, "that they are in harmony with those of Schopenhauer, without his bitterness; with those of Nordau, without his flippancy. His materialism is Haeckel's, presented with something of the charm of Omar Khayyám."

"Yes," chimed in Davis, "it answers the strenuous demand of our day,—dissatisfaction with an unjustified optimism,—and voices for us the courage of human philosophy facing the unknown."

I had a vague recollection of having read something like this somewhere, but so much has been written, that one can scarcely discuss any subject of importance without unconsciously borrowing, now and then, the thoughts or the language of others. Quotation, like imitation, is a superior grade of flattery.

"The Procrustes," said Thompson, to whom the metrical review had been apportioned, "is couched in sonorous lines, of haunting melody and charm; and yet so closely inter-related as to be scarcely quotable with justice to the author. To be appreciated the poem should be read as a whole,— I shall say as much in my review. What shall you say of the letter-press?" he concluded, addressing me. I was supposed to discuss the technical excellence of the volume from the connoisseur's viewpoint.

"The setting," I replied judicially, "is worthy of the gem. The dark green cover, elaborately tooled, the old English lettering, the heavy linen paper, mark this as one of our very choicest publications. The letter-press is of course De Vinne's best,—there is nothing better on this side of the Atlantic. The text is a beautiful, slender stream, meandering gracefully through a wide meadow of margin."

For some reason I left the room for a minute. As I stepped into the hall, I almost ran into Baxter, who was standing near the door, facing a hunting print of a somewhat humorous character, hung upon the wall, and smiling with an immensely pleased expression.

"What a ridiculous scene!" he remarked. "Look at that fat old squire on that tall hunter! I'll wager dollars to doughnuts that he won't get over the first fence!"

It was a very good bluff, but did not deceive me. Under his mask of unconcern, Baxter was anxious to learn what we thought of his poem, and had stationed himself in the hall that he might overhear our discussion without embarrassing us by his presence. He had covered up his delight at our appreciation by this simulated interest in the hunting print.

When the night came for the review of the Procrustes there was a large attendance of members, and several visitors, among them a young English cousin of one of the members, on his first visit to the United States; some of us had met him at other clubs, and in society, and had found him a very jolly boy, with a youthful exuberance of spirits and a naïve ignorance of things American, that made his views refreshing and, at times, amusing.

The critical essays were well considered, if a trifle vague. Baxter received credit for poetic skill of a high order.

"Our brother Baxter," said Thompson, "should no longer bury his talent in a napkin. This gem, of course, belongs to the club, but the same brain from which issued this exquisite emanation can produce others to inspire and charm an appreciative world."

"The author's view of life," said Davis, "as expressed in these beautiful lines, will help us to fit our shoulders for the heavy burden of life, by bringing to our realization those profound truths of philosophy which find hope in despair and pleasure in pain. When he shall see fit to give to the wider world, in fuller form, the thoughts of which we have been vouchsafed this foretaste, let us hope that some little ray of his fame may rest upon the Bodleian, from which can never be taken away the proud privilege of saying that he was one of its members."

I then pointed out the beauties of the volume as a piece of bookmaking. I knew, from conversation with the publication committee, the style of type and rubrication, and could see the cover through the wrapper of my sealed copy. The dark green morocco, I said, in summing up, typified the author's serious view of life, as a thing to be endured as patiently as might be. The cap-and-bells border was significant of the shams by which the optimist sought to delude himself into the view that life was a desirable thing. The intricate blind-tooling of the doublure shadowed forth the blind fate which left us in ignorance of our future and our past, or of even what the day itself might bring forth. The black-letter type, with rubricated initials, signified a philosophic pessimism enlightened by the conviction that in duty one might find, after all, an excuse for life and a hope for humanity. Applying this test to the club, this work, which might be said to represent all that the Bodleian stood for, was in itself sufficient to justify the club's existence. If the Bodleian had done nothing else, if it should do nothing more, it had produced a masterpiece.

There was a sealed copy of the Procrustes, belonging, I believe, to one of the committee, lying on the table by which I stood, and I had picked it up and held it in my hand for a moment, to emphasize one of my periods, but had laid it down immediately. I noted, as I sat down, that young Hunkin, our English visitor, who sat on the other side of the table, had picked up the volume and was examining it with interest. When the last review was read, and the generous applause had subsided, there were cries for Baxter.

"Baxter! Baxter! Author! Author!"

Baxter had been sitting over in a corner during the reading of the reviews, and had succeeded remarkably well, it seemed to me, in concealing, under his mask of cynical indifference, the exultation which I was sure he must feel. But this outburst of enthusiasm was too much even for Baxter, and it was clear that he was struggling with strong emotion when he rose to speak.

"Gentlemen, and fellow members of the Bodleian, it gives me unaffected pleasure—sincere pleasure—some day you may know how much pleasure—I cannot trust myself to say it now—to see the evident care with which your committee have read my poor verses, and the responsive sympathy with which my friends have entered into my views of life and conduct. I thank you again, and again, and when I say that I am too full for utterance,— I'm sure you will excuse me from saying any more."

Baxter took his seat, and the applause had begun again when it was broken by a sudden explanation.

"By Jove!" exclaimed our English visitor, who still sat behind the table, "what an extraordinary book!"

Every one gathered around him.

"You see," he exclaimed, holding up the volume, "you fellows said so much about the bally book that I wanted to see what it was like; so I untied the ribbon. And cut the leaves with the paper knife lying here, and found— and found that there wasn't a single line in it, don't you know!"

Blank consternation followed this announcement, which proved only too true. Every one knew instinctively, without further investigation, that the club had been badly sold. In the resulting confusion Baxter escaped, but later was waited upon by a committee, to whom he made the rather lame excuse that he had always regarded uncut and sealed books as tommy-rot, and that he had merely been curious to see how far the thing could go; and that the result had justified his belief that a book with nothing in it was just as useful to a book-collector as one embodying a work of genius. He offered to pay all the bills for the sham Procrustes, or to replace the blank copies with the real thing, as we might choose. Of course, after such an insult, the club did not care for the poem. He was permitted to pay the expense, however, and it was more that hinted to him that his resignation from the club would be favorably acted upon. He never sent it in, and, as he went to Europe shortly afterwards, the affair had time to blow over.

In our first disgust at Baxter's duplicity, most of us cut our copies of the Procrustes, some of us mailed them to Baxter with cutting notes, and others threw them into the fire. A few wiser spirits held on to theirs, and this fact leaking out, it began to dawn upon the minds of the real collectors among us that the volume was something unique in the way of a publication.

"Baxter," said our president one evening to a select few of us who sat around the fireplace, "was wiser than we knew, or than he perhaps appreciated. His Procrustes, from the collector's point of view, is entirely logical, and might be considered as the acme of bookmaking. To the true collector, a book is a work of art, of which the contents are no more important than the words of an opera. Fine binding is a desideratum, and, for its cost, that of the Procrustes could not be improved upon. The paper is above criticism. The true collector loves wide margins, and the Procrustes, being all margin, merely touches the vanishing point of the perspective. The smaller the edition, the greater the collector's eagerness to acquire a copy. There are but six uncut copies left, I am told, of the Procrustes, and three sealed copies, one of which I am the fortunate possessor."

After this deliverance, it is not surprising that, at our next auction, a sealed copy of Baxter's Procrustes was knocked down, after spirited bidding, for two hundred and fifty dollars, the highest price ever brought by a single volume published by the club.

The Doll

The Crisis (1912)

As an African American who came to adulthood in the post–Civil War North, Chesnutt had an obvious interest in— even a preoccupation with—the intersections of race and culture. For all his emphasis on racialized subjects, however, his fiction, especially his short fiction, very rarely relies on stereotypical characters or stock situations; his works, that is, are almost never fictionalized discussions of some arcane "Idea." Instead, Chesnutt recognizes and subtly explores race as a subject that both shapes and is shaped by a rich variety of social, cultural, and personal contexts. Consider "The Doll," for example, a story published in W.E.B. Du Bois's *The Crisis* in 1912. In it, an African American businessman's chance encounter with his father's murderer, several years after the fact, compels him to choose between revenge and his responsibilities as a father, a black businessman, and a model black citizen.

Published more than a decade after Chesnutt dejectedly realized his writing career could not sustain him and his own family, "The Doll" depicts the attempts of a successful black barber, Tom Taylor, to reconcile his keen desire for vengeance with a constellation of responsibilities: to his daughter, to his employees, and indeed to his race. When the murderer—Colonel Forsyth, now a Southern politician—comes to Taylor's barbershop one day and narrates his crime in excruciating detail while being shaved by Taylor, the reader might recall Melville's "Benito Cereno," another story in which a white figure takes a close shave from a justifiably angry black barber. Here, as Taylor holds the razor and looks down upon his father's murderer's upturned throat, he undergoes a series of violent reflections:

> under his keen razor lay the neck of his enemy, the enemy, too, of his race sworn to degrade them, to teach them, if

need be, with the torch and with the gun, that their place was at the white man's feet, his heel upon their neck; who held them in such contempt that he could speak as he had spoken in the presence of one of them. One stroke of the keen blade, a deflection of half an inch in its course, and a murder would be avenged, an enemy destroyed! . . . A few strokes more and the colonel could be released with a close shave—how close he would never know!—or, one stroke, properly directed, and he would never stand erect again! (207–8)

In terms of the plot, then, the story comes down to the barber's choice: should he take this opportunity to avenge his father or not?

As a self-made, substantially successful businessman[1] and largely self-taught writer and intellectual, Chesnutt had a deep psychological investment in the notion of an America that would support individuals who strove to make better lives for themselves, regardless of race. His "Ohio" or Northern fictions repeatedly make clear that investment: Grandison's skill in constructing "freedom" for himself; Mr. Ryder's ability to reconcile, at least partially, his past in the South with his future in the North; even Hal Skinner's capacity for redefining himself in "The Shadow of My Past." In "The Doll," Chesnutt places that impulse in the foreground again, this time in the form of a black businessman, Tom Taylor, who owns and operates "the handsomest barber shop in the city" (204). Like several of Chesnutt's other "Ohio" protagonists, Taylor has *made* himself: "Committed by circumstances to a career of personal service, he had lifted it by intelligence, tact and industry to the dignity of a successful business" (204). Once more, Chesnutt focuses on the life of a hardworking, industrious African American, one who has created a place for himself and his family by working in the North. Taylor, that is, has become a part of the social and business fabric of the (relatively) integrated North.

"The Doll" shares many similarities with Chesnutt's other Northern writings, but it has some fascinating differences as well. Like many of his other fictions—including "The Wife of His Youth," "Her Virginia Mammy," and "A Matter of Principle," to name only three—this story focuses on the ways in which African American families struggle to preserve or, just as often, to remake themselves in the tumultuous United States in the early years of the twentieth century. In those works, the characters must work to protect or put back together families splintered by war, slavery, and, paradoxically, Reconstruction. As a study of an African American family in the post-Reconstruction North, "The Doll" explores one emotionally charged day in the life of a successful black man whose life and business (on which depend the lives of many others) are threatened—as so often in Chesnutt's works—by the persistent echoes of a racialized past. The protagonist of the story, who grew up in the antebellum South, is confronted by a walking, talking reminder of the violent, unjust world of his youth.

But "The Doll" differs from "The Wife of His Youth," "Her Virginia Mammy," and "A Matter of Principle" in significant ways, too. While those stories focus on relatively private social matters—courtships and other highly personal social navigations—"The Doll" emphasizes, both dramatically and subtly, the public interactions of a new class of African American: the business professional. For, although Taylor's dilemma seems ultimately to force him to choose between vengeance for the murder of his father and his own fatherly duties, Chesnutt relentlessly reminds the reader that Taylor has other responsibilities as well. As he contemplates whether to kill his father's murderer, the barber comes to several realizations that temporarily stay his hand:

> The barber's glance toward the door, from force of habit, took in [his] whole shop. It was a handsome shop, and had been to the barber a matter of more than merely personal pride. Prominent among a struggling people, as yet scarcely beyond the threshold of citizenship, he had long been looked upon, and had become accustomed to regard himself, as a representative man, by whose failure or success his race would be tested. Should he slay this man now beneath his hand, this beautiful shop would be lost to his people . . . but he knew full well that should he lose the shop no colored man would succeed him; a center of industry, a medium of friendly contact with white men, would be lost to his people. (209)

Despite the obvious appeal of revenge, such a course, the barber realizes, would have far broader consequences than his own fate, and it is telling that Chesnutt chooses to depict those consequences in terms of a business ethos. The shop provides meaningful contact for the races, but a contact that is filtered through an economic prism. Indeed, this story seems to affirm, at least in part, Booker T. Washington's advocacy for the advancement of African Americans by gradual degrees, by embracing manual labor and vocational education as the means by which to gain access to the American economic system.[2]

In fact, Chesnutt's depiction of Tom Taylor's situation in "The Doll" relies on a familiar pattern in his Northern writings, most of which make pervasive references to the social and economic milieu of African Americans at the turn of the century. In this story, Taylor's ruminations about the loss of friendly "contact" merely touch the surface of the responsibilities he has toward his race. Still holding his razor above the throat of his father's murderer, Taylor ponders a second compelling reason not to take his personal revenge:

> Of the ten barbers in the shop all but one were married, with families dependent upon them for support. One was sending a son to college; another was buying a home. The unmarried one was in his spare hours studying a profession, with the hope of returning to practice it among his people in a Southern state. Their fates were all, in a measure, dependent upon the proprietor of the shop. (209)

In addition to providing the barber with one more reason not to kill his customer, this scene emphatically depicts subject matter utterly unfamiliar to white readers of the early twentieth century. For here, Chesnutt takes pains to disclose the specific ways in which African Americans—many of them, like the barber, only a generation away from slavery—were enacting the freedoms conferred upon them by the Thirteenth and Fourteenth Amendments. And it's important to recognize how, for Chesnutt, the exercise of those freedoms derives explicitly from economic options. Taylor's fellow barbers, that is, perform precisely the rights American citizens had already long taken for granted: to invest in housing; to send their children to college (as Chesnutt did, for his son and his two daughters); to study a profession, the mastery of which will presumably lead to even more social freedoms.

Ultimately, of course, the most compelling reason for Taylor to limit his razor to its officially approved business is the fate of his daughter, and it is the sight of her doll that forces him to make his decision. Although Taylor cannot avenge his father's murder or even verbally confront the murderer, Chesnutt nevertheless makes clear that he comes to his conclusion by reasoning based on his current situation as a black businessman and father. Thus, Taylor's inaction—which the colonel, typically, misreads as confirmation of his race "theory"—actually constitutes a statement on behalf on African Americans living in the North at the beginning of the twentieth century: a commitment to live in the present and for the future. Taylor, that is, escapes (although in psychologically painful fashion) the clutches of the past in choosing to remain in business and at home. In that way, at least, "The Doll" provides a compellingly optimistic (if not altogether "happy") view of black Northerners adapting to their surroundings.

Writing in their introduction to one volume of Chesnutt's letters, Jesse S. Crisler, Robert C. Leitz III, and Joseph R. McElrath Jr. call attention to Chesnutt's depictions of "upwardly mobile black entrepreneurs heeding the advice given by Booker T. Washington for advancement" (xxvii). Although they do not cite "The Doll," that story nevertheless serves as a striking example of precisely that impulse in Chesnutt. For, while the story putatively examines a civilized man's courageous resistance to the temptation of violent revenge, "The Doll" does much more than that: it provides a blueprint for African Americans living and doing business in the New North.

NOTES

1. Chesnutt often pointed out the disparity between his disappointing earnings as a writer and his business success. In an 1891 letter to George Washington Cable, for example, he writes, "My business for the past year has been very absorbing, and has netted me a handsome income. I stand at the parting of two ways: by strict attention to business, and its natural development, I see a speedy competence and possible wealth before me. On the other hand, I see probably a comfortable living and such compensations as the literary life has to offer" (*To Be an Author*, 72).

2. "The Doll" is an interesting work in this regard, because generally Chesnutt had serious disagreements with Washington's well-known emphasis on manual labor and vocational education. See, for example, the several letters that pass between the two of them, as collected in *To Be an Author: Letters of Charles W. Chesnutt, 1889–1905*.

The Doll

WHEN TOM TAYLOR, PROPRIETOR of the Wyandot Hotel barber shop, was leaving home, after his noonday luncheon, to return to his work, his daughter, a sprightly diminutive brown maid, with very bright black eyes and very curly, black hair, thrust into his coat pocket a little jointed doll somewhat the worse for wear.

"Now, don't forget, papa," she said, in her shrill childish treble, "what's to be done to her. Her arms won't work, and her legs won't work, and she can't hold her head up. Be sure and have her mended this afternoon, and bring her home when you come to supper; for she's afraid of the dark, and always sleeps with me. I'll meet you at the corner at half-past six—and don't forget, whatever you do."

"No, Daisy, I'll not forget," he replied, as he lifted her to the level of his lips and kissed her.

Upon reaching the shop he removed the doll from his pocket and hung it on one of the gilded spikes projecting above the wire netting surrounding the cashier's desk, where it would catch his eye. Some time during the afternoon he would send it to a toy shop around the corner for repairs. But the day was a busy one, and when the afternoon was well advanced he had not yet attended to it.

Colonel Forsyth had come up from the South to attend a conference of Democratic leaders to consider presidential candidates and platforms. He had put up at the Wyandot Hotel, but had been mainly in the hands of Judge Beeman, chairman of the local Jackson club, who was charged with the duty of seeing that the colonel was made comfortable and given the freedom of the city. It was after a committee meeting, and about 4 in the afternoon, that the two together entered the lobby of the Wyandot. They were discussing the platforms to be put forward by the two great parties in the approaching campaign.

"I reckon, judge," the colonel was saying, "that the Republican party will make a mistake if it injects the Negro question into its platform. The question is primarily a local one, and if the North will only be considerate about the matter, and let us alone, we can settle it to our entire satisfaction. The Negro's place is defined by nature, and in the South he knows it and gives us no trouble."

"The Northern Negroes are different," returned the judge.

"They are just the same," rejoined the colonel. "It is you who are different. You pamper them and they take liberties with you. But they are all from the South, and when they meet a Southerner they act accordingly. They are born to serve and to submit. If they had been worthy of equality they would never have endured slavery. They have no proper self-respect; they will neither resent an insult, nor defend a right, nor avenge a wrong."

"Well, now, colonel, aren't you rather hard on them? Consider their past."

"Hard? Why, no, bless your heart! I've got nothing against the nigger. I like him—in his place. But what I say is the truth. Are you in a hurry?"

"Not at all."

"Then come downstairs to the barber shop and I'll prove what I say."

The shop was the handsomest barber shop in the city. It was in the basement, and the paneled ceiling glowed with electric lights. The floor was of white tile, the walls lined with large mirrors. Behind ten chairs, of the latest and most comfortable design, stood as many colored barbers, in immaculate white jackets, each at work upon a white patron. An air of discipline and good order pervaded the establishment. There was no loud talking by patrons, no unseemly garrulity on the part of the barbers. It was very obviously a well-conducted barber shop, frequented by gentlemen who could afford to pay liberally for superior service. As the judge and the colonel entered a customer vacated the chair served by the proprietor.

"Next gentleman," said the barber.

The colonel removed his collar and took his seat in the vacant chair, remarking, as he ran his hand over his neck, "I want a close shave, barber."

"Yes, sir; a close shave."

The barber was apparently about forty, with a brown complexion, clean-cut features and curly hair. Committed by circumstances to a career of personal service, he had lifted it by intelligence, tact and industry to the dignity of a successful business. The judge, a regular patron of the shop, knew him well and had often, while in his chair, conversed with him concerning his race—a fruitful theme, much on the public tongue.

"As I was saying," said the colonel, while the barber adjusted a towel about his neck, "the Negro question is a perfectly simple one."

The judge thought it hardly good taste in the colonel to continue in his former strain. Northern men might speak slightingly of the Negro, but seldom in his presence. He tried a little diversion.

"The tariff," he observed, "is a difficult problem."

"Much more complicated, suh, than the Negro problem, which is perfectly simple. Let the white man once impress the Negro with his superiority; let the Negro see that there is no escape from the inevitable, and that ends it. The best thing about the Negro is that, with all his limitations, he can recognize a finality. It is the secret of his persistence among us. He has acquired the faculty of evolution, suh—by the law of the survival of the fittest. Long ago, when a young man, I killed a nigger to teach him his place. One who learns a lesson of that sort certainly never offends again, nor fathers any others of his breed."

The barber, having lathered the colonel's face, was stropping his razor with long, steady strokes. Every word uttered by the colonel was perfectly audible to him, but his impassive countenance betrayed no interest. The colonel seemed as unconscious of the barber's presence as the barber of the colonel's utterance. Surely, thought the judge, if such freedom of speech were the rule in the South the colonel's contention must be correct, and the Negroes thoroughly cowed. To a Northern man the situation was hardly comfortable.

"The iron and sugar interests of the South," persisted the judge, "will resist any reduction of the tariff."

The colonel was not to be swerved from the subject, nor from his purpose, whatever it might be.

"Quite likely they will; and we must argue with them, for they are white men and amenable to reason. The nigger, on the other hand, is the creature of instinct; you cannot argue with him; you must order him, and if he resists shoot him, as I did.

"Don't forget, barber," said the colonel, "that I want a close shave."

"No, sir," responded the barber, who, having sharpened his razor, now began to pass it, with firm and even hand, over the colonel's cheek.

"It must have been," said the judge, "an aggravated case, to justify so extreme a step."

"Extreme, suh? I beg yo' pardon, suh, but I can't say I had regarded my conduct in that light. But it was an extreme case so far as the nigger was concerned. I am not boasting about my course; it was simply a disagreeable necessity. I am naturally a kind-hearted man, and don't like to kill even a fly. It was after the war, suh, and just as the reconstruction period was drawing to a close. My mother employed a Negro girl, the child of a former servant of hers, to wait upon her."

The barber was studying the colonel's face as the razor passed over his cheek. The colonel's eyes were closed, or he might have observed the sudden gleam of interest that broke through the barber's mask of self-effacement, like a flash of lightning from a clouded sky. Involuntarily the razor remained poised in midair, but, in less time than it takes to say it, was moving again, swiftly and smoothly, over the colonel's face. To shave a talking man required a high degree of skill, but they were both adepts, each in his own trade—the barber at shaving, the colonel at talking.

"The girl was guilty of some misconduct, and my mother reprimanded her and sent her home. She complained to her father, and he came to see my mother about it. He was insolent, offensive and threatening. I came into the room and ordered him to leave it. Instead of obeying, he turned on me in a rage, suh, and threatened me. I drew my revolver and shot him. The result was unfortunate; but he and his people learned a lesson. We had no further trouble with bumptious niggers in our town."

"And did you have no trouble in the matter?" asked the judge.

"None, suh, to speak of. There were proceedings, but they were the merest formality. Upon my statement, confirmed by that of my mother, I was discharged by the examining magistrate, and the case was never even reported to the grand jury. It was a clear case of self-defense."

The barber had heard the same story, with some details ignored or forgotten by the colonel. It was the barber's father who had died at the colonel's hand, and for many long years the son had dreamed of this meeting.

He remembered the story in this wise: His father had been a slave. Freed by the Civil War, he had entered upon the new life with the zeal and enthusiasm of his people at the dawn of liberty, which seem, in the light of later discouragements, so pathetic in the retrospect. The chattel aspired to own property; the slave, forbidden learning, to educate his children. He had worked early and late, had saved his money with a thrift equal to that of a German immigrant, and had sent his children regularly to school.

The girl—the barber remembered her very well—had been fair of feature, soft of speech and gentle of manner, a pearl among pebbles. One day her father's old mistress had met him on the street and, after a kindly inquiry about his family, had asked if she might hire his daughter during the summer, when there was no school. Her own married daughter would be visiting her, with a young child, and they wanted some neat and careful girl to nurse the infant.

"Why, yas ma'am," the barber's father had replied. "I reckon it might be a good thing fer Alice. I wants her ter be a teacher; but she kin l'arn things from you, ma'am, that no teacher kin teach her. She kin l'arn manners, ma'am, an' white folks' ways, and nowhere better than in yo' house."

So Alice had gone to the home of her father's former mistress to learn white folks' ways. The lady had been kind and gracious. But there are ways and ways among all people.

When she had been three weeks in her new employment her mistress's son—a younger brother of the colonel—came home from college. Some weeks later Alice went home to her father. Who was most at fault the barber never knew. A few hours afterward the father called upon the lady. There was a stormy interview. Things were said to which the ears of white ladies were unaccustomed from the lips of black men. The elder son had entered the room and interfered. The barber's father had turned to him and exclaimed angrily:

"Go 'way from here, boy, and don't talk ter me, or I'm liable ter harm you."

The young man stood his ground. The Negro advanced menacingly toward him. The young man drew his ready weapon and fatally wounded the Negro—he lived only long enough, after being taken home, to gasp out the facts to his wife and children.

The rest of the story had been much as the colonel had related it. As the barber recalled it, however, the lady had not been called to testify, but was ill at the time of the hearing, presumably from the nervous shock.

That she had secretly offered to help the family the barber knew, and that her help had been rejected with cold hostility. He knew that the murderer went unpunished, and that in later years he had gone into politics, and become the leader and mouthpiece of his party. All the world knew that he had ridden into power on his hostility to Negro rights.

The barber had been a mere boy at the time of his father's death, but not too young to appreciate the calamity that had befallen the household. The family was broken up. The sordid details of its misfortunes would not be interesting. Poverty, disease and death had followed them, until he alone was left. Many years had passed. The brown boy who had wept beside his father's bier, and who had never forgotten nor forgiven, was now the grave-faced, keen-eyed, deft-handed barber, who held a deadly weapon at the throat of his father's slayer.

How often he had longed for this hour! In his dreams he had killed this man a hundred times, in a dozen ways. Once, when a young man, he had gone to meet him, with the definite purpose of taking his life, but chance had kept them apart. He had imagined situations where they might come face to face; he would see the white man struggling in the water; he would have only to stretch forth his hand to save him; but he would tell him of his hatred and let him drown. He would see him in a burning house, from which he might rescue him; and he would call him murderer and let him burn! He would see him in the dock for murder of a white man, and only his testimony could save him, and he would let him suffer the fate that he doubly deserved! He saw a vision of his father's form, only an hour before thrilling with hope and energy, now stiff and cold in death; while under his keen razor lay the neck of his enemy, the enemy, too, of his race, sworn to degrade them, to teach them, if need be, with the torch and with the gun, that their place was at the white man's feet, his heel upon their neck; who held them in such contempt that he could speak as he had spoken in the presence of one of them. One stroke of the keen blade, a deflection of half an inch in its course, and a murder would be avenged, an enemy destroyed!

For the next sixty seconds the barber heard every beat of his own pulse, and the colonel, in serene unconsciousness, was nearer death than he had ever been in the course of a long and eventful life. He was only a militia colonel, and had never been under fire, but his turbulent political career had been passed in a community where life was lightly valued, where hot words were often followed by rash deeds, and murder was tolerated as a means of private vengeance and political advancement. He went on talking, but neither the judge nor the barber listened, each being absorbed in his own thoughts.

To the judge, who lived in a community where Negroes voted, the colonel's frankness was a curious revelation. His language was choice, though delivered with the Southern intonation, his tone easy and conversational, and, in addressing the barber directly, his manner had been courteous enough. The judge was interested, too, in watching the barber, who, it was evident, was repressing some powerful emotion. It seemed very probable to the judge that the barber might resent this cool recital of murder and outrage. He did not know what might be true of the Negroes in the South, but he had been judge of a police court in one period of his upward career, and he had found colored people prone to sudden rages, when under the influence of strong emotion, handy with edged tools, and apt to cut thick and deep, nor always careful about the color of the cuticle. The barber's feelings were plainly stirred, and the judge, a student of human nature, was curious to see if he would be moved to utterance. It would have been no novelty—patrons of the shop often discussed race questions with the barber. It was evident that the colonel was trying an experiment to demonstrate his contention in the lobby above. But the judge could not know the barber's intimate relation to the story, nor did it occur to him that the barber might conceive any deadly purpose because of a purely impersonal grievance. The barber's hand did not even tremble.

In the barber's mind, however, the whirlwind of emotions had passed lightly over the general and settled upon the particular injury. So strong, for the moment, was the homicidal impulse that it would have prevailed already had not the noisy opening of the door to admit a patron diverted the barber's attention and set in motion a current of ideas which fought for the colonel's life. The barber's glance toward the door, from force of habit, took in the whole shop. It was a handsome shop, and had been to the barber a matter of more than merely personal pride. Prominent among a struggling people, as yet scarcely beyond the threshold of citizenship, he had long been looked upon, and had become accustomed to regard himself, as a representative man, by whose failure or success his race would be tested. Should he slay this man now beneath his hand, this beautiful shop would be lost to his people. Years before the whole trade had been theirs. One by one the colored master barbers, trained in the slovenly old ways, had been forced to the wall by white competition, until his shop was one of the few good ones remaining in the hands of men of his race. Many an envious eye had been cast upon it. The lease had only a year to run. Strong pressure, he knew, had been exerted by a white rival to secure the reversion. The barber had the hotel proprietor's promise of a renewal; but he knew full well that should he lose the shop no colored man would succeed him; a center of industry, a medium of friendly contact with white men, would be lost to his people—many a good turn had the barber been able to do for them while he had the ear—literally had the ear—of some influential citizen, or held some aspirant for public office by the throat. Of the ten barbers in the shop all but one were married, with families dependent upon them for support. One was sending a son to college; another was buying a home. The unmarried one was in his spare hours studying a profession, with the hope of returning to practice it among his people in a Southern State. Their fates were all, in a measure, dependent upon the proprietor of the shop. Should he yield to the impulse which was swaying him their livelihood would be placed in jeopardy. For what white man, while the memory of this tragic event should last, would trust his throat again beneath a Negro's razor?

Such, however, was the strength of the impulse against which the barber was struggling that these considerations seemed likely not to prevail. Indeed, they had presented themselves to the barber's mind in a vague, remote, detached manner, while the dominant idea was present and compelling, clutching at his heart, drawing his arm, guiding his fingers. It was by their mass rather than by their clearness that these restraining forces held the barber's arm so long in check—it was society against self, civilization against the primitive instinct, typifying, more fully than the barber could realize, the great social problem involved in the future of his race.

He had now gone once over the colonel's face, subjecting that gentleman to less discomfort than he had for a long time endured while undergoing a similar operation. Already he had retouched one cheek and had turned the colonel's head to finish the other. A few strokes more and the colonel could be released with a close shave—how close he would never know!—or, one stroke, properly directed, and he would never stand erect again! Only the day before the barber had read, in the newspapers, the account of a ghastly lynching in a Southern State, where, to avenge a single provoked murder, eight Negroes had bit the dust and a woman had been burned at the stake for no other crime than that she was her husband's wife. One stroke and there would be one less of those who thus wantonly played with human life!

The uplifted hand had begun the deadly downward movement—when one of the barbers dropped a shaving cup, which was smashed to pieces on the marble floor. Fate surely fought for the colonel—or was it for the barber? Involuntarily the latter stayed his hand—instinctively his glance went toward the scene of the accident. It was returning to the upraised steel, and its uncompleted task, when it was arrested by Daisy's doll, hanging upon the gilded spike where he had left it.

If the razor went to its goal he would not be able to fulfil his promise to Daisy! She would wait for him at the corner, and wait in vain! If he killed the colonel he himself could hardly escape, for he was black and not white, and this was North and not South, and personal vengeance was not accepted by the courts as a justification for murder. Whether he died or not, he would be lost to Daisy. His wife was dead, and there would be no one to take care of Daisy. His own father had died in defense of his daughter; he must live to protect his own. If there was a righteous God, who divided the evil from the good, the colonel would some time get his just deserts. Vengeance was God's; it must be left to Him to repay!

The jointed doll had saved the colonel's life. Whether society had conquered self or not may be an open question, but it had stayed the barber's hand until love could triumph over hate!

The barber laid aside the razor, sponged off the colonel's face, brought him, with a movement of the chair, to a sitting posture, brushed his hair, pulled away the cloths from around his neck, handed him a pasteboard check for the amount of his bill, and stood rigidly by his chair. The colonel adjusted his collar, threw down a coin equal to double the amount of his bill and, without waiting for the change, turned with the judge to leave the shop. They had scarcely reached the door leading into the hotel lobby when the barber, overwrought by the long strain, collapsed heavily into the nearest chair.

"Well, judge," said the colonel, as they entered the lobby, "that was a good shave. What a sin it would be to spoil such a barber by making him a postmaster! I didn't say anything to him, for it don't do to praise a nigger much—it's likely to give him the big head—but I never had," he went on, running his hand appreciatively over his cheek, "I never had a better shave in my life. And I proved my theory. The barber is the son of the nigger I shot."

The judge was not sure that the colonel had proved his theory, and was less so after he had talked, a week later, with the barber. And, although the colonel remained at the Wyandot for several days, he did not get shaved again in the hotel barber shop.

Mr. Taylor's Funeral

The Crisis (1915)

Appearing in W.E.B. Du Bois's magazine *The Crisis* in two install-
ments (April and May) in 1915—and thus one of the last works of
fiction Chesnutt published in his lifetime—"Mr. Taylor's Funeral"
suggests that a man's identity and reputation remain fertile ground
for interpretation even after his "death." Featuring one of Chesnutt's most peculiar plots, the story seems at times almost farcical
in its treatment of how a man's presumed death leads his friends
and family to interpret his life in comically divergent ways.
Despite its near-slapstick plot, "Mr. Taylor's Funeral" nevertheless reiterates many of the same issues and themes that pervaded
the works of its author in his literary prime. And although the
story reached print more than ten years after a dejected Chesnutt
had practically abandoned his financially disappointing literary
career and returned fulltime to his highly successful stenography
business,[1] the work also re-emphasizes and indeed expands upon
Chesnutt's commitment to depicting the lives of middle-class
African Americans living in the North at the beginning of the
twentieth century.

Set in "Groveland," Chesnutt's fictional version of Cleveland, "Mr. Taylor's Funeral" examines, in comically exaggerated
form, the consequences of a man's month-long disappearance,
which, along with several other factors, prompts his family and
friends to presume his death. Believing her husband dead, the
not-quite-grieving widow sets out to make funeral arrangements,
but she mistakenly engages two local ministers from competing churches to officiate at the ceremony. When, on the day of the
funeral, both ministers insist on performing the service, the undertaker, whom the narrator describes as "a man of resources" (223),
explains to the ministers his novel solution:

"Gentlemen," he said soothingly, "I think I can see a way out of this difficulty which will give each of you an opportunity to officiate and prevent the funeral from being spoiled. Here are two large rooms, opening by wide doors from opposite sides of a central hall. . . . The remains can be placed in the hall between the two rooms, where they can be seen from both. Each of you conduct a service in a separate room, and all the guests can be comfortably seated in a position to hear or participate in one service or the other." (223)

At the end of this laughably bifurcated service—including two ministers trying to out-eulogize each other and two choirs singing competing hymns—both congregations are startled by the appearance of the still-living Mr. Taylor, who has listened to two very different accounts of his life.

Here, Chesnutt literalizes, albeit comically, W.E.B. Du Bois's notion of the duality—or "two-ness," in Du Bois's own term—that all black Americans necessarily feel.[2] Like Du Bois's representative "Negro," Mr. Taylor has to confront the feelings of "double-consciousness, this sense of always looking at one's self through the eyes of others" (Du Bois, *Souls*, 215) that his funeral must generate. Clearly, Chesnutt concurred with Du Bois on this point, repeatedly building his fictions around characters defined by their divided identities, including Northern stories such as "The Wife of His Youth," "Her Virginia Mammy," and "The Passing of Grandison."[3]

Although the story is built upon an apparently absurd premise, "Mr. Taylor's Funeral" nevertheless allows Chesnutt to revisit many of the concerns that pervaded his works during his most productive writing years, between 1899 and 1905. The story is a comic tribute to the inscrutability of identity. Chesnutt returns again and again to this theme in his writings: he relentlessly dramatizes the profound complexity both blacks and whites face when trying to locate and articulate their relative positions in a confounding social landscape. His earlier works, however, bear more visibly the scars of his struggle with the theme. While the characters who populate most of his fictions suffer tangibly from their inability to craft meaningful identities for themselves and their families, "Mr. Taylor's Funeral" is a figurative shrug of the shoulders at a man's powerlessness to define himself. In short, the story reiterates, with a comic difference, Chesnutt's career-long interest in depicting the ways in which people define themselves and others, and it does so through the prism of a group of African Americans living in Ohio.

Like several of Chesnutt's fictions—including other Northern works such as "Cartwright's Mistake," "A Matter of Principle," and "The Shadow of My Past"—the story focuses on the ways in which a person's identity is formed and re-formed by his community. In this case, Mr. Taylor becomes the subject of (mostly faulty) interpretation for a host of "readers," including his wife, two ministers, and various of his friends and business companions. In essence, each member of the community reads Taylor in light of his or her own ideology and financial ambitions. One of the two ministers, for example, had envisioned the living Taylor as a romantic rival; he reads Taylor's "death," therefore, as an opportunity to marry his rival's attractive (and now wealthy) widow. The other minister views Taylor as the epitome of Christian probity, whose death has serious consequences for the church. Like Chesnutt himself, then, Taylor becomes for his "readers" an amorphous subject, one capable of sustaining wildly divergent interpretations. Chesnutt thus casts Taylor, the putative subject of the townspeople's interpretations, as largely irrelevant to those interpretations. For, as the omniscient narrator makes clear, those readings bear no resemblance to the truth about a character the narrator describes as "the absent man"(217). Such a characterization might just as easily apply to an author who, until lately, has been consigned to the periphery of a black tradition in fiction which he, in many ways, established.[4]

In "Mr. Taylor's Funeral," Taylor is physically positioned as a voyeur—he peers "curiously through the half-closed blinds at the scene within"(225)—who is able to hear two distinctly different versions of himself as formulated by the two ministers. As in "The Shadow of My Past," a central character is in effect defined by others, and he has little input into his identity until the end of the story. And, more figuratively, one might say that Taylor is also positioned between this and the nether world. In that sense, he has perhaps the most profoundly divided identity of any Chesnutt character.

Perhaps just as interesting, however, is the extent to which Chesnutt reasserts his interest in depicting the lives of black Americans living in the North. Although seemingly secondary to the comic intent of the story, the characters deployed here share more than merely an interest in Mr. Taylor's funeral(s). Unlike those of his fictions that rely on presenting the lives of African Americans whose experiences had been defined by slavery or Reconstruction (or both), "Mr. Taylor's Funeral" instead portrays a group of people shaped by their economic possibilities and responsibilities. The title character, for example, is introduced in the first paragraph of the story as a man whose career as a chief steward "upon a steamboat running between Groveland and Buffalo" has developed in him a businessman's ethos:

> The salary and perquisites made the place a remunerative one, and Mr. Taylor had saved considerable money. During the winter time he ran a coal yard, where he supplied poor people with coal in small quantities at a large profit. He invested his savings in real estate, and in the course of time became the owner of a row of small houses on a side street in Groveland, as well as of a larger house on the corner of the adjacent main street.(216)

Mr. Taylor thus epitomizes Chesnutt's interest in defining the lives of Northern African Americans in economic terms rather than historical ones.

And indeed, the story reiterates its author's interest in combining the racial and the financial in the depictions of the other characters in the text as well. Mr. Taylor's "widow," for example, had originally agreed to marry the much older Taylor because she "had a practical vein as well, and concluded that on the whole it would be better to be a rich old man's darling than a poor young man's slave"(217). Marrying on such a premise might seem a tad mercenery, but note how her thoughts, like those of her husband, are expressed in primarily fiscal terms, a focus which allows Chesnutt to wield his satirical knife throughout the story. Several other characters likewise envision Taylor's funeral not as a moral imperative but as an opportunity to enhance business: the undertaker, for example, "had expected to make a reputation by his success in directing [the funeral]"(222).

Chesnutt's focus here is telling. Although the story clearly reflects his continued fascination with the ways in which identity is constructed and understood in a multiracial society, he nevertheless satirically examines the greed and opportunism prompted by the premature funeral of a successful businessman in a self-contained African American community.

NOTES

1. In his introduction to *Critical Essays on Charles W. Chesnutt*, Joseph R. McElrath Jr. comments on Chesnutt's reasons for returning to the business world.

> By early 1902, it was clear that Chesnutt would have to return to stenography to make his living. With two daughters who had recently attended Smith College, a son who would graduate in 1905 from a no less expensive school, Harvard, and a wife, who, like her husband, was long used to upper-middle-class amenities, he could not afford to continue his indulgence in the lifestyle of a man of letters. His last published

novel, *The Colonel's Dream*, was written in hours stolen from business and conventional recreations. He would write other novels that never found a publisher during his life. (5)

2. In *The Souls of Black Folk*—which Eric Sundquist has called the "preeminent text of African American cultural consciousness"—Du Bois writes,

the Negro is a sort of seventh son, born with a veil, and gifted with second-sight in this American world,—a world which yields him no true self-consciousness, but only lets him see himself through the revelation of the other world. It is a peculiar sensation, this double-consciousness, this sense of always looking at one's self through the eyes of others, of measuring one's soul by the tape of a world that looks on in amused contempt and pity. One ever feels his two-ness,—an American, a Negro; two souls, two thoughts, two unreconciled strivings; two warring ideals in one dark body, whose dogged strength alone keeps it from being torn asunder. (214–15)

3. Chesnutt's novels, too, focus on those with deeply divided sensibilities: the mixed-blood brother and sister who attempt to "pass" as white in *The House Behind the Cedars* (1900); the tormented extended family—one branch of which is black, one white—in *The Marrow of Tradition* (1901); and the Southern business man who is both attracted to and repulsed by the South in *The Colonel's Dream* (1905).

4. Chesnutt's writings have recently elicited sustained and significant attention, resulting in what Joseph R. McElrath Jr. calls "an outpouring [since the 1960s] of interpretive studies of his contributions to both imaginative literature per se and social thought concerning the relationship between the races during the Reconstruction and the period that came to be known as the Jim Crow era" (*EC*, xi).

Mr. Taylor's Funeral

MR. DAVID TAYLOR HAD been for many years chief steward, during the season of navigation, upon a steamboat running between Groveland and Buffalo, on one of the Great Lakes. The salary and perquisites made the place a remunerative one, and Mr. Taylor had saved considerable money. During the winter time he ran a coal yard, where he supplied poor people with coal in small quantities at a large profit. He invested his savings in real estate, and in the course of time became the owner of a row of small houses on a side street in Groveland, as well as of a larger house on the corner of the adjacent main street.

Mr. Taylor was a stout mulatto, with curly hair and a short gray mustache. He had been a little wild in his youth, but had settled down into a steady old bachelor, in which state he remained until he was past forty-five, when he surprised his friends by marrying a young wife and taking her to live with him in the corner house.

Miss Lula Sampson was a very personable young woman, of not more than twenty-two or twenty-three. She had not been without other admirers; but Mr. Taylor's solid attractions had more than counter-balanced the advantages of these others in the way of youth and sprightliness. For Miss Sampson, while not without her sentimental side, had a practical vein as well, and concluded that on the whole it would be better to be a rich old man's darling than a poor young man's slave.

They lived together very comfortably in the corner house, and Mrs. Taylor enjoyed to the full such advantages as regular rents and savings-bank dividends carried in their train. Mr. Taylor had been for many years a leading member of the Jerusalem Methodist Church, in which he had at various times acted as class-leader, trustee and deacon, and of which he had been at all times the financial backer and manager. Mrs. Taylor had been brought up, so to speak, in the Mt. Horeb Baptist Church, and had at one time sung in the choir; but after her marriage she very dutifully attended service with her husband, only visiting the Baptist church on special occasions, such as weddings or funerals or other events of general public interest.

One day in May, 1900, a month or more after the opening of navigation in the Spring, Mr. Taylor left Groveland on the steamer *Mather* for Buffalo, on one of her regular semi-weekly trips to that port. When the steamer returned several days later without him, his wife and friends felt some concern at his non-appearance, as no message had been received from him in the meantime. Inquiry on the steamer merely brought out the fact that Taylor had not been on hand when the boat was ready to leave port, and that she had sailed without him; in fact he had not been missed until the *Mather* was some miles out.

When several days more elapsed without news from the absent man, his wife's uneasiness became a well-defined alarm. She could account for his absence on no hypothesis except that some harm had befallen him. And upon reading an item in a newspaper, about a week after Mr. Taylor's disappearance, to the effect that the body of a middle-aged mulatto had been found floating in Buffalo harbor, she divined at once that her husband had been the victim of accident, or foul play, and that it was his body that had been recovered. With a promptitude born of sincere regret and wifely sorrow, she requested the company of Deacon Larkins, the intimate personal friend and class-leader of her husband, and with him took the train for Buffalo.

Arriving there they found the body at an undertaking establishment. It had evidently been in the water several days, and the features were somewhat disfigured, but nevertheless Mrs. Taylor had no difficulty in identifying the body as that of her late husband. She had the remains prepared for shipment, and the day after her arrival at Buffalo accompanied them back to Groveland. She had telegraphed for a hearse to be at the depot, and when she saw the coffin placed in it she took a carriage with Deacon Larkins and drove to her home.

"Brother Larkins," she said, in grief-stricken accents, as she thought of her good friend and husband and of the narrow cell in which he must soon be laid, "I wish you would t-t-take charge of the arrangements for the f-f-funeral. I know my dear dead David loved you, and would have wished you to attend to it."

"I shall be glad to, Sister Taylor. It is the last service I can perform for my dear friend and brother. His loss will be a sad blow to the church, and to us all."

In pursuance of his instructions Deacon Larkins engaged an undertaker, inserted in the newspapers a notice announcing the date of the funeral, requested six of the intimate friends of the deceased to act as pallbearers, and telegraphed the pastor of the Methodist Church, who was out of town, to be on hand on Wednesday, at 2 o'clock in the afternoon, to conduct the services and preach the funeral sermon.

Several friends of the family called on Mrs. Taylor during the day preceding the funeral, among them the Reverend Alonzo Brown, pastor of the Mt. Horeb Baptist Church. Mr. Brown was a youngish man, apparently not more than thirty, and had himself suffered a bereavement several years before, in the loss of a wife to whom he had made a model husband, so excellent a husband indeed that more than one lady had envied his wife when living, and when she died, had thought that her successor would be indeed a fortunate woman. In addition to possessing these admirable domestic qualities the Reverend Alonzo was a very handsome man, of light-brown complexion, and with large and expressive black eyes and very glossy curly hair. Indeed, Mrs. Taylor herself had several times thought that if an overruling Providence in its inscrutable wisdom should see fit to remove her dear David from his earthly career while she was yet a young woman—which was not at all unlikely, since he was twenty-five years her senior—there was no man of her acquaintance with whom she could more willingly spend the remainder of her days and the money her good David would leave her, than the Reverend Alonzo Brown. Of course this had been only one of the vague day-dreams of a lively imagination; but it is not surprising, when the central figure in this vision called on her upon the heels of the very event upon which the day-dreams had been predicated, that the idea should penetrate even the veil of grief that surrounded her, and assume something of the nature of a definite probability.

Mr. Brown was a man of tact, and consoled the widow very beautifully in her bereavement.

"Yes, Sister Taylor," he said, pressing her hand with soothing friendliness, "your loss is indeed great, for your husband was a man of whom any woman might have been proud. You displayed excellent taste and judgment, too, Sister Taylor, in selecting as your companion a man of steady habits and settled character, who could leave you suitably provided for during the rest of your life."

The widow sobbed at the magnitude of her loss, but was not unmindful of the compliment to her own taste and judgment.

"But the saddest feature about our dear brother's taking off is not *your* loss;" he said, again pressing her hand consolingly, "it is what he himself has lost—the companionship of one who made his household a model for his friends to imitate, and the despair of those who could not hope to be so fortunate. It is true," he added, with proper professional consistency, "that he has gone to his reward; but I am sure he would willingly have waited for it a few years longer in this terrestrial paradise."

The minister, as he said this, looked around appreciatively at the very comfortable room in which they sat. There was handsome paper on the walls, a bright red carpet on the floor, lace curtains at the windows, a piano, a well-filled book-case,—and in fact all the evidences of solid prosperity, based on landed proprietorship. And by his side too, sat the weeping young widow, to whom tears and weeds were by no means unbecoming.

While he had been speaking an idea had occurred to Mrs. Taylor. She was before her marriage a member of his church. The pastor of the Methodist church, she had learned since her return from Buffalo, was out of town, in attendance on the general conference of his denomination in session at New York. It would be a very nice thing indeed to have Mr. Brown preach the funeral sermon.

"Brother Brown," she said, on the impulse of the moment, "I want you to do me a favor. Will you preach my dear David's funeral sermon?"

He reflected a moment. It was an opportunity to secure that influence which would enable him to lead back into his fold this very desirable sheep.

"If you don't think it will be taken amiss by his own church," he answered, "it would give me great pleasure to perform the last sad rites over our departed friend."

"There will be no trouble about that," she replied. "Elder Johnson has gone to general conference, and there is no one else whom I would prefer to yourself. I ask it as a personal favor."

"It shall be done at any cost," he said determinedly, again pressing her hand in farewell.

"And if you will ask the choir to sing, I shall be under still greater obligations," she said. "They are all my friends, and I have often joined with them on similar occasions, before I was married, and I'm sure you would prefer them."

About an hour after Mr. Brown went away, Deacon Larkins called to make a final report of the arrangements he had made.

"I've requested several of the brethren to act as pallbearers," he said, naming them, "and have asked the choir to furnish the music. Elder Johnson telegraphed this afternoon that he would be here in time to preach the sermon. He has already started, and will get here by half-past one, and come right up from the depot."

Mrs. Taylor scented trouble. "But I thought he couldn't come, and I've invited Elder Brown to preach the sermon," she said.

Deacon Larkins looked annoyed. "There'll be trouble," he said. "You asked me to make arrangements and I acted accordingly."

"What can we do about it?" she asked anxiously.

"Don't ask me," he said. "I'm not responsible for the difficulty."

"But you can help me," she said. "I see no way out of it but to explain the situation to Elder Brown and ask him to retire. Please do that for me."

Deacon Larkins grumbled a little and went away, intending to do as requested. But the more he thought about the matter the more displeased he felt at the widow's action. She had not only been guilty of disrespect to him, in asking a minister to conduct the services without consulting the man in whose charge she had placed the arrangements, but she had committed the far more serious offense of slighting the Methodist church. He could hardly think of a graver breach of propriety than to ask the minister of a rival denomination to officiate at this funeral. If it had been some obscure member of the congregation the matter would have been of less consequence; but to request the Baptist minister to preach Brother David's funeral sermon was something like asking Martin Luther to assist at the Pope's interment. The more

Deacon Larkins thought of it the less he liked it; and finally he concluded that he would simply wash his hands of the entire business—if the widow wanted to call off Elder Brown she would have to do it herself.

He wrote a note to this effect and sent it by his youngest son, a lad of ten, with instructions to deliver it to Mrs. Taylor. The boy met a companion and went off to play, and lost the note. His father was away when he got back home. In the meantime the boy had forgotten about the note, and left his father to infer that it had been delivered.

About a quarter of two on the day of the funeral the friends began to arrive. The undertaker in charge seated them. When the Baptist choir came it was shown to the place provided beforehand for the singers. When a few minutes later the Methodist choir arrived and stated what their part in the service was to be, the undertaker, supposing they were an addition to the number already on hand, gave them the seats, nearest those occupied by the Baptist choir. There was some surprise apparent, but for a while nothing was said, the members of the two bodies confining themselves to looks not altogether friendly. Some of them thought it peculiar that, if the two choirs had been asked to cooperate, there had been no notice given and no opportunity to practice together; but all awaited for the coming of the officiating minister to solve the difficulty. Meantime the friends of the family continued to arrive, until the room where the remains were placed was filled to overflowing, and there were people standing in the hall and seated in other rooms from which they would be able to see or hear very little of the exercises.

At just five minutes to two a livery carriage drove up to the gate, and deposited on the pavement a tall dark man, wearing a silk hat, and high vest, and a coat of clerical cut—it was Elder Johnson, of the Jerusalem Methodist Church. The elder paid the driver his fee, and went in at the front gate. At the same moment the pastor of the Baptist Church came in at the side gate and drew near the front door. The two preachers met on the porch, and bowed to one another stiffly. The undertaker's assistant came forward and took their hats.

"Which of you gentlemen is to conduct the service?" asked the undertaker, with a professionally modulated voice.

"I shall conduct the service," answered Elder Johnson in a matter-of-fact tone.

"I am to conduct the service," said Mr. Brown firmly, in the same breath.

II

Elder Johnson looked surprised, Mr. Brown looked determined, and they glared at each other belligerently.

"May I ask what you mean, sir?" said Elder Johnson, recovering somewhat from his surprise.

"I mean, sir, that I'm going to conduct the funeral exercises," replied the other.

The undertaker began to feel uneasy. It was his first funeral in that neighborhood, and he had expected to make a reputation by his success in directing it.

"There's evidently some misunderstanding here," he said, in a propitiatory tone.

"There's no misunderstanding on my part," said Elder Johnson. "I was telegraphed to by Deacon Larkins, at the widow's request, and have left important business and come five hundred miles at considerable expense to preach it, or know the reason why."

"There can be no possible misunderstanding on my part," replied Mr. Brown. "People may send telegrams without authority, or under a mistaken impression; but I was asked by the widow, personally, to conduct the funeral services, and I propose to do so."

"The deceased was a member of my church before the widow was born," retorted Elder Johnson, making in his warmth a mistake of several years. "I was requested by the widow's agent to conduct this service, and have come here prepared to do it. Every consideration of duty and decency requires me to insist. Even the wishes of the widow should hardly be permitted to stand in the way of what, in this case, is the most obvious propriety."

"The widow," said Mr. Brown, "is the principal one concerned. Her wishes should be sacred on such an occasion, to say nothing of her rights. I'll not retire until I am personally requested by her to do so. I received my commission from her, and I'll resign it to her only."

"Wait a moment, gentlemen," said the undertaker, hopefully, "until I go and speak to the widow."

The colloquy on the porch had not gone unnoticed. Through the half-closed Venetian blinds a number of the guests had seen the group apparently engaged in animated discussion, though their voices had been pitched in low tones; and there was considerable curiosity as to what was going on.

In a few moments the undertaker returned. "Gentlemen," he said in desperation, "something must be done. I can't get anything out of the widow.

She is almost hysterical with grief, and utterly unfit to decide on anything. You must come to some agreement. Why can't you divide the services between you?"

The rival clergymen set their faces even more rigidly.

"I can submit to no division," said Elder Johnson, "that does not permit me to preach the sermon. No man could know Brother Taylor as well as I did, and no man could possibly be so well prepared to pronounce a fitting eulogy on his life. It would be an insult to my church for any one but Brother Taylor's pastor to preach his funeral; in fact, it seems to me not only in bad taste, but bordering on indecency for the pastor of another church, of another denomination, to take advantage of a widow's grief and irresponsibility, and try to force himself where the most elementary principles of professional courtesy would require him to stay away. However, I'm willing to overlook that, under the circumstances, if Brother Brown will be content to read the Scriptures and lead in one of the prayers."

"I repel Brother Johnson's insinuations with scorn; their animus is very plain," said the Baptist minister, with some heat. "I will accept of no compromise that does not allow me to deliver the discourse. I was personally requested to do so; I have prepared a sermon with special reference to the needs of this particular case. If I don't use it my labor is wasted. My brother seems to think there's nobody to be considered in this matter but the deceased, whereas I am of quite the contrary opinion."

It was very apparent that no such compromise as the one proposed was possible. Meanwhile the curiosity on the inside was rising to fever heat; a number of eyes were glancing through the blinds, and several late comers had collected about the steps leading up to the porch and were listening intently.

Pending this last statement by the reverend gentlemen of their respective positions, the undertaker had had time to think. He was a man of resources, and the emergency brought out his latent powers. A flash of professional inspiration came to his aid.

"Gentlemen," he said soothingly, "I think I can see a way out of this difficulty, which will give each of you an opportunity to officiate, and prevent the funeral from being spoiled. Here are two large rooms, opening by wide doors from opposite sides of a central hall. There are people enough to fill the two rooms easily. The remains can be placed in the hall between the two rooms, where they can be seen from both. Each of you conduct a service in a separate room, and all the guests can be comfortably seated, in a position to hear or participate in one service or the other."

The two sermons came to an end almost simultaneously, and again the two audiences were led in prayer. While the eyes of the two ministers were raised on high in supplication, and those of their hearers were piously turned to earth, the man on the outside, unable to restrain his curiosity longer, stepped down from his box, came around to the front door, opened it, walked softly forward, and stopped by the casket, where he stood looking down at the face it contained.

At that moment the two prayers came to an end, the eyes of the ministers sought a lower level, while those of the guests were raised, and they saw the stranger standing by the coffin.

Some nervous women screamed, several strong men turned pale, and there was a general movement that would probably have resulted in flight if there had been any way out except by passing through the hall.

The man by the casket looked up with even greater wonderment than he had before displayed.

"Whose funeral is this, anyhow?" he asked, addressing himself to nobody in particular.

"Why," responded several voices in chorus, "it's your funeral!"

A light dawned on the newcomer, and he looked much relieved.

"There's some mistake here," he said, "or else if I'm dead I don't know it. I was certainly alive when I came in on the train from Buffalo about thirty minutes ago."

The drowning in Buffalo harbor of a man resembling Taylor had been, of course, a mere coincidence. It might be said, in passing, that Mr. Taylor never explained his prolonged absence very satisfactorily. He did tell a story, lacking in many of the corroborative details which establish truthfulness, about an accident and a hospital. As he is still a pillar in the Jerusalem Methodist church, and trying hard to live up to the standard set by his funeral sermons, it would be unbecoming to do more than suggest, in the same indefinite way, that when elderly men, who have been a little wild in their youth, are led by sudden temptation, when away from the restraining influences of home, to relapse for a time into the convivial habits of earlier days, there are, in all well-governed cities, institutions provided at the public expense, where they may go into retreat for a fixed period of time, of such length—say five or ten or twenty or thirty days—as the circumstances of each particular case may seem to require.

White Weeds

Unpublished in Chesnutt's lifetime

Set on a university campus located somewhere "in a strenuous Northern climate" (230), "White Weeds," one of only two stories in this collection not to have been published in Chesnutt's lifetime,[1] qualifies as one of Chesnutt's oddest productions. Although the story combines several of his well-worked topics—the importance of "blood," the intersection of race and love, and the costs of doubting one's spouse—it nevertheless comes across as remarkably unlike his other fictions. The first line of the work sets it clearly apart from other Chesnutt stories: "Students of Danforth University during the late Nineties may remember the remarkable events following the death of Professor Carson of that institution"(229). With such an opening, one might expect a crime mystery, perhaps, but then the focus of that first line becomes apparent—it is not the death of Professor Carson that strikes the narrator as "remarkable." Instead, he directs our attention to the "events following the death." The title, too, with its peculiarly Gothic feel, foreshadows something ominous to come. "White Weeds" focuses on the dire consequences that unfold when a man receives, on his wedding day, an anonymous letter asserting that his bride-to-be has "Negro blood cours[ing] through [her] veins" (241).

The plot of "White Weeds" traces the grim consequences of not trusting one's spouse. Although the recipient of the letter, Professor Carson, seeks advice in the matter, he nevertheless chooses to pursue the unhappiest path. Though wracked with uncertainty about the accusation—and dreading the possibility of its truth—Carson marries the former Miss Tracy *before* confronting her with the accusations described in the letter. When the now—Mrs. Carson learns of his uncertainty about her, not to mention a deathbed vow he made to his mother regarding precisely "'this sin'" (242), she is deeply offended and more: she refuses to assuage his fears. Because his perverse view of "honor" dictates so, the couple thus lives together, and indeed maintains the pretense of marriage, until his early death, which the narrator announces in language that recalls Hawthorne's "Young Goodman Brown" or "The Minister's Black Veil": "And she never did [deny the accusation]. . . . He was never certain, and in his doubt he found his punishment" (243). All of which serves as context for the "remarkable events following the death of Professor Carson": Mrs. Carson's production of the funeral. Rather than displaying "the customary trappings of woe, . . . [the] house [was] decked as for a wedding ceremony" (236), and rather than somber music befitting a solemn ritual, "a band associated only with pleasure parties was playing music" (237). And, at the climax of the funeral, "Mrs. Carson, clad not in widow's weeds but in bridal array, . . . moved in time to the music [the 'Wedding March'!] . . . and pausing before the bier took off her wedding ring and placed it in her dead husband's hand" (237–38).[2]

"White Weeds" is not Chesnutt's only story to play out, in dramatic (even melodramatic) terms, the vagaries of the so-called "color line." In such works as *The House Behind the Cedars*, *The Marrow of Tradition*, and "Her Virginia Mammy," he explores the potentially disastrous consequences of mixed blood as well as the controversial topic (for turn-of-the-century readers) of miscegenation. And in "A Matter of Principle" and "Uncle Wellington's Wives," he even touches on those subjects for comic purposes. Here, though, Chesnutt seems intent on making the professor's doubt the subject of this fictional inquiry. Carson never knows whether the anonymous accusation is true or not. Thus, the story provides a medium through which Chesnutt can contemplate what seemed to him the inexplicable emphasis on the notion of "race." When, near the end of the story, two academics who know of Mrs. Carson's story debate the psychological machinations of her husband, we catch perhaps a glimpse of Chesnutt's own race views:

> "It is curious," said Dr. Trumball, reflectively. . . . "Nature has set no impassable barrier between the races. A system which, assuming the Negro race to be inferior, condemns Mrs. Carson, because of some remote strain of its blood, to celibacy and social ostracism, or throws her back upon the inferior race, is scarcely complimentary to our own. The exaggerated race feeling of men like Carson is . . . more than a prejudice. It is an obsession."
>
> "A disease," returned Professor Gilman. "In all probability, had she given Professor Carson the answer he wanted, it would never have

satisfied him. The seed had been planted in his mind; it was sure to bring forth a harvest of suspicion and distrust. He would in any event have worried himself into a premature grave." (243–44)

While Chesnutt has made a psychological study of Carson's early death, this story also reflects arguments he made regularly in such essays as "What Is a White Man?" "The White and the Black," and "The Future American: What the Race Is Likely to Become in the Process of Time." In those essays, he argues that, ultimately, the amalgamation of the races is an evolutionary certainty—indeed, that race will become an obsolete concept. In "The Future American," for example, he writes that "the future American race . . . will be formed of a mingling, in a yet to be ascertained proportion, of the various racial varieties which make up the present population of the United States" (20). Thus, for Chesnutt, the doubt that brought Carson's life to a premature close was based on an illogical premise.

Now, one can only hope that the plot elements of "White Weeds" do not too accurately represent the behaviors of Northerners at the turn of the last century: Carson's disastrous sense of protecting a woman's honor; Mrs. Carson's macabre reenactment of her wedding at her husband's funeral; and, of course, the sending of anonymous notes to people about to be married. In any event, in "White Weeds" the reader is presented with typical Chesnutt elements transmogrified into the kind of chilling story one might expect from Hawthorne or Poe.

NOTES

1. It originally appeared in Sylvia Lyons Render's monumentally important collection, *The Short Fiction of Charles W. Chesnutt* (1974). No date of composition for "White Weeds" has been ascertained.

2. See Dean McWilliams for a discussion of how "[t]hese musical references form part of the profoundly paradoxical texture of the service Marian has constructed" (109).

White Weeds

STUDENTS OF DANFORTH UNIVERSITY during the late Nineties may remember the remarkable events following the death of Professor Carson of that institution.

At three o'clock one afternoon Professor Carson left his own apartments in Merle Hall and crossed the university campus toward the president's house. It was obvious to the few students whom he encountered during his short walk that Professor Carson was deeply absorbed in thought, because, ordinarily a model of politeness, upon this occasion he either passed them as though unaware of their presence, or responded to their respectful salutation with a very palpable perfunctoriness. There was reason enough, the students knew, for a certain degree of preoccupation on the part of Professor Carson, but hardly sufficient to account for an agitation so extreme as not only to disturb his usually grave and composed countenance but to make him forget his punctilious manners. A man might well be absent-minded upon his wedding day, but he need not look as though he were under sentence of death and straining every effort to secure a reprieve. For Professor Carson, as everyone knew, was to be married at 7 o'clock in the evening to Miss Marian Tracy, by common consent of the university faculty and the student body the most beautiful woman of her years in Attica.

It was a noble campus that Professor Carson crossed. Founded by a wealthy merchant of a past generation, before the days of colossal and burdensome fortunes, the university had never been regarded as a medium of self-advertisement, but as the contribution of an enlightened philanthropist to the training of youth and the advancement of science. There was a broad quadrangular sweep of velvety turf, crossed by two intersecting avenues of noble elms, while distributed symmetrically around the square were a dozen stately stone buildings, some ivy-clad, others beginning already to show, though the institution was only fifty years old, the markings of frost and snow and sun and which in a strenuous Northern climate so soon simulate the mellowness of age.

Professor Carson found the president at home and was ushered into his presence. President Trumbull of Danforth University was a suave and learned gentleman of fifty, in whom a fine executive mind had not overborne a zeal for scholarship, in which he had achieved deserved renown before assuming the cares of administration. A more striking contrast than that between the two men it would be difficult to imagine; physically they were almost the antitheses of each other. Professor Carson was tall and slender with fair hair, which he wore much longer than most men; the president was sturdy and his hair dark, with a very slight sprinkling of white, and ruddy of complexion. The professor's forehead was high and narrow, the president's lower but broader. The president's eye was gray, keen and steady; the professor's blue, weak and wavering. The one was the face of a man of affairs, who welcomed responsibilities as a fit exercise for high powers; the other that of a man lacking resolution and prone, in the crises of life, to seek the support and direction of stronger minds. It was, indeed, Dr. Trumbull's well-known decision of character which had brought Professor Carson, torn by conflicting emotions, across the campus to the president's house. Both were men of striking appearance, not to say handsome men, Professor Carson's manner being marked by a certain distinction, accounted for in some measure by his consciousness that he was of an old and distinguished ancestry. He was deeply wedded to his work, and punctiliously conscientious in its performance; he was professor of mathematics, a science governed by exact rules and requiring little exercise of judgment or imagination. He had been connected with the school longer than President Trumbull and was loyal to its ideals and traditions, with the tenacity of a vine which has thrust its slender roots into the interstices of a rock.

President Trumbull was in his study, in company with his daughter Marcia, a handsome and intelligent child of twelve who sat beside a window reading, while her father wrote at his desk. At a glance from his visitor, the president, with another glance, dismissed Marcia. Professor Carson, murmuring a request for permission, closed the door of the room and sat, or rather sank into a chair near the president.

"Well, Professor Carson, what can I do for you? I see that you have something on your mind."

"Dr. Trumbull," said the other, "I am in the greatest trouble of my life."

"Bless me, Professor! What can it be? Nothing serious, I hope?"

"Serious is hardly the name for it—it is more than serious. It is a matter that concerns my whole future—almost a matter of life and death. As you know, I am—I was to be married tonight."

"Yes, and to an exceedingly beautiful and charming lady."

This statement was made in all sincerity, and not without a certain degree of regret. Dr. Trumbull was a widower of less than a year's standing. Had Professor Carson waited a while longer, he would not have been without a formidable rival.

"Exactly," said Professor Carson, extending his hand with a gesture unconsciously tragic, "and an hour ago I received this letter."

Dr. Trumbull took the letter, and as he read it an air of astonishment overspread his features.

"An extraordinary statement," he exclaimed, "most extraordinary! But surely it is not true—surely you cannot believe it?"

"I—don't—know what to believe. It is possible—most things are possible."

"But, my dear sir, this is an anonymous letter—the weapon of malice—the medium of slander."

"I know it, sir. In the ordinary affairs of life I should have tossed it into the fire. But this is a matter vital to my happiness. And there is always the possibility that someone might wish to tell another the truth, without seeming to do an unkind thing. An anonymous letter *might* be written with the best of motives."

"The method throws suspicion on the motive. Is there no clue to the writer? Have you any enemy?"

"None that I know of," replied Professor Carson promptly. "I don't know of a man in the world who should wish me other than well."

"Or a woman?"

"Or a woman," came the reply with equal promptness.

"It is more calculated to injure the lady than you," said the president reflectively. "*She* may have enemies."

"She is the soul of candor, and popular with her own sex."

"She is beautiful, and popular with the other sex—sufficient reasons why she might be the object of envy or malice."

"The letter is from another city. It is postmarked 'Drexel.'"

"Drexel is forty miles away," returned the president. "One might take the ten o'clock train from here, post the letter at Drexel, and be back here by twelve o'clock. The letter would be here for afternoon delivery."

Professor Carson examined the envelope.

"It was post-marked at Drexel at eleven o'clock. The receiving stamp shows it delivered at the post office here at 12:15. It reached me in the afternoon delivery. It is typewritten, so there is no penmanship to afford a clue."

"I have passed the point of concern about its origin," returned Professor Carson. "It is the fact itself that worries me. The mere suggestion is torture. If the statement be true, it means the ruin of my happiness. If it be false—and pray God it is—I have no time, before the hour set for the wedding, to ascertain the fact. I must decide now, with such light as I have. As my friend and superior in office, what would you advise me to do?"

"Why not ask the lady?"

"I could not do it. If it were true, I could not marry her."

"Nor, as I understand, would you wish to. And if it were false, your mind would be at ease."

"But if I should ask her, she might not marry me; and if it is false, I would not lose her for the world."

"You would trust her word?"

"Implicitly. She is too proud to lie."

"Then, my dear Professor Carson, if you feel that way. . . ."

"Then you would advise me?"

"Is it so important?" asked the president, perplexed. "The world would never know it, even if it were true."

"Someone knows it—if it be true," returned the other. "And then, I should wish to have children, and it is of them I should have to think—it would be criminal not to think of them. The time is so short that I don't know what to do nor where to turn. I thought you might advise me—you are so prompt, so resourceful. I should wish to adopt a course that would protect myself, and yet in no way reflect upon the lady, or upon the university, or impair my usefulness here."

"Such delicacy was to be expected of you, Professor Carson. If it were my own affair, I could decide it promptly, but unless I could put myself exactly in your place, as perhaps I should be unable to do, I should hesitate to advise a man upon a matter so vital. Your problem is a difficult one from your own point of view—perhaps from any man's. You are engaged to be married, within a few hours, to a most charming woman, in whose worth and worthiness you have had entire confidence. The wedding preparations are made, the guests invited. Even now, in all probability, the bride is dressing for the wedding. At this moment you receive an anonymous letter, purporting to convey information which, if true, renders the lady ineligible for marriage with you. I see but three courses open to you as a gentleman—and those who know you would expect you to consider the subject first from that point of view. You can take the letter to the lady, ask her frankly if the charge be true, and marry her or not, as she may answer. A less frank but at least forgivable step would be to postpone the marriage on account of sudden indisposition—you are looking far from well just now. If she confirmed the statement of the letter, you would have to make some such excuse, in order to spare her feelings. A third course, which a man—some men at least—who loved the lady well enough would follow, would be to throw the letter into the fire and marry her."

"But which do you think—" began Professor Carson desperately, "which do you think—"

"I think," said the president, interrupting him, "that you had better choose between the three. A gentleman of your character and antecedents can hardly fail to select a course consistent with—"

"With honor," murmured the poor professor. "Thank you, sir," he added with dignity, "I shall trouble you no further. But whatever course I decide upon, I may ask you to hold in strict confidence all that I have said, and the contents of this letter?"

"You need hardly ask it. It is not a matter to be repeated. Whether the marriage take place or no, we should have no right to compromise the lady."

At 7 o'clock the same evening the marriage of Professor John Marshall Carson to Miss Marian Tracy took place at the latter's residence. Miss Tracy was alone in the world, having neither parents nor near relatives living. She had been a teacher in a ladies' seminary, and made her home with a distant connection who lived in the town. To the college world the event was a notable one. Professor Carson was, if not exactly popular, at least very highly esteemed by his colleagues. If he seemed at times to hold himself aloof from the other professors, his attitude was instinctively ascribed to a natural reserve rather than to undue self-esteem. If any new-fledged tutor or professor ever attempted to be familiar with the professor of mathematics, he was brought back to the conventional by a tact so delicate, a courtesy so refined, that no offense was taken, and respect took the place of what, at a ruder rebuff, might easily have been dislike. The wedding was attended by all of the professors and their wives, as well as by many of the townspeople.

The house was decorated for the wedding with red and white roses. Festoons of smilax ran from the chandeliers in the center to the corners of the rooms. The floors were covered with white canvas. Gorman and McAlee's orchestra, screened behind palms in the back hall, played a varied program of classical and popular music, ranging from Mendelssohn to ragtime. These details are mentioned because they are important to the remainder of the story. The bride,

> *"Clothed in white samite,*
> *Mystic, wonderful,"*

as Dr. Trumbull murmured when the vision dawned upon him—was radiant in the well-preserved beauty of thirty years, for Miss Tracy was no longer in her first youth. When she entered the front parlor upon the arm of her cousin, to the strains of the wedding march, there was not a man present who did not think Professor Carson an extremely lucky man. It was observed, however, by those who paid the bridegroom any attention, that he did not seem as happy as the occasion demanded; that the voice with which he spoke the irrevocable vows had not the vibrant ring that might be expected from the virile man united to his mate; that the hand which he gave to those who congratulated him was limp and cold; that while from time to time during the evening his eyes sought the bride's face with a look of longing, behind this lay a haunting distrust—that he seemed to be seeking something which he did not find; that at other times his manner was *distrait* and his smile forced; and that when the last guests were departing, his expression alternated between anticipation and dread. President Trumbull, the most distinguished guest, responded at the supper table to a toast in which he wished the couple every felicity. At no time during the evening did Professor Carson allude to the interview of the afternoon, nor did the president mention it to him then or thereafter. There had been no scandal, no sensation, and Dr. Trumball had no disposition to pry into another's secrets.

If there were any lingering curiosity on Dr. Trumball's part concerning which of the two possible courses open to him besides postponement of the marriage Professor Carson had adopted, it was not lessened by his observation of the married couple during the succeeding months. He went to Europe for the summer, but upon his return in the autumn to his duties, he met Professor Carson daily, in the routine of the university work, and the lady from time to time in the social life of which the university was the center. Only a few meetings were necessary to convince him that neither husband nor wife was happy. Professor Carson, at the end of what should have been a restful vacation, had visibly declined in health. Always slender, he had become emaciated. His natural gravity had developed into an almost sepulchral solemnity, his innate reserve into a well-nigh morbid self-absorption. The rare smile which had at times flickered upon his features seemed to have gone out forever.

His efforts to overcome this melancholy were at times very apparent. Mrs. Carson was fond of society, and they often went out together. On such occasions their bearing towards one another was perfect, of its kind. Professor Carson was the embodiment of chivalrous courtesy—a courtesy so marked that in the bearing of any other man toward his own wife it would have provoked a smile. The lady, in her demeanor toward her husband, responded in a manner so similar as to seem at times ironical. In a free and familiar society of intimates they were, when together, conspicuous. The lady when alone could unbend; but Professor Carson after his marriage never appeared in society alone.

In spite, however, of this elaborate deference toward one another, more than one observer besides Dr. Trumbull suspected that their union was not one of perfect happiness. Dr. Trumbull wondered, more than once, whether Carson had asked her, before their marriage, the question suggested by the anonymous letter, and, receiving a negative answer, had had his faith shaken after marriage, or whether he had loyally burned the letter, but had been unable to divest himself of the hateful doubt it had engendered, which was slowly sapping his vitality. That some cause was producing this unfortunate result became more and more apparent, for before the next summer vacation came around, Professor Carson took to his bed, and, after a brief illness, was enrolled among the great majority.

The number of those who were interested in the Carsons' household was largely increased during the two days succeeding the professor's death. Announcement was duly made that the funeral services would take place on Saturday afternoon—Professor Carson had died on Thursday—and were to be conducted by old Dr. Burridge, rector emeritus of St. Anne's. This in itself was a novelty, for Dr. Burridge was purblind and hard of hearing, and rarely performed any priestly function except some service where sight and hearing were not prime essentials. Some surprise being expressed that Dr. McRae, the rector in charge, had not been requested to officiate, it was learned that Dr. Burridge would act by special request of the widow.

This, however, was a trivial preliminary. The real surprise began when those who entered the house shortly before the hour fixed for the service found none of the customary trappings of woe, but on the contrary, a house decked as for a wedding ceremony. It required only a moment for those who had been present at Professor Carson's marriage a few months before to perceive with a sort of dazed wonder, that an effort had seemingly been made to reproduce, as near as the plan of the rooms would permit, the decorations upon that occasion. Roses, white and red, were banked in the corners; long streamers of smilax ran from the chandeliers to the corners of the room, and were twined around the stair railing. Where, at the wedding ceremony a floral altar had been reared, the body of Professor Carson, in immaculate evening dress, lay upon a bier, composed of a casket the sides of which were let down so as to resemble more a couch than the last narrow house of a mortal man.

The troubled wonder of the funeral guests was still further augmented when in the rear hall, behind a screen of palms, Gormand and McAlee's orchestra began to play Wagner's "O du mein holder Abendstern." For a moment, while the gathering audience were realizing that a band associated only with pleasure parties was playing music, which, while not exactly profane, was certainly not religious—for a few moments the audience was silent, and then the room was as murmurous with whispered comment as a wheat-field shaken by the wind.

One of the professors spoke to the undertaker, who was hovering, like a bird of prey, around the hall.

"What is the meaning," he asked, "of this extraordinary performance?"

"Don't ask me, sir. It is the widow's orders. I don't approve of it, sir, but business is business with me. It is the widow's orders, and, as the person chiefly interested, the widow's wishes are sacred."

While Dr. Burridge, in full canonicals, having taken his place before the bier, to which he was led by one of the ushers, was reading the first part of the beautiful Episcopal service for the burial of the dead, there was opportunity for those present to reach in some degree the frame of mind befitting so solemn an occasion. At that point, following the first lesson, where a hymn is sung or an anthem, the discomfort returned with even greater force when a hired quartet, which some of those present recognized as belonging to the neighboring town of Drexel, began to sing, to a soft accompaniment by the orchestra, not the conventional and the expected "Abide with Me" or "Lead, Kindly Light," but Graben Hoffman's exquisite love song, "Der schoenste Engel." As the words were German only a few understood them, but in the bosoms of the rest there was a vague intuition that the song was of a piece with the other unusual features of the occasion.

Good old Dr. Burridge, however, to whose dull hearing all music was the same, had neither seen nor heard anything to mar the solemnity of the service. He repeated the Creed, in which he was joined by those who were sufficiently collected, and added the fitting prayers. When he had concluded the portion of the service which could be performed at the home, and the undertaker had announced that the remainder of the service would take place at the cemetery, the guests instead of rising returned to their seats as though by a common premonition that there was something more to happen. Nor were they disappointed, for almost immediately the orchestra struck up the "Wedding March" from *Lohengrin,* and Mrs. Carson, clad not in widow's weeds but in bridal array, her face set in a tragic smile, entered the back parlor and moved in time to the music down the narrow lane which had been left between the chairs, and pausing before the bier took off her wedding ring and placed it in her dead husband's hand; took off her wreath of orange blossoms and laid it among the flowers by his side. Then, turning, she left the room by the side door. A few moments later, when the casket had been closed and the body was ready for sepulture, she came downstairs dressed in an ordinary street costume of dark cloth, took her place in the mourner's carriage, and followed the remains to the grave, by the side of which she stood like any ordinary spectator until ashes had been consigned to ashes, and dust to dust, after which she immediately entered her carriage and was driven away, leaving the mystified throng morally certain that nothing but pronounced mental aberration on the part of Mrs. Carson could account for so extraordinary, not to say shocking a funeral. To more than one the mad scene in Hamlet occurred as at least a distant parallel, though no one of them had ever dreamed that the stately Mrs. Carson had loved her middle-aged husband so deeply as, like Ophelia, to go mad for love of him.

So paralyzed with amazement had been everyone at the funeral, and brief had been Mrs. Carson's appearances, that not anyone had uttered a word of condolence or spoken to her during the afternoon. That very night she left Attica. Her house was closed and her affairs settled by her distant cousin, and it was learned that she had gone abroad for an indefinite sojourn. By the will of Professor Carson, which was presented for probate shortly after his decease, he left to his widow the whole of his estate, which amounted to some $20,000 in money and securities.

A little more than a year after Professor Carson's death, at the close of the school year, Dr. Trumbull, accompanied by his daughter Marcia—he had been a widower now for three years—left home to spend the summer in Europe. A few weeks later, upon stepping aboard the steamer at Mainz for the trip down the Rhine, he saw seated upon the deck, at a little distance, a lady whose outlines, though her face was turned away, seemed familiar. Having seen his daughter comfortably seated and their hand baggage placed, he went over to the lady, who, upon his addressing her by name, looked up with a start, and then extended both her hands.

"Why, Dr. Trumbull, what a surprise! You are the last person whom I should have expected to see!"

"And, I suppose, the one whom it gives you the least pleasure to see?"

"By no means! Indeed, I am glad to see you. One's home friends are never so welcome as when one meets them in a foreign land."

"Yes, I believe it is understood that a mere bowing acquaintance at home becomes an intimate friendship abroad."

"Now, doctor, I shall not follow your very palpable lead; you must take my friendship at its face value."

"My dear Mrs. Carson, I am only too glad to do so, and am sincerely delighted, on my part, that our paths have met."

The president's daughter, finding herself deserted, and recognizing Mrs. Carson, came over at this juncture, and was duly hugged and kissed.

"How tall you are growing, dear!" said the lady. "It is only about a year since I saw you, and you look three years older."

"My dresses are longer," said Marcia ingenuously. "Oh, I'm so glad we've met you. You know, I always liked you, Mrs. Carson, even before you were married."

"You dear child! And as for you, who could help loving you? But, there, how selfish I am! In my pleasure at our meeting, I had forgotten all about Professor and Mrs. Gilman. I'm traveling with them, you know. Professor Gilman has had his 'sabbatical year,' and I've been with them ever since they came over last July. At school Mrs. Gilman was my dearest friend, and they have been very good to me."

"And you never give up your friends?"

"Never! So long as they are good to me. But excuse me a moment, and I will look them up."

She returned shortly with her friends. The two gentlemen were old acquaintances and former intimates. Professor Gilman, an authority on medieval history, had been a colleague of Dr. Trumbull's at Brown, many years before. After the exchange of cordial greetings, the ladies, accompanied by Marcia, went over to the side of the boat, leaving the gentlemen together.

They spoke of their work and their travels, and then the conversation turned on Mrs. Carson.

"She is looking well," said President Trumbull.

"A fine woman," returned Professor Gilman, "a woman of character, capable of forming a definite purpose, and of carrying it out; and yet not at all hard, and in some ways exceedingly feminine. My wife loves her dearly, and we have enjoyed having her with us."

"I never thought," said Dr. Trumbull, "that she was quite happy with Carson."

"Happy! Far from it! I suppose, after Carson's remarkable funeral, that all Attica imagined her out of her mind?"

"Her conduct was unusual, certainly, and in default of explanation, such a suspicion might really have seemed charitable."

"Did it ever occur to you that there might be a reasonable explanation, without that hypothesis?"

"Frankly, yes, though I could never have imagined what it was. I happened to know something of Carson's antecedents, and of certain events preceding his marriage, which I have thought might in some obscure way have accounted for Mrs. Carson's eccentric conduct upon that occasion. But the knowledge came to me in such a manner that I shall probably never know any more about it."

"Did it concern a letter?"

"Yes."

"An anonymous letter?"

"Yes."

"Then I know it already. Mrs. Carson is my wife's other self—even I play only second fiddle. They have no secrets from one another. I know that Mrs. Carson values your good opinion, and since you know so much, I imagine she would not be unwilling for you to know all the facts—if you could dream them, say. Indeed, you ought to know them."

It was a warm day. Their cigars were good. The ladies left them alone for half an hour. The steamer glided smoothly down the Rhine. Two gentlemen in middle life, upon their vacation, might have dozed and might have dreamed. At any rate, before the ladies rejoined them, each knew all that the other knew of Mrs. Carson's story, and what they did not know required no supernatural wisdom to divine it.

When, after the wedding, the guests had departed and the wedded pair were left alone, the bride observed that Professor Carson was ill at ease, and that his embarrassment was serious. For a while he wandered about the room. At length he sat down beside her and began to speak.

"Marian," he said, "I have a very painful duty to perform. This afternoon, only a few hours ago, I received through the mail an anonymous letter, containing a certain statement with reference to yourself."

To say that his wife was surprised is a mild statement. She was not a child, but a mature woman, and the inference seemed plain; a wedding, an anonymous letter upon the eve of it. That he had not believed the statement, whatever it had been, was apparent, for he had married her. But right upon the heels of this conviction came the first false note in her conception of Professor Carson's character—a doubt of his taste. She had considered him the flower of courtesy—had looked upon his chivalrous deference for women as a part of his Southern heritage. It was this attribute of his, which, more than anything else, had attracted her. That having loyally ignored such a letter, he should now tell her of it was hardly to have been expected of him.

"I could not believe the statement," he went on, "and therefore, as honor required of me, I threw the letter into the fire, and fulfilled my contract."

Again the lady winced. It hardly required a sensitive mind to infer, from his language, that he had married her because of their previous engagement. His choice of words was at least unfortunate.

"I am sorry," she said with spirit, "that you should have felt under any compulsion."

"There was none," he replied, "except that of my love. And I did not believe the story."

"Then why mention it?"

"Because I must know," he replied, "and yet I dared not run the risk of losing you. Had I asked you the question before our marriage, your pride, which in my eyes is one of your greatest charms, might have made you refuse to marry me."

"Quite likely," she replied, with rising anger. "But since you ignored the letter, and disbelieve the story, why, oh, why, do you tell me now?"

"Because," he said wildly, "because I love you, and because my happiness is so bound up in you, and because this charge is of such a nature, that I can never shake off its memory until I learn from your own lips that it is false. I know it is false—I am sure it is false—it must be false; but I want your lips to give it the lie. Whatever you say, I shall believe."

She was a woman, and for a moment curiosity replaced indignation.

"And what," she asked, "is this terrible charge which I must meet, this crime I must deny?"

"It is a monstrous calumny. Could anyone, looking at your fair face, at your clear eye, your frank and noble countenance, believe that one drop of Negro blood coursed through your veins? Preposterous!"

His words were confident, but his voice scarcely rang true, and she could read the lingering dread in his eyes. This, then, that some unknown person had said of her, was the offense with which she was charged!

She was silent. He watched her anxiously.

"Suppose," she answered with a forced smile, "suppose, for the sake of the argument, it had been true—what then?"

"Ah, dearest," he replied, reassured by her smile, and drawing nearer to her, while she retreated behind a convenient chair. "I should have suffered a severe shock. For the sake of the university, and to avoid scandal, I should have lived with you, had you been willing, and to the outer world we should have been husband and wife; but to ourselves the relationship would have existed in name only."

"And you married me," she said coldly, "with such a doubt in your mind, and with such a purpose, should the doubt be wrongly resolved? It seems scarcely fair to me. I might have answered yes."

He explained his state of mind, or at least endeavored to make it clear, plainly surprised that he should find it necessary; for to his mind, the mere statement of the fact was its own explanation.

His father had been a planter, with wide estates and numerous slaves. His mother had suffered deeply in her pride and her affections, because of some poor unfortunate of color. With his mother's milk he had drunk in a deadly antipathy to the thought of any personal relation between white people and black but that of master and servant. The period of his adolescence had coincided with the tense years during which the white South, beaten on the field, had sought in the fierce and unreasoning pride a refuge from the humiliation of defeat, and with equal unreason, but very humanly, had visited upon the black pawns in the game, who were near at hand, the hatred they felt for their conquerors. Most of this feeling Professor Carson had overcome, but this one thing was bred in the bone.

"It is part of me," he said. "Nothing could ever make me feel that the touch of a Negress was not pollution. Beside my mother's deathbed I swore a solemn vow that this sin should never be laid at my door."

His bride was not flattered by the suggestion. She, a Negress, to whom his vow might apply!

"How white," she asked, "must one be, to come within the protection of the code of Southern chivalry?"

"There are no degrees," he explained. "To me, and those who think like me, men and women are either white or black. Those who are not all white are all black. Were I married in fact to a woman even seemingly as white as you, yet not entirely white, I should feel guilty of mortal sin. I should lie awake at night, dreading lest my children should show traces of their descent from an inferior and degraded race. I should never know a moment's happiness."

"Pardon my curiosity," she said, "but this is interesting—at least. What, may I ask, was to have been—my attitude in this marriage? In this state there would have been no legal objection to our union. We are both

Episcopalians, and our church looks upon divorce with disfavor. Was I to have submitted without protest to a plan which left me married, yet no wife?"

"It would have been for you to say," he replied. "I could not blame you for concealing your antecedents. For me to seek a divorce would have been to reveal your secret, which honor would scarcely have permitted, and the same reason, I imagined, might constrain you. But, let us thank heaven! I am spared the trial, and with your assurance that all is well we shall be happy all the rest of our lives."

He moved toward her to take her in his arms.

"You forget," she answered quickly, and still evading him, "that I have given you no such assurance."

Professor Carson turned white to the lips. She thought he would have fainted at her feet; he clutched the table beside him for support. She would have pitied him, had she despised him less.

"What," he faltered. "Can it be possible?"

"I shall certainly not deny it," she replied.

And she never did. They lived together according to his program. He was never certain, and in his doubt he found his punishment. When he died, she yielded to a woman's weakness. She was not a widow, but a bride. She owed Professor Carson no affection and felt for him no regret. He had outraged her finest feelings, and she had stooped to a posthumous revenge, which had satisfied her mind, while it only mystified others; indeed, she had cared very little, at the time, for what others might think. That having known her, and loved her, and married her, a prejudice which reflected in no wise upon her character, her intelligence or her beauty could keep them apart, was the unpardonable sin. She must be loved for what she was.

"It is curious," said Dr. Trumbull, reflectively, "how the fixed idea dominates the mind. Perfectly reasonable and logical and fair-minded upon every other topic, upon one pet aversion a man may skirt the edge of mania. Nature has set no impassable barrier between races. A system which, assuming the Negro race to be inferior, condemns Mrs. Carson, because of some remote strain of its blood, to celibacy and social ostracism, or throws her back upon the inferior race, is scarcely complimentary to our own. The exaggerated race feeling of men like Carson is more than a healthy instinct for the preservation of a type; it is more than a prejudice. It is an obsession."

"A disease," returned Professor Gilman. "In all probability, had she given Professor Carson the answer he wanted, it would never have satisfied him. The seed had been planted in his mind; it was sure to bring forth a harvest of suspicion and distrust. He would in any event have worried himself into a premature grave. His marriage, while the doubt existed, was a refinement of Quixotry—and of unconscious selfishness; to spare the feelings of the possible white woman, and to save her for himself, he deliberately contemplated the destruction of the happiness of the possible—Negress."

Across the deck, Dr. Trumbull studied the graceful contour of Mrs. Carson's figure, the fine lines of her profile. A widow, and yet no wife! It was interesting. It would be a brave man who would marry her—but surely she had never loved Carson.

Dr. Trumbull had always admired her, since he had known her. Had she been willing, and had she waited a little longer, she might have been spared the somewhat tragic interlude with Carson.

"I had always wondered," he said, reflectively, "which of the three courses open to Carson he adopted—to postpone the marriage—to burn the letter—or to ask her frankly whether its contents were true. It seems that he did all three—he asked whether or not the statement was true; he burned the letter and married her without mentioning it; and—he deferred the marriage—the real marriage. It was the order in which he did them that destroyed his happiness and shortened his life."

"And all," said Professor Gilman, "for nothing, absolutely nothing. What malicious mind conceived and wrote the letter, Mrs. Carson never learned, but there was not a word of truth in it! Her blood is as entirely pure as Professor Carson's could have been. My wife knew her people, and her line of descent for two hundred years is quite as clear, quite as good, as that of most old American families. But here come the ladies."

"Oh, papa," cried Marcia, "you and Professor Gilman have been so busy talking that you have missed the most beautiful scenery—the Lorelei, and Bingen, and Ehrenbreitstein, and—oh, my! If it hadn't been for Mrs. Carson, who has been telling me all the legends, I shouldn't have known anything about them."

"I saw you with her and Mrs. Gilman, dear, and knew it was all right. Perhaps Mrs. Carson will show them to me—some other time."

Appendix

Supplementing the fourteen stories that appear in the main body of this collection, this appendix contains four more of Chesnutt's Northern stories. These four works—"A Metropolitan Experience" (1887), "An Eloquent Appeal" (1888), "How a Good Man Went Wrong" (1888), and "How He Met Her" (unpublished but written before 1890)[1]—are generally brief, light-hearted pieces written early in the author's career. Each story nevertheless reflects Chesnutt's already-forming interest in presenting the North as a distinctive, vibrant place just before the turn of the last century. Although shorter than the other fictions in this collection, the works presented here reiterate, in compressed fashion, Chesnutt's examination of the ways in which people go about "making" their lives—finding love, starting a business, building a family—in the new North.

NOTE

1. See Sylvia Lyons Render's bibliography in *The Short Fiction of Charles W. Chesnutt.*

A Metropolitan Experience

Chicago Ledger (1887)

I HAD COME TO New York to seek my fortune. The path over which I was to pursue the fickle goddess was but vaguely defined, at least in regard to details. But I know what I wanted to do, and that was to practice my profession.

I had just finished a three years' course in a New Jersey medical college, during which time I had spent the greater part of my modest patrimony, which had consisted of three thousand dollars realized from an insurance on my father's life. My father had been a physician of fine skill, high ideals, and small practice, a not uncommon combination. I had no mother or sisters to keep me at home; our town was abundantly supplied with physicians; and, as I did not care to wait half a lifetime for a practice which would have barely supported me during the remaining half, I had determined to seek my fortune elsewhere.

On leaving a small town, it was natural that I should come to a large one. I knew that the greatest success, other things being equal, was only possible where the largest opportunities existed; and if I did not succeed in a large city, I could not reproach myself with the lack of opportunity. Hence I came to New York.

I secured board at a second-rate boarding house in the neighborhood of Washington Square. It was part of my plan of operations to study the city a while before hanging out my shingle.

With this object in view I spent a good deal of time on the streets and in public parks; and on pleasant evening I frequently sat for an hour or two in Washington Square. Seated there, on one of the public benches, often in close proximity to some bottle-nosed and ill-odored tramp, I would study the strange jumble of types in the stream of humanity that rolled through the park, which is more of a thoroughfare than a pleasure-ground.

Most of those who passed belonged to the shabbier classes of the metropolis; you could see there every variety of New Yorker, from the above-mentioned tramp to the shabby genteel clerk; only the wealthy and prosperous-looking were seldom met with.

One evening as I sat in my accustomed seat, absorbed for the moment in a calculation as to how long the human stomach could endure the food at Mrs. Van Hashelar's boarding house, I was dimly conscious of a female figure passing by. I looked up, but the lady had gone too far from me to see her face. What I did see was a slender figure, set off by a blue silk dress of a stylish cut, and though walking somewhat briskly, borne along with a graceful motion quite different from the usual wobble of a woman in a hurry; a charming back, above which rose a well-turned neck, surmounted by a head of hair of the color poets are popularly supposed to rave about, a ruddy gold, on top of which in turn reposed a most bewitching bonnet. This somewhat elaborate description but faintly pictures the impression she made upon me at the time.

I felt a sudden desire to see the lady's face; I was sure it would be beautiful and I have always been a great admirer of beautiful women, or rather of the beautiful in women—the distinction is obvious. I rose from my seat, and started down another path, running in the same general direction as she was going, intending to execute a sort of flank movement and meet her face to face on the other side of the park, where the two paths converged after a long curve. Just as I approached the point where the paths came together the lady slipped and fell, uttering a little scream. I rushed forward and assisted her to rise.

"Are you badly hurt?" I inquired in a sympathetic voice.

"Oh, no," she replied, thanking me, "it is nothing at all." But as she started off she came near falling a second time. I caught her and placed her arm in mine.

"Shall I call a carriage?" I asked.

"Oh, no," she said, "it is hardly worthwhile. I live only a short distance, and—if you will—"

"Certainly," I said, not waiting for her to finish the sentence, "I shall be very glad to assist you."

A few minutes' walk, and one or two turns brought us to a brick house of conventional style, and I helped her up the high stoop and rang the doorbell. As she did not release my arm when the door was opened, I could do nothing less than help her into the house. I deposited my fair burden on a cushioned armchair in the parlor, and, hat in hand, was beginning an elaborate parting bow, when she exclaimed:

"Oh, do sit down and rest a moment. How tired you must be carrying poor me such a distance."

I sat down. I may say here that she was quite as pretty as I had imagined her to be.

"I suppose we ought to be introduced," she said. "I am Miss Preston."

"And I am Dr. Scott, at your service," I replied. Our conversation had not advanced beyond this preliminary stage when the doorbell rang, and the servant girl entered a moment later with a telegraph message. Excusing herself, Miss Preston hurriedly tore open the envelope and glanced at the message. Her face took on a look of concern, and she said to the servant:

"Katy, is papa at home?"

"No, ma'am, he went to Boston this afternoon."

"Then telephone Uncle George's house and see if he is at home," and when the girl had gone out she continued, turning to me: "It's all about my

Cousin Harry. He is at Yale, and I am afraid is just a little wild. He tells me that through an unfortunate mistake he has got into a scrape, without any fault of his own, and that if I don't send him a telegraph money order for fifty dollars by nine o'clock, he is likely to be disgraced, and perhaps expelled from college."

I murmured my sympathy. The girl returned and announced that Uncle George had gone to Philadelphia, and would not be back until the next night. At this intelligence the expression of concern in Miss Preston's face deepened into dismay.

"Papa away—Uncle George out of town—and only twenty-five dollars in the house," she exclaimed. "Oh, what shall—"

I interrupted her: "If I can venture to offer you my assistance I shall be glad to lend you the money."

"Oh, no," she said, "I couldn't think of accepting a loan from a stranger—or, such a recent acquaintance," she corrected herself, blushing.

I assured her with some eloquence of speech that in a crisis like this the ordinary conventionalities of polite society should yield to the exigency of the moment; and in the end I persuaded her to accept a loan of twenty-five dollars.

"Papa will send a check when he returns tomorrow," she said, "or I will send the money by Katy, if you will leave me your card."

I felt for my card-case, but I had left it at home. I said it didn't matter; I often walked down that way, and would stop in a day or two, and see if she had recovered from her injury.

"Very well," she replied with a fine blush and an entrancing smile, "I shall expect you."

I went home with my head in a whirl. What a divine creature! What beauty! What grace! What refinement of sentiment! And to think that I had been able to serve this beautiful creature and to place her under an obligation to me, and that I was expected to call again. I felt much like a knight-errant of the olden time when he had rescued some captive princess, and had been rewarded for his valor with permission to wear her colors. My ecstatic condition was the more excusable by reason of the fact that I had no lady acquaintances in New York—barring Mrs. Van Hashelar—and had been for three years immersed in the dry details of my medical studies, and entirely without ladies' society.

I concluded that two days would be a reasonable time to elapse before I called to see Miss Preston. I spent the next two days in dreamland. If I sought my accustomed seat in Washington Square it was only to compare the women who passed with Miss Preston. It was very annoying to have to think of such an adorable creature in such a formal way. "Dear Miss Preston" would have looked very well on an envelope, or even as a spoken address; but to think of her as "Miss Preston" was maddening. I tried to supply the hiatus, and ran over all the pretty names I could think of without being able to decide upon any one which expressed all I thought her name ought to suggest. I suppose if I had known her name was Sarah, or Jane, or even Sarah Jane, I would have thought it very nice, but I gave up in despair the attempt to name such loveliness. To find relief from my restlessness I went up to the Astor Library and tried to read a bulky treatise on macrobiosis, which was my favorite study; but somehow the subject was less interesting than usual, and I finally found temporary distraction from my thoughts in Ouida's latest novel.

The two days finally ran out, and with winged feet I sought the home of my fair acquaintance. I was at first a little doubtful about the place, as on my former visit my absorption in the young lady had been such that I had failed to notice either street or number. However, by following the same course as before, I soon found the house and rang the doorbell. A servant girl admitted me, and asking my name, ushered me into the parlor. I had been seated but a moment when a somewhat elderly woman of angular build and severe countenance entered the room. In answer to her inquiring look I said that I had called to ask how Miss Preston was.

"Miss Preston? Why, there's no Miss Preston here," she said.

I looked around the room. It was surely the same room in which I had seen her last. There was the same ugly steel engraving of Abraham Lincoln signing the Emancipation Proclamation; the same chromo of Charles Sumner between the front windows, the piano occupied the same corner, and on it stood the same open sheet of music, the latest popular catch, "When the Chickens Come to Roost," or some similar title.

"But, madam," I said, "is not this the residence of Mr. Preston?"

"No, indeed," she replied, "this is Mrs. Ledbetter's boarding house."

"This is surely where I saw Miss Preston. But perhaps I am mistaken in the house, though it seems hardly possible."

"There are no Prestons in the block," she said, positively. Then a thought seemed to strike her. "Perhaps you mean Miss Weston; she and her father went away yesterday."

"Was she a blond, with dark blue eyes and very fine teeth, and did she wear a blue silk dress?" I inquired.

"Her exact description, only those fine teeth were false. They left yesterday, without paying their board bill. Twenty-six dollars, young man, is a large sum for a poor widow to be swindled out of."

I began to have an idea. "Do you know where they lived?" I asked.

"They said they were going to Boston, where they were expecting remittances, and all that. But it's my belief that they live wherever they can get board. That sort of people don't have any homes."

My idea had by this time developed into a theory. I remembered the stories I had read of the female sharpers of New York. I had been swindled. The sprained ankle was only a trap, into which I had fallen, like any common greenhorn. I made my theory known to Mrs. Ledbetter, and her opinion readily coincided with mine, which was further strengthened by several circumstances which she related. My theory became a conviction. I had been taken in, and I had myself to thank for it.

"Well, young man," said Mrs. Ledbetter, "you have my sympathy, but I don't see that that helps either of us. Where are you boarding?"

Having found out that I did not wish to change my boarding house, Mrs. Ledbetter at length permitted me to wish her good afternoon.

I was cruelly undeceived. My faith in humanity had received a shock from which I feared, in my youthful pessimism, that it would never recover. Henceforth woman lost her charm for me, and in every fair face I saw a possible Miss Preston. I steeled my heart against feminine attractions; I even changed my boarding house because I discovered in myself signs of weakening toward a pretty shorthand writer who came to board at Mrs. Van Hashelar's. My mind was made up; I would live and die a bachelor.

However, this sternness wore off, or, at least became softened with time, which takes the edge off the sharpest pain. I resumed my walks and character studies; but as my experience of Washington Square had been so painful I got into the habit of going up to Central Park to pursue my observations. One afternoon I sat on an iron bench just at the intersection of a carriage drive and a footway reading a copy of the *Herald*, which contained a graphic account of a great ball on Fifth Avenue the night before. I was wondering how long it would be before I could gain admittance to that enchanted sphere—I confess that I am given to day-dreams—when a carriage drew near, and an exclamation in a feminine voice caused me to look up. A hansom cab had stopped a few yards away, in which sat an elderly gentleman and a very good-looking young lady.

"Yes, papa," said the lady, "it is surely he; I cannot be mistaken." When she spoke I recognized Miss Preston. In the light of those eyes and the charm of that voice I forgot that I had been swindled, and blushed to the roots of my hair—I am not sure that my hair did not blush, but as it is naturally red I cannot be certain. I lifted my hat and advanced to the carriage, as her attitude showed that she expected me to do.

"Papa," she said, turning to the portly, well-dressed gentleman who sat beside her, "this is Dr. Scott, who so kindly helped me to rescue Harry from that very disagreeable predicament the other day; my papa, Mr. Preston. We have been looking for you ever since, and I have been, oh, so mortified that I could not learn your address. We got the directory and looked up all the Dr. Scotts, but could not find you. How could you be so cruel as to leave us under such a burden of obligation for so long?"

As I was trying to collect my thoughts, and to tell the truth without referring to my manifestly absurd suspicions, the portly and respectable father invited me to enter the carriage. I complied, and as we drove through the shaded drives on the beautiful metropolitan pleasure-ground, I explained that I had been unable to find the house.

"A very natural mistake," observed Mr. Preston, oracularly, "for one who is not familiar with great cities. To find a needle in a hay-mow is an easy task compared with searching for a person in New York without an address"—in which opinion I agreed with him; indeed, he could not at that moment have expressed an opinion in which I would not have concurred.

But why prolong the story? I accompanied them home; I got my money, though that was a small matter. My first visit was but one of many, and I now have an office in the basement of my father-in-law's residence. Mr. Preston is an alderman, and is interested in city contracts. He is already rich, and when his term of office expires we expect to move up on Fifth Avenue. As my wife is her father's only child, and will undoubtedly inherit his wealth, I am not obligated to enter the feverish race for money. I am at present engaged in the preparation of a work on macrobiosis which I expect will make me famous. There is but one drawback to our wedded happiness—Mr. Preston is a widower and I have no mother-in-law.

An Eloquent Appeal

Puck (1888)

A TALL TOLERABLY WELL-DRESSED and somewhat distinguished-looking colored man came into my office the other morning.

"Can you spare a moment of your valuable time?" he inquired, in excellent English.

"Certainly," I replied. (My time was not very valuable, but I didn't feel called upon to say so.)

"Sir," he continued: "you see in me the representative of a despised and down-trodden race. For centuries the race with which you are identified held my people in a bondage more cruel than death, and lived lapped in luxury while their black bondmen toiled beneath the burning sun."

"That's largely true," I remarked, as he paused. He fixed me with his eye, and continued:

"When at last the exigencies of war made the abolition of slavery necessary for the preservation of the Union, your statesmen reluctantly granted us the tardy boon of liberty."

I was not able to deny this, and he went on:

"You gave us a theoretical liberty, and turned us loose, penniless and ignorant, among the people who had oppressed us. Is not this true?"

"Substantially true," I assented.

"The catalogue of our wrongs is a long and bloody one. But I notice now a growing sentiment among the white people of this country—a feeling that, in merely giving the Negro back the liberty they had forcibly taken from him, they have not done their whole duty toward him, but that they owe him reparation for the wrongs he has suffered."

I remarked, at this point of the interview, that I had an engagement which would require me to leave the office in a very short time.

"Just one moment," he continued: "As a member of the dominant race, do you not feel it your duty to do what you can toward lifting my race to a higher level—toward repaying, in some small degree, the debt this country owes them?"

I remarked that I was willing enough, but that I happened to be financially embarrassed just at that particular time.

"You misconstrue me," he replied, with dignity: "I do not seek charity for myself, or for others. I mean business. If, for instance, you could confer a favor on my race, with profit to yourself at the same time, would you do it?"

I answered in the affirmative.

"Then," he said running his hand into his coat-pocket, "you will certainly take a stick of my 'Magic Corn Cure,' warranted to remove hard or soft corns on one application; or if used occasionally, to entirely prevent their formation. Will one stick be enough?"

Before I could recover from my astonishment, he collected a quarter from me, and left the office with a bow that would have done credit to any headwaiter in America.

⟞⟡⟟⟡⟞

How a Good Man Went Wrong

Puck (1888)

THE TREASURER OF WAYUP left town somewhat unexpectedly the other day, and in order to explain his absence to his family, sent a note home by a District Messenger boy.

The Treasurer had been gone about two weeks, when it began to be rumored about the City Hall that nobody knew where he was. An enterprising newspaper got wind of the affair, and a morning edition of the *Daily Screecher* came out with a four-column article, inquiring in guarded but significant language: "Where is Treasurer Barnstable?"

By noon the report was pretty general that the City Treasurer had absconded. By two o'clock a meeting of the city finance committee had been held, and an examination of the books had disclosed the fact that there was three hundred thousand dollars of the city's money in the Treasurer's possession.

At three o'clock an expert was called in to open the Treasurer's vault, of which the absconded official alone knew the combination. By four o'clock the rumored defalcation had been telegraphed to the four quarters of the globe.

In the gray dawn of the following morning, after a night of ceaseless toil, the expert succeeded in opening the vault. It was empty!

This discovery intensified the prevailing excitement. The defaulting Treasurer's bondsmen attached all his property. A warrant was issued charging him with embezzlement, and a description of his person was telegraphed all over the world. A crop of lawsuits sprang up; the newspapers flourished like a green bay tree.

When, on the morning of the eighteenth day of his absence, Treasurer Barnstable walked into his office, set his grip-sack on the floor, and hung his hat on its accustomed nail, you would have thought from their looks that the clerks in the office had seen a ghost. The news of his return spread like wildfire. In thirty seconds the Mayor was in the office.

"Barnstable, old man!" he exclaimed; "where *have* you been?"

"Why, I've been down in New Jersey, fishing. What's been going on? I hope I haven't been missed."

The Mayor groaned.

"Where is the three hundred thousand dollars?" he inquired, as soon as he could command his voice.

"The three hundred thousand dollars? Why, it's in the vault; where else should it be?"

"Don't ask me now, Barnstable, but show me the money; I'll tell you why afterward."

The Treasurer was mystified; but he knew his friend the Mayor too well to think he would ask anything of the kind except for some good reason. He unlocked the vault, entered it; and, taking down an old cigar box from an upper shelf, unwrapped a bundle covered with brown paper, and revealed to the glad eyes of the mayor three hundred thousand dollars worth of cash and good securities.

An explanation followed; and, as soon as the astounded Treasurer could pull himself together, he took a carriage and was driven rapidly to his home.

As he mounted the steps of his house, he met the messenger boy coming down; he had just delivered the message.

How He Met Her

Unpublished in Chesnutt's lifetime

FRANK HATFIELD WAS FEELING very comfortable as the Chicago express sped swiftly and smoothly westward along its iron track. He was off on a week's vacation and was going to Chicago to meet his sweetheart, who was coming with her mother from a far Western state.

Frank had first met Minnie West some years before at the home of her married sister in his native town, and the acquaintance then formed had been kept up by occasional visits which Frank made on his trips to the West in the interest of the large manufacturing establishment which he represented as traveling salesman. Frank was not the gay, careless drummer we read so much about in the funny papers, but a long-headed, ambitious young fellow, who went on the road because it paid well, and because he expected at some future time to be at the head of a business where his traveling experience and extensive acquaintance would be of great commercial value.

His acquaintance with pretty Minnie West had ripened into love. Minnie was not merely pretty; she was talented and industrious, and as teacher of a Western school had for several years been the sole support of a widowed mother—a gentle, inefficient woman of middle age who could easily enough manage their small domestic establishment, but who would have been utterly incapable of engaging single-handed in the struggle for existence. Minnie's industry, accomplishments, and devotion to duty, joined to a pretty face and a graceful figure, formed a combination of attractions which even the prospective burden of a mother-in-law could not offset, and to which Frank had willingly succumbed. A brief courtship, supplemented by frequent correspondence, had culminated in an engagement. Minnie had resigned her school and was on the way East to her old home, where the wedding was to take place the following month. Frank had arranged to meet them in Chicago and accompany them on the remainder of the journey.

Frank arrived in Chicago about eight o'clock in the evening. He went to a hotel, registered his name, ate supper, wrote a few letters, smoked a cigar, and about ten o'clock went to bed. The house was rather full, and the best room to be had was on the fourth floor. But Frank was a veteran traveler, and a varied experience of hotels had rendered him callous to considerations of altitude, amplitude or temperature; so when the bell-boy led the way to a room in which the traditional cat could with difficulty have been swung, and of a temperature more frigid than was exactly comfortable, Frank went calmly to bed without indulging in any unnecessary profanity, and was soon sleeping the sleep of youth and good digestion.

His dreams were pleasant. He dreamed that his marriage was taking place in a vast cathedral whose venerable aisles were filled with dim religious light which came through ancient stained glass windows. A priest, clad in his sacred vestments, performed the marriage ceremony, and a white robed acolyte swung a perfumed censer to and fro. Once he swung it too far, and the pungent smoke got into Frank's nostrils and made him sneeze.

The sneeze awoke him, and he found his room full of smoke—not from a perfumed censer, but from burning carpets and woodwork. Then the electric bell in his room began to ring, and as he hurriedly threw open the window, the roar of rushing engines and clanging fire-bells greeted his ear. The hotel was on fire. A glance along the side of the building showed that there was no fire escape within reach. Going back to the door, he opened it for an instant, and the cloud of smoke rushing in nearly blinded him. Closing the

door quickly, he hurriedly drew on a portion of his clothing. Then, opening his valise, he took from it a coil of cotton rope, small, closely twisted,
and knotted at intervals of a foot or more; he always carried this rope in his
valise, though he had never heretofore had occasion to use it. Then drawing the bedstead close to the window, he was in the act of fastening the rope,
when he heard a scream which sounded very near him. Hastily looking out
of the window, he saw at another window a short distance from his own two
women leaning out—one an elderly woman, who was frantically scream-
ing, and the other a young woman with her hair done up in curl papers. Both
women were in their night dresses, and the younger woman was with one
hand trying to throw a shawl around the elder woman's shoulders, while
with the other hand she firmly grasped the arm of the elder woman, who
looked as though she would jump from the window to certain death on the
stone pavement beneath. Far below the crowd surged, the engines throbbed,
and the streams of water rose into the air. The fire was yet mainly in the
interior of the building, and the firemen were trying to reach it from the
lower floors.

When Frank saw the women he paused in the work of fastening his
rope, and rushing back to the door, perceived that in a moment the fire
would reach his own room. He made a rapid estimate of the distance of the
room where the women were from his own, and seizing the rope, rushed out
into the thick smoke, and holding his breath, felt his way along the side of
the passage until he reached what he thought to be the right door. He turned
the knob, but the door did not yield. Looking back, he saw the fire almost
upon him, and threw himself with desperate energy against the door. By
this time the inmates of the room had heard him and unlocked the door,
which he entered and closed quickly behind him.

"Just keep cool," he said quietly to the excited women, "and you will
get down all right. Here is a rope."

Then with the aid of the younger woman he drew the bedstead to the
window, fastened the rope, and threw the end out of the window.

"Now, then, be quick," he said to the elder woman, "you go first. The
rope is strong, and the knots will keep it from hurting your hands."

But the old lady protested that she could never do it. There was no time
for argument, so Frank drew up the rope, and fastening it under her arms,
with the help of the younger woman lowered her to the ground. Then while
the people below were untying the rope, he assisted the young woman out of
the window and saw her nearly to the ground. Meanwhile the fire had burnt

through the thin door of the room and long tongues of flame were reaching toward the window. There was no time to be lost; Frank thought the rope would bear the weight of two. If he did not go at once the fire would reach the upper end of the rope and cut off all hope of escape. So he climbed out of the window and started downwards.

The young woman had reached the bottom safely, and Frank was about half-way down, when what he had feared took place. The rope was burned at the top, and giving way, precipitated him to the pavement below.

When he recovered consciousness he saw a fair and familiar face bending over him, in which tears gave place to a joyful smile as he opened his eyes and looked up wonderingly.

"O, Frank!" cried Minnie, "I am so glad! I thought you were dead, and that I had killed you." And a pair of soft white arms encircled his neck and a shower of warm kisses fell upon his face.

The Wests had arrived a few hours earlier than they had expected to, and had just retired when the alarm of fire was given. They had put up at the same hotel, and had seen Frank's name on the register, but in the confusion and terror of their flight from the burning building, had not recognized his face, begrimed as it was with smoke. For similar reasons Frank had not recognized them, especially as he had not expected them until the next day.

"I cannot understand," said Minnie, sometime after their marriage, with mock reproachfulness, "why you did not recognize me on the night of the fire."

"I had never seen you in evening costume before," replied Frank mischievously. "And why was it that you did not know me?"

"O!" she said, severely, "you had just come through the smoke, and you know I had never seen you in your true colors before."

BIBLIOGRAPHY

Primary Works

Chesnutt, Charles W. "Aunt Mimy's Son." In *Short Fiction*, 202–8.
———. "A Bad Night." *Cleveland News and Herald*, 22 and 23 July 1886.
———. "Baxter's Procrustes." *Atlantic Monthly* 93 (June 1904): 823–30.
———. "Busy Day in a Lawyer's Office." In *Short Fiction*, 73–74.
———. "Cartwright's Mistake." *Cleveland News and Herald*, 19 September 1886.
———. *Collected Stories of Charles W. Chesnutt*. Ed. and intro. by William L. Andrews. New York: Mentor, 1992.
———. *The Colonel's Dream*. New York: Doubleday Page, 1905.
———. *The Conjure Woman*. Boston: Houghton Mifflin, 1899; Ann Arbor: University of Michigan Press, 1969.
———. *The Conjure Woman and Other Conjure Tales*. Ed. and intro. by Richard H. Brodhead. Durham, N.C.: Duke University Press, 1993.
———. "The Doll." *Crisis* 3 (April 1912): 248–52.
———. "An Eloquent Appeal." *Puck* 23 (6 June 1888): 246.
———. "A Fool's Paradise." *Family Fiction*, 24 November 1888.
———. *Frederick Douglass*. Boston: Small Maynard, 1899.
———. "The Future American: A Complete Race-Amalgamation Likely to Occur." *Boston Evening Transcript*, 1 September 1900, 24.
———. "The Future American: A Stream of Dark Blood in the Veins of Southerners." *Boston Evening Transcript*, 25 August 1900, 15.
———. "The Future American: What the Race Is Likely to Become in the Process of Time." *Boston Evening Transcript*, 18 August 1900, 20.
———. "The Goophered Grapevine." *Atlantic Monthly* 60 (August 1887): 254–60. Rpt. in *Conjure Woman*, 1–35.
———. "A Grass Widow." *Family Fiction*, 14 May 1887.
———. "Her Virginia Mammy." In *The Wife of His Youth*.
———. *The House Behind the Cedars*. Boston: Houghton Mifflin, 1900.
———. "How a Good Man Went Wrong." *Puck* 24 (28 November 1888): 214.
———. "How He Met Her." In *Short Fiction*, 283–85.
———. Introduction to *Senator John P. Green and Sketches of Prominent Men of Ohio*, by William Rogers. Washington and Cleveland: Arena Publishing Company, 1893.
———. *The Journals of Charles W. Chesnutt*. Ed. Richard Brodhead. Durham, N.C.: Duke University Press, 1993.

———. "The Kiss." In *Short Fiction*, 306–14.

———. *Mandy Oxendine*. Ed. Charles Hackenberry. Urbana: University of Illinois Press, 1997.

———. *The Marrow of Tradition*. Boston: Houghton Mifflin, 1901.

———. "A Matter of Principle." In *The Wife of His Youth*, 94–131.

———. "A Metropolitan Experience." *Chicago Ledger*, 15 June 1887.

———. "A Midnight Adventure." In *Short Fiction*, 85–88.

———. "Mr. Taylor's Funeral." *Crisis* 9 (April 1915): 313–16; *Crisis* 10 (May 1915): 34–37.

———. "The Negro in Cleveland." *Clevelander* 5 (1930): 3–4, 24, 26–27.

———. "Obliterating the Color Line." *Cleveland World*, 23 October 1901, 4.

———. "The Passing of Grandison." In *The Wife of His Youth*, 168–202.

———. *Paul Marchand, F.M.C.* Ed. and intro. by Dean McWilliams. Princeton: Princeton University Press, 1999.

———. "Po' Sandy." In *Conjure Woman*, 36–63.

———. *The Quarry*. Ed. and intro. by Dean McWilliams. Princeton: Princeton University Press, 1999.

———. "The Shadow of My Past." In *Short Fiction*, 292–302.

———. *The Short Fiction of Charles W. Chesnutt*. Ed. and intro. by Sylvia Lyons Render. Washington, D.C.: Howard University Press, 1974.

———. "A Tight Boot." In *Short Fiction*, 58–61.

———. "Uncle Wellington's Wives." In *The Wife of His Youth*, 203–68.

———. "What Is a White Man?" *New York Independent*, 30 May 1889, 5–6.

———. "The White and the Black." *Boston Evening Transcript*, 20 March 1901, 13.

———. "White Weeds." In *Short Fiction*, 391–404.

———. "The Wife of His Youth." *Atlantic Monthly* 82 (July 1898): 55–61.

———. *The Wife of His Youth and Other Stories of the Color Line*. Boston: Houghton Mifflin, 1899; Ann Arbor: University of Michigan Press, 1968.

Secondary Works

Andrews, William L. "Introduction." *Collected Stories of Charles W. Chesnutt*. New York: Mentor, 1992.

———. *The Literary Career of Charles W. Chesnutt*. Baton Rouge: Louisiana State University Press, 1980.

Baym, Nina et al., eds. *The Norton Anthology of American Literature*, 5th edition, Volume II. New York: Norton, 1998.

Bone, Robert. *Down Home: A History of Afro-American Short Fiction from Its Beginnings to the End of the Harlem Renaissance*. New York: Putnam, 1975.

"The Book-Buyer's Guide." *Critic* 36 (February 1900): 182. In *CE*, 48.

Chamberlain, John. "The Negro as Writer." *Bookman* 70 (February 1930): 603–11. In *CE*, 134–38.

Chesnutt, Helen. *Charles Waddell Chesnutt: Pioneer of the Color Line*. Chapel Hill: University of North Carolina Press, 1952.

"Chronicle and Comment." *Bookman* 7 (August 1898): 452. In *CE*, 29.

Davis, Charles T., and Henry Louis Gates Jr., eds. *The Slave's Narrative.* Oxford: Oxford University Press, 1985.

Delmar, P. Jay. "The Mask as Theme and Structure: Charles W. Chesnutt's 'The Sheriff's Children' and 'The Passing of Grandison.'" *American Literature* 51 (November 1979): 364–75.

Du Bois, W.E.B. "Possibilities of the Negro." *Booklovers Magazine* 2 (July 1903): 2–13.

―――. *The Souls of Black Folk.* In *Three Negro Classics*, ed. John Hope Franklin. New York: Avon, 1965.

Duncan, Charles. *The Absent Man: The Narrative Craft of Charles W. Chesnutt.* Athens: Ohio University Press, 1998.

Ellison, Curtis W., and E. W. Metcalf Jr. *Charles W. Chesnutt: A Reference Guide.* New York: G. K. Hall, 1977.

Farnsworth, Robert M. Introduction to *The Conjure Woman.* Ann Arbor: University of Michigan Press, 1969.

Fraiman, Susan. "Mother-Daughter Romance in Charles W. Chesnutt's 'Her Virginia Mammy.'" *Studies in Short Fiction* 22, no. 4 (Fall 1985): 443–48.

Ferguson, SallyAnn H. *Charles W. Chesnutt: Selected Writings.* Boston: Houghton Mifflin, 2001.

―――. "Rena Walden: Chesnutt's Failed 'Future American.'" *Southern Literary Journal* 15 (Fall 1982): 74–82. In *CE*, 198–205.

Fienberg, Lorne. "Charles W. Chesnutt's *The Wife of His Youth:* The Unveiling of the Black Storyteller." *ATQ* 4 (September 1990): 219–37.

Gartner, Carol B. "Charles W. Chesnutt: Novelist of a Cause." *Markham Review* 1 (1968): 5–12. In *CE*, 155–69.

Gatewood, Willard B. *Aristocrats of Color: The Black Elite, 1880–1920.* Bloomington:Indiana University Press, 1990.

Glover, Katherine. "News in the World of Books." *Atlanta Journal,* 14 December 1901, sec. 2, p. 4. In *CE*, 84–85.

Heermance, J. Noel. *Charles W. Chesnutt: America's First Great Black Novelist.* Hamden, Conn.: Archon, 1974.

Howells, W. D. "Mr. Charles W. Chesnutt's Stories." *Atlantic Monthly* 85 (May 1900): 699–701.

―――. "A Psychological Counter-Current in Short Fiction." *North American Review* 173 (December 1901): 872–88.

Hurd, Myles Raymond. "Booker T., Blacks, and Brogues: Chesnutt's Sociohistorical Links to Realism in 'Uncle Wellington's Wives.'" *American Literary Realism* 26 (Winter 1994): 19–31.

Johnson, James Weldon. *The Autobiography of an Ex-Colored Man.* In *Three Negro Classics*, ed. John Hope Franklin. New York: Avon, 1965.

Keller, Francis Richardson. *An American Crusade.* Provo: Brigham Young University Press, 1978.

Lewis, Richard O. "Romanticism in the Fiction of Charles W. Chesnutt: The Influence of Dickens, Scott, Tourgee, and Douglass." *College Language Association Journal* 26 (December 1982): 145–71.

"Literature." *Washington, D.C., Times,* 9 April 1899, 2. In *CE,* 32–34.

Mabie, Hamilton Wright. "Two New Novelists." *Outlook* 64 (24 February 1900): 440–41. In *CE,* 50–51.

McElrath, Joseph R., Jr., ed. *Critical Essays on Charles W. Chesnutt.* New York: G. K. Hall, 1999.

McElrath, Joseph R., Jr., and Robert C. Leitz III, eds. *"To Be an Author": Letters of Charles W. Chesnutt, 1889–1905.* Princeton, N.J.: Princeton University Press, 1997.

McElrath, Joseph R., Jr., Jesse Crisler, and Robert C. Leitz III, eds. *Charles W. Chesnutt: Essays and Speeches.* Stanford: Stanford University Press, 1999.

———. *An Exemplary Citizen: Letters of Charles W. Chesnutt, 1906–1932.* Stanford: Stanford University Press, 2002.

McWilliams, Dean. *Charles W. Chesnutt and the Fictions of Race.* Athens: University of Georgia Press, 2002.

Nicholson, John B., Jr. "Biographical Essay about the Author." *Baxter's Procrustes.* Cleveland: Rowfant Club, 1966.

Olney, James. "'I Was Born': Slave Narratives, Their Status as Autobiography and as Literature." In Davis and Gates, eds., *Slave's Narrative,* 148–75.

Pickens, Ernestine Williams. *Charles W. Chesnutt and the Progessive Movement.* New York: Pace University Press, 1994.

Redding, J. Saunders. *To Make a Poet Black.* Ithaca, N.Y.: Cornell University Press, 1988.

Render, Sylvia Lyons. *Charles W. Chesnutt.* Twayne's United States Authors Series 373. Boston: Twayne, 1980.

———. Introduction to Chesnutt, *Short Fiction,* 3–56.

Sollors, Werner, ed. *Charles W. Chesnutt: Stories, Novels, & Essays.* New York: Library of America, 2002.

Stephenson, Nathaniel. "The Reviewer's Table." *Cincinnati Commercial Tribune,* 13 May 1900, 32. In *CE,* 55–56.

Stowe, Harriet Beecher. *Uncle Tom's Cabin.* 1852. Afterword by John William Ward. New York: NAL Penguin, 1966.

Sundquist, Eric. *To Wake the Nations: Race in the Making of American Literature.* Cambridge, Mass.: Belknap Press, 1993.

Taxel, Joel. "Charles Waddell Chesnutt's Sambo: Myth and Reality." *Negro American Literature Forum* 9 (1975): 105–8.

Taylor, Yuval, ed. *I Was Born a Slave: An Anthology of Classic Slave Narratives.* Foreword by Charles Johnson. Chicago: Lawrence Hill Books, 1999.

Wintz, Cary D. "Race and Realism in the Fiction of Charles W.Chesnutt." *Ohio History* 81 (Spring 1972): 122–30.

Wonham, Henry. *Charles W. Chesnutt: A Study of the Short Fiction.* New York: Twayne, 1998.

Wright, John Livingston. "Charles W. Chesnutt." *Colored American Magazine* 4 (December 1901): 153–56. In *CE,* 76–78.